Amelia Island's

VELVET UNDERTOW

The Goodbye Lie Series

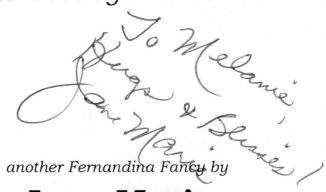

another Fernandina Fancy by

Jane Marie Malcolm

authorHOUSE®

AuthorHouse™
1663 Liberty Drive
Bloomington, IN 47403
www.authorhouse.com
Phone: 1.800.839.8640

First published by AuthorHouse 11/18/2009

ISBN: 978-1-4490-2920-3 (e)
ISBN: 978-1-4490-2919-7 (sc)

Library of Congress Control Number: 2009910258

Printed in the United States of America
Bloomington, Indiana

This book is printed on acid-free paper.

"I wish you'd develop a splash of patience!"

Ignoring her, Grey brushed past, instantly recognizing he'd interrupted something. His confirmation was her ruddy face and puffy lips. It was a blessed good thing he'd come along when he had. "Patience! I've been freezing my ass off outside, waiting for your highness like some lap dog. When you say five o'clock, I damn well expect you to be downstairs waiting for me at five o'clock. I sure don't have to ask what you've been up to. And where is this man who tempts you so much, you're willing to debase yourself at his mere beckoning?"

Carolena looked to the velvet pillows now crushed on the floor. Wadded in the corner was the blue dress. There was little sense denying it. Then again, who was he to tell her what was proper? He'd bedded hundreds of women, she was sure, so he had no room to talk.

Remaining calm, lest her feeling of guilt show, she told him, "Signor Alontti is attending to business. He sends his regards."

"Yeah? I'll just bet he does. Come on. Let's get the hell out of this lair before I find your lover and lay him out!"

-Amelia Island's VELVET UNDERTOW

Amelia Island's VELVET UNDERTOW is dedicated to the innocent souls who lost their lives and loves to the great 1889 Johnstown Flood in Pennsylvania, some of whom may have been distant relatives of this author. And to my sister, Nancy Harkins Kamp, who has guided and partnered me in my writing since 1992. Thank you, dear Nancy.

SENSES

I see a lake and dream I am
skimming the surface
on rose petal skates.
I hear music and feel myself
swirling around and down
a velvet mountain.
I smell lavender and
my vision turns
a matching hue.
My senses are mine no longer,
my love.
They are in your gentle hands, forever ...

- Jane Marie

THE GOODBYE LIE Series set on
AMELIA ISLAND

Amelia Island, Florida is the last in the chain of Atlantic coast barrier islands that stretch from North Carolina to Florida. Just south of the Georgia border, it is named for Princess Amelia, daughter of George II of England. The island is 32 miles northeast of Jacksonville and is naturally protected from hurricanes, most of the time. It is just 13 x 2.5 miles in size with an average temperature of 70 degrees Fahrenheit. Birthplace of the modern shrimping industry, the Victorian seaside resort of Fernandina Beach has a population of some 12,000 and is the only city on Amelia Island. Fort Clinch State Park, a pre-Civil War fort, sits on the northern tip of the island overlooking Cumberland Sound.

Late January 1889

Chapter 1

As a few breeze-blown clouds danced over the island town of Fernandina, Florida, intense sunlight grilled every surface that lay exposed. Sunshine poured through the Dunnigan dining room window. Today, a beam was intercepted and then intensified by the new crystal bowl on Miss Ella's sideboard. A concentrated ray pinpointed Carolena's tussie mussie, left from last month's holiday dance. The dried rosettes in the small bouquet smoldered and burst into a flaming golden halo of combustion.

Burning petals spit radiant sparks onto the sugar-starched doily beneath the bowl. The crocheted cotton speckled brown. It appeared to rot and, in seconds, transformed into a glowing black patch.

The blistering heat scorched Aunt Coe's nearby letter from her new home in Charleston. The pages curled, charred, and drifted onto the Oriental carpet, catching the braided fringe along its edge. The floral design darkened as the woven rug smoked and flashed.

The thick mahogany table leg resisted the fire, fighting for survival, but after a time, it also turned torch.

Old-rose colored draperies framing the window, whose glass had welcomed the rays of destruction, caught a spark. Flame spread onto the wallpaper. Or was it the petit point chair cushions? No matter. Each object in the room came alive to join the charge toward its demise.

The scarlet fire demon found the dining room too confining. Flames leapt onto Grammy's long braided rug in the hall and leapt again, crossing into the front parlor. Stroking the pump organ, the bellows moaned a final crackling cord. Sheet music surrendered without hesitation. Ashes floated around the room on currents of heat, landing on the green velvet sofa, the oak bookcase, the walnut desk, and Michael Dunnigan's favorite wingback chair. Family faces framed in silver blackened, then vanished, mercifully blind to the scene.

The lead flame split in the front hall. One lashing tongue entered the library and passed into the offices of Aqua Verde Passenger Line. Another raced up the carpeted stairs to the second floor. The fire punched through exploding windows, reaching for more players in its game of annihilation. Then the roof puffed smoke and blazed. The inferno seemed to sear the clouds above, changing the sky to twilight.

In less time than it had taken Michael to design his wife's pantry, their haven of three decades was swallowed by hell, and there was no one about to witness the scene but Clover, hired hand and loyal friend. All he could do was direct the horses and cows, the chickens and goat to the farthest pasture and pray the fire wouldn't catch the dry, yellowed grass and spread to his cabin, to Grammy and Peeper's little house, or to the Taylors' new home on the property. His silent plea was interrupted as he glimpsed Monstrose. The no-tail marmalade cat fled flat to the ground, his hidey-hole under the front veranda suddenly and curiously very hot.

Catching Blackie-White-Spots by the collar, Clover tried to hush his barking. "Shhh, dog. Shhh. Only thing holdin' down them loose porch planks was footsteps. Guess there's no need ta worry 'bout replacin' 'em now."

Together, man and animal sat in the sand, ignoring the prickling thistles and reflecting heat to watch the conflagration. The last screw securing the veranda's plaque lost hold and the carved sign reading *Dunnigan Manor,* thudded onto Miss Ella's hand painted welcome timbers corralling her shriveling pansies.

"Jesus God," Clover whimpered and closed his eyes. "That seals it. We got nothin' left."

***

"There! I'm all done!" Nora Duffy slammed the lid on her deerskin trunk. "For the last time, Carolena, please get up. Have you even begun packing yet? You'll take forever doing it. You're too fussy about your duds, you know. I just threw in my things. I'll worry about wrinkles when we get back to Fernandina. I'm too excited to be as careful as you always are."

Not pausing to take a much-needed breath, she added, "I'm starved for some sticky buns. I'm so glad Captain Taylor insists his ships serve your family's recipes. You're not still feeling under the weather are you? I thought sure Peeper's ginger tea would settle your stomach. You look fine. Please hurry."

Carolena Dunnigan, in bed in the ship's stateroom she shared with her cousin, pushed off the covers, sat up and gulped the fresh air blowing in through the porthole. "I'm up, Nora. I'm up and feeling fine. And why are you awake before me? That's never the case."

"True, true, but today is such a lovely day, and although January means winter on the calendar, it surely feels like spring here in Florida. I'm hoping for a little romance on the beach later to go along with the fine weather. Walking barefoot, arm-in-arm ..."

Her imagination wafted away and just as quickly, she returned to the present. "Of course, I haven't a candidate with whom to share a beach moment, but one will happen along. I know he will."

The talking continued as Carolena readied herself for the new day. Jabbering was always Nora's way, and her friends got used to it. Carolena realized she'd likely miss the nonstop gabbing if it weren't a daily occurrence.

"Ready, yet?"

"Would you quit asking? I'm having an awful time. I can't get this darned shoe buttoned. I'm not accustomed to the handle on your hook. Wonder where the dickens mine has gone."

Impatient, Carolena struggled to secure her boot without bunching and creasing her skirts. "Honestly," she said, "I'm as anxious as you to get to the beach, but you do realize it isn't seemly to go without foot cover unless you're in a proper swimming costume, don't you? That *is* what you were thinking, isn't it?"

"This is 1889, for goodness sake, Cary, and it's the beach. I always walk naked." Her eyes opened in mild shock for having said such a thing. Instantly recovering, "Oh, you know what I mean. I walk barefoot no matter what I'm wearing." She added, daringly, "If anything."

Realizing Nora was unusually full of empty talk, Carolena let that particular subject pass without further comment. She said instead, "Since I only brought my small steamer trunk with me, I finished packing last evening while everyone was playing for shuffleboard champion. It just proves I wasn't missed."

"You were too missed. We thought you were strolling the upper decks with Grey. Don't tell me you were wasting your last night at sea folding dresses and stashing toiletries. Please don't tell me that."

Neither confirming nor denying, Carolena responded, "Golly Ned! Folks sure are ready to see us as a couple. Why are they always pushing us together? I admit he's handsome enough. Perhaps a little too handsome."

Nora interrupted, "Now really, whoever heard of someone being too handsome? It's completely impossible!"

"Maybe," Carolena gave in. "Even dismissing his good looks, we haven't the same interests. Where I love to read, I'd bet the last book he picked up was the dictionary, and that was only because his teacher demanded it."

"Are you being fair? I think his occupation as an engineer requires a lot of study to keep those engines and all that nasty, oily equipment running on this brand new ship or any other. By the way, don't you just love the name, *Coral Crown*? It really expresses the magnificence of the boat we're riding in."

"Hmm? Yes, it's quite the perfect name." Carolena was still considering differences between Grey and herself. "What about religion? I may not be as devout as some; still, it does mean a great deal to me, and I rarely see him in church."

Nora defended the gentleman, "It isn't because Grey doesn't want to attend. Being out on the ocean most Sundays gives him ample cause not to be there." Expecting an answer, she asked, "Well?"

"I suppose it's as good an excuse as any. When he is in church, his bass voice is so powerful, it's almost embarrassing."

"I don't understand why you're so critical. You never sing a note yourself."

"It's because I can't carry a tune in a bucket." Carolena recalled the time Sister Josephine, although sweet about it, had told her to move her lips when the other children were singing so no one would guess she was tone-deaf.

"You always say that. How do you know it's still true? No one's heard you sing in years. Now that you're grown, maybe you've improved. One thing's for certain, Carolena. If everyone were as reticent as you, well I'm just glad they aren't or we'd have no choir. Then the only accompaniment to the church organ would be old Mr. Winders' snoring. Bless his heart, he's so decrepit, his skin is almost transparent!"

Nora prattled on, "Oh, I forgot to tell you. A few weeks back, as we were all leaving church, I saw Uncle Michael clap Grey on the back and then say," Nora lowered her voice in imitation, "'I've got to admit, boy, you're one hymn-singin' sonofabitch.'"

"Nora!"

"Those were his exact words! I swear!" Slightly insulted her cousin could think she would make up such a thing, Nora sighed and immediately forgot the offense. Pouring herself a glass of water from the carafe on the nightstand, she found the upholstered chair in the corner. With her legs dangling over the arm, she leaned back, sipping.

"Anyway," Carolena proceeded, "I consider myself reserved and dignified and frankly, Grey's down right bold in his deportment. Besides, he has a temper, I've heard. Any fight he's in, he's probably the one to toss the first lick."

Nora shrugged, indicating a so-what kind of reaction.

"And his choice of acquaintances, for the most part, would certainly never be invited into my parlor."

Nora judiciously gave her analysis. "I now realize your problem, Cary. You lead a constipated existence."

Astounded at such a determination, the blonde Carolena scolded the redheaded Nora. "You know how much I despise being addressed as Cary. I've told everyone, time and again, my given name is Carolena. I find it unique. So please, do me the small courtesy of abiding by my wishes. *Cary* just isn't the image I want to present."

Nora casually examined the twist of one of her curling tendrils. "My point exactly."

"Humph! Nevertheless, I can't see the day when Grey and I'll unite. There are simply too many differences. While we talk over anything and everything in the world when we're together, he doesn't show the least inkling of interest in me - that way. Yes, I took notice of him around town when he first arrived. Just like all the girls, I was taken by his physique. Had it not been for us working together, I doubt we'd have spoken except in passing. And that's only because my sister is married to his best friend, the all around wonderful Captain Waite Taylor," she said unreservedly. "Since Breelan and Waite built their home behind our Dunnigan Manor, Grey visits him, not me.

"I only wonder what woman will finally snag him," Carolena added. "How many times have we seen others prostrate themselves at his feet? I think it's simply degrading. He's not flattered by feminine pursuit. I see him as an aggressor, and that's how it should be."

This wasn't their first conversation along these lines, Nora realized, wondering why Cary was so brittle about things. She hoped one day her straitlaced cousin would recognize life had more to offer than reading books. There was so much romance out there for the taking. Nora smiled to herself at the thought of some young man holding her in his arms and ...

"Nora, are you listening to me?" Carolena was impatient. "Here I am telling you some of my deepest, most personal feelings, and you're not paying attention."

"I am. I am!" Nora squawked back. "Don't get in an uproar."

"I'm sorry." Carolena couldn't contain herself any longer. "Oh drat! I have to admit the truth. I'm captivated by the man and have been since the first day he walked into my line of sight. Despite our dissimilarities, what I really, truly want is to find common ground, solid enough to support a mutual love."

Glad her cousin had fessed up to what they both already knew, Nora instructed, "You're going about this backwards, Cary. Did you ever think love might be the common ground and the obvious differences between you would only enhance that love? Make it more entertaining, more fertile and enjoyable somehow?"

"I guess we'll never know because up to this point, there's been no spark from him to ignite the love, let alone any flirting with me. To Grey McKenna, I'm a capable, intelligent woman and a good friend. It's normally not my fashion to tease. Seems I've changed because when he's around me, I'm like any other lovesick female. I have to force myself to smother my coquettish leanings. Were he to reject me ..." She shuddered once. "Dunnigan pride is a power unto itself, so with all my strength, I refrain from initiating any intimacy between us. And I'll continue to deny my attraction to him to everyone, except you. Needless to say, I have your word this conversation between us is private?"

Nora nodded, honored Carolena had confided in her. She picked up a magazine to occupy herself while the troubled woman she loved like a sister quietly straightened the bedclothes on both beds.

Daydreaming as she worked, Carolena hoped for all the writing and all the talking of it, there was more to love than the tingle of a random kiss. She craved to encounter all aspects of passion, and for her, passion was Grey McKenna.

She wouldn't let herself dwell on it further. Turning to Nora, "Now, about last evening. After I packed my trunk, I got restless. Since I'd read all the books I brought from home and I'd already been through what would be the ship's library while they were building her, I went for a walk. I wanted to think. I'm working on the new yacht for that musician from

Charleston. He seems impatient to get our ideas. As I understand it, he has the fortune to expect quick results. Though this trip's been wonderful, it's put a crimp in the business of design. It's made me fall behind schedule."

"Carolena! You're simply too dedicated for your own good. Captain Taylor and your dear father, Uncle Michael, took the time off and pleasure owed them for having worked so unceasingly to get this ship through her sea trials before she was christened at the beginning of the year. Now here we are, family and friends, enjoying her first-ever private sailing. It's the only chance we'll have this beauty all to ourselves. She goes public next week, as you know. Why can't you take a break from your all-consuming job until we get home?"

Nora took hold of Carolena's arm to still her. "And why can't you let the maids tidy our room? You'll put them out of work, for holy sakes!"

"Don't be a silly-billy. They'll change the linens and clean the staterooms once we dock in Fernandina, the same as they'll do for all passengers each day at sea. I'm so fussy about the way things look because the responsibility for the embellishment of these rooms, of the whole ship, was left to me. I have a hard time seeing them less than just right. I guess I consider them like my, um, pets."

Nora eyed Carolena then scrutinized their compartment, taking in the comforters of gold threaded brocade, which shown as the sun's rays set them sparkling.

"I almost said I consider them like my children. However, never having had any babies, I'll not use that comparison."

"If you don't take some time for yourself, you'll never get the chance to have those children with Grey or any man for that matter." Nora had started; she might as well speak her mind. Now seemed the perfect opening. "And while we're on the subject, I must tell you, I'm ashamed of you."

Caught off guard, Carolena pricked her ears. "Ashamed of me?"

"Yes, ma'am. I haven't told a soul before this, but I'm at the end of my rope with you. May I elaborate?"

"Please do." Carolena readied herself for Nora's onslaught.

"You're sullen so much of the time, and you're, you're just plain dull! You act superior and talk superior. You're impatient and curt and can take the fun out of everything. We all try to include you, encourage you to join in. Often, you seem as if you can't be bothered. You're so stiff, you look like you'll crack. You make everyone around you uncomfortable. You act like we're all stupid, and we're not, none of us." Tears were in Nora's eyes. "It's because I love you I say this. Carolena Michelle Dunnigan, you're a bore!"

Hurt, the accused never thought to defend herself. Her reply was simple. "I never realized."

Nora went on while the target of her words closed her ears and again became pensive. She was used to being criticized for working too hard, too intently, but never had anyone called her a bore! A bore?

She made a silent examination of her recent past. Since graduating from Florida Women's College in Tallahassee, Carolena desperately needed to dedicate her life to something. A body could only tolerate so much housekeeping and cooking and stitching, especially when done in the family residence. She was long past ready to have a home to call her own. She had toyed with the idea of moving to a room in Mrs. Steinberg's boarding house in town, a few miles away. But her parents carried on so, it hardly seemed worth upsetting them. As an incentive to keep her at home, the entire attic, except for a quarter left for storage, was converted to a spacious bedroom. She had planned it, and her father had two of his ship's carpenters execute the work. So, in theory, she did have her own place. Of course, the entire family, including her Grammy and Peeper, as well as Nora's parents, Aunt Noreen and Uncle Clabe Duffy, were all aware of her comings and goings. There was little privacy.

Her father, an architect, and his son-in-law, Captain Waite Taylor, sailor and master pilot, had joined skills to design and construct ships for their Aqua Verde Passenger Line and a few select clients. With Michael Dunnigan's knowledge of building and Waite's experience with ship's construction and sailing, it seemed inevitable. Since Waite and his wife Breelan lived on the Dunnigan property, Michael moved his architecture business from downtown Fernandina to an added-on wing in his home, creating a convenience for everyone.

After a time, Carolena was invited to join the firm, having proven her talents in the accoutrements of *The Miss Breelan*, the first ship of the line. Long ago, Carolena discovered her artistic leanings, which manifested in interior design. She saw an empty room in her mind and sensed the personality of each space. She could envision the colors and textures of fabric, wood, masonry, glass, and paint that, when combined, would present a pleasing effect.

Other members of the family, too, held vital positions in the company. Miss Ella, Michael's wife and the mother of four, had final approval over all foodstuffs and beverages served. Breelan, second oldest daughter and ship's namesake, was a former reporter for the weekly *Fernandina Mirror*. Currently, she was director of sales and marketing for the business, writing all advertising copy. Only son, Jack Patrick, going on 16, was under the part-time tutelage of both his father and Waite, the captain being something of an idol to him. The last of the Dunnigan children, Marie, was doing just what any ten-year-old did. Although bashful, she wavered between a curiosity about boys and playing with dolls. What started as a sole male venture had developed into a prestigious family owned business. It was a pleasant atmosphere in which to work for all involved. Close to the wives, grandmas and children for love, and close to Miss Ella Dunnigan's nourishing and delicious meals.

True enough, Carolena's life was filled with work. Yet, like most women, she wanted a husband and children. She often marveled at the enjoyment Breelan found with her family. Carolena was an aunt twice over, first to Breelan's sixteen-year-old adopted son, Mickey, and most recently to Halley, Breelan and Waite's young daughter. The cherished lad and lassie brought zip, zest, and mischief to the Dunnigan family with each utterance and prank.

But Carolena would never marry in haste. She would hold out for Grey as long as possible. She yearned for his discovery of her. She imagined how their romantic gathering of knowledge, each of the other, would inevitably lead them on a climactic journey to the altar. Ideally, by the time she wed, she would come to understand beyond the physical why she loved the man and know, to the depth of her being, he would be true. True in heart, true in his love for her, and true to his honor toward himself and their family. She would settle for nothing less.

Then again, if Grey didn't respond to her in due course, she would not deprive herself of matrimony. She would make do with a second choice husband. Surely there was another man somewhere for her, wasn't there? To think such a thought saddened her already laden heart.

The pressure to marry was often ungraciously veiled. She'd overheard her Aunt Noreen comment to her husband, "Around their house, I'm sure the Dunnigans call a hope chest, 'Carolena's God only knows when chest.'" Defending his niece, Uncle Clabe, bless him, had been abrupt and cutting in his reprimand of his wife, reminding her their own daughter, Nora, had yet to marry.

Mrs. Ickles, Fernandina's most meddlesome resident, had advised, "Miss Carolena, being the oldest Dunnigan girl, I'm sorry to say you're starting to show your age. You'd have married long ago if you'd only get off your bluestocking high-horse and accept the favors of one of the hard working, respectable beaus who seek your favors."

Those bitter memories only made Carolena more determined. She wouldn't settle until all hope was lost. Grey would come to her some day. Pray God, he would.

Nora's voice penetrated Carolena's thoughts. Miss Nora Duffy was best friend to Carolena and confidant in most things, just as she'd been to Breelan before the younger sister married. Minutes earlier, Nora heard Carolena admit how she wanted Grey. Had she told Nora too much? Carolena worried her loose tongue might have gotten the best of her, but Nora agreed to keep the secret. And her word was golden.

Carolena interrupted Nora's seemingly never-ending lecture to say, "You know, I should be mad at you for speaking so harshly to me."

Nora's bottom lip trembled.

"Now, don't get upset. You're right. I am too serious. I do look down on people, and I can be, no, I am dull. I promise I'll try to be more frolicsome, more carefree, more spontaneous!"

"Then you don't hate me for being so frank?"

"Of course not! You spoke out of caring." Carolena grabbed Nora by the hand. "Come on! Time for Mama's massive breakfast. I could do with some picture eggs and sausage gravy. Ooh, and maybe if we go about it the right way, the staff might produce a dish of spiced apple rings. Do you think they'd let us have vanilla ice cream on top and a benne seed cookie on the side?"

"Ice cream and cookies for breakfast?"

"Sure, Nora," Carolena said. "Why not? The worst they can do is kill us for asking, but that won't happen. We could end up with what we want!" She held open the door, and they went in search of the compelling scents of first-class home-style cooking.

Their pace brisk, probably too brisk to be considered lady-like, the young women reached the end of the passageway in scant seconds. At the sudden sound of a familiar male squawking, they halted, spun round, and returned to the cabin two doors from theirs.

"Warren Lowell!" bellowed Nora, anxious over the cries coming from her younger brother. "Warren Lowell?" Jerking her hand from Carolena's, she beat on the door with both fists. "Are you all right in there? Let me in!"

When Carolena's baby brother, Jack Patrick, answered, he was wearing that annoyingly transparent smile of his. Nora looked past him to see Warren Lowell standing in the copper bathtub, frantically tying a white bath sheet about his dripping middle.

"Well, I should have expected I'd find you making trouble." Carolena's hands were on her hips.

"Hey, Nora. Hey, Aunt Carolena," piped up Breelan's son, Mickey. "No harm done. Just a minor skirmish." His attempt to conceal his laughter was useless.

"What's all the noise about?" Carolena eyed Jack Patrick with suspicion. "What have you done this time, Pat?"

"Why do you automatically assume I'm the culprit?"

"Why indeed!" Her arms shifted to cross her chest.

Attempting to divert attention from any crime, Mickey asked, "Have you women no modesty? Can't you see there's a man in a state of undress here?"

"Remember, I changed his diapers," answered Nora.

"Yeah," Jack Patrick's defenses were up. "I've heard how you and Breelan babysat the poor boy. How you two poured perfume down his dirty pants to keep from changing him. And how—"

"Enough!" shouted Carolena at the disgusting story she knew to be true.

Embarrassed at her youthful transgression, Nora exclaimed with impatience, "Warren? We demand to know what you did."

"It was nothing." Warren Lowell stood strong. "I won't tell on my friend."

"Me neither!" Mickey was a sworn member of the band known wearily by the Order of the Sisters of Saint Joseph, their teachers, as "The Terrible Threesome."

Nora glared and said, "If you don't speak up, I'll tell Mother you all are up to no good, and then you'll know the true meaning of confession."

"Okay. But please don't tell Aunt Noreen," Jack Patrick pleaded. "You know how your mother can be." Hating like the devil to give in and realizing the utter necessity of it, he conceded. "Mickey and I have been waiting on Warren Lowell for an hour. He's so dang slow at dressing and primping, and we're starved. So I thought of a way to hurry him up some. I peed in his bathwater."

Carolena's eyes bulged.

"Oh, is that all?" Nora remained calm. "Next time, please try to keep the screaming under control, would you, Warren? You liked to have scared us to death. Remember, if there's no blood or bone, we don't want to hear about it. See you boys upstairs at breakfast. If there's anything left," she added, closing the door and pushing a still wide-eyed and speechless Carolena out in front of her. Oh well, Nora observed, so much for a carefree and frivolous Carolena.

Chapter 2

In the Grand Salon of the *Coral Crown*, all passengers assembled to feast on the breakfast being served.

"So far so good," Ella Dunnigan told her husband Michael. "No one," she whispered, "not even Noreen, has turned green from the food."

"You worked out any kinks. You always do, Miss Ella. Relax, would you? After all your efforts getting ready for this first three day run, you deserve it." With some difficulty, Michael propelled his large form from the marble-topped table, leaving only the slightest residue of evidence of his elegantly prepared breakfast on the new bone china plate. He sighed with contentment, despite being stuffed and uncomfortable. "If only a fellow had something to eat," he told everyone jovially. Since this was often his remark after a meal, no one paid any attention. He'd have to come up with some other clever comment, he guessed.

Right now, he desperately wanted to loosen the belt on his trousers, as he'd do in the privacy of his home. Though only family, close friends and crew were on this cruise, his ladylike wife would be mortified, not to mention his sister, Noreen. He chuckled to himself at the commotion Noreen would cause if ever he really let go and was his genuinely disgusting self. What silly machinations man adopted to be called civilized.

Michael focused on Grey McKenna seated beside Leo Rockwell, former captain of the *Miss Breelan*. Michael realized there was no love lost between the two. But despite their different styles of command, they respected one another and got their jobs done. That was all that mattered.

Grey listened while Rockwell spoke in humorless paragraphs. Yes, the man was a committed leader. Yes, he could handle difficult maritime situations, but he was so strident and unyielding. Why were they so unfortunate as to be seated next to each other on such a joyous occasion as this?

Looking for relief, Grey surveyed the room around him, analyzing his newly appointed fellow crew members. First Officer William Tracy, second in command, was a good man, proud of his family of five children. Second Officer John Armstrong, the navigator, was sharp as a store-bought razor. First Lieutenant Dale Wishes, who had worked his way up the ranks, was a tough gent, and from his reputation, the female passengers would be as well tended as the ship. Purser Jacob Diebert was as watchful and honorable with his professional accounts as he was with his own. Over all, they were a grand bunch of men with whom to be working.

Grey's eyes found Carolena next to her mother at the far end of the table. Framing her golden radiance was the splendid backdrop she had created. Carolena's imagination was unequalled. At first, he'd thought her extravagant until he discovered her father had given permission to spare no expense in decorating the *Coral Crown*. She'd taken full advantage of that.

Refinement without ostentation was the motto of the Aqua Verde Line. The new ship was a floating palace.

Despite the importance of this gathering, the atmosphere was informal. Yet, when Grey stood, silence fell as all took in the big man. The casually undulating muscles beneath the fabric of his crisp black uniform could not be ignored by any woman nor dismissed by any man. Wise eyes, the color of Caribbean waters, shown bright beneath the shock of coal-colored hair combed back from his tanned features. His skin was flawless, his brows roughly sculptured, his nose thin. He was unaware of his appealing powers, but others were not. His demeanor left him at ease, easy-going, and easily liked. His naturally relaxed manner reeled in strangers, turning them into acquaintances, and if they were lucky, into friends.

Grey spoke. "My fellow passengers, we cannot let any more time pass without remarking on the beauty of our ship. The twenty-foot stained glass windows, the mosaic murals, the fluted columns. Grandeur lies before us, and it is due solely to the genius of Miss Carolena Dunnigan, queen of the *Crown*. Let us raise our glasses in her honor. She is truly the *Coral Crown*, personified. To Miss Carolena!"

The hosannas surprised and flattered her though the best part was Grey leading the praise. His words sent ripples of hope coursing through her heart. She'd never known such adulation. Coffee and teacups toasted the young woman whose hair was pinned high to expose a slender neck. Her bright smile spoke her appreciation to Grey. He recognized her devotion to detail, and she was fortunate to have him as champion.

Grey read her thanks and returned a slow bow. He recalled how he'd come to join this group, and he was damned proud to be here. Six years past, Grey heard a brand new passenger ship, the *Miss Breelan* out of north Florida, was looking for experienced hands. He'd found the owner, a Captain Waite Taylor, to be a tough taskmaster, but also a fair and decent man. Upon interviewing with Captain Taylor, he'd discovered they had many of the same credentials. As young boys – too young, both served in the Civil War, known here in the South as the War Between the States. Although on opposite sides, both sailed the Atlantic seaboard. One contrast between the two, Grey was raised in Pennsylvania and Waite in Florida.

There was another difference between the men. One had married. One had not. As co-president with his father-in-law of the Aqua Verde Passenger Line, Waite was able to juggle his time to work out of Michael's architectural office, oversee the boat yard, occasionally sail on the *Miss Breelan* and best of all, as he told Grey so often, to sleep in his own bed in Fernandina with his beloved Breelan.

Except for the pick-up and discharge of passengers in Fernandina, the *Miss Breelan's* run kept Grey away from town. With every docking at the marina, he monitored the construction of this second ship of the line's development. He'd been as anxious as any to board the finished product.

After nearly two years, the *Crown* was christened and launched on

January 3, 1889. Grey remembered the big question of the day back then was who would take her helm. Grey was not privy to that information, so kept his own council and didn't ask. In his innermost recesses, he hoped for the job himself, but recognized his own limitations. After all, he'd never captained a ship and combined with his reckless air, it left him little confidence he would win the position. Besides, rumor had it Captain Taylor himself would return to the sea as the new craft's skipper. Grey waited like everyone else for the announcement.

Despite the sticky, humid air, the Fernandina marina was congested that night in January as it had never been before. The surrounding waters of the twenty-seven foot deep Amelia River were filled with varying types of bobbing vessels, each jockeying for a better view of the launching. It seemed to Grey every resident of the area, including those from St. Mary's, Georgia and even Brunswick, Jacksonville, and Lake City, had come to witness the spectacle - if only to tell their grandchildren they had been there. Flags flew and the Fernandina Concert Band played rousing music punctuated by their signature sour notes. Spectators hung from open windows, and trees and the rooftops swarmed with the interested townspeople.

With the *Miss Breelan* resting comfortably on the water and her even more resplendent sister perched upon her launch cradle, Michael Dunnigan climbed the steps to the makeshift stage and waved his hands to hush the crowd. After a fifteen-minute oration on why and how and what the passenger line meant to him, Michael expressed his gratitude to all who had contributed to bringing the ship to this triumphant point.

Turning the podium over to Captain Taylor, he shook his son-in-law's hand as the multitude cheered. "I realize there has been much speculation as to the command position aboard our young beauty here," the captain said. "It took no effort on our part in deciding because the reward of authority is justly deserved. Time and again, he has proven himself to be a capable leader with an unblemished record. We would have no other. With complete assurance and confidence, I am honored to announce the captain of our new ship is Leo Rockwell."

All except the immediate family were surprised. Grey was disappointed he didn't get the job, but realistically knew he didn't deserve it. On the brighter side, he thought how he'd be out from under the thumb of *Rockwall,* the name he mentally substituted for Rockwell, who was most times uncompromising. He'd gladly serve any one else on the *Miss Breelan.*

Once the cheers subsided, Waite announced the rest of the crew of the *Crown.* Grey heard his name and the title of chief engineer. Damnation! He liked his job where he was. He would hate leaving. Still, to work on the new ship, to get her performing to perfection as he'd done on the *Bree,* would be a welcome challenge. He was glad to have been chosen though his excitement was dampened by the fact he would once again answer to

Rockwall.

When time came to publicly respond, the same as the other appointees had done, Grey remembered his wonderful mother's lessons in the importance of the spoken word. Curbing his sailor's tongue and as graciously as he was able, he accepted his new position. The people roared, and their happy cries split the stars. Despite recognizing much of the hoopla was due to the alcohol many in the crowd had drunk, Grey was genuinely touched by their support.

At long last, Miss Ella was accompanied to the platform by her children, a bottle of champagne cradled in the crook of her left arm. There were a few lewd whistles directed toward Breelan and Carolena, who seemed even more dazzling than usual as the flicker of torchlight illuminated their faces.

Grey and Michael noticed Jack Patrick scowl toward the crowd, trying to locate the offenders. The boy was ready to defend the honor of his sisters against any man.

Restraining the lad with a tug on his sleeve, Michael made mental note to praise him for his courage. With a deliberate nod in the direction of the ruckus, Michael indicated his son should observe. Pat watched while the crass behavior was quickly silenced as three odious fellows were none too gently conducted from the festivities by a few stalwart citizens. "We are Dunnigans, my boy. Remember, we have a name in this community. Just watch 'em scramble!"

Grey and Jack Patrick eyed one another, both thinking scramble an odd choice of words for Michael Dunnigan to use. It made him sound condescending, which wasn't like him. This being no time to question his father, Pat said only, "Yes, sir."

"Look to your mother. She's the real beauty here tonight."

With a clear, strong voice, Miss Ella spoke. "I christen thee the *Coral Crown*! May God guide this ship and grace those who voyage on her with a safe and secure passage." Then she smashed the champagne bottle against the point of the bow. The ship's bonds were cut, and the massive *Crown* slid slowly from the wooden ways that had held it, the friction so great it left steam streaking the clammy night. The *Crown* was truly alive with spirit, with stability and strength, and indeed, with dignity.

So here was Grey, reveling with those who'd accepted him as kin. He'd come to love them all as just that. He kept the details of his past to himself. That didn't mean those memories weren't revisited and often. His own people had long since passed away. His mother, Leticia, a farm girl, young and without intrigue, had married Gene G. Powell. After the birth of a son, Grant, their happy marriage was short-lived when Gene succumbed to pneumonia. Lettie's life turned melancholy. Alone, with no adults to share her feelings or ease her troubles, her mourning knew no limits.

Two years later, the future brightened as she came to know and love Peter Fitzmorgan McKenna, owner of McKenna Mines, major supplier of coal to the eastern United States. With his encouragement, Lettie's positive outlook on life returned. McKenna moved his new wife and her four-year-old boy into his Pennsylvania family home. Grant was soon adopted by Peter and another baby boy, Greyson, surprised his parents five years later.

Peter McKenna lavished gifts upon his wife and together they decorated the mansion in tasteful fashion. She learned the intricacies of socializing and charity work so as to share their privilege with others.

Even after ten years of marriage, Lettie retained much of her naiveté. One quick pleasure trip to Pittsburgh changed many a life. Before a matinee performance at the theater, Lettie discovered yet another love token on their buggy seat. It was a square powder compact encased in pink leather with her initials carved into its gold cover.

After Peter, considerably older than his wife and weary, retired early that evening, the innocent Lettie left the hotel, unaccompanied, to fetch his tonic at the drug emporium she'd seen from the window of their suite. The next morning she was found in an alley, raped, her neck broken. Clutched in her fist was the new compact, its mirror shattered. Her husband took his life at the news, leaving Grant and Grey orphaned at ages fourteen and five.

Both sons had adored their parents and dealt with their grief individually, offering little comfort to one another. Although, he became embittered at the world for having his happiness torn from him so suddenly, Grant realized the only useful thing he had left was money. He was young, but sufficiently worldly to understand that with no living relatives and without proper supervision, the courts would see him and his half-brother placed in an orphanage, despite their funds. Therefore, he instructed his stepfather's head attorney, James Z. Jaxmyer, to hire the best tutors. Uncle Jax, as the boys called him, thought it a sound plan and did as requested. A judge approved, appointing Jaxmyer guardian. The lads were permitted to continue living in the family home.

Grant took to the schooling, certain his cherished mother would have wanted it so. He did his utmost to glorify all recollection of her and Papa Peter. Blotting away their ugly deaths, he wanted to remember, retain, and recapture the memories of their sweet life as a happy family.

Grey was a different case. He chose to speak little of his dead parents. The pain of their loss was almost unbearable for him. He endured Grant, the nagging teachers, and the boring lessons. The only thing he thrived upon was his sporting instruction. Fencing, pugilism, riding, tennis, swimming, golfing, and shooting turned him from an average boy into a prematurely brawny young man.

Battles raged between the brothers whenever Grant imposed his will on the independent Grey. The fighting became less frequent once Grant's attentions turned to women. Foolish as he knew it was, Grey felt neglected. His home held little happiness for him. After years of the life Grant wanted,

Grey had enough. He fled the mansion, fled the state, fled the country. He crossed the Atlantic Ocean as a stowaway. Having the proportions of a full-grown powerful seaman, he got a job loading cargo onto freighters until, at 17, he returned to America to fight for the Union in the Civil War.

Over time, Grey sent a few letters to his brother back home. His only response was from Uncle Jax, now caretaker, who replied Grant, too, had left. With no further correspondence from Grant, Uncle Jax explained there were more than sufficient monies in the McKenna accounts to keep the house up indefinitely. Uncle Jax loved the boys like his own, staying on between his travels.

Jax and Grey mourned Grant, lost no doubt to war as one of many valiant unknown soldiers. Both prayed he'd found solace in the beyond with his beloved parents. As for their homestead, it held only sorrowful memories for Grey. He could never see the day when he would live there.

Grey's thoughts of the past were invaded by a prestissimo rendition

of *Boat Song* being wildly whacked out on the piano. Most heads in the dining salon turned to take in the music. Feet tapped as they enjoyed the lively tune,

even at this early hour. Peeper, the short, round, self-appointed grandmother to the Dunnigan children, and Grammy, Miss Ella's mother, sat side-by-side, drumming time upon the white damask table covering despite their crippled-up fingers. All the while, their eyes never left the three boys huddled in the corner.

Jack Patrick, Warren Lowell, and Mickey were in heavy discussion. However, it wasn't the melodious cadence they were analyzing. Due to the family voyage, they'd been excused from school for a week. They'd heard there would be new seat assignments when they returned and debated who would sit next to Mary Jo Bestner. Jack Patrick trusted the teachers would seat everyone alphabetically. Mickey hoped they'd be grouped according to reading ability, and Warren Lowell just prayed his spectacles wouldn't conceal too much of his own good looks.

Rising from his chair, Captain Rockwell addressed his second in command, "Mr. Hastings, see to it the broom flies high from the mast. I declare this passage a clean sweep!"

"Aye, sir."

Hoots and hugs went around and it was a proud season in the history of Dunnigan.

"Grey, my friend," Michael called out over the din, meaning the classification in earnest. "We need your words of wisdom."

Wearing his infamous impish grin, the engineer replied, "Let me remind you all that a freckled mermaid never cooks squash."

Once everyone recovered from Grey's absurdity, the unflappable Michael continued. "How is it a man from Pennsylvania crews on not one but two ships of a Florida fleet? Tell me that."

The tone delivered was received as teasing, and the response was similar. "Must be that special Canadian blended whiskey I personally deliver to you, Mr. Dunnigan, and your acquaintances every time we dock in Fernandina."

The ladies let forth a collective gasp as Grey laughed aloud at their predicable response. Midst the disgusted murmuring, Grey said, "If you listen, you can hear the birds squawk. It can only mean landfall is near. I must return to my duties." Standing, "See you all topside as soon as I'm able." As he read his pocket watch, noting they were right on schedule, he left the splendid room, his dark cap secure under his arm.

Michael and the rest of the men folk were left to reassure and appease the women.

"Why, Clabe Duffy," Noreen accused her husband, her face pale. "Do you mean to tell me all the times you, an honest banker, said you were out giving financial advice, you were, in truth, gulping liquor?"

Nora felt sorry for her father, yet hoped it might be true and he'd enjoyed himself when he was away from her mother's nagging.

"Major Fairbanks!" said Heleen Cydling, his society columnist. "Let's hope this scandalous news remains within these walls, shall we? I'm concerned we may lose subscribers to *The Florida Mirror* if they find out the former editor is a hard-drinking man."

"Father Kilcoyne!" Peeper was addressing the parish priest of Saint Michael's. "At least we're aknowin' for certain you're an ignoramus concerning this matter." She paused. "Ain't we, Father?"

Breelan kept her face expressionless. She listened to Waite Taylor, her strong, strapping husband, rattle off his guarantee he was no alcoholic, as did the other men. "For God's sake, Bree," he implored, "you're with me damn-near every night and well aware of my habits."

Bree's laughter ruptured her serious façade. She threw her arms around her captain's neck. Realizing the joke, he responded, feeling a little foolish he'd felt it necessary to plead his innocence before her in the first place.

All the women followed suit, likewise unable any longer to reprimand their men. They'd played along with the engineer's jest. Only the men were foolish enough to have taken the matter seriously, the men and Noreen, of course.

Crackling mirth reached Grey's ears. He imagined the flurry he purposely left behind as he went below decks. Donning his blue coveralls, he spoke with Second Engineer Ray Casey who accompanied him on inspection. To a hand, his men were always glad to see him. If criticism were in order, they realized it was coming from an experienced sailor, and they looked upon it as information they needed to know. They'd heard how he'd argued hard with Captain Rockwell on their behalf to shorten the rotation in the boiler and engine rooms where heat exhaustion was a critical consideration. Since assigned tasks were done well and quickly, the captain accepted Mr. McKenna's decision. It was common knowledge Rockwell didn't appreciate the popularity of his chief engineer.

Many minutes later, Grey was at the rail, with the rhythmic meter of the pistons still in his thoughts.

"It was some joke you pulled on Captain Taylor and my daddy, Grey," Carolena told him. "Weren't you the least bit afraid it might backfire on you? That the ladies would demand your resignation because you were a bad influence on their husbands, that they didn't want your kind around them?" She couldn't understand why the tall man before her had deliberately endangered his position with the firm.

Watching the bow effortlessly slice its way through the soft chop, he answered her. "Ah, Miss Carolena. I see your concern for my blunder is genuine. I'm only surprised you haven't realized by now that I often toss caution over the side."

"You're sometimes foolhardy, but I don't understand how you were so certain everyone would see your humor."

She looked completely baffled, and he could stand her sweet confusion no longer. "All right. After all this time, I know the men and women in the dining room pretty well. And they know each other. Yet, the men forgot that fact for a moment. The ladies enjoyed seeing their husbands squirm. I figured it would be a matter of only a few minutes before they'd all be laughing at my statement and from the sound of it, they still are. Rest comfortable, little one, I can look out after myself."

His calloused hand patted hers as if he were her older brother. These platonic gestures left her doubting herself and her femininity.

Taking binoculars from their swinging case on a hook behind them, he looked west. "Land ho," came his words, strong and clear.

Using her hand to shade her moss-colored eyes, Carolena followed his line of sight. "Won't be long till we're all home, again," she said, naturally including him as if Fernandina on Amelia Island were his birthplace.

Chapter 3

As Grammy focused on the shoreline, her white-hair wispies were set free by the wind and whipped from beneath her bonnet, tickling the wrinkles on her cheeks. "I see the masts of ships in the harbor and the outline of the depot!" Her eyesight wasn't keen, so she wasn't certain if she really saw anything.

Home. Fernandina was her second home. When she counted, she was amazed to discover she'd lived there nigh onto eighteen years. After her husband, Pap, so named by their children, was killed in a fall from the roof while shoveling off a heavy snow, she'd allowed her younger daughter, Ella, to persuade her to leave Pennsylvania and move to the Deep South to live with the Dunnigans. Grammy objected, mostly because it put her so much farther from her older girl, Coe. Coe was married to Fries Dresher of Dresher Leather, originally out of New York City. Now, Coe and Fries lived in Charleston, making the distance bearable. It helped that Coe had kept her vow to write bimonthly and visit her mother a minimum of once a year and, too, living with Ella enabled Grammy to watch her grandbabies grow up.

Another reason to move south was the overflowing creeks of Johnstown, Pennsylvania. Situated in the foothills of the Allegheny Mountains as the town was, melting snows raised the river waters and washed the front stoop, and sometimes worse, of every home in the valley each spring. Pap was forever replacing ground floor boards, which over time would sponge up the muddy waters. It was all part of life if your husband was determined to live in the house his father built.

Wanting always to be with her family, Grammy had come on this trip to test the new boat. This one was a beaut, to be sure. Yet, with all its luxury, the short voyage had been a trial for her. Grammy wasn't feeling her best these days. She'd kept still about it, but the seas, though generally smooth, left her out of sorts. By God, she had a right. She was eighty-two years old! She was the oldest woman she knew of. And Grammy liked being the matriarch of both her family and the entire town of Fernandina. There would surely be a grand turnout at her funeral. She would put money on it if she were a gambling woman.

"Mother," said the ever-attentive Ella, "Please come out of the chilly breeze and sit over there under cover of the upper deck. Your little nose is getting pink."

Grammy smiled at her girl's ministrations and took Michael's arm as he led her to the cushioned chair.

"Here, Mother, let me put some bee's wax on to sooth the burn."

Sheltered from the wind and harsh rays, Grammy was almost comfortable. Close as she could tell, everyone had finished their breakfast and was on deck; all anxious to touch dry land. Watching the array of good folk before her, she folded her hands upon her lap and smiled peacefully.

Miss Ella and her husband walked to the stern of the ship. Standing behind her, Michael encircled her with his arms, his hands grasping the teak rail in front of them.

"Happy?" she asked him.

"I have more fish in this life than I can skin, my darlin'. If I were any happier, they'd have to charge an amusement tax." As they stood watching the wake slip away, he whispered so no one else would hear. "Then again, there is one thing that would make me giddy with delight."

"And what would that be?" Miss Ella inquired, feigning innocence.

"To play hide the ..."

"Hush," came her artificial reprimand. "Someone may hear." She should be aghast at his comment, but found it funny. It was a game they played. Michael was forever toying with her, trying to shock her. She never discussed remarks such as this with other women, yet guessed her husband was not so unusual. Most men probably had a secret side to them. She was glad hers did.

Grammy saw the loving exchange and was grateful her daughter was content. She spied The Terrible Threesome, at it again, slapping each other about, then running off, disappearing down the steep stairs, popping up around the next corner. Those boys have too much energy for their own good, she worried. No, she was happy the boys had so much stamina. It meant they were well on their way to becoming strong, capable men, men like Ella's Michael and Breelan's Waite. She saw Clabe Duffy. Let's see, Grammy wondered, what relation is he to me exactly? Since his wife, Noreen, is the sister of Michael, doesn't that make him my ... She thought on it for a time, gave up, and decided he wasn't anything to her except a kind and good friend. And how he endured his wife all these years was well beyond understanding.

Grammy noticed Halley with her father, her thumbs covered with Peeper's freshly applied pepper lotion to keep them from being sucked raw. The little girl's arms were filled with her homemade dollies, one applehead, one pew baby, and one wooden spool man. At the same time, the child was twisting around in an effort to count the number of "ornaments" she wore on a string tied about her waist.

"Daddy, please help me see behind my back. My eyes can't reach that far." Her father smiled at his little girl.

"Did Jack Patrick give you permission to borrow his furry rat tails?"

"Yes, sir. But you're silly. They're not furry rat tails, they're squirrelum tails. He said I could have 'em if I kept 'em clean."

"Oh, squirrelums. Hey, thanks for keeping me straight. I get confused sometimes," Waite replied indulgently crediting Monster, the family cat, for leaving behind such perfect treasures for imaginative children.

Grammy heard Carolena shout over the wind to her mother, "Mama, would you like to use my parasol?"

"I'm good, baby girl."

"If you're sure. Hey, stand over here, you and Daddy, and you, too, Marie, and you'll all be able to see better."

Gallantly forgetting he'd designed the ship, Michael replied, "You may be right, child. Thanks for looking out for your old ma and pa."

Grammy's eyes darted from familiar faces to spectacular scenery and back again. Giggling off to the side of the pilothouse was Nora, now joined by Carolena while Noreen kept vigil on her daughter. Grammy admired Nora for holding her tongue, most of the time. After all, she was a grown woman and having a controlling mother like Noreen, well, …

Peeper sauntered over, hickory walking stick in one hand, ear trumpet in the other. She plopped onto the chair beside Gram, saying, "Brr! Ever notice how wind on the water is so much cooler than on shore. Cain't wait 'til we go apicnicin' on the beach again. Them children needs ta burn off some extree energy." She looked at Waite and Halley. "I heard somewheres how the Irish say there's no man worn a scarf 'round his neck warm as the arms a his child."

"Amen," agreed Grammy.

Letting out an uncomfortable sigh, Peep said, "One of these days, I'm agonna' quit stuffing myself so. Then again, what pleasures in life is left an old woman like me? Ya know, I could hardly traverse stairs. These knees a mine is likely ta go out from under me at any time. They get ta painin' me so much, my heart hurts. And I got the bumble foot this morning, too. My feet feel like puffy little bald-headed men with headaches."

"I thought you soaked your corns last evening in that batch of hartshorn." The older woman recalled the stench of the ammonia preparation, as potent as smelling salts.

Peeper put her black trumpet to her ear. "What's that you say?" She could hear as well as the day she was born, but there was little use in accusing her of it. She liked the sympathy and visual flair the horn presented. It made folks slow up a tick or two and pay special attention to an aging female.

So Gram, herself confirmed partially deaf by Doctor Tackett, increased the volume of her speech. "I say, I thought you had a foot-soak last night?"

"I did, but these corns is harder than usual. This time, it'll take a while." She laid her hearing instrument in her lap and thought of the discomfort she was bearing so bravely.

Grammy whispered under her breath, "If you weren't so gull-derned vain and bought your shoes two sizes larger, you wouldn't be having corns in the first place."

Peeper expelled an insulted snuffle from flaring nostrils. She wasn't supposed to have heard this slander, so she couldn't comment upon it. Gram was the one person she'd allow to get away with little jabs. A'course, Gram did likewise. That's what proved they were friends. They were able to let things ride.

Peep closed her eyes against the glare of the water. Afraid she'd miss something, she opened them just as quickly. "And speaking of Saint Michael's, why that new organ rumbles like thunder! If you ask me, the way Mona Slider plays, sounds more like she's acallin' up the devil himself 'stead a the good Lord!"

The always loving, often grousing conversation rocketed from subject to subject. A stranger was frequently lost. Grammy, never. But entering a church, any church, for her was like entering the heart of God. Therefore, she felt it her duty to scold Peeper to save her soul from any more scarring. "Why Gaylee Maude! You've said some outrageous things in your time, gal. You'd best be glad Father Kilcoyne didn't hear you. Your last remark would try the patience of—"

Interrupting as was her usual, Peeper asked, "Didn't you sleep good last night? You was floppin' like a trout." Before Grammy could speak, Peeper declared, "Take a look over yonder, Gram. There's a big old thundercloud arisin' up. Looks like it's on the east side of the island, out near our place. We could use a bit a dampness. This past season's been so dry. Your own periwinkles wilted the one day Clover forgot to put water on 'em. Hard ta remember a much crueler month in recent years."

Captain Taylor took his brass spyglass from Halley. "Let your daddy see, would ya, baby girl?"

She relinquished the telescope to him. Devoted, she always did his bidding without hesitation.

"Go to your mother, Halley."

Breelan gathered the child to her and although his words were casual, his wife caught a concern in them that made her look up into his strong face. She saw his jaw clench once he'd adjusted the glass into focus. Breelan asked no questions.

"Mama," said Halley. "I saw all the people waving at us! They're welcoming us home!"

"Isn't it grand of them?"

"I hear a ringing, too!"

"Yes, angel, I can hear it."

Carolena was nearby now and listening. She wondered whose bell was ringing. People struck their bells for many reasons, a downtown merchant hawking a sale, the birth of a baby, the calling of a church service or chow time, a fire. She hoped it was ringing for any purpose other than the last. The fire of '76 burned the wooden structures of Fernandina from the docks to Third Street. More recently, another in '83 destroyed the south side of Centre Street, the main road of town, from South 2nd Street to South 3rd.

The interior designer looked about for Grey then remembered he'd told her he'd be back in the engine room until they were fully and safely docked. She glanced around to see Captain Rockwell scowl from the pilothouse, the creases across his forehead running deeper than usual. Of course, she assured herself, it was because it took great concentration to guide such a large ship as the *Coral Crown* into her slip. A slapdash job of it would create little confidence in any future passengers who might be observing.

Nora and others on board waved their arms from down low at one side, round about to the other, in order for the distant throng to see. The teenage boys aboard were all swinging wildly with accompanying whistles. Deciding not to fret and simply enjoy the impressive view from this watery approach, Carolena joined in, wagging her limbs and grinning, copying the others.

As the ship skillfully slid closer to the pier, those along the shore grew silent. Only the shrill clang of the bell was heard. It seemed to stifle the natural sounds around them until it, too, stilled. The breeze disappeared and sunshine drenched everyone in their own perspiration.

"Mama?" asked Marie, gaining in height toward the five-foot one-inch Miss Ella. "Is there something the matter? Why are the people on the docks so quiet and not smiling at us? And where's Clover with the buggy to take us home? He's so punctual about everything. I think we're pulling in on time. Mr. Grey said we would."

Miss Ella's thoughts turned back to the days of the war. Faces were sad then, too. She gripped the rail, answering her daughter, "I don't know, sweetsie. I don't know."

Hearty hands tied the hawsers, securing the ship to the heavy brass cleats on the pier. Even Nora's attention was torn from the brawny sailors and, unthinking, she reached for Carolena's hand. Michael Dunnigan and Captain Waite were the first to disembark. Although several male faces seemed anxious to talk to them, only Doctor Tackett, their family physician, stepped forth.

Not hearing his words, the passengers left on board understood one thing. There was something wrong and desperately so.

Michael was the first to turn around and when he did, his shoulders stooped and his head hung low. Waite, with the obvious intent to assist, took his arm and together, they climbed the gangway back onto the *Crown* with the doctor close behind.

Miss Ella rushed to her husband and everyone followed. "Tell us, darling. Whatever it is. We're all here. We'll all pull together." Her words were not hollow. Those aboard vowed to help, despite not knowing the particulars.

When Waite looked into Michael's blue eyes, he saw tears threatening to overflow the rims and realized his partner hadn't the words. The captain spoke instead. "I need you all to remain calm." Weighing every syllable, he said, "Clover is safe. But, we've just been informed there was a fire."

The intake of breath on the ship was audible from the shore.

He continued, his words staggering the explanation. "A fire has broken out on the Dunnigan grounds."

"Well, by God, what in hell are we all doin' here?" hollered Jack Patrick, already running down the plank just laid. "Come on, lads!"

Waite shouted his name but one time. The boy returned.

Though he was annoyed at the forced delay, he asked respectfully, "Sir?"

"I'm sorry to tell you this. The fire happened early this morning. From the little I know about it, by the time the water truck got there, the place was pretty much engulfed."

There was no more to say, and no need to say more.

***

A parade of ten or so buggies carried the disembarked passengers and those who hoped to help in some small way. Headed due east away from the port and toward the Atlantic Ocean, Waite and Grey drove the family. Overflow, including a miffed Aunt Noreen, followed in Major Fairbanks' rig.

"No offence, Major, but I should at least be in the second buggy, if not the lead carriage. After all, it's my brother's house that's burned to the ground."

"Yes, ma'am," was his reply as he wondered at his luck at having to escort Noreen Duffy. At least she was in the back seat.

"I see you've got your prayer book with you, Father. From what I've heard, we'll be needing it."

"I know we will, Major. I know we will."

There was little conversation. An occasional sea gull let forth an irritating caw. No one noticed. All attention focused on the massive smoke cloud hanging in the air. Finally turning right onto Dunn Avenue, the caravan passed three recently built homes.

To Carolena, it seemed the neighbors, either on their front porches or standing in their yards, were paying last respects to the passing funeral cortege.

Then the cloud lay before them, and there was little option but to enter the murk. Although it was still a sun-filled morning, the dusk of tragedy added to the nightmare. Most began coughing. Retrieving their delicate lace handkerchiefs from their reticules, the ladies covered their noses and mouths against the acrid air. Halley wriggled as Breelan tried to protect her with a shawl. Marie protested when Miss Ella instructed her to bury her head in her skirts.

The next house on the right was the brick Duffy home, still strong and sturdy. A barking dog ran from the porch toward the buggies. Despite his soot-darkened coat, he was recognizable as Blackie-White-Spots. Jack Patrick jumped from the wagon to meet him. Thrilled to see his master, the mongrel took no heed when commanded to stay and behave. His joy at his family's return was no reason to begin obedience.

Reality loomed. The showplace Michael designed and built to honor his bride was gone. Consumed. All of it.

Friends and volunteer firemen, townsfolk, and strangers stood about, not speaking. Their faces and bodies were dark with soot, like the dog. They were one with the surroundings. Only glowing wood and smoldering ash were left, save for five tall brick chimneys. Those towers rose like markers in an ebony graveyard designating the place where every Dunnigan possession lay burned or charred. The little house out back, a smaller version of the mansion, where Peeper and Grammy lived - gone. The four-year-old Taylor home beyond that - gone.

But there was Clover! Alive. He'd removed his hat, his tears washing a trail through the ash on his black face. "Clover's barn," as everyone called it, was gone too, as was his nearby cabin. He had lived there next to the stable, which had housed all his critters. Those animals were running loose now, frightened of their unaccustomed freedom and the unnatural smell of smoke, yet interested most in their next feeding and watering.

Carolena looked to the south, straining her eyes to see through the dark haze and saw Clip and Clop, their two gray horses, searching for fresh grass among the dried weeds and nettles in the sand. There was Noir, Breelan's beloved mount. He was headed their way. Afraid, he'd come too near the hot remains and with Halley still in her arms, Breelan climbed from the buggy to meet him. She set her little girl on her feet and pressed her face into the horse's mane, soundlessly screaming. She hugged his muscled neck as her daughter gripped her mother's knees.

Breelan's movement stirred the group. Miss Ella, as usual, took charge. She desperately wanted to draw a cleansing breath. It was impossible. With uncontrollable tears still falling, she told her grandson, "Mickey, take Halley, Marie, Peeper and Grammy to Aunt Noreen's and stay with them. They've already breathed too much of this caustic air."

He had never seen his grandmother so shaken, nor felt as childlike as he did now. He didn't know what to do, and so he did as any young man should. He listened. He gathered his charges, all but one. Grammy.

Miss Ella didn't need an argument. "Mother, I want you out of this smoke."

"Think I'll sit up here a time, and then I'll be going. I want to be with you all, not apart."

"But Mother —"

"If'n Grammy's astayin', so am I," proclaimed Peeper. She wasn't about to leave her dearest friend.

"Oh, for God's sake!" Frustrated, Miss Ella waved Mickey away to escort the children across the cropped field toward Duffy Place.

The wind picked up to swirl the smoke, letting in the barest inkling of clean, fresh air to permeate the stench. Father Kilcoyne thought this was a sign. "Please, everyone," he called. "Please, come together and pray with me."

As if heavy chains wrapped their legs, they dragged themselves to him. It took no effort to bow their heads. They were already low.

"In the name of the Father and of the Son and of the Holy Ghost. Dearest Father in Heaven, we come together this day to ask for Your aid in what seems to be a world torn apart by flame. We are blessed, however, that by Your Hand, the lives of Your children have been spared. Yea, though this is a sad time for the family Dunnigan, that which is lost is only manmade and of this earth. Please let this be a special time that might bring them closer to one another and to You, precious Lord. With each defeat, there is victory, victory of mind and victory of spirit as we gather as one to scale the challenge before us. We know not why we have been presented with such a test. Only You, great God, hold the reason. It is not ours to question our fate. It is ours to do what needs to be done to recover. And in our recovery, we will please You."

Most of the gathered thought him through. He continued.

"Blessed be the name of the Lord. As with all things, beloved Creator, Your wisdom is beyond our understanding. May we not question. May we instead praise and thank You. Therefore, let us follow Your teachings and in doing so, with Your guidance, we shall find peace. For goodness comes when we walk with You, our Lord and Savior. Lead us to that goodness as we praise Your Name, oh God, remembering always, Thy will be done. Thank You for all You have done and will do for us, now and forever. To Your glory and honor, in Jesus' name, we pray. Amen."

"Amen."

The people's response was automatic, and the gentle father wondered if his words were helpful. He hoped they would be remembered and absorbed and somehow comfort.

"Well, goddamn!"

Although the voice was readily recognized, brows snapped up to attention.

"Thank you, Father Kilcoyne," cooed Michael Dunnigan. "I, for one, can't tell of the solace your words have brought me. Hell, let's indeed thank the Lord for all His works."

"Michael, dear," his wife pleaded. "Darling, come away from here. We'll—"

"We'll what, Ella. Go where? Shall we stay next door at my sister's? Let's see. How many in one house would that make? Fourteen, fifteen? No, sixteen with Clover. Of course, we haven't been invited to stay."

Noreen Duffy said nothing. She couldn't imagine and didn't want to think about having to share her spotless home with an invading horde.

Major Fairbanks, city father and kind man, spoke into the hush, "Michael, please stay with me at Fairbanks House. You know how huge it is. With ten fireplaces in the house, there's plenty of heat if we need it. Miss Ella can decide the menu every day or just sit back and rest. My library is as yet untapped by Carolena, and Marie will enjoy the playroom over the kitchen. The boys are welcome to sleep in the tower if they like."

Clabe Duffy spoke up. He loved his brother-in-law. The thought of so many in one place did seem unsettling. No matter, they would get by. "Michael, you should know you have a home with us. We would have it no other way. There just hasn't been a chance to say so. The latch string is always out."

Dismissing the invitations, Michael continued, "Can you imagine? Just picture Noreen. Why she'd be in one dither after the next every time someone neglected to hang up a hat or dented a cushion or dropped crumbs on her carpet."

Noreen was aghast her brother would speak so of her and in front of other people, too! And why wasn't Clabe standing up for her, for land sake?

"Michael. Stop it. You don't mean what you're saying. Please stop."

He heard his wife speaking, and every vowel and consonant from her sweet voice, reminded him of what they'd lost, what she'd have to live without. "The business is gone. What a fine idea I had to move the office to our house. Not only are all our possessions an unrecognizable crisp, all our drawings, all our calibrations, all our records and equipment are, too."

Waite spoke. "You only did it, sir, so we could be near one another. We all thought it was a fine idea. It'll take time, a lot of time, but we'll rebuild. We'll rebuild the houses and the business."

Michael looked hard at his son-in-law. "And how shall we pay for all this, my boy?"

Waite and the others were puzzled. Insurance, naturally. Blessed fire insurance. "Since the land was given you by your brother, Fitz, and the house paid off long ago, the insurance will pay for a fine new place." Waite was trying his damnedest to keep up a good front for everyone.

"Ah, but that's what you don't know. We have no insurance, and the whole complex was mortgaged to pay for the passenger line." There was no excitement in Michael's tone or panic, just statement of fact. Ugly, horrible fact.

It was then friends turned away and strangers left. They knew this was not for their ears, nor did they want to learn more. This tragedy would continue well beyond the devastation of the flames. All those leaving went away counting their own blessings.

This time it was Waite whose features faded from tan to pale. The breeze had cleared a goodly portion of the smoke away by now, and the sun was blistering. It went unnoticed. Michael had begun a tale no one wanted to hear though they realized they must listen.

Michael continued, "You all thought me so good at ciphering. The truth is we didn't have the extra capital going into the ship building business the way we should have. I wanted to do it anyway, and I could see how much everyone else wanted it. So many other families never get along. Not us. We were an innovative, motivated, enthusiastic group, but we severely under-budgeted the start-up cost. Or rather, I did. Then, short of bank robbery, I had nowhere to turn. So, Father," he eyed the priest, "I put all my trust in the Lord. I bet on divine intervention while things only got tighter. I had no choice. I mortgaged our place to get the funds we needed. The business started off slow enough. Some of you know that. Despite a pick-up in bookings, the profits have never caught up with the debt. I got in arrears with the fire insurance installments on the property, and the policy lapsed one week before we left on this trip. I hoped to reinstate coverage with the monies we got from the first cruise booked on the *Coral Crown*. We're sold out, and I thought with two ships running, we'd soon be in tall cotton, soon turn the corner.

"Don't you all see? I've been juggling the ledgers, paying only the creditors who would cause us the most grief, and stalling the others. You often asked me why I used suppliers from out of town when it would be less costly to use resources closer by. You believed me when I told you I found the goods were of better quality and only the best would do for our company. I was simply trying to cloak our financial position. Local merchants would have spread the word the Aqua Verde Passenger Line was a bad risk, that we didn't pay our bills. I dreaded getting the mail everyday for fear of another threatening demand to pay up. If you remember, I always did watch for the mail so no one would see the nasty correspondence."

Michael seemed to never draw a breath. Spilling the sobering truth, he straightened, as if each word of confession chipped the weight of burden from his shoulders.

"Before you say anything, Clabe, since you're a financial officer at the bank, I know you're wondering how you never heard a thing about this. It was easy. I have some dirt on the bank president, your boss. I threatened to disclose that information if he told anyone how I'd gotten the money to build the *Crown*. He handled the deal personally.

"I guess, Father, I got my divine intervention after all. Your good Lord is telling me to pull my proud-ass neck back into my shoulders, huh? In a mixed up concoction of false pride and love for my family, I ruined the lives of the very ones I hold dear." Then, saying no more, he walked away.

Miss Ella didn't try to stop him. She was in shock, as was the rest of the family, a shock that was real, total, complete, and jarring.

Carolena didn't know quite what to do. She was aware there were people who were poor, people who did without. Now she was one of those people. She had no roof over her head, no bed in which to sleep, no food to eat, no clothes to wear except the few in her trunk, no books to read, no soap with which to cleanse herself, no photographs to remember, no trinkets to treasure. She had nothing.

She looked at those standing before her and realized they, too, had nothing. All the years. All the mementos. Everyone would have to start over, a task she speculated would be somewhat easier the younger one was. Youth has an innate sense of optimism, or at least she hoped it was so. What about Gram and Peep? What about her dear mother and father?

At no time did it occur to Carolena that her father had really done anything wrong. After all, he was a father, and they handle situations. That's exactly what this was. A situation. Her daddy was only distraught. Everyone was. Things would get better. Father Kilcoyne was right. They had been spared their lives. That had to be remembered, and the good Lord praised for it.

"Look what I found!" cried a triumphant Warren Lowell. "It's all fouled with soot, but you can make out it's a tin-type!" He wiped the char with his clean sleeve, leaving Aunt Noreen aghast at the filth.

"Really, Warren. You've just ruined that shirt, and it's one of your newest."

Ignoring her, Warren Lowell said, "I found it in a metal box. The box must have protected it, Gram. Don't know exactly who it's a picture of. Looks to be two adults and a child."

"Let me see, boy." Grammy raised herself to stand in the buggy and reached for the picture. She recognized the photo at once.

Jack Patrick was close behind, anxious to see for himself. His sudden running footsteps combined with the alien air and surroundings to startle one of the mules hitched to the wagon. It lurched forward a few feet. Always somewhat top heavy and never really possessing much balance, Grammy tumbled off, hitting her chest against the wheel before thudding to the ground.

"Mother? Mother!" Miss Ella called out and in a moment was holding the old woman in her arms, rocking her back and forth. "It's alright, darling, I'm here," she said, kissing her mother's brow. "Grey! Waite! Hold those animals still! Get her back up into the rig. Lay her flat. Be gentle with her! We'll take her to Noreen's. We've got to get her out of the heat."

Well, I like that, tsked Noreen to herself. And after the way my brother insulted me. Without an apology, they expect me to up and forget what he's said and be nursemaid to Grammy. It isn't Grammy's fault what comes from Michael's mouth, I guess. But they could have asked me. She sighed.

"No, Ella. Let me be, dear." A tiny bubble of blood, dripped from the corner of Grammy's mouth. "These old bones have cooked in the heat before. It won't do any harm. I could surely stand a drink of water though, if one's handy."

"Certainly." Ella frantically looked about for some refreshment for her suffering mother.

"I'll get some water from the well out back," yelled Jack Patrick.

"No time. No time," Grammy exhaled.

Clover was running toward them with the end of the fire hose in his hand. The firemen had left their drained wagon in a hasty departure to give privacy to the family. Clover held the nozzle near the grandmother's mouth, and the last slow-falling drops caressed her dry lips.

"Smart fella, that one." The shriveled woman mustered a wink at the sad man and saw tears drip from his chin.

"Peeper?"

"Yes, Gram. Right here." Though her knees were hurting her something fierce, she knelt in the hot sand. Forgetting her own pain, she ignored the coarse breathing and the chain of claret bubbles her closest friend emitted with each labored breath. Her prayers were with Grammy. Clasping hands, the two looked upon one another for the final time.

"Peep, I want to thank you for taking in a grumpy old Yankee and treating her like a sister. You'll never know all you've meant to me. Never. Now gather round, the rest of you."

Peeper Clegg hadn't felt so heartsick since her own child died many years past. Who would she have to complain to? Who would tell her when she'd crossed the line with her sassy tongue? Who would be there to fuss at and share with?

The family shaded the two elderly women with the comfort of their love, and Grammy continued to speak, her voice an ugly rasp. "Breelan, you're a fine wife and mother. Carry on with your writing, darling. Remember, whether everyone in the world reads your stories or only your family, know the time you spent writing them brought you pleasure, and you'll leave a proud legacy for your children. That's what's most important."

The brunette hadn't suspected her grandmother knew she had written much more than newspaper articles and advertising. Her lips curved in a gentle smile as her tears dropped, leaving dark polka dots on the precious woman's blue print dress. She shouldn't be surprised. Grammy always said she knew what her family was thinking.

"Waite, just keep on treating my grandchild here the way you have been, and I'll go happy."

Grammy was taking slow, painful gasps. It was obvious to the adults that, in the fall, her ribs had hit the wheel and broken, piercing her lung.

Captain Taylor put his arm around his wife's waist and hugged her close. He turned his eyes toward Duffy Place. He had to. He was having a time with this one. Jennie Eckert had become his grandmother, too, and he would miss her welcome advice.

"Carolena, there's a good man in your future, and one day you'll find each other. Until that time comes, help your family in the business. You be the solid one for your father. You are blessed with a fine brain. Use it well."

You be the solid one for your father. That was what Carolena heard, appreciating the mighty commission Grammy had given her.

"Tell Marie and Halley, they've been my heart's delight. And tell Mickey he's made a fine addition to our family. I'm mighty proud of him.

"Are the Duffys about?" Squinting, "Yes, I can see you. I've come to love you as my children. Do what you can to help out, and the Lord will grace you for it."

Noreen put on a limp grin as she envisioned her own future. At least Grammy has the polish to appreciate what we're about to do for the Dunnigans.

"Jack Patrick, my dear, dear Bird of the Earth. Remember, I used to call you that when you were a little boy?"

He nodded, wanting her to go on calling him the silly, endearing name.

"Be good to your sisters. And Ella, you are the strongest of the lot. You'll have to be. Don't let the family split over this loss. Look for the good."

"I'll try, Mother. I promise to try. We didn't split before. We won't now." Futilely wiping at the bloody drool spilling onto her mother's throat and back toward her ear, Miss Ella murmured, "Mother, I forgive you."

Some listening especially hard wondered what heinous act Grammy had performed to be needing pardon on her deathbed by her daughter.

Miss Ella was afraid to speak further for fear her words turn to wails. How can I be strong, Mother, without you here to help me?

"Tell your sister, Coe, her mama was thinking of her at the last. Tell her, too, I'm anxious to see your father up yonder. He's waiting for me, I'm sure of it." She paused a moment, smiled and then said clearly, "I see seven little angels sittin' on a fence, pointin' the way." Grammy closed her eyes and was gone.

Ella tried to do as Grammy asked. Removing the picture from the slackened old hand, the daughter laid it over her mother's heart, where all energy and courage had vanished. Ella put her head on the soft bosom, stilled for all time, and wept. As her own heart splintered, so did many more around her. No one cared to hide his pain. Not the girls, not the women, not the boys, not the men.

Patting Ella's shoulder, Noreen was the first to speak. Amidst forced, dry sniffs, she said, "Come, dear. Let's take your mother from beneath the sun. We'll spread her out on my dining table. She always did like my cooking." The stout woman confided to her husband, "If Michael had built his house of brick, not wood, like we did, they could use their own table."

Clabe Duffy slapped his wife for the first time in his life. Nobody questioned whether she deserved it. Most wondered why it hadn't happened sooner.

Chapter 4

The days that followed were challenging. So many living so closely, there was no space for a private conversation. Cabin fever was contagious; its victims easy prey. Few held strong. Most gave into it with increasing frequency.

"God Almighty!" Noreen screeched as she fiddled with the black jet dove-shaped brooch at her throat representing Grammy's resurrection to heaven. It secured the removable black collar of her matching mourning gown. "I'm certain Peeper did it on purpose."

"Did what?" Clabe asked, following her down the stairs and into the parlor while wondering what sin dear Peeper could have committed this time.

"She used hot water to wash my neck pieces and spare cuffs, too, and now they've shrunk. This thing is so tight, I'm close to choking! She's such an evil creature. I wish she had died instead of Grammy. You won't see me wearing black for that one. Everyone knows I'm a stickler for tradition, and I'll wear these gruesome clothes for Grammy, but not for Peeper. Before I do, I'll be the one in the casket!"

"You don't say," Clabe mumbled, thinking that might not be such a bad idea.

"Excuse me?" his wife inquired.

"Pretty day."

Noreen was on a rant that wasn't finished. "And it looks like someone picked up this house and shook it! This disarray is getting the best of me, Clabe. I don't know how much longer I can remain still on the subject. Why, Ella would never let her own place look like this. If only Grammy had left her piddly fortune to her daughter instead of the church, maybe Ella and Michael could rent a house."

Clabe listened to his wife's tirade as he had all the long years of their lives together. To counter her grousing, he concentrated on his own thoughts, nodding occasionally in her direction. It had worked thousands of times before. But recently, her grumbling had begun to penetrate his senses. This time he heard the words and said, "Noreen, hush! What if someone tells Ella what you've said? It will embarrass her to the bone. That woman has stood so much already, she doesn't need you applying more pressure."

Shocked at her husband's defense of the untidy intruder, Noreen almost screamed. "At this point, I honestly don't give a tinker's damn if she hears the word from me or the grapevine. The camel is getting his nose under the tent for certain."

"What does that mean?"

"It means I know my brother. He never does things in half measures. When he eats, he overeats. When he drinks, he gets drunk. Now that we've given him an inch of our house, he'll take over the parlor, the kitchen, the front porch—"

"And you call yourself a good Christian woman?"

"Don't be twisting matters to make me out the villain. The entire situation is getting out of hand, Clabe, and I don't mind saying so. You can't tell me you're enjoying this–this invasion of our home, can you?"

"Of course not. This is no way for anyone to be living. But the Dunnigans would feed and shelter us if the situation were reversed. For God's sake, you're speaking of your own brother's family as if they were—"

"You can try and give me the guilts all day long. It won't work. I'm warning you, I won't be able to tolerate much more before I burst!"

From out of nowhere, Peeper's voice was loud and clear, "Some folks would complain if they was hung with a new rope."

Uncomfortable, Clabe faced his wife squarely. His soothing voice disguised his temper. "Noreen, your life has been richly blessed, yet you harp on how Michael and Ella's situation is a hardship on you. In truth, your complaining only demonstrates to the world what a selfish, spoiled, uncaring bitch you really are!"

Noreen fell into the rocking chair, her excessive weight tipping it back so far it nearly toppled over. Clabe offered no assistance to right it and turned away when he saw the white of his wife's petticoat, the thought of intimacy with her raising bile to his throat.

Planting her thick feet firmly on the hand-woven Oriental carpet, Noreen stood. Ignoring her husband's cruelty, she continued, her tone sawing forth the words. "The Dunnigan name stands, or rather used to stand, for something in Fernandina. Rumors are flying that the family business is in serious trouble due to Michael's mishandling."

"Enough!" screamed Clabe in a thunderous whisper. "You may feel cold and heartless toward your kin, but I forbid you to show it any longer! If you utter one more insulting word about—"

Noreen would not be forbidden to do anything, not by her husband or anyone. Her head listed slightly to the right. "Just what punishment would you inflict upon your wife, dear Clabe? Perhaps another slap across the face in public? I must say, that did much to bolster the Duffy name. Should you ever, ever again lay a finger on—"

"Good morning all," said Miss Ella, as cheerfully as she was able. Despite the black crepe gown and mourning cap she was obliged to wear for a year and a day, she smiled. She thought how, after this sad period passed, she would don the gray or dark purple dresses as a sign of half mourning. It was the way of things, and Grammy had been such a wonderful mother, especially in these last years. She deserved the respect signified by the armbands, dark clothing, dull jewelry, and bracelets made of Grammy's own braided white hair. Tired of all the sadness, Ella wanted to complain, the same as everybody else, though pretense was the mode of the hour.

"It's bottling time again," Miss Ella commented. "The day's so pretty, let's just bottle it up, shall we?" As she talked, she scurried about the front room, picking up Halley's paper dolls, which Peeper had cut from Aunt Noreen's latest issue of *Godey's Lady's Book* magazine.

"Shhh!" Noreen hissed. "What's that noise?"

An unrecognizable pinging sounded, followed by her unexpected squeal when something hard hit the side of her broad heeled shoe. The aunt's eyes traced the path from which a rolling marble came to find Monstrose curled in the center of the Chinese checkerboard left on the floor by The Terrible Threesome. "You should have drowned that monster cat long ago," the callous hostess declared. "He is aptly named. Michael has shown me the scars on his forearms. If your children weren't so softhearted toward animals ..." She looked at Miss Ella. "And you and my brother, right along with them ... Oow, I can't abide him rubbing against my skirts. I have cat fur all over me. We all do, wearing this black business."

I'd rather be softhearted than be a viper like you, Noreen, Miss Ella wanted to say. Compared to you, our Monstie would win first prize in a charm school contest.

For his current amusement and without straining his neck muscles by lifting his head, the feline subject of disharmony, lay on his side among the scattered marbles. With the most minute of efforts, one huge paw batted a tiger eye, then a bismuth, then a hematite sphere, sending the marbles thumping against the papered wall, the low sill of the window, the bookcase, the Bible stand, a slipper, and whatever lay in the way.

"Don't look at me like that, you nasty critter," Noreen warned. "I've had just about enough from you. Why you're almost more trouble than Halley is." She'd temporarily forgotten houseguests surrounded her. "Oh, of course, I love that little girl, Ella. It's just that Clabe and I aren't used to wee children under foot who cause commotion far into the night."

By this time, Miss Ella wanted her sister-in-law to advance on Monstie so he could give her a good comeuppance with his claws. However, her ingrained godly spirit would not permit it, and she was quick to grab Noreen's arm before she made a move to snatch up the cat and toss him from her house.

"Move along, Monstie darling," Miss Ella told him. His eyes half closed, he did her bidding when she gently prodded him with a rolled newspaper. Miss Ella concluded the disgruntled cat would find another inappropriate location soon enough, his labors at Chinese checkers having been interrupted.

Halley entered the room, tracking in sand.

"Now look at that mess, and Nora swept in here only last evening," Aunt Noreen whined.

With a big smile, Halley wanted to include her aunt in family activities, an often difficult task since Aunt Noreen didn't like to play games or with dolls. "There's more sand in the kitchen for you to clean up, too,

Auntie!"

"My stars. Ella!" screamed the witch of the house.

"Get the broom and dustpan, Halley, and you can help me."

Confused why she would help her grandmother and not her aunt, the child walked back into the kitchen.

A tense silence followed. Miss Ella filled it with small talk. "I have to say the sleeping arrangements seem to be working out pretty well." She chatted on, thinking she'd just told a whopper of a fib since everyone was pretty much uncomfortable. With her daughter, Marie, taking the window seat in the guest room she shared with Michael, there was no opportunity for privacy for mother and father. Nora and Peeper shared the bed in Nora's room with Carolena crowding in on a cot. The late-night rumble from the old woman's clogged sinuses kept the two girls half-exhausted. Neither spoke of it for they would never hurt the feelings of their ancient friend or make her self-conscious.

Jack Patrick and Mickey had set up a tent outside, battling the mosquitoes and other insects, with plans to make pallets in the attic if the weather demanded it. Since Breelan, Waite, and Halley had Warren Lowell's room, Warren was relegated to the parlor sofa. To his relief, his father finally prevailed against his over-protective mother, and he was granted permission to sleep out of doors with his cousins. Although he scratched his bug bites each morning, Warren Lowell found it a marvelous adventure. Clover hung a hammock in the Duffy bunkhouse where their man, Justice, made his home. The only two not dislocated were Clabe and Noreen. It was a temporary arrangement for everyone else. The problem was no one could define "temporary."

"I believe Peeper has made muffins for breakfast. I can smell them now," said Clabe, rubbing his hands together in anticipation of the fine treat to come. "It's a bonus Peeper and Miss Ella are wonderful cooks."

Noreen was left waiting for a culinary compliment. None was forthcoming.

"Thank you, Clabe. Tell me how you slept last night, Noreen," inquired Miss Ella, not particularly caring.

At that moment, Halley returned without the broom. Instead, she was holding her Uncle Clabe's fragile leaded glass kaleidoscope, a birthday present recently given him by his wife. "Show grandma what you've got, darling," Miss Ella coaxed while not taking her eyes off her sister-in-law's puckered lips. "Thank you. Are you all washed up and ready for breakfast?"

"Yes, ma'am. Peeper told me if I eat all my food, she'd let me peel the eggs!"

"How exciting for you," commented Aunt Noreen with a snarl.

Miss Ella felt her teeth might crack from the pressure she applied to them. She was grateful Breelan and, dear God, Waite, hadn't heard the woman's attitude toward their daughter. They would have pulled their tiny family out of the Duffy house so fast ...

Clabe spoke. "We slept just fine, thank you, Miss Ella."

Seeing the look of warning cross her husband's face, Noreen defied him by saying, "After dark, it's like lights out in the reptile house." She sighed. "That's to be expected, I suppose, with so many of us. I heard doors slamming in the middle of the night, and voices, too."

"I'm sorry you were disturbed. I believe the children were up once or twice to avail themselves of the facilities. That's always the way with the younger ones."

"And with a few grown-ups I know, too." Clabe remembered his wife leaving their room twice.

"Well, I was hungry," Noreen declared. "My stomach wouldn't let me sleep. By the way, guess who I ran into in the kitchen? Michael. He polished off the last of the ham I was saving for lunch today. We'll have to rework the noon meal now that the meat has been eaten."

Mortified her husband was caught plundering the icebox, Miss Ella apologized, again. "I'm sorry, Noreen. You know your brother has quite an appetite."

"If he ate less, his trousers wouldn't fit him so snugly and ..."

Clabe broke in, stopping his wife mid-sentence. "What are your plans today, Miss Ella?"

Thankful for her friend's interruption, "After I rework lunch with Peeper, there's paperwork."

"I want vegable soup, Gamma, with no vegables!"

Never appreciating spontaneous children's chatter, Noreen gave her unsolicited opinion. "Great day, girl. The word is pronounced veg-e-ta-ble and you can't have vegetable soup without the vegetables."

"I can so. My mama always makes it that way for me." Halley was near tears. Still, the tiny child stood toe to toe with her great aunt.

Miss Ella took hold of her granddaughter's shoulders, turning her in the direction of the kitchen. "Run along to Peeper, sweetsie, and tell her what you want. She can open a jar of tomatoes for you quick enough."

"Can I help her mash 'um, so they disappear?"

"I'll bet she'll welcome your help."

"She always does, Gram. Just like you do."

"That's my dearest girl. Go on now."

Before Noreen chewed the subject of soup to death, Miss Ella detailed her upcoming day's plans. "Yes, Clabe. I have much paperwork to do. With having to let go Michael's secretaries, I've all the correspondence, reservations, and ticketing to tend to. I'll be spending much of my time working on that."

"What a beautiful morning it is!" came Breelan's bright appraisal.

"Good morning, dear niece," her uncle greeted. She quickly kissed him on his whiskered cheek. "And how will you fill the hours today?"

"I'll be busy, busy. Peeper said she'd watch Halley for me while she cleaned. You know her and pot-walloppin'. She sees a dull kettle and won't let it be until it's bright as new."

Noreen sensed an insult. If her kettles weren't as shiny as they used to be, she had good reason. Some of them were decades old! Well, if the silly old woman wanted to wear her elbows out rubbing, so be it.

"Then she's going to make a fresh batch of sugar starch and go to work on your doilies, Aunt Noreen."

Noreen replied, "Had it not been for the fire and the expense of extra company, Clabe was going to get me a maid, you know. He hates to see me doing menial chores, don't you, dear? They're best left to the uneducated. What with so many open mouths around here, we decided to wait on my maid until after you're gone." Noreen noted the others in the room were speechless. Good, she thought. I've gotten my point across. They need to realize they're a burden in our happy home. It may motivate them to work harder to get out.

Breelan shook her head to recover and staunchly continued. "Anyway, with Halley occupied, I can get the advertising copy off to New York. We've had success in the past with minimal advertising. Word of mouth has worked well. Right now, we need more passengers and fast. We'd like both the *Miss Breelan* and the *Coral Crown* fully booked to hasten our return to ..." Breelan was unable to find the words. And she was responsible for attracting customers to their business with her prose? It was such a daunting and important task, she realized.

Her mother finished Bree's sentence. "... until we're back on our feet."

"Speaking of feet, where are Michael's?" Noreen looked about theatrically.

Miss Ella grimaced. Not again! "Your brother had difficulty sleeping. He must still be in bed."

Suddenly the front door flew open behind them and in came the man himself wearing not his usual dark suit, but a work shirt and loose trousers. "What's everyone doing in the parlor? I've been out gettin' a worm wet." He proudly held high five red bass and three flounder. "Don't I warrant a howdy-do from anybody?"

Miss Ella and Breelan rushed to greet him.

"After I clean them, a little cornmeal and garlic on these beauties and they'll be plenty enough lunch for all of us." Drawing a deep breath of air, Michael said, "While I was casting, I thought of another idea for a new design for a house. Can't wait to get started. First things first, though. I smell breakfast. Let's go get some, shall we?" And he led the way into the dining room like the place was his.

After eating, Miss Ella dried while Peeper washed the dishes as they discussed rose pruning. "You'd best be tending them white climbers of 'yourn, Noreena, or all you'll be agettin' is green leaves. They need ta be dead-headed regular-like."

Noreen sat in the kitchen sipping her third cup of coffee, annoyed her fleshy forearms were resting on crumbs. "You've forgotten to wipe off the table," she reminded Peeper.

The eldest lady balled up a clammy dishrag and threw it at the mistress of the house, just glancing her topknot of hair and knocking it slightly askew.

"Peeper Clegg! You mean old crone!" Noreen shrieked. "Someone should have blistered your behind as a child. How dare you?"

"How dare I?" Peeper mocked. "I'll show you how I dare." She picked up a knitted potholder, dipped it in the pan of sudsy water and lobbed the dripping projectile at her intended target. This time it missed and hit the window, sliding down to the sill. "Hmm. I need ta be aworkin' on my wrist action. My aim is off ta the right, just a whit."

Noreen stood, brushed off her elbows, pushed back the fallen hair in her eyes from the first attack, and ordered, "Clean up the mess!"

"Certainly, I'll clean up after ya, ya crab ya! Lord knows you'd be asteppin' over a spot a mud or grease sos you dasn't git your hands dirty. If it tweren't for your sweet Nora, and now me, this house ud be nasty. Ya remind me a somethin' ma pappy used ta say. Fits ya perfect."

"You know who your father was?" Noreen rebutted.

Like water off a duck, Peeper ignored then educated, "Never try ta teach a pig ta gargle. It's a waste a time, and it done irritates the pig."

Miss Ella jumped at the chance to escape by answering the twist of the front bell. "I'll get it."

Sore disappointment filled her at the sight of the always-tattling Mrs. Ickles. With her spectacles delicately balancing on the tip of her pointed nose, Mrs. Ickles' expression looked as if she had just smelled some offensive odor.

"Do you know what your son has done this time?" she hollered in Miss Ella's face.

"Good day to you, too."

"Apparently, you don't. Let me enlighten you! He and his cousins smeared my front door with honey last night. The buzzing of the all those dirty flies woke me from a dead sleep! I had to use my back door to get out of my own house!" She went on. "Then I go into town to learn he and those other savages have been hanging dead snakes from the tree branches across South 3rd and Broom. When the ladies pass underneath in their buggies, why, I myself have seen two faint dead away! And one of them was driving alone. Her horse saw the snakes, bolted, and ran the whole rig into the iceman's wagon, spilling huge chunks all over the street. What with the screaming and whinnying, it was one disagreeable agitation, I can tell you. It was so bad, we've had to cancel this morning's meeting of the Literary League, and we have our annual Buy a Book sale in two weeks time! Frankly, Miss Ella, that boy of yours is the meanest white child in Fernandina!"

Having learned of her son's antics from Mrs. Ickles far too often, Miss Ella kept her voice tranquil. "I'll check into it. I promise. Goodbye." She closed Noreen's black wreathed door as gently as possible, refraining from slamming it, which was exactly what she wanted to do. She usually didn't take such things to heart. After all, Jack Patrick had been a rascal all his life, but this time she felt embarrassed. "I must be getting old and tired," she confided to herself.

After one heavy sigh, Jack Patrick came into the parlor by way of the kitchen. He spotted his mother sitting in his aunt's rose velvet upholstered rocker. "Hey, Mama. Peeper is sulking again. Did she have another run-in with Aunt Noreen?"

His mother didn't answer his question. "Pull up that stool, Pat, and sit next to me."

Jack Patrick preferred this nickname, given him by his brother-in-law, Captain Taylor. It was so much more grown up, he thought. "What's the matter?" He hated to see his parents upset and, lately, that seemed to be their usual condition.

"Mrs. Ickles was just here."

He cut her off. "Oh. Was it about the snake thing?"

She nodded.

"And that honey on the door thing, too?" He didn't wait for affirmation. "Holy cow. That sack of fussy feathers didn't waste much time, did she?"

"You should know by now she never does, son."

"We'll go back and clean up the snakes and scrub her door off."

"You certainly will, young man, but why do you do such pranks in the first place? Why?"

Pat never lied when confronted with accusations, most of which were true. "I did it because you hate the things. So, we decided to go on a snake kill. We thought we were helping you out."

"Who are you trying to fool? I can believe the part about doing it for me, and I appreciate it. It's the part about hanging the nasty things from the trees that's tough to swallow."

He hesitated for a second. "That was my idea. Mickey and Warren Lowell only went along with it 'cause I threatened to spread word among the girls that whoever didn't help me had a terrible case of gas."

Miss Ella reached out for her son's strong neck and pulled him to her, laughing until tears were rolling. He was laughing, too, and glad his mother's mind had turned from seeking his motive for honeying Mrs. Ickles' front door because he hadn't a nice-sounding reason for doing it. He was still thinking of one.

***

After an evening of a none too friendly family card game, there came

45

the familiar screech, "Who let the god-awful cat back in my room?"

Clabe grinned at Noreen's earlier reaction to Monstie's wake up call. He guessed that having a purring ball of fur with fish breath lick your eyebrows would startle anyone from a sound sleep.

"It's not funny!" Noreen pointed to the coverlet on her bed, "You know I take extreme pride in making a tight bed. Now look. There're kitty footprints all over the spread, and he's shed so much, it looks like someone's picked orange cotton in here. I promise I'll take a broom to him the next time I see him. I mean it!" she reinforced in a gravelly tenor.

Clabe could shake the covers out the window and be done with it as far as he was concerned, but there was no sense offering to help tonight. Noreen was in a mood. Sure as the sunrise, that mood would last through till daylight when poor Miss Ella would get an earful.

Once the commotion passed, the house settled down for the long dark hours ahead, or at least most of the house settled. Michael was not home yet. Picking up the alarm clock, Miss Ella held its face toward the still burning candle on the nightstand. 3:40 in the morning. As the weeks crept by, she had tried to find peace in their situation. Tonight, she finally admitted the truth to herself. There was no foreseeable departure from the Duffy home. The money just wasn't there. Whether from worry or the too soft mattress, she couldn't sleep. Pushing aside the covers, she found her wrapper and Noreen's old slippers in the darkness, and tiptoed down the steps.

Crossing the dining room to the sideboard, Miss Ella lifted a daguerreotype photograph from its easel to stare at the sepia faces. Unable to see well enough, she carried the picture to the window where the moonlight struck it. She'd insisted a photographer ride along during the *Coral Crown's* sea trial. Despite tearing eyes from the brilliant sun and the usual complaining at having their picture made, the family was happy then and all together. The women were seated with the men standing behind. The older children were kneeling or sitting on the deck. Halley, in her father's arms, was frantically reaching for her stuffed Martha Bear, which she'd dropped. Frozen in time, her silent wails for the cuddly white creature seemed faintly audible.

Seated in the center was Grammy. This was the only image Miss Ella possessed of her mother now. And next to the lives of her children, it was her most treasured possession. Her sister, Coe, had written saying she would send copies of old photos. None would look like this with Grammy's face covered in the telling crinkles of life's down-winding clock. Miss Ella would remember her mama as the woman pictured here.

The sightless stare of Noreen captured Ella's attention. Her husband's sister was awful more than she was nice. Try though they did to ignore her hateful gibes and comments, everyone, including the children, felt uncomfortable. Poor Nora was so embarrassed by her mother's remarks, she'd run out of apologies.

Moving through the parlor, Miss Ella sought the rocking chair yet again. Maybe the steady back and forth of it would lull her tangled thoughts. She turned to sit down and was met by a protesting resistance. Adrenalin shot through her veins until she heard Monstie's moan. "Come on, fat cat, let's sit a spell and chat."

She lifted his bulk and once he adjusted himself on her lap, she whispered, "So it's like this, my furry friend." Miss Ella needed to tell someone or something of her woes. "Lack of sleep these days is showing itself as dark circles beneath Carolena's beautiful green eyes. If she isn't bent over her drawings, she's talking about them or thinking about them. They seem to be her only interest. Should things continue like this, she might never marry." An ache for the girl filled her mother's heart. Marriage and children had been the best of blessings for her. Then again, independent Carolena might just be happy alone. Other single women were although she didn't know many.

Miss Ella petted the cat's head and after the fourth stroke, he began to purr. "Since the disaster, there seems to be almost constant tension between Breelan and Waite. I've heard them arguing about what to do with the insurance money they got for their own incinerated house. Waite wants his private life back. He, like the rest of us, is desperate to get out of Duffy Place. I confess I listened, although I shouldn't have. Waite suggested they rent a house or apartment. Breelan considers leaving as family desertion. Since he's not about to accept Noreen's alms, especially when they're so resentfully bestowed, Waite's going to make weekly payments for room and board for himself as well as us.

"My God, how humiliating!" She caught her inflection on the rise and retuned to near silent tones. "At least Waite is helping us out of love, without reservation, whereas my foul-natured sister-in-law took us in out of cold, uncaring obligation. She's afraid folks will talk if she turns us away. Clabe says compensation isn't necessary, that they're well fixed. He's a banker, so I'm very certain our staying here isn't the hardship Noreen leads us to believe. Still, starting Monday morning at 8 a.m. sharp, Breelan will make a payment to her carping auntie, and I can guarantee every Monday, that auntie's hand will be out, palm up, clutching for the cash. With the balance of his fire insurance, Waite wants to start construction on a new home for himself and Bree."

Feeling suddenly warm and a bit claustrophobic, Miss Ella, removed the heavy cat from her lap. Her left leg asleep, she stood and wiggled her foot to awaken it. She walked to the front door, opened it to look outside into the cool darkness, and exited to sit on the cushioned white wicker chair on the porch. In two twinkles of an evening star, she and the cat shadowing her were again settled. Her tale continued. "My Breelan has different ideas. After deducting rent, she wants to reinvest the balance in the Aqua Verde Line. She thinks the sooner the business is up and running efficiently, the sooner Michael can begin rebuilding Dunnigan

Manor. I'm sure Bree will win out because Waite will do anything for her, but it won't leave him happy. Nor will Bree be happy because she's gone against her husband's judgment. I know them both, and she'll spend long hours reassuring Waite he's not second in her life after her parents, although I don't believe he would ever think ill of us."

Monstie rolled onto his back and stretched his neck so she had access to his throat. This was the most vulnerable position any animal could assume. It made her feel good that, despite his displacement, he was feeling safe with the people he knew loved him.

"If you haven't seen Waite around the last few weeks, Monstie, it's because he's taken over command of the *Miss Breelan* to save paying a salary to anyone else. The only good to come of this mess is Waite can hear the slap of waves against a hull instead of the clash of wills within a house other than his own.

"As for Breelan, she's run ragged raising their children and working on advertising and promotion for the ship line. She's of a different, more modern generation. She'll probably continue working as her family grows up." She gave a soft snort. "Look at me. I was raised to be a homebody. Any other career, let alone a full-time job, to my mind, was always strictly for the man in the family. Now here I am. As honored as I am folks rave about my recipes, I'm equally scared." She stopped to slap at a buzzing mosquito. "The pressure to get it all right is tremendous. Cooking for a large family can't compare to overseeing the preparation of meals for hundreds, not to mention the overall presentation.

"Oh, and the paper work. My lands, the paperwork!" She brushed her salt and pepper hair back from her cheek. "Since we let most of the office staff go, the majority of everyday work has fallen to me. Thank goodness for little Marie. She's so good about helping me lick the stamps and seal the envelopes. Trouble is, she'll soon get bored with it all and want to play. For the love of heaven, she's just a child and that's exactly what she should be doing - playing like other girls her age.

"Jack Patrick ..." She corrected herself. "These days, Monstie, he wants to be called Pat. We have to remember that. The boy has such wonderful sweetness and gentleness of character, but he's a constant concern. Our Bird of the Earth seems to never stay out of mischief."

She wondered at the hour, trying to ignore any and all of the horrible possibilities why Michael still wasn't home, wasn't back, she corrected. In the middle of the night, she was powerless to do anything. Good sense wriggled from beneath the weight of worry. She hoped her exhausted body would win out and put her mind to sleep.

"Come on, Monstie. I don't give a damn if Noreen doesn't want you upstairs in the bedrooms. This is one night we're making an exception!"

***

"There's absolutely no need for Mama to know about this particular episode of Daddy's. Agreed?" Carolena watched as Jack Patrick, Nora, Warren Lowell, Mickey, Clover, and Justice all nodded their promise of silence.

"I'm sorry, Clover, to always put it on you, but Justice's bunk house is best for looking after him while he sleeps it off."

"No, Miss Cary. Mr. Michael's always been good to me, and I'm glad to help you children out whenever I can. It's no bother. Right, Justice?"

"No bother a'tall, Clove. Heck, you've seen me skunk-faced and helped me out. I can do the same for your friend. I'll sleep out back under the stars tonight whilst you all do what needs ta be done. No chance a rain, I'm thinkin'."

"Thank you. I remember a kindness." Clover replied.

Justice waved off the gratitude. "See all y'all, in the mornin'."

"Daddy's pretty far gone," Jack Patrick assessed. "I say we each take a watch in case he needs something. That way, we'll know he's safe and hasn't wandered off, and none of us will lose much sleep."

All but Clover drew straws to determine which would be their hour of custody. It seemed logical he take the last stretch so he could help clean up his employer when he woke.

Clover settled himself in his nearby hammock. Soft sounds of a gitfiddle floated in through the open window as Justice strummed his guitar. It helped sooth the disquieted spirits of those within hearing. And while Miss Nora breathed endearments to her mother's drunken brother who lay sprawled on the only bed in the next room, Clover realized, yet again, how close a family this was. He was proud to be a part of it, in good times and in bad.

Chapter 5

The next morning, Miss Ella awoke late. She gathered her wrapper, feeling guilty she hadn't helped in the preparation of breakfast. Just outside the kitchen door, she peeked around the corner to see who was in the room. She found her normally clean-shaven husband at the breakfast table under attack from his big sister, ever bigger in girth as years passed. Relieved Michael was safe, Miss Ella hung back in hope of hearing of his whereabouts the previous night. She also realized she was doing a lot of eavesdropping these days.

"You can't possibly imagine you look better in a beard," needled Noreen. "And your eyes are all bloodshot, Michael. What's the matter with you? You're not getting sick? Oh my God! If anyone gets sick in this house, we might as well consider it an epidemic. Everybody will get it, and Doc Tackett will quarantine the place!"

Peeper, also present, glanced about and cupped her hand to her ear to listen hard. She wanted to be sure there were no children around before she laid into Noreen, an experience she thoroughly enjoyed despite her Christian conscience. "What in the holy hallowed halls is the matter with ya, woman? You's without doubt the most ice-hearted bein' I dun ever heared of. And you's atalkin' about your very own brother. Noreena, Noreena, Noreena. You're a disgrace. Shaaaaamme on ya." Peeper dragged out the pronunciation for dramatic effect.

"Go ahead, old woman, put your hands on your fat hips and shake your head at me. That won't change the fact if one gets ill, we all do. When you're ailing and too sick to pour your elixir fixer remedies down every gullet that can swallow, you mark my words. You mark my words."

"My fat hips? Your backside's so wide, ya take up near all a one church pew yourself!"

"I'm not sick," Michael reported coolly, ignoring the two. "I just didn't get much shut-eye last night. You said that was a new mattress we're sleeping on? By all the saints, you were taken when you bought the saggy thing. They should have named it 'The Crippler' because it kills my back." He would not let his sister defend her purchase and immediately said, "As for the beard, Noreen, I haven't had one since my university days. I thought I'd give it a try." He shoved his chair back with an abrupt push of his legs, carried his plate to the drain board, took the newspaper from the table where Clabe had left it, and headed toward the back stairs. Finding his wife, he walked past without a word.

"Good morning," greeted Peeper when Miss Ella entered the sunny kitchen.

Noreen started in at first sight of her next victim. "Some of us have been up since dawn, Ella. Perhaps you're setting a bad example by sleeping so late. You don't want the children or Clabe to think you're taking advantage of our generous hospitality, do you?"

Peeper grinned, ready to wage another skirmish. "My Miss Ella is the best lady in this house, that's for sure. Ask anybody who's aknowin' her. She works so hard, she's entitled to a few minutes extra rest if'n she needs it. No one but a pinched face old prune like you would be begrudgin' this good woman her due."

Difficult though it was to admit, Noreen recognized Peeper was right. Ella was a hard worker. Yet, sleeping in when she, herself, had to slice Peeper's fresh baked bread while her nieces were primping upstairs, well, it just wasn't fair. So she covered, "Everyone knows Ella generally does her share —"

"More than her share," Peeper interrupted.

Noreen pursed her lips. "I just mean if she's so tired, she needs to go to bed earlier."

Finding her eyes had closed of their own volition, Miss Ella opened them and offered, "You're right, Noreen. Early to bed and all."

Noreen crossed her arms over her full bosom and gave a smug nod in Peeper's direction.

"Phttt," replied the adopted grandmother in disgust. "What'll ya be awantin' for breakfast, missy?"

"Hmm? Oh, thanks, Peep. Just a cup of coffee and a slice of bread. I'll take it back up to our room and eat it while I dress. It is late."

"Is that all? How about some of my orange jam spread real thick?"

"No thanks. Just bread and coffee. Where is everyone?" She looked out the window to realize it was a pretty day. "It is Saturday, right?"

"It surely is," Peeper told her and explained the whereabouts of the rest of the family.

While Peeper poured coffee, Miss Ella cleared the dirty dishes from the table and tried to block out the yammering of her sister-in-law.

"Here ya go, Miss Ella." Peeper presented a full tray with tomato juice, bacon, scrambled eggs, toast slathered with orange jam, and coffee. "I was athinkin'. How does some sweet potato candy sound to ya? It's been a spell since I last made some."

Miss Ella took the tray, smiled and leaned over to kiss the cheek of the woman who knew only one way - to spoil those whom she loved. "If it makes you happy, Peep, we'd love some." She headed back upstairs with Noreen's parting words blasting her ears.

"Don't spill that juice on the carpet in the bedroom, Ella. I'll never get it out!"

"As if Miss Ella is the least bit clumsy," Peeper challenged. "She's not like you. You're so ham-handed, we just might as well take all these here teacups a yourn and throw 'um ta the floor right now. You'll be abustin' 'um up soon enough."

Turning from the sour tempers, Miss Ella sought the room in which she slept, her pace slowing as she neared it. These days she was never sure what personality she'd find because Michael Dunnigan was a changed man. Their quarters were always tidy though it wasn't because of anything Miss Ella did. For the first time in their lives, Michael picked up after himself, even making the bed before his mate had a chance. He changed the sheets, helped Peeper put up the clean wash and occasionally made supper - his specialty, a tender stringy-meat roast and mashed potatoes that were so rich with butter they glowed golden. He seemed to have reversed occupations with his wife and was content doing so. Though no adults in the house spoke much about Michael's curious condition, they'd forgotten what blabbermouths their children could be. Word got out how Michael had taken over the female household chores.

Carolena had confided to her mother she'd overheard Mrs. Ickles insult her father to his face, calling him "an old fool." Michael hadn't defended himself then nor did he take offense. He seemed to not care if the town teased him about his pastries or his technique for the removal of fruit stains with a soaking of whiskey.

By day, liquor was a household help, by night a household destroyer. Too often these past months, Miss Ella perceived the Dunnigan patriarch spent his limited funds on brew. Once known for his homemade wine, now his presence was often found in any of the twenty-some saloons around Fernandina.

As for their ship line, Michael didn't talk about the business of it and would hear little of the detail of things. His deliberate ignorance left the burden of responsibility on Waite. The partnership between them, though still legally in force, had dissolved emotionally. Michael asked no questions, wanting no answers. Conversation about the company arose frequently around the dinner table because the success or failure of the Aqua Verde firm would determine when or if the Dunnigans would regain the lives they once knew. Often during these discussions, Michael would say, "I need some air," and get up and leave. If he did remain, he made no comment. Instead, he quietly filled his face while Noreen glowered at his gluttony. He let everyone do their job and his. Occasionally, he rode aboard the *Miss Breelan* with Waite or the *Coral Crown*, but only as a passenger. He gave no advice and, after a time, none was requested.

Many weeks passed and Miss Ella noticed his passion, his only passion, returned to architecture. He set up a makeshift desk in their room where he sketched house plans. Michael's designs were detailed, and elegant. Every one was a massive mansion that could easily house an extended family of twenty or more. Curiously, each drawing contained a site for a solid steel door drop to cordon off a section for privacy. After all they'd been through, Miss Ella loved the thought of seclusion, but Michael's dream of it was extreme.

The plans were too expensive for the Dunnigans' personal use or even to be marketable. Though the war was long past, there was still much recovery going on, and any money made would be in the peddling of simple designs in quantity to average American families. Even if his blueprints were commercially viable, he would not bother.

Dear Lord, how Miss Ella needed his help and comfort. Since her only education in business was picked up over the years at the dining table or serving refreshments to Michael's cronies, she scoured her memory for any useful information she'd inadvertently heard or read about in the newspapers pertaining to commerce, negotiation, and industry. She happily accepted advice from all sources, yet she had to be especially careful. Only the family could have knowledge Michael was a total non-participant in his business. Miss Ella remembered people had turned away and left after the fire when Michael began his tirade. She hoped no one witnessed his confession other than immediate family. Details of their situation would only serve to fuel ugly speculation. So many rumors were already flying, the least of which was all was not well with the Dunnigans. The kinder townsfolk assumed the family was deeply mourning Grammy and still distraught from the fire.

The most difficult thing of all was Michael's altered behavior. Miss Ella couldn't put this down to drink because he was stone cold sober whenever it happened. In the presence of friends and family, he presented cheer and confidence. He appeared intrepid despite ample reason to be disheartened. It was only in the private hours shared between husband and wife that his callous indifference showed. Miss Ella never imagined the man she'd married so long ago and this man could be the same person. She didn't believe Michael capable of cruelty, particularly toward her, the woman he'd worshipped thousands of days and nights before. That he was able to formulate insults toward her, let alone voice them, was incomprehensible to her.

As she balanced the tray on one hip and turned the doorknob to their room, she hoped today would be a better day.

"Good morning, darling. Look what Peeper dished up. If I'd let her, she'd have me weighing 500 pounds."

"Dammit! Don't talk to me when I'm reading the paper," Michael scolded sourly.

Miss Ella closed the door quickly.

"This house is too small to swing a cat! I come in here to escape Noreen's constant griping! It was all I could do not to up and leave Tuesday past. I heard her call me *shanty Irish*. How any kin of mine could talk down about their own— She may consider herself *lace curtain Irish*, but the truth is—"

He stopped himself. "I love my granddaughter," he said, changing subjects, "but if Breelan doesn't take a firm hand with Halley, she'll turn into one first-class monster. She's already a spoiled whelp. I'm up to my eyeballs playing tea party with her. That's all she pesters me to do! And have you seen the way Breelan strains the girl's orange juice?"

She set the tray on the straightened bedspread. "I just made the bed, Ella. Why must you always go around after me messing things up?"

Dismissing his accusatory manner, "Did you see the pretty flowers Halley picked for us?"

Michael looked at the vase on the dresser. He warned, "If that child pulled them out of Noreen's flower bed, we'll have hell to pay."

Upon his words, his wife realized the white roses, bearded iris, and daffodils could have come from nowhere else. "Oh dear." Racking her brain, she said, "How about if we ask Noreen for a tiny patch of her flower bed that will be specifically for Halley to pick from. I'm sure she won't mind, and that will solve everything."

"And if frogs drank beer, they'd burp bubbles!"

"You're right. Noreen won't ever go for it. We'll just have to stake out a small spot for Halley on our property and help her plant seeds and show her how to tend them. That's what we did with her mother so she'd learn flowers don't just appear but must be grown. She'll appreciate them even more this way."

"And when will you have time to farm?" Michael demanded, as if she would be shirking her other duties to help their grandchild.

Miss Ella had enough. "What is the matter with you? This room is my escape, too. It's as if you don't want any part of me around. Like you care more for the furniture than you do for your wife."

He didn't deny it. "I'll tell you why I want everything where it goes and in good order. I'll tell you once and never speak of it again. It's because this is the only place left in the world where I'm in control. The only place! This 15 by 20 foot room is my refuge and, by God, I will have order. Is that understood?"

He rose to open the window. "Step aside! I can't get away from you, Ella. You always stand too close to me. I can't breath with you so near."

He looked hard on his wife, and his eyes were jagged blue crystals. He'd torn a hole in her soul with his brutal biting words.

Resolute, for she had no other choice, Miss Ella tried a different subject, "As of last evening, the receipts for the week were down."

"What good will it do to hear how badly things are going? Will it change anything?" he asked her. "Or do you just want me as miserable as you are?"

"Of course I don't want to add to your misery, Michael," she answered, "but occasionally talking over problems instead of ignoring them would help me. If we share the hardships, we might formulate solutions. As long as I'm not alone, I can bear anything."

"You love to wallow in all this shit. You thrive on it. It's all you talk about. You're at your best when there's trouble."

He seemed to resent any strength she showed. Her mouth agape, she listened to his harangue, not fathoming his reasoning. "If it's all I talk about, doesn't that show it's all consuming? It's our lives and the lives of our children, I'm fearful for, Michael."

"Well, have at it, my dear. You're so damn smart. Saint Ella, that's you. Go ahead; take control. You handle matters. Bury yourself in our misfortune if it will keep you off my back!"

Then she cried.

"You're wasting your time if you're trying to impress me with tears. They mean nothing to me. There are more pleasant things to be concerned about than you."

Her skin chilled. Her face paled as it did of late when his attacks came. With each one, so increased a tingling in her left arm that ran from her elbow down to her thumb. Doctor Tackett told her it was merely tension, and to try to calm herself. He prescribed Spirited Milk Punch. Once a day, Peeper mixed two tablespoonfuls of Clabe's good brandy, with his permission, into six tablespoons of milk with a bit of sugar and a sprinkle of nutmeg. The patient drank the brew, but the occasional slug of alcohol was insufficient to salve her nerves.

The destruction of her marriage was invading her body and threatening to break her health. Her own husband was destroying her love for him the same way the fire had leveled their home and livelihood. If she didn't so adore him, she might be able to fight back with equally cruel words, or even leave him. So far, she'd found hatefulness and abandonment were not in her. She wanted to make him understand how the nights they laid together, after Marie was sound asleep, felt like nothing more than sharing a bed with some indifferent being. Such telling would be wasted effort. For the only time in all their wedded years, she felt unloved, unappreciated, and unwanted. She was becoming desensitized. Unconsciously, her ever-hardening armor of self-preservation had taken over. She would never again be the woman Michael Dunnigan had chosen as his bride.

Tears dripped from her face to land on her toast. Her heart replayed Grammy's dying words, goading her to do the right thing. *Don't let this split the family. Don't let this split the family.* Miss Ella ran a napkin across her chin and prayed, dear God, if it's Thy will, please, please keep me on course.

Although Duffy Place was sturdy, the walls were not soundproof. Everyone wondered where all this would lead.

***

Carolena sat in the rocker in Nora's room, resting her eyes. Nora and Aunt Noreen were off to their "once ta-month Orchid Society meeting," as everyone called it, so Carolena savored the moments alone.

She opened her eyes to see the sailor's valentine Grey had presented her two days earlier on Cupid's special holiday. She'd hesitated to accept it only because she was officially in deep mourning for her grandmother and gifts were not seemly during sad times. Grey would have been reluctant to approach her with it had he not mentioned making it to Grammy before her death.

Carolena thought how, in the late of night aboard the *Coral Crown*, Grey's powerful fingers, fingers that held iron wrenches and had broken men's jaws when fisted, had crafted this complex patterned heart of delicate, colorful seashells encased in a wooden frame. Hand scripted in the center he'd written:

Recall the Joy

Although his words were simple, the sentiment was meaningful to her. Grey wanted her to focus on what made her happy. No matter if the hardships overwhelmed, she had fond memories of her family and of fun times with Grey. He was a dear and his thoughtfulness left her smiling.

Carolena needed a distraction from her work. Her hope was to sell her interior designs for extra income to anyone interested and wealthy enough to afford a luxury boat. She had one serious customer so far.

She would rather have been trolling the beach for shells and sharks' teeth with Breelan and the children, but Grammy often said handwork freed the mind for pondering. Carolena reached into the basket on the floor to pull out what she hoped would end up a pretty shawl. This knitting business was new to her. Peeper said making the broomstick lace pattern was within her capabilities. Clover found what was left of a broom in the rubble from the fire. After sanding the whole thing smooth and clean, he whittled the handle into a knitting pin. Aunt Noreen contributed leftover multi-colored scraps of yarn and the result, so far, was an appealing rainbow of warmth meant to wrap her mother's weary shoulders.

Footsteps on the landing took Carolena's attention from her tangle of yarn. She listened hard to establish it was her mother who entered the next room to slam the door behind her. As if she'd been in the same space with Carolena, Miss Ella's panic was clear. There was no masking her voice to keep information a secret. "Look what Peeper just found on the desk in Clabe's office. I guess he figured you might drop by and see it. Lord knows you haven't done any work sitting there."

"What the hell is it?" Michael wanted to know.

"It's word from Pat! Our son has run off to Georgia somewhere. He hopes to get a job as a field hand picking cotton or shaking the dirt from peanut plants and stacking them to dry. His goal is to send his pay home."

"Damnation!" Michael cursed. "Maybe if you hadn't called in my marker, *my* marker, Ella, not yours, and let Garfield hire him for a night job, the lad wouldn't have been so exhausted and fallen asleep at the switch. His humiliation and firing at causing that caboose to jump track helped in his decision to go off."

Michael was right. Miss Ella countered with, "Well, what about his getting caught drinking communion wine? I guess he figured if it's good enough for dear old dad, a little sip of the grape won't hurt any." She softened, "You forget he's just a boy."

"Aw, a little drink every now and then will make a real man of him."

"Like it's doing for you, Michael? You're gone every night. You don't give a fig about your family."

Carolena fled Nora's room and dashed out the front door. She hated hearing her parents argue, and now Pat had run off. How utterly awful!

She didn't care that the air had turned chilly as she walked down Dunn Road toward the main street that ran between Amelia Beach and the downtown marina. She didn't care that dust showed on her dark skirt either. She didn't' care about anything but righting this whole horrid situation.

On top of everything else, Peeper was washing other people's dirty clothes. Mickey and Marie refused their allowances and were doing odd jobs. Worst of all, the entire Dunnigan family was depending upon a resentful relative. Carolena's self-respect slithered down her throat until she felt she might choke. There was little time to dwell on lost pride or disgruntled emotions. In fact, no time at all.

Being the oldest child and well educated, it was her place to take on the most responsibility. She had finally completed the plans for a private yacht for a Signor Paolo Alontti from Charleston, who'd requested them the previous fall. For many months, they'd mailed drawings back and forth, with her reading his scribbled suggestions, a glass wall here, a planter there. She'd redesigned and tweaked and tweaked some more until she could look at the plans without feeling something was off, something was not quite right. So, with confidence and a long prayer, she'd mailed a copy of the final blueprints along with color swatches to the gentleman.

She realized she'd been staring at the toes of her shoes as she walked north into the wind. When she looked ahead, she saw a young man riding toward her wearing the uniform of the telegraph office.

"Telegram for C. M. Dunnigan."

"I'll take it. I'm Carolena Dunnigan."

"Yes, ma'am," he grinned, gap-toothed, at the pretty girl. "Have a nice day." Having no coin to spare, she offered a sweet smile. It was sufficient. He doffed his cap and spun on his heel. She heard the sound of his humming fade as she stared at the sealed telegram. She turned, too, and headed to Duffy Place.

All seemed quiet as she mounted the stairs to Nora's room. Sitting down slowly upon the bed, Carolena opened the envelope with her finger, trying not to rip it. She read.

WESTERN UNION   16 February 1889
    TO: C. M. Dunnigan
    Aqua Verde Passenger Line
    Fernandina, Florida

    FROM: Paolo Alontti
    Charleston, South Carolina

AM IMPRESSED WITH PLANS FOR YACHT STOP HOWEVER FACE-
TO-FACE CONFERENCE A MUST TO DISCUSS ALTERATIONS
STOP EXPECT YOU IN CHARLESTON ON 18 FEBRUARY STOP

She checked the dates. He wanted her in Charleston in two days time! What arrogance! As if I've nothing better to do than respond, posthaste, to his whim, she thought, never appreciating orders from anyone. This time she must go because she desperately needed the work. She could not afford to thump any free melons, as her father always said. The *Crown* would be docking tonight, then heading north. She'd have to leave in a few hours!

Carolena's heart pounded. The opportunity she'd longed for was upon her. Her breathing stopped. What could he possibly want to alter in her designs? It was her best work so far. Vulgar combinations of hues and textures exploded in her mind's imaginative eye. Well, he was the fellow paying, so at this point, if he wanted a merry-go-round in the water closet, she'd just have to smile and nod and do it. Her family needed the money.

She glanced at the telegram yet again, and her initials glared back at her. She remembered boldly signing them instead of her given name on the blueprints and in her correspondence. It appeared more professional. They were the same letters as in her father's name. The total truth was she'd done it because she wasn't certain a prosperous gentleman from the grand city of Charleston would look seriously upon sketches if he knew a woman from a small town drew them. If she could persuade him she was capable, allow him to change her design to something less than perfect and stand it, convince him the firm would oversee the completion of his yacht in Fernandina with their already established crew of shipbuilders, and have him advance half the cost of the ship to build it and the rest upon completion - if, if, if! But it was exactly what the Aqua Verde Line needed. Floating capital, literally! It would give her mother some breathing room to more easily deal with creditors, maybe even catch up a little. As part of the contract, she would guarantee 100% satisfaction. Things were done that way at reputable firms. She had to deflect any negative rumors, which might be out there. It all had to be perfect in her customer's eyes. It had to be because she would have no funds to actually return. They would all go toward household expenses.

The family would fight her trip to Charleston. They would say she shouldn't be conducting business so close to losing her grandmother, but her own mother did what was necessary to keep the office open. Carolena would as well. They would protest her traveling alone, the way they had an unmarried Breelan years before on a trip to New York City. Her sister had solved that concern by taking Nora. Of late, Nora was enamored with Austin Gage, a volunteer fireman she'd met that awful day of the fire in January. Carolena was pretty certain her cousin wouldn't want to be going on any out of town trips any time soon, not to mention Nora was in mourning for Grammy, too.

She walked to her trunk stashed in the corner, semi-hidden behind a parlor palm. She'd been keeping most of her clothes neatly folded inside her luggage since Nora's armoire and bureau overflowed with her own gowns and other dainties. Carolena would have no need for any grand dresses for a long while. Instead, she retrieved her spare collars and cuffs and a second black dress Aunt Noreen had grudgingly dyed for her and packed them in one of the carpetbags Peeper had made to sell. She added two pairs of black stockings, a stiff black petticoat, a simple black fan, three white handkerchiefs with black borders, gloves, and a bonnet. Just in case of chilly weather, she set an old cape of Nora's and a warm scarf on top of everything.

Where to stay? She'd have to impose on her mother's sister, Aunt Coe, and her husband, Uncle Fries Dresher. Carolena couldn't keep from chuckling at her childhood remembrance of his nickname, Uncle Igloo, Iggie for short. She'd come up with it to help her friends and others remember his surname was not pronounced like the *fried* in fried chicken, but rather *freeze* as in the freezing cold of an igloo.

Thank goodness he'd moved his leather goods business from New York to Charleston two years earlier. Carolena hadn't seen them since she'd finished school. They were getting along in years, and she'd try to cause as little disruption in their lives as possible. Oh, matters will work out one way or another, Carolena thought. They usually do.

Throughout the morning, she bustled about, completing her preparations, deliberately telling no one of her impending journey.

Chapter 6

The table was set for the noon meal. With no activity currently happening in the dining room, it seemed to Monster to be the most private and coziest place possible. Jumping up, he trod among the plates and silver, knocking over the pepper mill as he kneaded the tablecloth, bunching it into a suitable nest in which to rest his fat form. Leaning against the centerpiece, a pink flowering African violet, Monstie basked in the heat of the incoming sunshine until Aunt Noreen spotted him there. Saying nothing, she stiffly marched over and picked him up in order to heave him out the door yet again. Startled from his comfortable position, he did as cats naturally do. He unsheathed his claws, catching the cutwork and taking with him the Irish linen table cover. The shattering of china and the resulting scream brought forth family from every corner of the house and from outdoors, too. Monstrose, never appreciative of being held round his plump middle, wriggled, kicked his powerful hind legs, and left Auntie with two slight scratches on her wrist. Anyone would have thought he'd severed her arm from the yowls the woman emitted.

Clabe, who had just arrived home for his mid-day dinner, attempted to hush his wailing wife, taking her upstairs to dress her wound. Peeper was a sight as she chased the perpetrator through the house. The fly-flap she waved wildly did little more than stir the air. Her short plump legs were no match for Monster's fast and furry stems. He thought all the fuss was yet another game the old woman was playing with him. In fact, next to Aunt Noreen, Peeper was his favorite playmate.

Miss Ella and Breelan, along with an exhausted Peep, collapsed on the haircloth sofa after finally cornering the cat in the pantry. The embarrassed Dunnigan women barred Monstie from the Duffy house, a thing they should have done long ago.

Surveying the damage, they realized they had been fortunate. The dishes had fallen onto the patterned carpet so casualties were lighter than they could have been. Two goblets, one bread plate, one dinner plate, and a teacup were all that had broken. Miss Ella added their replacement cost to her list of debts owed.

Having requested her usual remedy for nerves, bread twelve hours old, an egg and black tea, Aunt Noreen remained in bed the entire of the afternoon, sending word she was so emotionally exhausted, she was left-handed.

As Miss Ella and Breelan actually were left-handed, they braved the comment, merely shaking their heads.

That evening Aunt Noreen wore a sling crafted from a paisley silk scarf to dinner. Her suffering was apparent to all, and she said, "This is my very best scarf because I need cheering so desperately."

Misery, however, didn't lessen Noreen Duffy's inspection of those about to be seated at her table. Her eyes narrowed at the children as she checked for comb tracks through their hair, shiny faces and hands, buttoned collars, tucked in shirttails, and tied bows and sashes. She waited for her husband to pull out her chair and sat down with all the dignity of a pretender to the throne who just received word her chances at becoming queen had markedly improved.

When Mickey gave an involuntary hiccup, he was skewered into his chair by his great aunt's stare.

"Young Michael," Aunt Noreen said, "What have you heard me say about making disagreeable noises at the dinner table? Snorting, hacking, scraping, pounding, lip smacking, and slurping will not be tolerated."

"Ah gee, Aunt Nor," the boy whined. "How's a fellow expected to enjoy his meal if'n he ain't allowed to make some bit a noise?"

"Don't be difficult, boy. And mind your English. It's atrocious! Has the entire world dismissed the value of table etiquette and proper speech?"

Once that episode passed, the chatter over supper was superficially pleasant. Bickering was veiled with forced smiles, though tension remained at a critical level. When the clash of personalities finally did collide, it would be ugly, unforgettable, and unforgivable. The question wasn't when, but who the combatants would be.

Tonight, Warren Lowell began the mischief with Marie as his target. "Look everybody, old whisker-tooth herself!"

As he spoke, the mortified girl pulled a bright green celery strand from between her front teeth. The children all laughed at the joke. Although Aunt Noreen should have called her boy down for his rude remark, she was quiet, the only time since the meal began. Fortunately, all the other women at the table held their tongues.

Then Peeper queried, "What's the matter with you, Noreen? My Miss Ella spent time she didn't have apipin' them deviled eggs extra fancy, and there you are aspreadin' the yoke flat as a pancake with yur knife." She shook her head in disgust. "Noreena, Noreena, Noreena. Tsk, tsk, tsk."

Glaring at Peeper, Noreen responded, "One reason your brood is so wild, Ella, is the influence of that one." She continued, "Don't gump your milk, Marie. Do slow down. And for mercy's sake, you'll turn over the glass if you don't stop dunking your chicken leg in it. Where ever did you learn such a trick?"

"Really, Noreen." Clabe's attempts were futile at controlling his wife.

"I was only trying to cool it off quicker so I'd be done eating when Peeper serves her sweeties," answered Marie, bravely bucking the bombardment of criticism. "Warren Lowell said he'd for certain sure eat mine if I wasn't finished."

Knowing her son could never be so piggish, Noreen replied, "Be careful when you set down that big glass. Who filled it so full anyway?" Suspicion in her eyes, she looked for the criminal. No one would fess-up. "It's so difficult to get up every last spatter of the stuff if it gets carelessly overturned. You wouldn't want a sour milk smell left in your auntie's carpet, now would you? Would you, child?"

Her innocent heart aching, Marie dropped her gaze to her lap, felt her wet white mustache with her tongue, quickly wiped it away with her linen napkin and, near tears, admitted in a soft breath, "No, ma'am."

Striving for humor, Mickey made another regrettable contribution, never intending harm. Holding a teaspoon, he displaying the knuckles of his first two fingers on the back of its bowl. The effect resembled buttocks. "Hey! There's Halley bending over the edge of the bathtub!"

"How dare you bring such vulgarity to my table, you impudent rapscallion!"

Correcting another woman's child in times past, would have been noted but accepted because children did as they were told by adults, particularly if he or she were kin. These days, Miss Ella and Breelan resented Noreen's intrusion and took it to mean they were failing at disciplining their own, that they needed assistance. "Noreen," Miss Ella was the first to speak, her perfect posture stiffening.

"Yes, my dear?" Pausing to garner sympathy, Noreen caressed her bandaged arm, her defiant expression dared any and all.

Something had to be done before all family fondness was forgotten or, Lord forbid, broken beyond repair. Carolena spoke. "Everyone. I have news I think you all will find exciting!"

Creamed corn dripped from spoons, lima beans tumbled from forks, as utensils froze mid-way to mouths. Vicious thoughts disappeared as tongues stilled. At last, something good! Everybody craved glad tidings and, at this point, didn't care how insignificant they might be. Good news was good news.

***

Explaining her plans, the adventurer repelled objections like a shield deflects arrows. "I've got it all figured out," Carolena told her family or most of them. Her father was absent from the table, again, and no one asked his whereabouts much anymore. "Clover has wired Signor Alontti for me, alerting him I'll be arriving on the *Coral Crown* because I must be in Charleston in two days time. Since the *Crown* is docked in Fernandina, I'll board her tonight. I could wait and take the train up in one day, but that would cost us fare, and I can travel on the *Crown* for nothing. Although my sketches are finished, if I have the extra hours traveling, I may come up with an even better presentation.

"I'm sorry to leave so much of the burden of the ship line on you and Breelan, Mama, but I've weighed the worth of my project. If I'm successful, it will put a mighty dent in our financial problems. Remember everyone, the entire reason for my journey is to sell a luxury yacht."

Breelan spoke up. "Who better to show and explain your work than you yourself? You'll do well. I'm sure of it!"

Aunt Noreen agreed, saying, "The best of luck to you."

Faces wore shocked expressions. Kindness coming from Aunt Noreen?

Noreen completed her thought, "Your father is of little help."

Nora got back to the subject at hand. "Your work is not only wonderful, it's unique," she told Carolena. "How can this Signor Alontti think anything else?"

"Thanks, Nora. Now listen. I'm sure Grey will see I get to Aunt Coe's in good order, so you needn't worry, Mama, or you either, Peep."

The adults around the crowded table were titillated at the prospect of income. Encouraging as always, no matter what, Peeper said, "The good Lord awillin' and the rain don't hurt the rhubarb, this man you're gonna be aseein' has gotta love ya. You're so smart, you'll dazzle 'um, just by atalkin.'"

Those older remembered past out-of-town family excursions. They were less concerned about finances and more concerned with their girl's well-being. Thus, the drill followed on how to behave and how to survive in the city with advice fired from all sides.

When she spied Aunt Noreen capturing the last chicken leg from the platter, licking it and sticking it in the pocket of the apron lying across her lap, Carolena could bear no more. Weary of contention and counsel, she excused herself and gathered her things. Exiting the house to look for Clover, she heard little Halley's voice screaming at Aunt Noreen, "Eat it all, by Jesus!"

The ensuing words from the adults were loud, angry, and accusatory. For a short while, the upcoming trip was forgotten by those who would be left behind.

Carolena climbed into the buggy with her old friend who was waiting for her with her carpetbag stowed. "Thanks, Clover, for sending that wire to Signor Alontti confirming my appointment with him."

"Glad I could help out, Miss Carolena. You mind you're careful, ya hear?"

"You, too?" she chuckled. "I'll be careful. I promise."

Carolena was pleased she had an hour and a half to spare before the *Crown* departed. Her brain was crammed with random contemplations. Right now, it was how her friend Clover smelled of wood smoke and bacon grease, a combination Carolena always found comforting.

All at once, her mind had only one thought. This was an emergency! "Stop, Clover! Turn the wagon around. I forgot something!"

Slowing the horse, "Miss Carolena, we're almost on top of the wharf. Sure you cain't get along without whatever it is you left behind?"

"I'm afraid I can't. Please, Clover."

No sense arguing with this one, he thought. He knew her stubborn ways. "Yes, Miss Cary. With all this here traffic, best to just drive around the block."

"I know. I know. Remember, I've lived here my whole life!"

Patience was not always Carolena's way. Clover understood she meant no disrespect.

"Okay. Git-up there, hoss. Clip, you mind me now if you want an apple for your trouble. Hear?" Clover's mild tone guided and reassured the strong, sensitive creature.

How could she have left her drawing case with the measuring tools? Without them, any new sketches would only be rough estimates, and how much confidence would that instill in a prospective client?

Once in front of Duffy Place, Carolena held her skirts and jumped from the buggy, not waiting for assistance from Clover. Blackie-White-Spots came to greet her. He got no petting. Up the front steps of the porch, she sprinted. The front door and windows were closed. Maybe those in the house hadn't heard the horse arrive. Hoping the heavy wooden door was well oiled, she opened it a crack and listened. She didn't want to be detained. She heard a commotion coming from out back. Uncle Clabe often built a fire in the brick pit near the gazebo in the rear, and that must be where they all were eating tonight's dessert, Miss Ella's peach pie. Quietly closing the door behind her, Carolena sneaked up the carpeted stairs, gathered her instruments, and was tiptoeing back down when she heard voices coming from the front parlor. Blast!

"I understand, Ella." It was a man's voice. Uncle Clabe.

Then her mother was sobbing. She'd never before known her mother's guard to be down like this. Still, Carolena was glad Miss Ella had someone to talk to. Her father was so distant these days.

Having little time for dallying yet not wanting to be found, Carolena waited impatiently behind the blue velvet swags framing the square arch into the parlor. The sobs eventually subsided due to the tender words from her uncle. Then silence fell. Moments passed. To be certain they were gone, she cautiously peeked between the gold tassels edging the drape.

Her mother was kissing her uncle! He wasn't forcing her! She wasn't struggling! She was willingly accepting his lips until the sound of her daughter's intake of breath startled them apart.

"Cary!" Shame and fear were apparent in Miss Ella's voice.

"How could you?" Carolena accused in a hushed scream, offended to revulsion. "No matter how impatient Daddy's been with you, how could you do this to him? Don't you know he's helpless? When he needs you more than any other time in his life, you betray him! And your own mother is hardly cold in the ground!" Carolena looked away, hoping if she turned from the disgusting couple, the picture of them would be forgotten. She realized she was playing a child's game. The thought of her uncle's fat fingers against his mother's slender throat was so revolting she wanted to flee.

Miss Ella stepped toward her daughter, and Carolena spat out her disgust. "Don't come near me ever again! Nothing would ever cause me to do this to my husband. I'm ashamed to call you mother!"

The daughter she'd tried to raise to be kind and understanding was more cruel and vicious than Miss Ella thought possible though her head told her it was a just cruelty, one she rightly deserved.

"Dearest, I'm sorry. I'm sorry I failed you and your father. But you don't understand. There's more than you know. Judgment is so easy. I used to say the same thing, about how there was nothing in this world that could separate your father and me. I've learned the bitter truth. We're all living a fragile existence, and like it or not, we don't always have control. If you'll let me—"

"What? Let you try to weasel out of conduct so disgusting only death will erase this vile memory from my soul! And you know well I can hold a grudge. It may not be the Christian thing, but I don't care. I'll never forgive you. Never!" In immediate reaction backed by powerful anger, Carolena's hand, which was once held in childhood and over time had developed a graceful grasp meant solely to create, caress, and console, that hand, slapped the satin cheek of its earthly creator, Miss Ella.

Mother and daughter recoiled, one from the other. What was happening? Carolena had seen Uncle Clabe strike his wife. Here, she found herself performing the same ugly deed. An unspeakable offense had been done to her father. If he were not here to defend himself, his daughter damn sure was.

A feeling of isolation consumed Carolena. The last remaining security, her parents' devotion to one another, would never, could never, be the same. She fled the house, pushing away Blackie who was pawing her dress, then sprang into the buggy. Snatching the reins from Clover and seizing the whip from its stand, she cracked it over the back of the horse.

Clover tore it from her, retrieving the leather ribbons from her tight fists.

"Whoa there, boy. Take it easy. I've got cha," he called out to the spooked animal. Welcoming the familiarity of his master's voice, Clip did as bidden. Clover urged a swift steady pace, using only the fervent pitch of his spoken word. Whatever had happened in the Duffy house, he didn't want to know.

Chapter 7

The ride to the *Coral Crown* gave Carolena little time to reestablish her composure. She knew she must try. The shame of the actions of her mother and uncle must be kept between the three of them.

The ship's engineer, supervising the last of the coal being loaded aboard, but ever aware of his surroundings, called out, "Cary! What are you doing here at the docks? And with your satchel in tow. I thought you'd be housebound for a long time mourning Grammy. Need a vacation from Aunt Noreen, do you?" he teased.

Grey was busy. Still, his remark, although partly true with regard to Aunt Noreen, could not be ignored. "Grey McKenna! I'm hurt you'd think me so selfish as to desert my family in their time of sorrow and need. I hoped you thought more of me than that." She really meant what she said. She was disappointed he would ever consider her doing such a selfish thing, although she didn't get the quality of loyalty from her mother. Mother. She forced herself not to frown at the thought. Mother would never again hold the sweet meaning it had.

"Hey, I meant no harm. We're about to pull out, so no time to talk. If you're coming, Cary, get your tail up the ramp. Now!"

When he took her bag from her, she glared at him for his crass language, not to mention his use of her horrid nickname. She just hoped nobody heard him. Had anyone else spoken like that to her, she'd happily assault them with a scathing attack they'd not soon forget. Grey was a friend and right now, she couldn't afford to lose any more people she trusted.

Carolena didn't know what cabin arrangements to expect and decided patience was reasonable. Choosing a deck chair, she settled herself in a corner while waiting for Grey to finish his work. Once the *Coral Crown* was piloted away from Fernandina and out in deep waters, he'd come get her.

She tried to concentrate on the sun's slow-motion dive into darkness as Amelia Island faded in the distance. The hours passed. Passengers strolled about; she never noticed them. Stewards offered blankets of woven plaid and warm bouillon to sip, served from silver, but she sent them away. Captain Rockwell stopped by, and she assured him she was fine. When her eyes closed and her head nodded from emotional exhaustion, her miserable meditation didn't abandon her. It lurked inside her dreams.

A low, long sounding "whooo" entered those dreams. It brought her around and once she deduced it was the bleat of the foghorn, she remembered where she was and why. Her gown was damp from the humid air, and she found herself shivering. Fully awake, anger surged through her. Well, I like that, she seethed. Grey McKenna has completely forgotten me! It certainly seems I have little chance to stir romance in him if he can't even remember I'm on board!

She rose and stretched her stiff limbs as inconspicuously as possible. She wondered if this was what Peeper felt like in the mornings when she arose, forever grousing about her achin' this or that. Carolena smiled as she fondly thought of Peep's squawking complaints of constant ill health.

Her pleasant musings quickly faded. Complain! She would find Mr. McKenna and complain a tad herself! She left her satchel behind the chair and went in search of him. He couldn't escape her on this floating island if he tried! She walked down to the engine room. Straining her voice to be heard against the powerful equipment, she learned from Mr. Casey, who was polishing the bright work to a fine fare-thee-well on some clanking machinery, that it had been approximately fifty minutes since he'd seen Grey. Back up she climbed, her anger firing her impatience.

She made one pass around the promenade deck, asking several porters if they knew the whereabouts of her prey. She was answered with the same shrug and some vague, "Sorry, ma'am. Last I saw of him, he was in the pilot house."

She headed to the pilothouse. There, she was steered to the dining saloon. She took in the savory smells and asked for Grey from the man who held the door for her entry.

"I believe, ma'am, Mr. McKenna was called to the library. There was a ruckus of some sort. If you go down this corridor and take the first left, you ..."

"Thank you, steward. I know the way." Of course, she knew the way. For a quick moment, she felt a twinge of guilt for having sounded so curt. Oh, she hadn't the time for apologies. A ruckus in the library? Strange. And to call for Grey particularly? Making a quick pass throughout the room, Carolena saw only an old man in a rocking chair, three frumpy-looking ladies and a teenaged boy and girl, who obviously had come to steal kisses between the stacks. She paused to spy, envying the young lovers. Grey wasn't in the library, so she would try the gaming room. He liked to watch the cards even if he couldn't play while on duty.

The place was lively with piano music, murky with cigar and pipe smoke, and loud with laughter and the sound of clinking chips, toasting glasses, and spinning roulette wheels. She caught sight of the playing cards imprinted with the Aqua Verde crest and thought them to be an elegant amenity. Grey was not in here either.

Carolena would check every compartment on this ship if she had to, asking each member of the crew when last they'd seen the engineer.

The boat deck grill smelled so good and the banjo strumming was so spirited, she was tempted to have a seat and look for Grey later.

She advanced to the winter garden. The glass enclosure was overfilled with lush foliage, exotic caged birds, butterflies, and an aquarium, all meant to impose spring and summer on the passengers year round. Grey was not there.

On to the gentleman's smoking room she'd furnished with leather wing chairs, the shooting gallery, the kennel with its own sun deck, the indoor swimming pool of enameled sandstone and mosaic wall friezes, the small hospital, the barber shop, the chapel, able to be transformed for multiple denominations with the sliding of a silk screen, the theatre where tonight's presentation was a musical comedy, the boutique, the print shop that was putting to bed the *Crown's* own daily newspaper, and even the children's playroom where the audience was enjoying a *Punch and Judy* puppet show.

The only thing left to do was to find the First Officer, Mr. Hastings. He would direct her to a cabin. She desperately wanted out of her limp clothes.

Then she remembered one more place she hadn't checked, the men's gymnasium. Rushing down two decks, she found herself looking at the thick polished oak doors. A gleaming brass plaque declared her destination reached, but Carolena suddenly wasn't certain if she should be so bold as to enter the room. She'd been here many times during construction, yet this was different. Men would be in degrees of disrobement and perspiring to boot!

Oh, pish-posh! Tugging open one door, she noted the paneling and wished it were daytime so the added illumination from the portholes would show off the high quality equipment in the room. There were a few fellows in short pants inside, all preoccupied with exercising. One guest was using the rowing machine, his full face flushed from exertion. Another, quite attractive with banana-blonde hair and soft blue eyes, was furiously punching a bag as if it were his mortal enemy. Realizing she was staring, Carolena's eyes turned to the pommel horse, which went unused as did the brass lion's head mounted on the wall, which held pull-ropes tied to weights. In the far corner, two men wearing mesh-wire facemasks and chest protectors parried, their fencing instructor shouting praises and corrections intermittently.

Disheartened at not having found Grey, Carolena pushed against both heavy double doors the same instant they were opened from the outside. She fell into the man who was intent upon entering. Grey!

He was quick to catch her in his arms. It took her a few breaths to recover her composure. Then she laid into him. "Where have you been?" she shouted. "All I can say is thank you ever so much for leaving me out in the dark and the cold and damp. I may have caught my death for all you care. And have you gotten me a cabin? Or did it slip your mind that my tail, as you so coarsely put it, was even on board? I've been everywhere looking for you so I could give you a good-sized piece of my mind."

Grey was amazed at Carolena's shrewish tone, and she was surprised when he lifted her to her toes by her upper arm and rushed her away from the door and into the passageway.

"Let me go! Just because you wrassle equipment and engines and things on this ship, gives you no leave to bully me!"

He released her once they were a distance from any ship's activity. The smile on his face was gone. "I don't give a good goddamn if your daddy and brother-in-law own this ship, missy, I won't tolerate you talking to me like that." His head cocked as if at the point of discovery. "Fascinating if you don't sound exactly like that Aunt Noreen of yours. Pity the poor fool who finally marries you." His searing look intensified. "It's a lucky thing you're a woman. If you were a man, I'd pound you flat!"

"How dare you?" she responded. "Handle me ever again, and I'll have your job!" She was upset. She was so mad, she could spit mud.

Grey's eyes narrowed, and what Carolena witnessed in him frightened her. Her temper disappeared, replaced by bewilderment. Was she afraid of him?

Speaking softly and slowly, "No one, not man nor woman, threatens my job." He leaned in closely. "You want to run things, do you? Well here, my dear, I give you full dominion of my responsibilities on the *Coral Crown*," adding, "with my compliments."

Grey pulled away. He ripped the golden crossed anchors from the collar of his uniform, seized her wrist, and slapped them onto her upturned palm. A casual about face and he walked away, leaving her alone in the corridor.

She stood trembling, unsure of what to do. In all her ups and downs, she'd never before felt faint. At this moment, she was quite certain she was near to it. It was clutching at her, pinching off the breath to her brain. She leaned against the wall to recover. She straitened her sleeve where he'd twisted it on her arm and righted herself. In the event anyone witnessed the spectacle, she spoke aloud, "If that insolent oaf wants to quit and leave hundreds of passengers stranded in the event the ship breaks down, then he's simply showing his true colors. No loyal crewman would abandon his obligations if his feelings got bruised." How I've misjudged him, she thought. He's neither the kind man nor true friend he purports himself to be. He's a beast!

Calm down, Carolena, she ordered herself. I'll just have to put Second Engineer Casey in charge, and that's that! Then it came to her. Who was she to be putting anyone in charge? Yes, she knew about the ship, but all she knew was its interior design. Of its basic construction, she understood only that burning coal in the fire room produced steam, which pushed piston-things, and they turned engines. Her tongue had gotten away from her, and her interference had caused Grey to quit his post.

Would Casey take over without talking to Grey? She doubted it because the chain of command was inbred in him the same as in any faithful sailor. When he and the captain learned the reason for the resignation, oh God. What if word gets out among the passengers and back in Fernandina? I can only imagine the rumors. And when it gets back to Waite and Bree and Daddy, I'll be so ashamed, they'll probably ask me to leave the business, and rightfully so. When I was a little girl, I remember Daddy telling me respect can only be given. It can't be demanded.

What have I done to myself, my family, and the reputation of the Aqua Verde Passenger Line? Beast or not, I need Grey.

***

Grey McKenna dwarfed his cabin and the furniture in it. He leaned on his forearms and peered into the square mirror hanging above the washstand. He wanted to see a man of honor, always. But he was sometimes hard pressed to live up to that standard. And tonight, he'd failed again.

Few saw his raw anger or heard his biting retorts these days. More times than not, he'd successfully kept control, masking his temper with a cheerful façade. Prior to coming to Fernandina, he'd been in many, too many, fights. Unconsciously, he massaged his right bicep where it still bore splinters of a bullet from one such incident. Yes, he'd kept control for some while now. Until this. The splayed threads on his collar, where he'd so violently torn away his rank, were a reminder of what had just happened.

Blue eyes surveyed his face. It had been a while since he'd looked hard at himself. Shaving his beard clean was a daily necessity, a habit requiring no particular attention to his features. As a young man, he'd heard girls whisper he was attractive. He never cared about that. He'd had women over the years. So many in fact, their faces blurred as he tried to summon each. He figured he'd been favored because he could be entertaining when he made the effort.

As Grey studied himself, he didn't really see handsome. He saw only age. He looked older than he felt. His straight black hair had fallen over his forehead and gray was beginning to salt his temples. His eyes were bright, while the furrow between them was deep, as were the creases in his brow. He moved from the mirror, deciding his reflection wasn't helping his disposition any.

Sitting on the bunk, he remembered the day he and Carolena were formally introduced. From the first, she settled in a warm place in his heart. Hair a pale yellow, her carriage regal, she was a damned handsome woman, very attractive, and very complicated. She could also be a downright bother, too serious and too intense. He horsed around in front of her just to see if she were capable of laughing. She was determined, single-minded, and family loyal. Those were all good things, he guessed, but now she'd humiliated him, or tried to, and he wouldn't stand for it.

Reluctantly, he admitted his pride was hurt. Carolena had attacked so fast, and he really didn't understand why. She'd said something about *leaving her in the cold and damp. Did he forget her tail was aboard?* For God's sake! He had forgotten! No wonder she told him where the hog bit the punkin! The poor little thing probably froze to a cocked hat out there in the sea air. As he thought on it, her hair was bedraggled and her clothes didn't have their usual crisp look to them. He chuckled at her slovenly appearance until he realized she really could catch her death in her damp dress. Hell, hadn't she shown up out of nowhere? So, of course, she had no cabin assigned to her. He owed her one massive apology.

As he went to exit his room and find her, there was a soft knocking at his door. He opened it and before him was Carolena. Her hair was still bedraggled and her collar limp, but her eyes looked directly up into his.

Carolena never thought it would take courage to speak to Grey. Uncertain how to address him, she remained still for a brief second while she decided. If she called him Mr. McKenna, he might think she was being impudent and accepting of his resignation. So, she just said, "Grey?"

"Yes, ma'am?" He was being as polite as possible.

She took his calling her "ma'am" as sarcasm and pooched-out her lips, then unconsciously chewed the inside of her cheek until she tasted the iron of blood. "I'm afraid I overstepped my bounds when I told you I would have your job. I have no authority to say such a thing. I request you continue your duties on the *Coral Crown*. I shall speak no further on the matter." But *you* will, she thought. "Agreed?"

He realized she had never actually spoken the words "I'm sorry." Carolena would rather do anything than say that. He would give odds she was only taking back her rash words for fear of hurting the family business with the gossip of a disgruntled crew. From her cold demeanor, he could tell she didn't care if she'd insulted him or hurt him.

He had to get something out of all this fuss. Maybe he could make this fun. He turned away from her so as not to break into a grin. "Agreed? Agreed? Your tongue got ahead of your good sense, did it? We're all responsible for what comes out of our mouths, or haven't you heard?" Giving her no opportunity to answer, "Apparently not. And here you are, thinking you can get me to save your hide just like that." He snapped his fingers with a startling crack for effect. "It'll take a heap more than your request," he spat forth the last word, "to get me to stay on this ship. You know, if I breathe one syllable to the crew, most will quit right along with me, and then you'll be up a creek." Now, it was he who bit his cheek, but to keep from laughing aloud. "Think you can maneuver the ship, make the repairs, feed, tend, and pamper the passengers single-handedly? I'd like to see you try. You and that mouth of yours will have a fine time talking your way out of this one, princess."

He heard a sniff. She was crying! He hadn't meant to go so far as to make her weep. He turned to see her and felt like a heel.

Carolena hated it when she cried. And most times, she had no control over it. It was the Irish in her, same as in her sister. She and Breelan often spoke of it. Tears for happy occasions, tears for sad, tears of anger and, at this moment in time, tears of frustration. Their father once said there was enough salt water between them to float the *Miss Breelan* down a dry riverbed. It was just the way they were put together, and it was forever embarrassing. She despised Grey thinking he had such power over her. He would and did, and there was no way around it.

She wiped her streaked face with the still damp sleeve of her black gown. "You've got me. I'm nailed to the wall." Faltering, she forced the words from her lips. "I need you." There. She'd admitted it. "The company can't afford another blow to its reputation. I don't know what else you want me to say or do. Tell me and I'll do it, but please, please don't quit on me. Please." As she spoke the last words, her legs remained locked despite her jagged breathing. Although she was scared he would refuse her, she faced him strong.

"Cary. I'm sorry. Please understand, I never meant to make you cry. Once I returned to this cabin, I remembered I'd left you unattended. Finally, I understood why you were so mad and came after me. My only excuse is I was ..." He hesitated, not wanting to tell her of his concerns. "I was occupied in another part of the ship. It took longer than I thought it would. I simply lost track of time. I never meant to slight or neglect you."

Silent, she hoped only to hear he would remain on station. Right now, she didn't much care why he'd forgotten her. It wasn't important.

"You were such an overbearing dickens, I wanted to give you a taste of it back. That's why I've been going on about you commanding the ship yourself once all the crew quit. Think on it a minute. Do you honestly believe I'd do that to the Dunnigans or to Captain Taylor? My loyalty can't be broken by one reaming out, even if it is by you. I am honored to render my humble service unto the *Crown*."

She flew across the cabin and jumped into his arms. He hugged her close as she clung to his muscled neck. "Oh, thank you, Grey. Thank you. I'm so relieved I think my heart will burst!"

He gave her a good squeeze, released her and steadied her gently on her feet. Offering his hand to her, "Friends?"

"You bet! Friends to the end!" Her smile was brilliant. But while his embrace left her warm inside, she was beginning to shiver again. Chastising herself, she thought, I was so ready to throw away everything and dismiss my caring for him because of one stupid argument. I know my love has to be stronger than that. Maybe there will be times ahead when I don't like him very much. That's natural, I guess. Deep down my devotion will never waver. Not like my mother's.

He saw her chill. "Of all the passengers on the ship, my boss should have the best service. And here she stands soaked, cold and, I'll bet, very hungry. You need to get out of those wet rags. What say I find you a stateroom without delay?"

"Sounds wonderful. Grey, let's get one thing right between us. I'm not your boss." She couldn't help herself. She had to add, "And you're not mine."

No use fussing any more with her, he decided. This back and forth contest of wills could go on until who knew when. He was proud to be the bigger man, er person, he decided.

Chapter 8

"Where shall we put you, Cary? Sorry to say, though only for the sake of your comfort, we're fully booked."

She let the nickname pass. "We're full, Grey? That's fabulous! Might I find accommodation in a double cabin with a lady traveling alone? How many single women this trip? You always know where they are."

He smiled. "There are only two women alone, I'm afraid. I wish I had more of a choice for you. One is nearly bed-ridden and the other ..." His expression soured and Carolena, as fatigued as she was, didn't pay any mind.

"Let me apologize up front. Had I any choice other than sticking you in confined quarters with this ..."

She waved his concern away. "Don't be silly. It'll be fine. Come on!" she grabbed his hand. "Let's go meet Miss ..."

"Pence," he completed the name for her. "Miss Peachie Pence."

In a short time, Grey and Carolena were at the door of stateroom 304. He glanced down at the pair of women's gold leather shoes waiting to be picked up by the cabin boy for polishing. They had large mother-of-pearl heart clips on the toes and faded pink and purple striped sachets inside. Tearing himself away from contemplating the boy's task, Grey knocked on the door. There was no answer. "She must be out for the evening." Rapping again, he took his master key and let Carolena inside. The light from the corridor sliced a path through the dark room and before anyone could speak, a shrill cry for help exploded in their ears, quickly followed by a flash and the crack of gunfire!

Grey knocked Carolena to the deck and threw himself over her. His weight was crushing and Carolena had difficulty breathing. Instead of fear, shame engulfed her from having doubted his loyalty. And his body felt good. Very good.

Grey wondered why she was wriggling. His deep respect for Carolena left him embarrassed at so intimate a position. He hoped this unexpected closeness didn't embarrass her as well.

Footsteps came running. A calm voice spoke the order. "This is Jacob Diebert, purser on the *Coral Crown*. Drop your weapon, or I'll fire!"

The next sound was the hard thud of what might have been a gun hitting the carpet. A whimpering and whining followed.

Diebert cautiously flicked a match to see a body cowering on the bed. He reached to turn up the gas of the brass lamp on the wall and beheld the chief engineer on the floor atop Miss Dunnigan. His hand held his own gun steady as he bent over Grey.

"We're fine, Jacob. Thanks." Grey helped Carolena to her feet. He was angry, "Who the hell fired at us? Please don't tell me it was ..."

"Yes, Mr. McKenna," came the nasal voice. "It was I, Miss Pence. Had

I known it was you breaking into my room, and everything, I would never have refused entrance." The welcoming gaze she cast over him required no interpretation.

He gave her a sharp glare.

Visions of the spindly female and the brawny mechanic entwined in embrace nearly sent an already cold, tired, hungry, and traumatized Carolena into uncharacteristic convulsions of hysteria. The woman's appearance caused Carolena to stare. A pink nightgown hung from the boney shoulders of her roommate whose skin bore an ashen-green cast dotted with brown freckles. It must be the lighting, Carolena thought, never having seen such a pigment. The eyes were unusual, too. With few lashes, they had large dark flecks, making them almost polka dotted. Her head was topped with thin black curls matted around and between irregularly spaced coils of light orange hair so wiry, they stood out from her skull like loose bedsprings. A straight row of short curly fringe hung over her low forehead, making the woman appear as if she were wearing a wig, which had slipped forward out of position. Not even Peeper's elixirs and face creams could help this poor woman, Carolena realized.

Grey saw Carolena's straight face and read her crinkled eyes and compressed lips. He was pleased to see her in this silly mood. However, his response toward their assailant was not as hers. For all his professional good humor, he'd never felt less like laughing. He wanted to throttle Miss Pence for endangering Carolena. Remembering he was an officer and duty-bound to remain reserved whenever possible, he erased his grimace. "Why did you shoot at us, Miss Pence? I knocked twice and you gave no response."

"I didn't hear you because I had in my ear plugs, and everything. I was counting sheep when I saw the door swing open. It frightened me. I feared being attacked by some unattractive stranger, and everything." She sniveled. "Praise the Lord, I only fired a warning shot out the porthole. Had I wounded you, and everything, you of all people ..."

Grey had heard enough. "Things are fine, fortunately." His tone was barely civil.

Picking up and examining Peachie's two-shot derringer, Grey introduced the women. "I've brought a companion to share your quarters. Miss Carolena Dunnigan, this is the notorious sharpshooter, Miss Pence. You may have heard of her. Taught Wild Bill Bedstead all he knows."

Recovered, Carolena wondered why he sounded so nasty.

Peachie only heard what she chose, and she chose to take Grey's words as flirtatious teasing.

The higher-ranking officer addressed Diebert. "Please take Miss Pence's pistol and see it's locked in the ship's safe. She may retrieve it when she reaches her final destination."

"Aye, Mr. McKenna." The purser left the room, dispersing the curious crowd in the passageway.

74

Grey had to stop the foolishness. "Miss Carolena must get into dry clothes. Cary, where did they leave your bags?"

"Just one and the last I saw of it, it was by one of the lounges on the starboard side of the promenade deck."

"I'll have a steward see your belongings are brought here at once. I have to report this incident to the captain. Should take about half an hour and then I'm off duty. When you've changed clothes, how about meeting me for a late supper? You must be nearly starved."

Spotting the hurt look upon the ogling woman's face and feeling pressure from Carolena, Grey felt obliged to add, "Needless to say, that invitation includes you, Miss Pence. We'll understand if you decline. We can see you've already retired for the night."

"Call me Peachie, and thank you, Mr. McKenna. Don't worry about me. I can sleep anytime, anywhere. I'll be there in a jiffy. Wait until you see me in my newest frock, and everything. I assume you'll be wearing another dull black dress, Miss Cary. May I call you Cary? Who died, by the way? And I'll call you Grey. How would that be? Oh, we can talk about all that later. I hope I don't show you up in all my fancies."

Within the hour, Grey in dark uniform, Peachie in purple and rust-color diagonal stripes and fur wrap, and Carolena in her second black dress supped in the informal Boat Deck Grill. The pigskin covered walls gleamed with wax. The violin selections were soft in volume yet light in composition. It would be a divine arena for romancing, Carolena was certain. She'd designed it for such occasions. They were three of some fifty passengers in the room who nibbled from the buffet.

As they ate, Carolena decided to avoid mention of her home and family whenever possible. She had to remember her objective, to sell her designs to make money for the family. She would not allow her mother's actions to ferment in her mind.

As Grey devoured smoked ox tongue and au gratin potatoes, he noticed Carolena seemed to have little appetite. "Why aren't you eating? Don't tell me you're seasick."

"Gracious no. After years fighting it, I've finally found my sea legs. No, I'm just tired."

"Tired?" Grey asked. "How can you be tired? You slept on the deck, remember?"

Why did he have to be such a stickler for detail? "It wasn't a deep sleep. I'm tired, I said."

"Okay, okay. Sorry. I just thought you might be coming down with something, and I wouldn't want that."

"She said she's worn out, Grey. I'm not," supplied Peachie. "I can stay up as late as you want me to."

Grey made no reply. To this point, he had not focused on Miss Pence. He realized people couldn't help what they looked like. It was all in the stars when it came to your parentage. Still, in his mind and to his sensibilities, there was no excuse for a human being, especially a woman, to smell the way she did, like a sour washrag. Everyone, no matter how poor, could afford a bar of soap, his mother used to say. And then there were Peachie's disgusting manners. Talking non-stop, saying "and everything" so frequently, it almost tempted one to count the number of times in a minute it was repeated. Almost. She babbled with food on the way to her mouth, with food in her mouth, and with food dripping from her mouth.

"And you haven't even mentioned a thing about the new ensemble I'm wearing."

"It's very nice," he lied.

"I thought so. Have I told you about one of my silly little quirks?"

"You have only one?" Grey inquired innocently with Peachie unaware of his jab. "What quirk is that, Miss Pence?"

"I'm so glad you asked!" she squealed. "Should I have any bad experience while wearing a particular gown the first time—"

"Excuse me?" Carolena asked, unconsciously covering her nose with her napkin to keep from smelling Peachie's unpleasant odor. Why hadn't she smelled it earlier in their cabin? Ah, yes. The porthole had been open and, out of necessity, would remain so tonight if she had anything to say about it. "What do you mean by bad experience?"

Peachie leaned into them as if telling a state secret. "It can be an array of things, such as a rude servant, a broken heel, a loud child, a bumpy buggy ride, no matter. Any experience that makes me uncomfortable or upset, whatever I'm wearing, I destroy it!"

Grey raised his brows. "That would be pretty costly for a normal woman. And don't you have to carry extra clothing with you, should something or someone give you a hard time?"

"It might be expensive, and everything, if I were that normal woman. I give you credit for discerning I am far from normal. People who know me avoid doing me ill. Most don't like to mess with my sensibilities, especially men."

"I see," replied Grey.

"As for this fabulous fox I'm wearing ..." She lifted the pelt to her cheek to feel its softness only to leave behind a residue of face powder on the silken hairs.

Her audience of two was bizarrely curious where this conversation was leading.

"It was given me by one of my suitors. I call such items trophies, and everything."

Carolena was shocked. Grey was not surprised.

Near the end of the evening, Carolena was glad she sat at a ninety-degree angle to Peachie instead of across from her, as was Grey. Several times, she'd glanced over to watch the food flying from her roommate's mouth. And with all the meaningless chatter, there was hardly a single second left empty of conversation in which to enjoy the music.

In desperation, Grey stood up and took Carolena's hand. Looking intently into her eyes, there was pleading in his voice. "I'm sure you don't think it proper to be dancing while in mourning, Cary, and I'll understand. However, would you consider one slow waltz? Remember how Grammy loved to hear a waltz.

"Grey," Peachie inserted. "It's not right to put Cary in such a position. I'll dance with you."

"Thank you. I'll be happy to dance with you, Grey," Carolena replied, leaving a stricken Peachie behind.

As they glided to the sweet strains of the one, two three, one, two, three rhythm, Carolena whispered up to her partner. "You looked so distressed, I worried you might drop to one knee and beg me to get you away from our companion."

"What made you dance with me besides Peachie? I honestly never expected you to, being in mourning and all."

"That was a major part of it. I thought how Grammy and Peeper would disapprove then almost chuckled to myself at the expression of horror Aunt Noreen would wear to see her niece commit such a crime." Carolena's mother came to mind, a mother who'd apparently do just about anything. "I'm sure somewhere someone has danced while dressed in black for reasons less dire than Peachie Pence. No one on board knows I'm a Dunnigan or my family owns the line. No one but Peachie, that is, who managed to get the details of my life out of me. How does she do that, Grey?"

"We answer her questions in hope she'll stop talking, that's how. She's windier than a goat with a can of beans."

Carolena giggled. "Maybe, too, I'm dancing because you and Nora both told me I need to be bolder and not so serious." She added, "And you needed my help."

His eyes flashed happiness as they circled the floor.

Glancing over at a sullen Peachie, Carolena tried to be charitable. "You know, everyone is someone's baby. Even Peachie, at one time, was an adorable little girl." They looked at one another and couldn't contain their laughter!

Carolena was thrilled to be in Grey's arms and wished he'd hold her tighter. Unfortunately, she'd committed sufficient social faux pas for one evening and kept her distance from him as was proper. She settled for the heat of his hand on hers and across her back. Enjoying each swaying rhythm, they were hard put to return to the table until the last possible moment when the music ended the late evening. It was clear Peachie longed for a dance, and Carolena whispered, "That dress has to be one of a kind. Shouldn't we try to save it by keeping Peachie smiling? What do you say, Grey?"

"We'd be doing the world a favor if she destroyed it. It stinks so badly of her and her curdled perfume, who would want it?"

Carolena giggled. "It's only that I can't be deliberately cruel, no matter how irritating she is."

"You're too nice, Carolena." He sighed. "I won't dance with her, but if you can stand her, I guess I can."

Once they returned to the table, Peachie's chatter-recommenced.

Carolena waited for an opportunity to say she was going to their cabin. It never came. Finally, she looked at Grey who was returning her gaze and loudly interjected over Peachie's prattle, "I must call it a night, Grey."

"I'll see you tomorrow, Cary. We'll visit then."

"Oh?" asked Peachie. "What time shall I meet you for breakfast, and everything, Mr. McKenna?"

Good Lord, thought an exasperated Grey. Will I have to take a club to this woman? With difficulty, he maintained his manners saying, "I have a ship to keep in running order, Miss Pence. I'm afraid I'll be unable to eat with you in the morning. If you'll excuse me, I'll walk Miss Carolena to her cabin. Good night."

"Silly you. It's my cabin, too! I'll just take your other arm, shall I?" She seized his forearm in a death grip.

One little boy, up past his bedtime, was heard to say, "Look Mommy. There's the princess and the wicked witch from my storybook!"

Upon hearing that, Carolena felt sorry for Peachie, Grey tried not to laugh aloud, and Peachie, hearing only the word *princess*, nodded with approval that such a small lad was able to discern her unique beauty.

***

Carolena was slow in awakening the second morning, blaming it on a disturbing dream of her mother and uncle together as well as exhaustion at trying to stay warm. The cold from the open porthole was a trade off for fresh smelling sea air. At least Peachie was not in the room now, and for that, Carolena was most grateful. Somewhat stiff, she knelt on the bed, pushed aside the gold curtains, and checked the weather conditions. Small wonder she was cold. Snow was in the air! Still, it was February. She closed the porthole until Peachie's return and was glad she had brought Nora's cape.

As if she were wearing leaden slippers, Carolena plodded about the cabin, whittling the hours away until she heard one long, loud blast of the ship's whistle. They were pulling into Charleston, South Carolina.

As she tried to tie the black ribbons of her bonnet into a pretty bow under her chin, she realized she hadn't seen Peachie since the night before. Her vibrant multicolored most-personal and not-so-personal things were still scattered around the cabin. "Who knows with that one?" Carolena said aloud. In speaking and swallowing, her throat was scratchy. "I hope I haven't caught a bug," she told the face in the mirror as she secured the hat with a single-headed jet hatpin for extra measure. Her arms dropped to her sides. Her limbs ached and her head was throbbing. Her skin hurt, too. She hadn't been hungry for breakfast and dawdling, had no time for lunch. Her empty stomach announced its displeasure.

When Peachie burst through the door to stuff her traveling case for departure, Carolena found her a somewhat welcome distraction from her own discomforts. At once, the air in the cabin fouled with Peachie's presence, and Carolena could stand it no more. "I'll see you upstairs. It's getting a bit close in here."

Peachie slammed her huge case closed. "Wait for me, Cary. I'm ready, too." She opened the door and hollered down the corridor to an elderly man in uniform, "Steward. You there. Steward! Come here at once and tend our bags. If you do so in prompt fashion, I may give you a tip. I may not, too."

Carolena cringed, smiled, and shrugged, mouthing the words *I'm sorry* to the gentleman who could have been her grandfather.

He returned the smile and walked past them on his way to their stateroom. "Nice trip, ladies?"

"Very nice. Thank you," Carolena answered. "I've left something on the dresser for you."

"Thank you, ma'am."

"Grey will be standing just inside the exit to the main deck across from where the gangway is hung, Peachie." Carolena explained. "That's usually where the men of rank say goodbye to departing passengers during inclement weather."

As they walked through a glass-enclosed passage, Peachie pointed out the snow. "I just love it when it's cold. More reason for cuddling, huh?" She clicked her tongue twice for emphasis. "How about you, Cary?"

Carolena didn't protest her nickname because, right now, she wasn't up to the bother of it.

"I've not had much experience in snow."

Grey kept a watchful eye for Carolena and Peachie, as along with the captain and other officers, he thanked each passenger who was leaving, inviting them to travel aboard the *Crown* in the future. Finally, he spied the odd pair coming his way and steeled himself.

"Oh Grey," Peachie began, extending her hand to his. "This has been a most memorable voyage for me, and everything. I feel I know you well enough to tell you my little secret. I'm in love!"

Grey hoped his grimace at the news was internal and didn't show on his face. "Miss Pence, this is one trip I won't soon forget either."

"I'm right! I'm right! You feel the very same way about me! I could tell from the moment we met."

Enough! He had to drop the ax on this bizarre happening. "Miss Pence. Please. Listen to me. I'm flattered you've chosen to bestow your charms upon me. However, I'm sorry. As a member of the crew of the *Coral Crown*, I am strictly forbidden to fraternize on a familiar level with the paying passengers."

Her hands covered her face.

This was going to be one hell of a distasteful display. Grey looked to Carolena who was putting her arm about the heaving shoulders of her roommate. She was far more sympathetic than he ever could be. Walking to a nearby bench, Peachie seated herself. Grey called for the steward to bring water as a crowd began gathering, partly from the spectacle and partly because they didn't want to venture outdoors until it was absolutely necessary. It was then Peachie removed her hands, revealing not tears of sadness, but tears of laughter! She sprang from the seat and attempted to speak between giggling gasps for breath.

"Grey, my poor deluded Grey! I just knew your company regulations were the only thing stopping you from advancing on me, and everything. Oh you foolish, foolish man. I'm flabbergasted you thought I was interested in you romantically. Why, all this time you've been under the misconception I want you? That way? No, no, no, no, no." Her voice trilled the rejecting word as if she were bestowing the most gracious of compliments upon him. Controlling her chortles at last, "Don't get me wrong. You are a fine looking fellow, and everything, but my heart belongs to another."

Grey stood there, his back straight, his pride punctured. It seemed at least a hundred passengers surrounded them by this time and they, too, sniggered in accompaniment to Peachie, with him the butt of their laughter.

Carolena's heart went out to Grey. She, as well, had been sure Peachie had fallen hard for him. There was little she could do to help except, "Peachie, you mentioned something about catching a cab? You'd better be doing it before they're all snatched up."

Calming herself at last, "Yes, you're right, Cary. Oh, first I must put on my nose warmer. I don't want my wee sniffle-flute to get frostbitten." Odd looking yet functional, the knitted contraption had two ear loops attached to a teal blue triangle that covered the nose. Peachie straightened the short tassel at the tip just so, and then said to Grey, "Goodbye, good sir. You've been a delight." Looking about, she snagged another man in uniform. "Steward. Yes, you. I've an appointment to keep with someone special, and everything! Come along." With that, she was gone.

The crowd dispersed, many still smiling. Grey asked permission from Captain Rockwall to be excused. To his surprise, his boss, who'd witnessed the commotion from a distance, gave his official nod, doing what he could to help ease the awkward situation.

Grey walked off, leaving Carolena standing alone. "Grey. Grey! Wait up." She hurried to catch him, summoning all her energy to do so.

He slowed his steps, and as she took his rigid arm, he stopped and turned to her. They were alone, except for the last few departing guests who, fortunately for him, had missed the entire humbling episode. "She got me a good one, Carolena. The gospel is, I'd have put money down she had a hankering for me. After suffering her rude ways, I took pleasure in imagining the most brutal of words to tell her we had no future together. Then when the time came, I couldn't be so mean. I'm not as hard-hearted as I think. I set myself up for her to lay me wide open."

Listening, she waited as he reflected further.

"Guess I needed a good comeuppance, huh? Still, of all the people in the world to make a buffoon of me ... You know, I can't really remember ever having felt so foolish."

"Sweet, Grey." Carolena stroked his smooth cheek with the flat of her gloved palm. "Please, don't let her do this to you. At first, I didn't understand why you were so cold toward her. After spending ten minutes with her, I figured it out. I think she really does have a terrible crush on you, and I think this last announcement of hers was self-defense. The entire time her hands were covering her face, she was scheming on how to get back at you. She turned her tears inward and saved herself. Don't you dare feel badly," she ordered him.

He looked down on the beautiful face. Her efforts to restore his spirits were sincere. Taking both her hands in his, he pulled her close, placing her captured fingers against his hard chest. His gaze reached into the glistening depth of her moss green eyes, "Thank you, Cary. You know," he thought for a moment, "you've been the single most constant friend I've ever had."

His remark surprised and touched her heart. "Until now, I hadn't thought about it." She analyzed his remark. "Although Nora is my best female friend, you're the closest male friend I have, too. Hey! The hour's gotten away from me! I have to hurry and hire a cab."

Releasing her hands, Grey grasped her by the shoulders. "Carolena. I thought we agreed our signalman would flash a communication to shore and have it delivered to your uncle saying I'll take you to his house?"

Although she relished his touch, she expected a debate. Casually stepping away from him, "Oh, my plans have all changed. I was so busy fending off Peachie, I forgot to tell you. Signor Alontti is apparently a busy man. He sent word to the ship asking me to meet him sooner than planned. I, in turn, sent a message to my aunt and uncle that I wouldn't be going to their house straight away, and I'd let them know when to expect me once I found out." She pulled aside her cape to look at the watch brooch pinned to her bodice. "I must go directly to the meeting."

Casey interrupted them. "Mr. McKenna, excuse me, sir. We're having a time sealing that steam leak."

Realizing the serious danger to his crew since super-heated steam was often invisible, Grey responded calmly in front of Carolena, "I'll be right there."

"Aye, Mr. McKenna."

"They can't get along without you, Grey. Ah-choo!"

They exchanged beaming smiles. "Bless you. You alright?"

"Sure."

He walked her back to the door exiting the ship. "It's been an interesting trip."

"I'm not certain just how long I'll need to stay here in town. I'll probably ride home with you next week when you dock. If I'm not ready to leave Charleston then, I'll let you know. Maybe you can come by to visit. My family would love to have you, I'm sure. Only if you have the time though, and want to. And if you do, I can report the progress I've made with my client."

"You be careful, Cary. I worry about you. I'm just glad your uncle lives in the city to keep an eye on you. I'm anxious to get to know him."

"Are you? I'm so glad. You'll love him. He and Aunt Coe are such dears." She bundled herself up tightly. "Oh, I must run! Signor Alontti shouldn't be kept waiting." She stretched to peck him on the cheek, taking care to hold her breath. She didn't want him to catch the cold, or whatever it was, she'd contracted.

He encircled her with his long arms, nearly crushing her in his hug. "Remember, men are men."

"Don't be silly. This is business. I'm excited."

"You must be. Your face is flushed. Sure you're feeling well, Cary?"

"Now, Grey," she warned sweetly. "Bye-bye!" Walking as fast down the runway as her weary body and the slick ramp would allow, "And the name's Carolena!"

Grey laughed at his hardheaded friend and watched her descend the gangway.

Chapter 9

The icy wind slapped Carolena's warm cheeks. She'd never been in weather this harsh. Snow had hung in the air once or twice in Fernandina with a few scattered flakes landing on the sandy soil until they melted in short order. She'd never actually walked on the stuff. Her shoes weren't meant for these conditions, and she worried they would soak through.

To take her mind off the cold while she waited for her bag, Carolena recalled the last time she'd been in Charleston. She was sixteen and her father had brought her along on business. Before their arrival, she'd studied up on the place, the sights, the food. Because their stay had been short with no time for sightseeing, her recollection was only of the busy streets. It was now as it was then. People were everywhere. The way they bustled, each seemed to be late for an appointment.

Her carpetbag was finally brought to the foot of the dock. She was glad she'd wired Uncle Fries, telling him he needn't pick her up, that she'd catch a cab to his house after the meeting. Talking with Grey made her one of the last passengers to disembark. All attempts at waving down a hack proved futile, so Carolena settled herself inside the wooden cabstand for protection. The cold air managed to whirl up and under her skirts despite her ample petticoats. Her legs chilled, and she shivered. Pulling the hood of her cape forward over her bonnet, she bound the black woolen scarf around her neck as tightly as she could without choking. With it covering her mouth and nose, only her eyes were left exposed to see what was happening.

Accepting she would more than likely be late in seeing Alontti anyway, Carolena was about ready to return to the ship to get out of the weather when a boy whistled to her, holding open the door of a cab. After giving a coin to the lad and her destination to the driver, she gratefully entered the relative warmth of the enclosed carriage. Rolling herself into a tight ball, she drew the rabbit skin lap robe provided to her shoulders and hunkered-down. She put aside her own aches and pains and focused on her mission. This Paolo Alontti would be met with confidence because she offered him a quality product.

Hearing a persistent pounding and unable to ignore the annoying sound, she was forced to acknowledge it.

"Miss? Miss! Are you all right in there? We've arrived, Miss. Miss?"

She'd fallen asleep, and on such an important day, too! "Yes. Thank you," she shouted, her heart pounding from being startled awake.

After paying, she saw the driver none too carefully deposit her bag on the sidewalk. Carolena exited the carriage, holding onto the grab bar and placing one shoe on the granite stepping block. It was slick with ice; so to prevent slipping, she quickly jumped to the sidewalk, landing in a puddle of brown slush up to her ankles. Her attention was distracted from her discomfort by the building in front of her. It was a huge theatre. Had the man taken her to the correct address? She looked for a street number and finally saw it marked in small red iron characters on the etched pilaster to her right. Glancing up, she blinked to keep the snow from settling on her thick brown lashes, and read the vertical sign: ZEUS THEATRE. A short fellow in a dark blue cape, hat, and gloves was in the process of cleaning the outside glass of six sets of double brass doors, while a man in white cleaned the inside. Gas jets hissed at the dim sun in an attempt to illuminate the marquis. Bold black letters spelled out CHARLESTON PHILHARMONIC on three sides. Just as boldly on the panel facing the street, the second line read CONDUCTOR - PAOLO ALONTTI.

Carolena was impressed and very cold. She turned to ask the driver to carry her carpetbag to the door. She'd been so engrossed in her perusal of the building, she hadn't noticed he'd left. She couldn't leave her bag on the curbstone, so dodging the passersby, she struggled, dragging it behind her. The cleaning man offered no assistance. She had to try four different doors to find one unlocked.

The custodian inside said with indifference, "You can't leave your belongings at the door, lady."

Ignoring him, she walked deeper into the warmth of the theatre. The entrance hall was vacant. The first thing to catch her curiosity was a placard perched on a brass easel easily three feet taller than she was. She expected to see a photograph of Signor Alontti, but it told only of some after-performance affair tonight, the time of the function, where, and the price of a ticket. Who would pay that much for tickets to go to a party to see this conductor, she wondered.

As she walked, Carolena discovered the walls along the sixty-foot or so lobby were painted with murals of Shakespeare's plays. Engaged by the detail of them and taking time she didn't have, Carolena identified each one. Overhead was the most massive chandelier she'd ever seen. It was suspended inside a dome painted a soft sky-blue with all manner of colorful flying birds. They looked so alive, she smiled as she found herself listening for their twittering. Empty refreshment areas periodically lined the walls, each bordered with live ferns and palms in gleaming brass planters. Lace covered shelving held row upon row of wine glasses. Ahead was a staircase, at least 20 feet wide, which she assumed led to the loge. It was carpeted in an intertwining geometric pattern of claret, purple, and yellow that gave the impression one must be prepared to bow down before the royal inhabitants who might, at any minute, descend in flowing robes of spun gold. The iron balustrades cascading on either side framed a path for regal footsteps to tread. Beneath the stairway, Carolena saw a horizontal wall of polished cherry doors. She imagined them thrown open to let loose the audience who would hail the wonderful productions on what she was certain would be an elegant stage.

Faint music caught her attention. As quietly as possible, she pulled a door open and slipped into the auditorium. The only lighting was from the stage, and the shadowed interior appeared palatial. The theatre walls were huge chiseled blocks of stone, like those of a castle. There were turrets on either side of the stage and the viewing boxes therein seemed to be windows looking out onto a courtyard. Colorful triangular flags hanging from twenty-foot brass poles floated to notes Carolena did not recognize. The music sent chills up and down her spine. It was like nothing she'd ever heard, and she walked halfway into the hall without realizing she'd even moved. Determined not to miss a thing, she scanned the musicians and their instruments.

She noted the conductor standing on a simple wooden box painted a flat black. Fascinated, she watched his silver hair whip wildly in, on and over his collar as he punctuated his musical instruction with a head toss. Squared shoulders twisted and snapped. Muscular arms and legs could not be ignored despite the full-cut fabric of his black clothing. A baton seemed a natural extension of his right forefinger, accenting note after note, punching the air, prodding, wanting, expecting, and receiving more. The music was a living creature, and it was this man who breathed life into it.

"This is a private rehearsal. If you'd like to view a performance, it will cost you a ticket, same as any other member of the public."

Carolena was sorely tempted to hush the woman speaking to her back. She hated severing herself from this symphony of skill, stamina, and strength. With no alternative, she turned to see a tight-lipped older woman dressed in navy pinstripe, her hands on narrow hips. The strained expression on the woman's face reminded Carolena of one of Peeper's prunes.

Carolena said, "I beg your pardon." It hurt her throat to raise her voice but because of the music, she found it necessary. "My name is Carolena Dunnigan. I've a meeting with Signor Alontti."

"Run along, little girl, before I find it necessary to call the law. I know just what kind of meeting you'd like with him. Bothersome fans like you have been trying for years to, well, they simply are not tolerated by the maestro."

"How dare you speak to me as if I were a woman of the streets? I repeat, I am Carolena Dunnigan, and I was wired to be here, at this address, on this day at 2 p.m. I can assure you, my purpose is strictly business."

"I am familiar with Signor Alontti's calendar, and you are not on it. What kind of business do you have with him?"

This was insulting! "I am a professional—"

The woman cut her off. "A professional what?"

When the music suddenly stopped, the woman was shouting. Carolena envisioned the entire orchestra and their conductor watching and listening. She was mortified.

Carolena's dignified posture held firm until her physical distress penetrated her stubborn resolve. Her skin felt so hot, she expected her clothes to flame. Mesmerized by the beauty of her surroundings, she'd never loosened her wraps once inside the theatre. Now, she couldn't seem to free herself fast enough. She stopped when the voice of the conductor entered her hearing.

"A fine rehearsal, everybody. Tonight's performance will be extraordinary if we do half as well. Thank you, all."

Carolena was surprised. He was an American! With a name like Alontti, she'd expected him to speak English with a rich Italian accent.

The sour appearance of the woman was gone, replaced by an almost – almost winsome expression as she looked up to the stage. Carolena turned around and understood.

The conductor was facing the empty theatre, his eyes downcast, gazing at a composition in his hands. This man was a dozen years older than she, and most appealing. Even from a distance, she could see his black lashes were so long, their shadows extended almost to the hollow of his cheekbones. His thick hair was a perfect pewter. Loose strands had fallen to his brows, and he unthinkingly pushed them back. He lifted his chin, and Carolena was stunned by the structure of his angular face.

He spoke again. Blinded by the bright lights illuminating his face, he shielded his vision. Still unable to see into the vacant auditorium, he called out, "Miss Gwenier? Gwenie? Are you about?"

"Yes, Paolo." Quick stepping toward the stage, she left Carolena behind in the dark.

"I think we ran a little long. Is there an appointment waiting for me?"

Looking over her shoulder then back to him, Carolena could hear disgust in the voice of this Miss Gwenier.

"Yes. There's someone up the aisle."

Without hesitation, "Thank you, Gwenie. I'll see you this evening."

Being discharged brought no pleasure to the aloof woman who marched past the intruder, purposely and roughly brushing Carolena's shoulder. However upset or insulted, Carolena got the idea it would take much for Gwenie to cross Signor Alontti.

He set aside his music, ignored the steps on either side of the stage, and handily jumped across the footlights, landing on the same level as Carolena. He advanced up the inclining aisle toward her with long slow strides. Her heart was pounding, and she didn't understand why.

He stood toe to toe with Carolena while the stage lighting framed him in its halo. He looked down, seemingly absorbing the contours of her face. She reckoned his scrutiny was because he was surprised C. M. Dunnigan was a female.

She didn't object to his inspection until she remembered how windblown and disheveled she must be. Her cape was unbuttoned at the throat and her scarf was hanging unevenly from her neck. She was still so blessedly hot. The huge surrounding room started shrinking in on her.

She grabbed hold of the closest thing - no, the second closest, for she could never touch a perfect stranger. Finding a seat back secured to the floor, she took two small steps to square herself behind it.

He reached out to her as the lock of her knees broke and she collapsed onto the cushioned chair. Reaching for the reticule hanging from her wrist, she jammed her hand into it and felt around for smelling salts. Peeper always insisted she carry them, and how glad Carolena was to have them with her.

Remembering Paolo Alontti, Carolena's eyes found him kneeling beside her. She felt weak and feminine. She didn't mind being feminine, yet she did despise weakness, particularly in herself. Her collapse proved how little control of this situation she possessed. Then she asked herself if it were really necessary to be in full control one hundred percent of the time.

Taking her hand, Signor Alontti removed her glove. She uttered no protest while he rubbed her cold fingers, stirring their circulation. This was more than a devotee's near faint, he recognized. The girl was ill. He gently slipped his right arm between her and the seat back. His left found the crook of her knees. Lifting her, he tipped her so her head naturally leaned into his shoulder. Now, he used the stairs to access the stage. Transporting her through the side curtains, he carried her into the recesses of the massive building.

Carolena didn't understand. He was taking her to a destination of his choosing. With her silence, she was a willing party to - to what? At this moment, she didn't care. Later. There was always time to protest, to turn away. Yes, later.

Up a stairway, they went. When they reached a door bearing his name stenciled in gold leaf, he entered what she assumed was his dressing room. He kicked the door closed behind them with his boot, and they were in near darkness except for weak sunlight casting a soft light through a large window. The snow outside was like flying shards of crystal whirling in the air.

Carolena Dunnigan was in the arms of a famous, powerful, obviously wealthy man. Signor Paolo Alontti was holding her close to him. She wished at that instant she had removed her cape and hat, and not because she was still so hot. She wanted to feel him touching her. Surely she was delirious or why else would she crave this familiarity? Then, to her immediate disappointment, the gentleman laid her down on his settee in front of a stone fireplace.

Transfixed, she watched as he reached to turn the key on an electric lamp with an elaborate Tiffany shade on a nearby table. He seemed to think better of this and found a match in his pocket. Crossing to the baby grand piano in the far corner of the twenty-by-thirty-odd-foot room, he lit five white candles in silver candelabra. Placing them on the mantle, he bent to build a fire.

Carolena was absorbed in the scene. She was a few feet from him, yet still heard his pounding heart in her ears or was it her own? She was acutely aware everything in the room, from the furniture to her, was his if he chose. She should feel out of place. She did not. He was master, and he wanted her there. Nothing and no one would dare speak otherwise. Why would they? He was a benevolent possessor.

The flickering candlelight left dancing shadows on every surface. But Carolena stared at Alontti, watching his form as he retrieved, stacked, and lit the fat pine to entice the dry logs to flame. Balancing on one knee on carpet that matched the lobby's, he prodded the reluctant blaze with a glistening brass poker.

That done, the signor's attention returned to her. Untying her bonnet and finding the hatpin, he lifted her head to remove both. This beauty before him seemed alert enough. Her big eyes took hold of him, never once leaving his body. Still, she was sick with fever. He discarded her cape and wet shoes, disturbing her as little as possible. Hair of gold was damp with perspiration and her moistened bodice was clinging to her. She needed help. Covering her with the mohair throw from the arm of the sofa, he moved to use the telephone on the wall in the room. He was appreciative of the privileges his fame afforded him, particularly in this instance.

A log popped as it burned and acted like a slap to her face. This man must think her what Gwenie accused, a loose fan overcome by celebrity. She had to try to regain some credibility. "Signor Alontti," she called to him. "Please forgive my awkward entrance."

"Miss Dunnigan, I believe?"

Her heart soared as he addressed her. She nodded, feeling inexplicably childlike at his correct identification.

"There is no need for apology. I can plainly see you've taken ill. I'm just telephoning for a doctor."

"Oh, no. Please don't bother. I'm a little chilled from this weather, is all. I'm a Florida girl, and quite unaccustomed to it. I'm fine. You have a performance tonight." As she spoke, she pushed the blanket off in order to stand. "I imagine time is tight for you. So let's get to it. My bag has a copy of your yacht plans. Where is my bag? Oh no! I left it by the front door of the theatre."

"My people will bring it here."

Her hand to her chest, "I'm so relieved. Now, where will I be able to lay out the drawings so we might discuss the alterations you wish? I've already caused you enough delay."

His only response was, "Lie back down. You're sick."

He cranked the telephone a few times. Talking into the mouthpiece, he said, "Operator? Yes, it is. Thank you. Yes. Yes. Excuse me, but I need a doctor at once." He paused while she spoke. "No. I'm fine. I need the doctor for a young woman who has fallen ill. Is Doctor Renninger on call?" He listened. "Good. Ask him to come as quickly as he can to the stage door of the Zeus Theatre. Have him knock loudly on the door, and the janitor can let him in and direct him to my dressing room. Do you have all that? Good girl. Thank you."

When Signor Alontti hung up, Carolena insisted, "Really, I'm fine. Please call back, and say the doctor needn't come."

"No, ma'am."

If she were honest, seeing a doctor probably wouldn't hurt. No more was said because Signor Alontti moved to his piano and played. His technique was engrossing, and the soothing music lulled the ailing girl to sleep.

By hour's end, the physician had arrived. The conductor waited in the hall while Carolena was examined.

All the while asleep, Carolena knew nothing of the doctor's visit until she was startled awake by another loud crack from a log in the fireplace. She heard voices and immediately recognized one belonging to Signor Alontti. She strained to hear as they spoke softly at the far end of the dressing room.

"Are you certain, Doctor?" the signor asked. "Why? Why, when I've just found her?"

Carolena thought she heard him say, "When I've just found her." She was confused. Surely, he couldn't be speaking of her.

"I've been a doctor for a long time, son. I've seen several of these cases, and they follow the same pattern. Sad to say, these things can creep up on a person over the years. A normal, healthy childhood is no guarantee one won't be struck later in life. I'm sorry, but an irregular, weak heart cannot be strengthened, only coddled."

Carolena! Carolena! She screamed her name in silence. What are they saying? A weak heart? Dear God! A weak heart? She felt her heart beating wildly in her chest. Her heart couldn't be weak because she felt so strong. Her current sickness was just temporary. She'd picked up a bug somewhere. She'd pushed herself to get her work completed, to get to Charleston on time. She was worn out, wet and chilled. It was just a cold. A simple cold! That was what was wrong with her. She stilled her breathing to a minimum, listening for more information.

"I can understand your anxiety, Signor. I do. It's times like these, I feel so helpless. No medicine I might prescribe will change the condition. Remember now, a frail heart can survive long if delicately treated. Avoidance of stress and relaxation, that's the best medicine. It's all dependent upon attitude. You can live a longer life with a sedate existence or one that is shorter and more pleasurable. It's a conscious decision only the patient can make."

"Is there any time frame you can give me?"

"How long is impossible to say. It's out of my hands."

She heard more that didn't register. All she understood was her heart was bad and there was no telling how much longer she had to live. Had to live! She felt her cheeks tickled by falling tears. She was still so young, only twenty-eight. She hadn't married nor had children. Even if she could wed tomorrow and have a baby in nine months, she wouldn't. She wouldn't bear a child to desert it with her early death. She always thought she had time to have all life offered. She'd been wrong. So very, very wrong.

The doctor reached into his little black bag for medicine, and paper and pencil. "I am writing out a list of instructions. I see little need for hospitalization. You may want to hire a nurse to insure proper care. I'll return in two days to see if she's better."

Better? She inwardly bristled at the word. She would never be better again.

"Thank you, Doctor."

"Keep me informed, Signor Alontti. You know where to reach me."

Carolena's eyelids were heavy. Paolo saw she was barely awake. Still, he told her, "You're to gargle every few hours with this strong solution of chlorate of potash, and take one of twelve sulfur and cayenne pepper capsules every three hours. Doctor Renninger has provided some camphorated oil to rub on your throat, too."

The musician thought hard on what to do. It was only sixty-five minutes until he was due on stage. He could hear the behind the scenes crew working their magic, along with an occasional riff from his musicians. If only he didn't have his performance tonight, he would care for her himself. He decided he would ask Gwenie to stay with Miss Dunnigan while he was forced to be away from her. Gwenie never denied him anything. The rest of the time, he would deal with the girl alone. To the best of his ability, he wanted, he needed to make her comfortable.

There was a knock at the door. The woman he'd known for so long rushed in, talking non-stop. "Paolo, my dear. The house is sold out once again! Why is it so dark in here?"

"Shhh," he said.

"What's all this? Let me turn on more lights. By the way, what did that young woman want with you this afternoon? As if I need to ask," Gwenie added sarcastically. "I don't know how you stand all the annoying female fans." She stopped dead still when she spied the fan in question stretched out on Paolo's settee. Gwenie looked to him for explanation.

"I'm as surprised as you. The poor creature collapsed in the theatre. The doctor has come and gone. He left a list of things we're to do for her and some medicine. I'll handle it all myself except when I'm on stage."

Had he said *we*? Gwenie didn't want to hear this. How often had his emotions been governed by a pretty face? He'd searched for true love so many times, and so many times his fantasy was destroyed once he got to know each woman. When he ended it, there were very few willing to graciously accept his decision. It was ugly scene after ugly scene. Gwenie wanted to spare him or try to - again.

"Paolo, please." She was almost pleading. "There's no need for you to take this on. I'll see this wanton is moved to a hotel, and I'll hire a nurse. I'll do whatever is necessary. Don't worry."

"No."

The single word had fierce meaning behind it, and Gwenie feared his heart was already captured.

"Listen well." His tone was stern; his eyes dark. "You will never again say a disparaging remark against her. She cannot be taken out of doors until she's better. Unfortunately and to her discomfort, she will have to remain here in my dressing room to wait for that day. Meanwhile, I want a bed brought in here, a full-size bed, so she has room to move. Once the doctor pronounces her well enough to travel, she can stay in the guest room in my apartment. For now, we will make it as restful as possible for her."

The white-haired woman heard *we* a second time and winced at the idea of it all.

His temper turned more reasonable. "I realize I'm asking a lot, but I do ask. While I'm on stage, would you please sit with her? She should stay asleep the entire time. Just in case, call Edward at home and have him bring food for her and us. I'll relieve you after the performance."

"Are you forgetting you are the guest of honor at the after-party?"

"Damnation! It slipped my mind."

"That, too, is sold out. And if you do stay with her, where will you sleep? On the floor? And suppose you catch whatever it is she has? Be reasonable, Paolo. Let me hire someone. You're too busy to minister to her." She added one more thing. "Did it cross your mind she may resent you caring for her in such an intimate manner?"

Despite his looking away, Gwenie caught the sparkle in his rich blue eyes. "Somehow, I don't think it will be a problem. Order a cot brought up here for me when your order her bed, would you? As for tonight, I know you were planning to attend the affair. You've been to so many; you must find them a bore. Would you stay with her then, too? If you honestly want to attend, go after I get back. I promise I'll only make a short appearance, no more than half-an-hour, just enough of a showing to appease everyone who purchased tickets. If it weren't for charity, I'd cancel the whole thing, last minute notice or not."

Gwenie could see it was useless to argue. Although she wouldn't like it, she'd do as he wished.

Chapter 10

"Fries," Aunt Coe told her husband, "ample hours have passed for Carolena's meeting plus her travel-time to get here. Where the dickens is she? It's dark out and so late now, and there is still no sign. What should we do?" She paced the floor. With every pass of the window, she stopped, pulled the lace drapery aside and peered into the night.

Yet again, her husband placed his monocle to his left eye, retrieved the message from his niece from the breast pocket of his black vest and read:

TO: Fries Dresher
C/O Fries Leather Goods
Charleston, South Carolina

FROM: Carolena Dunnigan
C/O Aqua Verde Passenger Line

CHANGE IN PLANS STOP HAVE APPOINTMENT ONCE CROWN DOCKS STOP NOT CERTAIN WHEN I WILL SEE YOU STOP DO NOT WORRY STOP

"Granted, it is rather vague. We don't even know with whom Carolena's appointment is. Therefore, we've no idea where she's gone. She doesn't know herself when she'll arrive at our door. The only thing to do, my dear, is go to bed. Should she show up tonight, she'll ring the bell. Come now, let's retire, and try to get some rest. She's a grown woman and smart as a whip to boot. She wouldn't want us fretting over her like this. We'll hear something soon. I'm sure we will."

Aunt Coe felt less charitable toward Carolena than her mate did. Her sister, Ella, had brought her children up to be more considerate than this. To cause undue worry was not right. Her husband's pinched brow told her he, too, was seriously concerned. Still, he was right. He needed his sleep. His arthritis was bad these days.

As she helped him up the stairs to their bedroom, a swift tear came into her eye. Ella's family was precious to her. When Coe got word of their horrible fire and loss of everything, her prayers went out to all the Dunnigans. Michael had refused the one thing they really needed - money. Fries tried and tried to give them a large sum, free and clear. Michael would have none of it. Pride was a powerful sentiment.

Folding the sheet back over the blanket's edge to keep it from becoming soiled or frayed before its time by her husband's whiskers, she tucked the covers under Fries' chin. Lying beside him, it came to her how having Carolena for a visit was so little to do toward helping her baby sister. Now, she wasn't quite sure what to expect. She marveled. Despite living several hundred miles away, the Dreshers still managed to get tangled in the middle of Dunnigan family dilemmas. But then, that was Coe's definition of family.

***

Thirsty, Carolena didn't want to swallow because her throat hurt. And coughing pained her ribs. She was miserable. Yet, she was experiencing a sense of pampering. Strong fingers with a tender touch, their warmth slathering on cool balm, were massaging her. What was it? With her nose stopped up, she couldn't really smell anything. She focused on the decadent sensation, loving it.

Carolena blinked back the bright light of morning to see Paolo Alontti bent over her! What he was doing to her was most personal and intimate, still she did not think to protest. A cotton nightie she didn't recognize was untied several inches at the neck, exposing her skin. As he stroked and petted, he brought a new experience of … she didn't know what to call it.

This was lunacy for him. He didn't care. Here he was, a complete unknown to the girl and she lay before him, seemingly welcoming his touch on her ivory flesh. His hands brushed the bunched fabric of her nightdress. He was aware if he ventured a centimeter or two lower, he would feel the swell of her breasts. Sorely tempted, he kept his eyes on hers.

"Are you feeling better this morning, Miss Dunnigan?"

"A bit," she told him none too convincingly.

"The doctor told me to watch your illness doesn't settle deeper in your chest. Now you can understand why I'm lathering you with this camphor. It will help clear your lungs."

He left the room and returned drying his hands on a white towel. Tossing the cloth over his shoulder, he said, "Breakfast should be here shortly." Adroitly, he retied the pink ribbons at her throat and straightened her tatted collar. A soft knocking sounded at the door. "Ah, right on time."

Weak, Carolena struggled to sit up as Alontti accepted a basket from a skinny, near-hairless man, who, bundled-up as he was, had obviously delivered it especially for her.

"Thank you for all your trouble, Edward," Carolena managed to say when they'd been introduced.

"No trouble, Miss. May I say, you're looking much brighter today."

Alontti dismissed his butler with a lift of his brow and then adjusted Carolena's pillows to support her back. He placed a linen napkin at her neck. In spite of her sore throat, she forced down the bland farina and milk punch he fed her. It could have been Beef Wellington. She couldn't taste a thing. She puzzled as to why her host was spoon feeding her. Why would a famous man, obviously well off, go to all this trouble? She couldn't fathom the reason. No matter. She found the experience so indulgent, she almost forgot the overall ache of her muscles and the rawness of her throat.

After breakfast, Signor Alontti suggested a bath. She tensed at the idea, alarmed he'd take liberties. Her guard up, she let him wash her face, arms, and legs to halfway up her calves. He discreetly left the room while she completed the most personal of ablutions. She had anguished unnecessarily. Happily, he was a gentleman.

Her sleep was restless, haunted by dreams she couldn't remember. She awakened unnerved and had difficulty pinpointing why. She felt sure it was something beyond the tempest raised in her when this man neared. To save her life, she couldn't imagine what it was.

Then there was Gwenie, a constant interruption. On occasion, she made a snide remark out of earshot of the boss and directed toward the patient. "I have better things to do with my time, dearie. I'm no rag picker nor maid servant either," or "How much longer do you plan to milk this sickness of yours. You're nothing but a leech."

Carolena concluded Miss Gwenier was a most possessive woman.

One day passed, then the second. Carolena tried to speak of business. Paolo would not permit it until she was one hundred percent better. In truth, time was rushing by too quickly for her. She didn't like the idea this cocooning could and would end.

***

The sea was wicked with churning this night, causing delay in the *Coral Crown*'s arrival in Baltimore. Refusing to risk his passengers or his ship, Captain Rockwell determined to sail offshore until the dawn, hoping the harsh weather would break enough for the ship to pull into port.

Passengers who had not expected a free night's accommodation, some disgruntled, some pleased at the extended holiday, were lured to late night dancing on the pitching parquet ballroom floor. Everyone anticipated this pleasure to be short lived in the current conditions. Nevertheless, as was the custom when off watch, the single officers were expected to play gallant hosts. Grey McKenna rarely found this task unpleasant because he loved women, short, tall, thin, or ample, even the elderly spinsters. Of course, a pretty face and form were the ultimate. But beauty and spinsterhood were often a thing apart, unless you were independent or professional or pigheaded.

Carolena Dunnigan entered his thoughts as he took care not to step upon the undoubtedly bunioned feet of Mrs. Viola Claymore, the middle-aged gentlewoman in his arms. He wondered if Carolena would ever find a man who could put up with her serious ways and get her to relax enough to show her there was so much more to living than books. There was adventure, surprise, spontaneity, humor, and most importantly, tenderness wrapped around passion.

As the minutes wore on, the floor increased its rolling, making dancing nearly impossible. Grey caught the eye of the steward in the doorway, pale with seasickness and waving a small paper in his direction. Keeping balance for himself as well as Mrs. Claymore, Grey walked more than waltzed her to the cushioned bench against the wall. "They are coming around with oil of peppermint, ma'am. Just place a dab behind each ear to help settle any stomach upset. If you'll excuse me, I have to attend to duty."

Reaching the steward, Grey heard, "Urgent communiqué for you, sir."

"Thank you, Shepherd. I'll bet Herlocker had a devil of a time reading the off-shore signal in this snow storm."

"Yes, sir, he did. It took him seven repeats before he could make out the message sufficiently to confirm it."

"I'll thank him in person the first chance I get. In the meantime, you're looking a little peaked. Report to sickbay if you need to, or at least open a porthole and get some cold fresh air in your lungs. It may help you feel better."

"Can't, sir. Too many passengers are down with illness. They're even lying on the staircases until they can be helped to their quarters."

Grey turned around to see there were no more couples dancing. The music had been reduced to one violinist who looked as if stroking the strings with his bow was almost more than his weak arm could accomplish.

"I will remember your dedication to the captain. Thanks again."

"Thank you, sir."

Intrigued, Grey opened the handwritten dispatch. Whatever it was, he was glad to be only a mile from shore and able to receive it, despite the snow. The *Crown* was rolling some 10 degrees or more off center now, he guessed, and he found it necessary to steady himself against the bulkhead as he read.

TO: Chief Engineer McKenna
C not arrived. Want no police or family worry. Too infirm myself. Please help.
    Dresher

Grey's response was immediate. He grabbed one of the foul weather capes hanging near the exit and put it on. Wailing wind and ice-spiked snowflakes attacked when he opened the door and stepped over the three-inch tall threshold. He reached for the rail so as not to lose footing and through squinted eyes, took in the sloshing salt water on the teak deck.

Grey found Captain Rockwall in the pilothouse, checking weather conditions and shouting orders loud enough to be heard over the gale, sounding only mildly less loud than outside.

"You've got the particulars, Mr. Wolfe. Follow them to the letter."

"Aye, sir," the watch officer yelled back, immediately conveying the order to the helmsman who was fighting the wooden wheel.

"Mr. McKenna," the captain said when he saw his chief engineer. "I'd hoped you'd be leading the dancing though I don't imagine there's much of that going on anymore."

"No, sir. None."

"Why did you come up here? You know the standard drill for rough weather. We drive the bow into the wind and take the waves head on. I just pray this weather passes by sunup so we can pull into Baltimore's harbor." Checking his watch, he read twenty-one-forty hours. "It'll be a long night."

"Captain Rockwell, may I have a private word with you, sir?"

"Aye, Mr. McKenna. Certainly." Without pause, "Mr. Wolfe?"

"Aye, sir?"

"After I confer with Mr. McKenna, I'll be in the Grand Salon, should you need me."

"Grand Salon, aye, sir."

"Shall we step into the passageway or would you prefer my office?"

"The passageway will do, sir." Grey caught the door for his superior when the roll of the ship would have slammed it closed.

Rockwell nodded his appreciation and then listened.

"First, I want you to know Steward Shepard is himself sick and tending the passengers despite it."

"Noted. Anything else?"

"Yes, sir. I have just been handed urgent word from the Aqua Verde office on the Baltimore shore. I must ask for a leave of absence. It's an emergency."

"What is it, Grey? Family?"

Although he felt as if the Dunnigans were his kin, in truth, they were not. "No, sir."

"I must have a reason. I don't need to tell you your presence is crucial to the running of this ship, especially when conditions are poor. Without a solid reason, I'm afraid your request for immediate leave is denied. You will have to wait until we dock in home port in a few days."

"I appreciate your thinking me valuable, sir. However, I assure you my second engineer is plenty capable. I mean no disrespect, but I cannot give you my purpose. I've been asked to keep it private. If I wait to depart on my mission until we return to Fernandina, I will be squandering precious time retracing wasted miles. I must be in Charleston as quickly as I'm able." He was caught between his concern for Carolena and his loyalty to her family's company.

"I repeat. Without a sold reason, I cannot give you leave."

By this point and in any other circumstance, Grey would have peppered his response with cursing. Determined to control his temper because they were professional sailors and gentlemen, he said, "Then I regret what I'm about to say, sir, yet say it, I must. You can transfer me, furlough me, or fire me, but short of locking me in the brig, I will disembark the moment we pull into Baltimore, hopefully at first light."

Although his demeanor was still unruffled, Captain Rockwell's words were grave. "Great God, man. I can charge you with disobeying a direct order, dereliction of duty, and anything else I can come up with. Even more, I can let it be known far and wide that you left your post without permission. You'll never find a position on any private line of consequence again. Are you willing to surrender a fine career for this objective?"

Unwavering, Grey answered dispassionately, "I am."

"So be it, Mr. McKenna. For the sake and reputation of the ship, I will not make a disturbance. You have been forewarned of the consequences of your impending actions. I hold you solely responsible. Is this clear between us?"

"Aye, sir. I understand fully."

"Very well then. Send for the second engineer, and I will inform him of the situation."

"As you say, sir."

"How long do you expect to be gone?"

"I have no idea, sir. I will report to you as soon as I'm able. At that time, you can proceed as you see fit. Just know I'm doing what I feel I must. I'm sorry, sir."

"I am, too, McKenna. Very sorry."

Grey touched his fingertips to the brim of his cap in formal salute. The captain returned the same. No more was spoken, and the two turned, stiffly parting, each to his chosen course.

Chapter 11

As the clock on Signor Alontti's desk ticked from early to mid-morn on the third day, Carolena had another visit from the doctor. This time, she'd been completely awake and aware. The sound of the doctor's voice brought fantasy to a screeching halt. She'd been playing make believe these past days, pretending she had no real problem. Her dreams unmasked, she could no longer ignore reality. Her heart was somehow malfunctioning.

Doctor Renninger pretended cheer and seemed enthused as to Carolena's progress. "I find her fit enough to travel from here to your guest room, Signor," he pronounced. "Just be sure she's properly protected from the elements. Telephone me in a few days to let me know she's well."

Why wasn't she told what to do and not to do to live as long as was possible? Unless - unless the Signor, unless Paolo - had made the decision she was not to know of her terminal ailment. Once again, she puzzled as to why he was so interested in her care.

The conductor noticed Carolena seemed less animated once the doctor had gone. Despite her illness, her attitude had been a happy, positive one. Now, she was so restrained. Had she heard the ugly truth? No, that was impossible. She'd been in a fever and unconscious when the physician was first here. He considered how she might object to staying at his apartment. Yet, in their brief time together, she'd not protested about anything except wanting to start back to work.

An hour later, Paolo helped her on with her cape. Securing her bonnet and scarf, he tugged on the cuffs of her gloves making sure no bare skin was exposed. Handily into his arms, he carried her down the stairs to the stage door. An elegant enclosed carriage waited in the alley. Once she was seated next to him, Carolena's body felt the warmth of his thigh against hers, despite the layers of cotton and wool between them.

It hadn't snowed too much over night, so it only took fifteen minutes to get to Paolo's place. During the ride, Carolena watched the passing scene, not speaking, only enjoying his nearness. The snow was turning dirty from foot, horse, and carriage traffic. Gray smoke from hundreds of chimneys smeared the blue sky.

They arrived under an ionic-columned portico as icy rain began falling. Paolo refused help from the doorman in carrying Carolena to the elevator. She had never been in such a contraption. She'd read of them in magazines and here she was, really going to ride in one! She was very glad to have the distraction from her problems. Seated on the burgundy-tufted bench inside, she watched while the operator in white gloves closed one crosshatched brass gate, then another.

"Nine, please," Paolo requested.

Paolo smiled down at Carolena's eager expression. When the gates parted, a polished brass number nine gleamed before them.

Again, Paolo scooped her up. With a brief word of thanks to the attendant, he exited the lift to the left, not stopping until he'd reached the door at the end of the ornately decorated corridor. Carolena noticed there were no markings on any of the doors they passed. Paolo bent slightly to depress the latch of his residence with the hand supporting the crook of her knees.

His butler hurried to greet them. "Good morning, Signor Alontti, Miss. Much better, are we?"

"I'm fine, Edward."

"Is Miss Carolena's room ready?"

"Yes, sir. Just as you requested, and a meal is waiting whenever you're settled. Lovely to see you again, Miss."

"That will be all for now, Edward," Paolo dismissed, adding, "Thank you."

"Very well, sir. Please ring when you require my services."

Paolo, still holding Carolena, passed through the open mahogany doors into a huge parlor filled with natural light. At the far end, three small steps led to a raised platform with a grand piano. This one was a pristine white.

"Paolo. Please put me down. I can walk."

He did so only because she asked. To this point, she had not called him by his given name to his face. Her voice, now normal, pronounced the words with such familiarity, it was as if she'd been his acquaintance for years.

She scanned the room while removing her scarf and bonnet, and unbuttoning her cape. The elaborately carved black marble mantle held triple vases filled with multi-colored roses. She hurried to the windows located on three sides. The view stole her breath. Through rain clouds, she discovered the magnificence of Charleston. Silver ribbons of rivers eventually emptying into the ocean tangled over the panoramic canvas. In the near distance were other tall buildings. Had she a spyglass, she'd be able to peek at the goings-on of others in their offices and apartments, a most unseemly thing to do.

A blush crossed her cheeks, and Paolo saw, wondering its cause. "Carolena," he paused, awaiting any disapproval she might have at the use of her familiar name, without a *Miss* before it. Her radiating smile was his answer. "Let me show you to the guest room. Doctor Renninger insisted you remain in bed for another day. I don't want you having a relapse."

Her inclination was to argue. She was nearly well, free of the simple fever, chills, and cough. A bad heart knew no cure.

Banishing her sad fate in favor of happier thoughts, she inspected the richly appointed room with its vaulted ceiling of criss-crossed walnut beams and jungle of live plants as she followed Paolo. Individual oval rugs of lush forest green every few feet did not completely hide the high-glossed random-planked oak flooring.

Counting the doors as they went so as not to look childish by mistakenly entering the wrong room later, she stopped behind Paolo at the third on the right. He held the door, and she passed into a maiden's garden! Windows, hung with gossamer coverings of rose silk lined with lace under-curtains, ran an entire wall. To her right stood a canopied bed, swagged in yards of white lace fastened back with ribbons of rose silk. The lace sheeting topping the mattress wore tiny pink bows, securing its layers into one thick comforter. Splashes of pale yellow in three loose bed pillows accented the chamber. Tied in were the matching fainting couch, vanity skirt, and matting of the floral oil paintings. Bouquets of yellow roses lay across the bed, on the dressing table, and several bunches were left scattered about on the yellow and mauve patterned carpet.

As Carolena stepped over one bunch, Paolo lowered the timber of his voice in annoyance. "That Edward. What an idiot to leave flowers on the floor so you'd have to watch where you walk! He's always trying to add special touches. And for you, of all people. That's what you do professionally."

Carolena was taken back a bit that Paolo didn't see the sweetness in Edward's efforts. She smiled. "I'll have to tell him how much I appreciate his creativity."

Paolo lost his irritation when he saw his guest was not displeased. "Don't you dare. If you flatter him, who knows what we'll be crawling over next time?"

She laughed with him as she again enjoyed the view. Here, high up in the cold, brittle air, the fresh flowers, the whole of the décor gave Carolena the sensation of a sweet day.

Her spirits lifted in spite of her ill health. "Paolo, although my trade is interior design, this may easily be the most soothingly attractive room I've ever seen. Who decorated it?" She desperately hoped it was not Gwenie. She didn't want to think that woman possessed sufficient sensitivity to create this beauty.

He hesitated

"Do tell. I need to speak with her, to try and understand her inspiration."

He chuckled, "Very well. But it's not a her."

"Don't tell me it was Edward!"

"Certainly not. I'm the culprit."

This masculine gem before her was not and could never be effeminate. He only appreciated beauty and delicacy. She was pleased as well as confused.

"Needless to say, I love what you've chosen. So why, in heaven's name, did you seek me, or anyone for that matter, to decorate your yacht when you obviously are quite capable yourself. What use am I to you?"

"I'm flattered by your compliment. The truth is you're schooled in the ways of design, whereas I only know what appeals to me. I'm never certain if what I like is pleasing to others. Since the yacht will be large and used for entertaining as I originally wrote you, I wanted the advice of a professional. About six months ago, I took a trip on the *Miss Breelan* and learned you were the one who'd done her interiors. It convinced me I wanted you to do the job for me"

"You've known all along C. M. Dunnigan was a woman?"

His expression was mischievous and he left no moment for discussion. "Enough of this. It's time you rested until luncheon. If you're up to it, after I return from tonight's performance, we'll dine on Edward's Oriental Pork Delight and fresh applesauce. Sound good?"

"Mmm. Yes, just perfect."

"I'm sorry to see you're in mourning. May I ask who passed away?"

"My grandmother."

"On whose side?"

Carolena didn't want to use the word *mother*, and replied, "My maternal grandmother."

"Were you close?"

"Yes. Grammy was very dear to me."

"I'm sure. Again, I'm sorry. Selfishly, I'd hoped to see you in the audience one night soon. Frankly, I'm a bit surprised you're even here if you're in deep mourning. I would have guessed you'd remain housebound for at least several months."

"I should, but sometimes social customs can't always be followed."

"Do you mean you might attend a performance?"

"I really shouldn't. It's only been weeks since Grammy left us. I loved her so much, I don't want to show disrespect in any way."

"May I suggest you wear a dark burgundy gown or gray instead of black? You will still show respect with half mourning, and you'll be able to come out in society a bit."

Carolena thought hard. It wasn't as though she were a widow or daughter. She might meet potential customers who would, in turn, help the family. What would her mother say? Her mother? Carolena felt no obligation to care what her mother thought. Maybe once upon a time. No longer.

"Well, I could consider it for professional reasons, that's true." Her face sagged with disappointment. "I've nothing else to wear except this mourning garb. If I'm seen in public in it, it would only cause ugly stares." She sighed, "Thank you for wanting me at your concert though."

"There is a solution to everything. I can have a tasteful dark gown with dull beading ready by tomorrow if I request it now."

"Oh no. I can't let you do that."

"You can pay me back from the money you'll make when my yacht is complete. As for the seamstress, she and her co-workers are on retainer. I always need repairs or new clothing for the orchestra. I'll put a call into Mrs. Morris right now."

"Are you talking about me attending tomorrow evening's performance?"

"Only if you're feeling up to it."

Reminded of her heart, it was now or never. "I feel very well and am determined to be in the same state tomorrow."

"Good. It's settled, doctor's permission pending. You lie down while I call our lady of the fancy needle."

Carolena sat in the gold velvet chair and untied the laces of her boots. She was careful not to wrinkle her dress when she lay on the soft bed that both welcomed and warmed her. Repeating a soothing gesture from childhood, she wove the satin blanket binding over, under, and between her fingers.

What have I done, she wondered? She answered herself with a *you know exactly what you've done* frown. You've rationalized the situation so you can attend a performance by the famous Signor Paolo Alontti. She smothered her guilt with visions of the concert. She wanted to go to the theatre and, by might and mirth, she was going!

Carolena panicked when she felt her heart take an irregular romp. She knew an instant and consuming terror. Dear God, would the rest of her life be like this? Which moment of excitement would finally stop her heartbeat? How excruciating would it be? Would her expression be twisted in torturous pain at the last? Where would she be when it happened? Would she linger or go quickly? The family. How devastated they would be. She paled and buried her face in a pillow.

Paolo's telephone call completed, he peeked through the door he'd left ajar to see if Carolena had fallen asleep. He burst in when he saw her and heard her weeping. Prying the pillow away, "What is it? Where does it hurt?"

In kindness, he wanted her ignorant of her illness, and she would oblige. What good would come of speaking of it anyway? She would try not to dwell on it. She would try. "Oh no. It's nothing like that, Paolo."

Tears were in her eyes. He was completely confused. "Then what?" He demanded an answer.

She thought quickly. Now was the perfect time to confess. "Paolo. I've done a terrible and very selfish thing."

He couldn't envision her kind of terrible. He sat on the edge of her bed. "What are you talking about?"

"You don't know how thoughtless I am to have not told my family of my illness. They must be beyond worry! It's just that I was sick at first and didn't remember. When I did remember, you were so nice to me and ..." Her face tear streaked, she said, "I didn't want to leave."

At her admission, his soul filled with joy.

She propelled herself from the bed and raced into the parlor. "I've got to go to them this instant!" Grabbing her cape from the chair where she'd casually tossed it, she headed for the front entrance.

In her panic, she'd not realized Paolo was right behind her. His hand covered hers as she laid it on the latch to leave. "Slow down, little one." Despite his soft tone, she grasped the power of each syllable. He wasn't going to let her leave his apartment.

Carolena was adamant. "You don't understand. I was to stay with my aunt and uncle while I'm here in town. They have no idea where I am."

"Listen to me. Cary, listen to me!"

Why did his use of her nickname sound endearing, almost intimate? He took hold of her shoulder and turned her. His hands on her face, he looked down into her wide, wet eyes. "Calm down. Now give me the pertinent information. Have they a telephone?"

"I don't know for sure. Probably at his leather goods store."

"That's fine then. I'll see he's contacted by wire if not telephone."

Paolo took her to the sofa, retrieved a small note pad and pencil from the inside pocket of his jacket and took down her uncle's address. Promising him she'd stay put, he left to walk down the hall to his office.

She heard him talking on the telephone, yet couldn't quite make out his words. Still concerned for her aunt and uncle, Carolena promised herself to visit them soon. Right now, she only wanted to rest. Forgetting she'd pledged to remain on his couch, she wandered to her bedroom and collapsed on the mattress. Her medicine had finally taken effect. Drifting off, she hoped for comfort in sweet dreams.

Paolo returned to the empty parlor. Startled, until he saw her cape lying there, he was pleased and once again entered the bedroom where Carolena now slept. He took the yellow blanket and covered the slender curve of her hip. All he wanted was to do for her and be with her.

***

The late winter weather offered little let-up as Grey traveled south from Baltimore to Charleston. On one occasion, it became necessary for the railroad crew to clear snow from the tracks.

By early afternoon of the second day, he found the Dresher residence. The woman who answered the door held a feather duster and put him in mind of an older Miss Ella. This had to be her sister, Coe.

"Don't tell me. You're Grey McKenna. Please come in. Come in. Oh, I wish Fries were here to meet you. He's at work. We weren't certain you'd received our message." The parlor was cozy, and she showed him to the fireside to take the chill off as she brushed the snow from his cloth cape over her arm.

"Yes, ma'am, I did. I didn't return a signal from the *Crown* to the ship line office because your husband wants to keep the situation as private as possible as I understand it. I didn't want the crew to know my plans. Once I reached land, I caught the first train south."

"I'm just glad you're here. We so appreciate your coming, Mr. McKenna.

But I've yet to tell you the good news. Our Carolena is safe!"

"Thank God." He was surprised at the great degree of relief he felt. "Is she upstairs? I'd like to see her."

"No. No, she's not." The dainty woman motioned for the large man to sit on her floral printed settee.

"Can I get you some tea, Mr. McKenna? Perhaps a cup of hot cocoa?"

Grey's taste buds stirred. "If it isn't too much trouble, ma'am, the cocoa sounds wonderful. I haven't had any since my mother made it for me when I was a boy. And please call me Grey, would you?"

"Only if you call me Aunt Coe. Ella and Michael have told me they think of you as one of their own."

"The feeling is shared, ma'am."

"Make yourself to home. I'll be back in a jiffy."

While she was in the kitchen rattling her cups and saucers, Grey walked about the room. He didn't notice the green upholstered chairs with their individual tapestry ottomans. Nor did he pay attention to the two hand painted oriental vases displayed on the walnut mantle. What Grey found fascinating was the photograph of Aunt Coe and a man, obviously Uncle Fries. Between them was a much younger Carolena. What a pretty girl, he thought to himself. What an irritation she can be, too.

"Here we are, Grey. And I've brought some sand tarts with almonds. I hope you enjoy them. Will this be enough to tide a big fellow like you over until dinnertime? We're having Grammy's chicken-pot-pie. Have you had it before?"

"Yes, ma'am. Miss Ella has served it. It's one of my favorites."

"Good."

The cookies were delicious and curbed his always-tremendous appetite. As he finished a sixth cookie, Grey could tell Aunt Coe was concerned about something. Since he'd laid eyes on the lady only minutes before, he didn't press her. "Where is Carolena, by the way?"

Aunt Coe hung her head to her chest and the velvet skin of her wrinkled neck bulged slightly. "I'm afraid she isn't here. We haven't seen her yet."

This didn't sound good to him. "You told me she was safe."

"When I said safe, I meant alive. I may have used the wrong word because, well, where she is, there's no telling how much danger she's in."

Alarmed now, he did his damnedest to remain patient with the woman.

"You see, we received a wire from a Signor Paolo Alontti. I understand he's here for a spell as resident conductor and pianist for our symphony. Anyway, Carolena was taken ill when she met him for her appointment. You have heard that's why she came to town, to do some work on a boat for him, right?"

Grey nodded. "She was flushed when I saw her last. I thought it was from all the excitement of arriving in Charleston. What's the matter with her?"

"From the wire, it was a cold of some sort, nothing too serious."

He cursed himself silently. It's my fault she fell sick. I'm the one who left her in the damp air that first night aboard the *Crown*.

"She's under a doctor's care," Aunt Coe continued. "She should soon be well. My concern lies with where she'd been recuperating."

Grey didn't particularly want to hear what was coming.

"Apparently, for whatever reason, this Alontti fellow didn't know she was to stay with us, and so he tended her himself. She was in his dressing room. Now she's in his apartment."

This seemed a little too convenient. "What do you want me to do, Aunt Coe?"

"That headstrong child should not be staying in a man's apartment. It's improper! I'd like you to bring her back here where she belongs. She can work with this man during the day and return to her family at night. Of course, Uncle Fries would like to drive her. He and I, especially me, feel he just isn't up to it. It's all he can do to get through a day of work at the leather shop. He knows his limitations. That's why we moved south to Charleston from New York. There was a business for sale here, much like the one he ran up north. We reckoned the warmer weather had to be better for him than all the ice and snow up there. The way it's been of late though, I'm not certain it's worth it. The wind is biting cold off the ocean here." She envisioned Fries, sitting by the fire, shivering beneath his shawl.

"Do you have the address where Carolena is?"

"Yes, I do." She handed him a folded piece of paper from her skirt pocket. Her words were halting, but her voice did not waver. "Bring her home, Grey…before this situation turns difficult."

"I'll do my best to have her sitting at your dining table tonight." He wanted to add, if I have to hog tie her and stuff a rag in her grumbling mouth, she'll be here.

Chapter 12

"The doctor said you can go to the theatre only if you rest most of the daylight hours before we leave," Paolo had explained.

Staying in bed will seem like forever, Carolena told herself while the seamstress re-pinned the bodice of her new burgundy silk gown.

"I'm so very weary of lying about I could scream. My sniffles are gone and my throat doesn't hurt any longer. I'm all better!"

"I'm pleased to hear that, miss," said a sincere Mrs. Morris, the olive skinned grandmother. Hesitating, "If I may say, miss is thin as a broom handle. Don't lose any more weight, or you'll float away and then how will Signor Paolo ever find you?"

Carolena blushed to the bone. "I may have lost a pound or two. Happily, my appetite is coming back."

"Good thing. We're done. I'll have this ready for you in plenty of time for the performance."

After Mrs. Morris left and while Paolo was at the theatre rehearsing, Carolena was alone in his apartment except for Edward. She strolled from room to room, fingering all the scrumptious fabrics decorating Paolo's home. It came to her how light his touch had been on her skin and how she was unable to enjoy it fully when she was not feeling her best. She liked his attention. His concern seemed much more than casual. It would be easy to let him take over her life. He could relieve all her financial difficulties and comfort her during what was left of her life. Could that be his ultimate goal? Marriage, short lived though it might be? Surely, she was being a silly female and reading far too much into his attention toward her.

She crossed to the window and looked at the stars. She didn't think she'd ever been at such a high altitude as this before in all her life. She'd always lived at sea level. Here, the stars looked larger than she remembered them from home. Home. She took a chill and sat in the rocking chair near the fire.

Carolena's mind turned to Grey, as it periodically seemed to do. At this point in their relationship, he was just a friend. He wasn't responding to her in the way she truly wanted. It looked as if he never would. She felt disloyal to him for finding Paolo attractive, and then wondered why. There was no sign of a commitment from Grey and now, she allowed, there never would be. She wanted, no needed, romance in her life. With the new knowledge of her fatal infirmity, she craved to understand the fullness, the complete pleasure of love. If not with Grey, she wouldn't be settling for second best with Paolo. He was handsome, strong, famous, wealthy, and so talented. She would always wonder what life with Grey would have been like, but it was not to be. She would learn to live without him the same as she would learn to live with each uncertain tomorrow.

By God, she'd best take advantage of her high stamina level while she still had it. She would experience all the joy and fun she could in the time left her! There was no predicting the future, so why not lust after life with all her strength? Right now, she was feeling energized! Was it because she'd come to grips with her situation, was almost rid of her illness, was in only half-mourning, and going to the theatre tomorrow night?

Whatever the reason, Carolena rushed to the piano, her black skirts whispering with each sway. She sat down and played *Linden Quickstep* from memory, demonstrating the same dash her mother had taught her. Her mother - to the devil with her and Grey, too! Carolena Dunnigan was alive and determined to spend her days the way she played this music, *con spirito*!

***

Edward worked his way around the apartment with more vigor than was his usual due to the carefree tune the girl was playing. His boss never seemed to choose such pieces. Most times, his were in the key of somber. Hearing a knock on the door, Edward crossed the room to answer it.

Grey raised his voice over the loud piano. "Is Miss Carolena Dunnigan here?"

Rattled by the abruptness of the man, Edward asked, "Who may I say is calling?"

"Just tell her it's Grey."

"Very well, sir. Please remain here in the foyer while I announce you."

Grey was not used to being formally announced and did as asked. After many long seconds, he grumbled, "The damn butler must be waiting until that annoying song is over." He was in no mood to hear the rest of some rollicking ditty. He entered the parlor and his eyes found Carolena. Her head was down, her hands flying over the ivories. She was completely engrossed in her symphony of one and didn't seem to be anywhere near the end of it.

As suspected, Edward stood listening, his toe tapping, until Carolena was through. Impatient, Grey dismissed the small man with a wave of his hand. The butler was not about to challenge the big man, no matter what he was being paid. He chose flight. At his own room in quick steps, he closed the door behind him. As an added precaution, he threw the lock, checking it twice.

Grey called her name. Carolena didn't respond. He called her a second time. The result was the same. He grabbed her wrist.

"Oh piddle!" She shouldn't be impatient with her host whose piano she played, but she was having such a good time. "I'm sorry for my rudeness, Paolo. It's ..." When she turned to look, she spun on the bench. Shocked, she shot up. "What are you doing here?"

"You thought I was this Signor Alontti? And you're calling him Paolo?

107

Already? From your expression, you looked disappointed I'm not him. And may I add you appear to be in pretty good health to me? What's all this trash about you being sick? And how much work have you done with your client? Very little would be my guess."

She whipped her arm from his grasp because his attitude was brutish and because he was pinching her skin in his grip. If her face wore a frown, it was because her rhythm had been interrupted. She was very glad to see Grey, or at least she had been until he'd opened his mouth.

While he walked the room in circles, he seethed. "Are you involved with this man? How can you be so gullible, let alone indiscreet? Don't you know you're just juicy fodder for this Italian Romeo? You're one of many. I'd bet money on it. Don't tell me I don't know what I'm talking about. I don't care if I've never laid eyes on him. If you don't believe a thing I say, believe this. Men are all alike. We've no scruples. These famous types have an advantage over us mortals. Their power and prestige beguile female fans with no effort on their part. Handmaidens beg to be exploited. Then there's your aunt and uncle. They are sick with worry over you. And not a word. How inconsiderate can you be? They messaged me on the *Crown* to come find out what happened to you. When I met Aunt Coe, she was busy cleaning like Jesus was coming, she's so excited to see you. And here you are, acting the part of a woman possessed by some unmarried musical master! At least, I assume he's single, or else he has one hell of an understanding wife somewhere. Worse yet, you're not just visiting, you're living here!"

"I'm sure I'm not the first lady to break with tradition." So long as it wasn't illegal, she reasoned, maybe some traditions were meant to be challenged.

Appalled, he asked, "Have you forgotten all the values your dear mother taught you?"

Carolena was furious. Grabbing the closest thing she could, she strangled the flower arrangement and snatched it from its cut-glass vase. Letting the stems fall to the rug, she cast their slightly slimy water into his face. The liquid dripped from Grey's long lashes, spotting his dark cape. Her hand found the brass candlesnuffer atop the piano. She drew back and heaved with all her might. Her aim was good. It caught him low on the jaw. Before she realized what was happening, he had her hands behind her back in an unbreakable clench. His breath was hot on her face and, had she any sense, she would have been frightened out of her skin. Her defiance destroyed her reason and nourished her daring.

Grey was full out enraged. So much so, he didn't as yet feel pain from the fresh gash he wore. As she watched the blood from his wound trickled onto her bodice, she decided she had nothing to loose. Charged with anger, she kicked her former friend in his tender shin.

"Shit!"

He released her. Off balance, she fell to the floor. Not offering to assist her back to her feet, he headed toward the hallway, disappearing from the room. She arose in a less than ladylike fashion, panting and pining her tousled hair back up into its chignon while she heard doors and drawers slamming.

After a brief time, Grey returned with her cape and hat in hand. "Put these on. You're coming with me!" He tossed them in her direction. "I'm returning you to your aunt's house tonight. I promised her I would. Once that chore is performed, I don't give a goddamn what you do or where you go!"

Deliberately not catching the garment, she let it fall at her feet. She watched him dab at his weeping wound with his white handkerchief, staining it crimson. She almost, almost felt badly she'd hit him. Not because she was sorry, but because it might leave a scar on his handsome face. Who cares? I don't any more, she screamed inside herself. If I ever had a worry I'd never get over you, Grey McKenna, it's in the past. You've done me a service by this last tirade. Thank God, I never let you know how much I cared. Thank God!

"I'm coming with you, you say?" she flipped back at him.

His frustration was at its maximum. His face hurt. His shin ached. Had it been any other person but Miss Ella's sister he'd promised, he'd have left the instant he saw for himself Carolena was alive and well. What a shrew! Just like that biddy, Noreen. He had expected more from Carolena, then again, blood was blood. Too bad.

"I know you're not so stupid as to provoke me further, Cary."

"Just what will you do to me?" she challenged. She also didn't wait for his reply. Grey was glad because he really didn't have a response.

"And don't you ever call me anything but Miss Dunnigan," she ordered. "No one except my most intimate friends and family may use my given name. You're obviously no longer my friend, and you're certainly not my family, so that goes double for you."

"Does Alontti call you Miss Dunnigan?" His face twisted. "I think not."

She glared at him.

"You know, I used to admire your intellect and class. Ha!"

"What do you mean *ha*?"

"You figure it out. Now put on that rag before I stuff you in it! We're going to your aunt's house. We'll send for your valise later."

"I can see there's little use in arguing with you and your sorry self. Once a tyrant always a tyrant."

He let the remark pass.

Her eyes narrowed to slits as she gave in. "Very well. However, I must leave a note for Paolo." She licked her lips in full view as if the name were honey and she was rolling it over her tongue to savor its full sweetness.

He looked away because the thought of her being used so willingly sickened him. "Write your note quickly, or I'll write it for you."

She knew he meant it, and could only imagine what vile message he'd leave. She finished her short letter, deliberate in her signature, in hopes of needling Grey a bit more. She dropped the note to the floor, guessing he'd retrieve it.

Anxious to get out of another man's place, Grey bent and snatched it up, reading the script.

Paolo,

Am staying at my aunt's. Will get in touch with you soon. Thank you for everything.

Cary

He flung the paper from him, the same as he would garbage. It landed on the center of the piano. Taking Carolena's arm, the sailor pulled her along with him out the door and into the future.

***

As she tended him, Aunt Coe realized Grey had not explained the origin of the gash on his jaw. "Honestly Grey. I promise this application of Peeper's all-purpose furniture varnish won't hurt your wound. The first dab only burned like fire because it went directly into the cut. You've got on a protective layer this time."

"Don't be a baby," Carolena cooed. Grey imagined she hoped it hurt like hell.

While tipping the brown glass bottle to saturate another wad of cotton, Aunt Coe wondered what the vessel held in its previous life. Peeper preached the value of reusing containers once they'd been subjected to a vigorous shaking of broken eggshells and soapy water. As she corked the bottle, Aunt Coe observed a small rust colored stain on the front of her niece's dress. Was there a connection to Grey's injury?

Carolena was made to rest by the fire. Her aunt and uncle quizzed her as she attempted to explain how she'd grown too ill to think to wire them and how a famous man like Signor Alontti had been kind to her. "After all he's done for me," Carolena concluded by saying, "I feel I owe my benefactor a great debt."

It was all Grey could do to keep from interjecting his views on the subject.

As they sat down to dinner, Aunt Coe chatted, "I'm so hoping you will enjoy my last minute entrée change. I just didn't feel chicken pot pie was a fine enough dish to celebrate Carolena's safe return home, so we have shrimp au gratin, potato pancakes, and baked onions."

Uncle Fries returned to Carolena's last few days. "Tell us more about your business, Carolena."

She slipped a tender onion drizzled with butter between her lips, enjoying its sweetness. "We haven't actually begun examination of my plans for his yacht yet. With my illness and his performance schedule, there hasn't been enough time. Now that his engagement is nearly up at the Zeus Theater, Signor Alontti has chosen to take an extended vacation. That's when we'll begin our daily work together." Knowing she hadn't, she innocently asked, "Oh! Did I show you his calling card? Quite elegant, don't you agree?"

"May I interest anyone in another cup of coffee to go with the fruit with cream cheese dressing I've made for dessert?" Auntie asked, noting how the conversation between Carolena and Grey seemed strained. It was obvious they'd had a falling-out of some sort.

"Thank you, ma'am," Grey answered. "Can't eat another bite. If you'll excuse me, I think I'll step outside for a smoke." Hearing no objections, he exited the front door. After a few minutes, he felt the last gasp of winter through his light wool shirt, but still didn't go back inside. Carolena's presence made him uncomfortable.

"Thought even a strapping man like you could use his coat out here."

"Oh? Thanks, Uncle Fries. Isn't this cold weather bad for you though?"

"Coe swears it is. You know women. To tell the truth, I find it invigorating. Believe it or not, I miss the long winters up north. Turns a place cozy. This is like a day in May compared to New York City."

They fell silent, puffing their cigars and standing sentry as carriages rolled by.

"Did you hear Cary say she'd be working every day with this Alontti fellow?" Fries paused, waiting for a reaction from Grey. When there was none, he added, "And that she can't afford the expense of a carriage to travel from our place to his? That it wouldn't be professional to expect him to come to our house to work on the plans for his damn boat? Well, she's refused to take money from me. Worse yet, she wants to go back to his house to stay, she says to save cab fare. Sounds like a pretty shallow excuse to me." The older man blew on the tip of his cigar so it glowed red in the darkness. "I know this is asking a lot, Grey. Damn it, I have to ask. I can see plain you and Cary aren't getting on too well. I don't believe that's always been the case. So for the sake of the Dunnigans, if not for Carolena herself, will you remain in town a spell and look after her? Stay with us or there's an inn on the next block. I'll pick up your tab if you just say the word. You can take me to work in the mornings and then drive Carolena to and from her business appointments. She won't like it much, but I will. These girls can get into more mischief than they can get out of. Believe me, I know from experience."

He didn't elaborate and right now, any sordid affairs of the Dunnigans were the last thing Grey cared to hear.

Fries, holding high his hand to silence any protest he anticipated Grey would make, added, "Before you say no, Carolena received a wire from her mother while she was missing. Since she wasn't here, I read it.

Apparently, your captain on the *Coral Crown* wired Michael and told him you deserted your post when he refused you permission to take leave. I sent Ella and Michael a letter saying it was I who asked for your help, explaining the whole situation. We all understand you disobeyed a direct order for that girl in there and for her family. You weren't going to tell us of your sacrifice, were you?"

"I ..."

"No need to say a word, boy. You've risked your entire career for us, and we aren't about to forget it." Touched to the core, Fries caught one dripping tear on the point of his thumb and flicked it away. "Hell, you've already left your ship. Seems to me the punishment will probably be the same whether you're gone one day or one month, and you might be saving a foolhardy young woman from the worst mistake of her life. Would you at least sleep on it tonight?"

Grey had often heard the Dunnigans speak of a case of "the guilts." It seemed manipulation was a deliberate and viable means of getting desired results for relatives by marriage, too.

***

Paolo Alontti relaxed against the leather seat of the carriage he shared with Gwenie as it delivered them to their respective apartments. He took a deep breath, expecting a negative reaction from her for what he was about to say. "After this week, I'd like you to cancel my performances for the next two months at least."

Gwenie lost her power of speech for five seconds. Then she made light of his pronouncement "You're just exhausted from tonight's appearance is all."

"No. Remarkably, I'm not really tired."

"You can't be serious then. Quit teasing. That's not nice. You gave me a fright."

"I am serious."

He didn't see her nostrils flare in the dark of the cab.

"May I ask why?" she inquired, anticipating his reason and hating it.

"Let's just say I need a vacation."

"Let's just say you've lost your head over that blonde creature with the brilliant smile."

"Here it comes."

"You're absolutely right. Here it comes." She tried not to raise her voice so the driver wouldn't hear. "Paolo, be reasonable. People have bought advance tickets. The rest of your shows are sold out. Do you know how much trouble it will be to refund all that money? Not to mention the travel and hotel arrangements. We've booked them and will have to pay whether you perform or not. And what about the musicians and the contracts with the vendors?"

When he didn't reply, she asked, "Are you as selfish as that?"

He was hard in his tone. "I didn't say I'd stop performing all together. Just for a while. Yes, it will be a bother to refund the tickets and, yes, we'll lose money on the halls and all. I understand that, and I am honestly sorry for the inconvenience to everyone. One thing the musicians won't object to is a holiday with pay. They need some time off, and so do I, Gwenie. I can't remember the last time I didn't answer to some damn show schedule. And yes, I hope to be in the company of Miss Dunnigan. She's a lovely, intelligent woman."

Gwenie wouldn't give up easily. "Be reasonable, Paolo. At least finish the season. After that, you can take a break in the summer."

"No."

Angry, disappointed, and having no choice, Gwenie said softly, "I will carry out your wishes."

"Thank you, dear one." Paolo kissed her cheek. "We're here at my place. I'll see you tomorrow. And don't worry. Things will work out, one way or another. They always do."

As the carriage took her away, Paolo decided Gwenie was acting as if he'd committed a crime. It sometimes drove him crazy. Still, how would he get through life without her?

His step was brisk as he left the elevator and headed toward his front door. He found a dark parlor with but a single candle burning on the piano. He surmised Carolena must have gone on to bed. He wanted to look in on her. No, that wasn't it. He needed to. Sleep would not be his tonight if he didn't lay eyes on her face. He crossed to blow out the fiery wick when he saw the note.

"Edward. Edward!"

His butler came stumbling in from down the hall. His tie was askew, his jacket wrinkled, his few strands of hair hung over his eyes.

"Sir?"

"How could you let Miss Dunnigan leave?"

Edward stammered something unintelligible.

"Answer me, by thunder!"

"Well sir, a--a man came and took her away."

"What man? Her uncle?"

"No. I don't think it was her uncle because he wasn't old."

Paolo grabbed Edward by his collar. "Who was it? Did you just let any stranger into my apartment?"

"No, no, of course not! Miss Dunnigan recognized him." Edward thought he was in enough trouble already so he used his standard strategy and feigned ignorance. He wasn't about to admit he'd witnessed a fight. The unreasonable musician would probably have expected him to intercede on behalf of Miss Dunnigan. He loved living too much to attempt a futile gesture against such a formidable mountain of a human being. "I was brewing a pot of Ceylon tea and preparing a tray with cakes for them. By the time I returned to the parlor, they were gone. The only explanation I found was the note."

Paolo pushed him aside and dropped to the sofa, his hands covering his face. "Do you at least remember his name when he introduced himself at the door?"

"Ah--Ah--Mac something. Mac--Kenna. I believe it was McKenna. Yes, a Grey McKenna." He thanked the heavens for his quick memory, certain the signor would be pleased he'd recalled the name.

With a heavy sigh, Paolo said, "Since she went willingly, I may as well wait until morning to seek her out. No sense disturbing her rest because I can't sleep." He rose and left the parlor.

Surprised and relieved his hide was intact, Edward extinguished the candle and headed toward his room. Donning a red nightshirt spotted with black silhouettes of wild animals, Edward checked in the looking glass for bruises about his throat where he'd been accosted. He wondered at the maestro's erratic moods of late. Feeling bold because he was alone, he decided he would not stand for such abuse and would give notice if any more unpleasant incidents occurred. In reality, he knew he would remain whether the situation was pleasant or not. Wherever again could he find such effortless employment at such a large salary? He should be used to the temperament of the man with the money by now.

Edward plumped his pillow thinking of the spoon player who'd caught his fancy last week at the Lavender Brickyard Saloon. He closed his eyes and smiled, hoping for saucy dreams.

Chapter 13

Again, the skies let loose. A look out the window often meant a gaze into a gray fog of water. Streets were flooded, snapped branches lay scattered like undernourished driftwood. Alley cats were scrawny in their saturated coats. And the smell of earthworms was abundant. So many showers back to back were a record in Fernandina, the old timers said. With the humidity at 100% and the temperature ranging from the mid-forties after dark to the low eighties, one didn't know how to dress. These dismal days did little to lift Miss Ella's mood.

"Oh Ella," Noreen called when her sister-in-law came through the kitchen's swinging door. "Have you heard what my dear friend, Mrs. Ickles, said about some man living on the south end of the island? About him having a two headed chicken?"

"No. Can't say I have."

"Is that possible, Mama?" Nora asked.

"If Mrs. Ickles says it's so, you can take it to the bank."

"Yes, ma'am." The reputation of the notorious nosey-poke, Mrs. Ickles, had to come from somewhere. No sense starting trouble over a two-headed chicken Nora quickly decided.

"What deliciousness are the two of you cooking up?" Miss Ella asked, appreciating the clean smell of lemon.

"It's a recipe from Mrs. Ickles for her delicious ambrosia pie. Three pies in fact. Enough to feed everyone. My Warren Lowell is crazy for lemon. He's had such a time of it, being unable to sleep in his own comfortable bed, I thought he deserved a treat."

Miss Ella didn't rise to the taunt and instead thought of her own kitchen where the fresh herbs used to grow outside in the window boxes Michael built. She thought, too, how everyone had favorite places in or about the manor. Breelan and Waite sat in the fern garden while they watched their daughter play and grow. Carolena read the books in her father's library. Peeper had her medicinal garden. Jack Patrick and Mickey roamed the barn where, under Clover's vigilant eye, they pounded nails, tended animals, and spent hours sharing secrets as only the best of friends do. Marie was nervous now, lacking the security of familiar surroundings. Michael, though he never said so, obviously ached more than anyone. He'd been the one to envision and create the beautiful manor, watching it sprout from sandy soil to become a showplace. Poor, poor Michael. Ella would have much preferred to be testing desserts with her own girls rather than scribbling on ledgers in Noreen's dining room. Now, she almost enjoyed being with Noreen because Nora was in the kitchen along with grandbaby, Halley. Seated at the table, she read aloud from *Pigger Parker Prune, the Doggie Who Wouldn't*.

Miss Ella bent over the counter where the handwritten recipe lay and noted the instructions for Ambrosia Pie. She hoped the pie turned out well for the Duffy ladies. Maybe it would do to serve aboard the *Miss Bree* and the *Coral Crown*. Of course, she'd have to credit Mrs. Ottilie Ickles. The idea made Ella shudder.

"Don't tell me you're catching a chill, Ella," Noreen accused.

"No. Not at all."

"Now don't be getting sick," ordered the pushy female. "With us all living like pinched toes in a baby's boot, one cough could wipe out everybody!"

"Yes, I heard you tell Michael something along those lines," Miss Ella reminded her.

"You forgot about my elixir fixers," Peeper challenged. "Your brain's so small, Noreena, you couldn't cuss a monkey!"

Absurdity rules this house, Miss Ella determined. She was pleased to hear the postman's whistle sound. "I'll get it." Stretching, she straightened her stiffened spine. Ouh. She was getting older. Reprimanding herself for complaining, she switched her focus to hope there might be a letter with happy news for everyone.

The mail had already fallen through the drop slot and hit the floor. She pulled open the door, brushing the correspondence aside. The mail carrier was ever recognizable in his blue uniform, round hat bearing a postal badge, and thick-soled black leather shoes. Ella inquired, "Mr. Auguss. Why the rush? Trying to dash between raindrops are you?"

"Yes, ma'am, but more especially I'm anxious to deliver this package to Miss Cydling at the *Florida Mirror*. It's clear from Siam!" Holding it aloft to display the foreign postmark, he quickly returned it to the dry security of his satchel. "I'm hoping she'll tell me what it is. You know she's doing that series of articles on cultures around the world for the paper."

"Yes, I'd heard. How exciting for all of us! Don't get too hot in your rain slicker, you hear?"

"I gotta admit I saw a dog chasing a cat and both of them was walking, it's so hot and steamy today."

"That's for certain sure. When you come by tomorrow, why don't you stop and have a quick sip of raspberry iced tea?"

"Thanks, Miss Ella. If I have the time, I'll surely try."

"See you, my friend."

Ella could tell with a glance that the stack of mail she'd collected was thick with bills. Then she saw a letter sandwiched between the statement from Dotterer's Grocery and an overdue notice from the ship line's linen supplier out of Tallahassee. It was from Charleston, but it wasn't from Coe. It was from Fries and addressed to Mr. and Mrs. Michael Dunnigan! In all the 30-odd years Ella had known her brother-in-law, he'd never written himself. She sat on the settee in the parlor and, with dread, tore at the thing, not using the letter opener. The envelope ripped into three pieces, and she let them flutter to the floor. Her eyes dashed across the squarely scripted lines on the plain white paper.

Refolding the letter, she laid her hands in her lap and leaned back into the pine needle back cushion covered in plush green velvet. So Grey, once more, showed himself honorable. He didn't leave his post because Rockwell refused him leave. He was on a mission to save the reputation of my Carolena. She closed her eyes and thought how delicate matters, as contained in this letter, matters of affection, of infatuation and romance, were one thing no soul could build stamina for or fortitude against if they didn't work out as desired. She might not be able to spare Carolena from a tragic mistake of the heart if Fries' concern was to be believed. Yet, she had to try. Her main purpose on the earth was to protect and defend her children. No matter if Carolena rejected her, she would never, could never give up.

Breelan can run the business in my absence, Miss Ella calculated. Bree's young and strong. Peeper can care full-time for Halley. We can wire Jack Patrick to return home now we know he's outside Savannah. If he's told his mother has an emergency, surely he'll come back. Maybe Michael will accept some responsibility. Maybe. She wondered what city her husband was in today. He'd been gone as long as Carolena this time.

In any case, "I have to go to Charleston," she told herself. "To the devil with the Aqua Verde business! No matter we're about dirt poor, the Dunnigans will survive." Her inspiring words deflated as she thought how a broken heart could ruin a woman or damned near.

***

"Ooh!" Carolena nettled, irritated her skirt had twisted beneath her as she slid across the seat of the buggy driven by Grey McKenna. She was disappointed she'd been unable to attend Paolo's performance as planned. The tension in the Dresher house caused by her unchaperoned time spent with the conductor had been too great to press the issue. She'd sent her regrets, and Paolo had been most understanding in his reply.

"What is your difficulty now, Miss Dunnigan?" Grey was filled to capacity with Carolena's whining. Alone with her in the carriage like this, he expected more of the same.

"You! You are my difficulty." Still flopping about trying to straighten her clothing, Carolena sputtered, "I can't believe you bullied my uncle the way you did. I'm sure he was perfectly willing to pick me up from Signor Alontti's. But no. You had to be the big boss. We're not some of your subservient crew who has to take orders or get shot for disobedience."

"Like it or not, you might as well quit fuming because things aren't going to change. I'll be the one to take you there and return you safely to the bosom of your aunt and uncle." Grey stood firm. "And we don't shoot people in the private passenger liner business. Of course, a bit of a body beating every once in a while doesn't hurt a thing."

"Speaking of the crew, why aren't you on the *Coral Crown*? That's your job, isn't it? That's what we're paying you for, aren't we?"

Her nose crinkled as she glared at him, and he plainly saw the bratty child within her. He took a deep breath and let it out slowly. Clenching his teeth, he closed his eyes and took another slow breath. The morning air was still cold and stimulating, and he tried to concentrate on its chill inside his warm lungs.

"I asked you a question, Mr. McKenna? Have you forgotten all your manners? Haven't you the courtesy to respond to a lady's inquiry?"

His tolerance vanished. Pulling the reins up short caused the horse to halt with a displeased whinny. "A lady? You think yourself a lady? Hell, the whores in the saloons have sweeter tongues than you! As for my job, I've taken a leave of absence." As a condition of his staying in Charleston, Uncle Fries was not to tell Carolena she'd caused him to jeopardize his job. Grey didn't want her beholden to him. Since she hadn't asked him to do it, she'd probably laugh and call him stupid to sacrifice his career for her anyway. He simply said, "I needed to get away. I've worked non-stop for years. But this time with you is certainly not what I imagined a peaceful holiday to be. I'd sooner go back to hearing Captain Rockwall complain than listen to carping from beautiful lips like yours. I don't understand you. The way you insisted your old uncle haul you around in this weather was plain selfish. If you weren't so self-involved, you'd have noticed your Aunt Coe's pleading looks at you." He shook his head in disappointment at her, concluding, "You'll have to learn to live with the situation because I'm driving you anywhere you need to go. Period."

Clucking the horse into a fast walk, Grey waited for her response. None came. He glanced her way. Carolena was looking straight ahead. Her profile seemed almost wistful! There was no telling what she was thinking.

Grey was right, although she'd never admit it to him. She'd been dreadful of late and angry with him for taking over. Her stubborn streak had grabbed hold again and didn't let lose until she heard his compliment. He thought her lips were beautiful. It left her feeling pretty. She needed that. She realized she'd rolled all her miseries, financial, physical, and emotional, into one ghastly personality like Aunt Noreen!

Now, here she was being spontaneous with Paolo, and all she was hearing was how everything was so improper this and improper that. She could do what she wanted because she was - good Lord Almighty, here it was again. The imperious Carolena fiend was surfacing. Why was it a constant fight to gain control? Why couldn't she be nicer, more gracious like Breelan? Am I just plain bad-tempered? Pray God I don't end up like Aunt Noreen, she thought.

They pulled up in front of Paolo's apartment. Not waiting for Grey to come around to her side of the carriage to help her out, Carolena jumped down with her carpet bag in hand, her designing tools rattling inside. "I should be finished around five o'clock. I'll see you then." As an afterthought, she looked back over her shoulder, smiled, and said, "Thank you, Grey."

He drove off, confused at her sudden turn-around in temperament. Dismissing it for lack of any reasonable explanation, he wondered what he would do with the rest of his day.

***

Carolena was anxious to see Paolo, but asked the elevator operator if she might ride up to the top floor and back down several times for fun. Appreciating the enthusiasm of the young woman, he obliged and asked, "Are you and your father having a nice holiday?"

Mortified the man thought she and Paolo were father and daughter, she found herself speechless. What must others think seeing them together? Then Carolena's usual independence presented itself and her dismay vanished. At this stage in her life, what earthly difference did it make? She and Paolo were the only people who counted here. There was no need, no need whatever, for embarrassment or explanation. She answered simply, "Yes, a lovely holiday, indeed."

That done, Carolena left the lift and walked to Paolo's door. Knocking softly, she expected Edward to answer and was pleased to find she was wrong. A handsome face greeted her, his gaze intense.

"Welcome, Miss Dunnigan. Your eyes are full of green sparkle this morning. You are better, aren't you?"

"Oh yes, Paolo. I feel just grand!" She was determined those words would be true for as long as she had left to live. This was one time her stubborn steak would be of benefit to her.

"Please, let me have your wrap. I don't want you to get overheated."

"Thank you. May I ask a favor?"

He stepped close, and she smelled his cologne. It was a new scent to her and its fragrance contributed to his mysterious persona.

"Anything."

"Oh, it's not as serious as that." She giggled at his anxious expression. "Please, just treat me as if I'm not ..." She redirected her speech in hope he would not suspect she knew of her fatal illness. "I'm all better now, so you needn't hover over me any longer. I can't imagine what a chore nursing me has been."

"Does my hovering, as you call it, make you uncomfortable?" He was still close and had taken hold of her hand. She felt his warm breath on her up-turned palm, and her insides stirred. His lips touched her flesh. She'd never had her hand kissed by a man so early in the day. It was almost depraved.

"As long as you aren't doing it because you fear I'm frail. No, I don't mind your being, uh near."

"Does that mean you won't mind if I kiss you?"

She wanted to cry out, please, please do!

"Good morning, Paolo." Gwenie entered from the direction of the kitchen, happily recognizing she'd interrupted something. "Shall we begin? There's much work to finish so Miss Dunnigan may return to ..."

She paused not certain of the pronunciation. "Fernandino? Fernandinia? Wherever it is you live. Yes indeed, much to do so your company can start construction on the signor's new yacht. Isn't that right, Paolo?" She judged this entire affair was going too fast for everyone involved, including her.

Except for the thinning of his mouth, Paolo successfully masked his irritation at the intrusion. "Gwenie," he said, stepping back from Carolena, "What on earth are you doing here? I told you I wouldn't need you until this afternoon."

"Thank you, dear. You're always so thoughtful, but I overheard you discussing your plans last night, and I realized I might be of some help here. Besides, tell me when you last completed any project without my assistance. You know you always marvel at how efficient I can be."

Not wanting to make any more enemies, Carolena said, "She's right, Paolo. Miss Gwenier could be a big asset in taking notes of any changes or ideas."

Gwenie didn't need some young thing testifying on her behalf. Yet in this instance, she welcomed the support because she could see the reined in lust in Paolo's eyes.

"Very well," he acquiesced. "Have you had your breakfast, Carolena?"

"Oh, my yes. If you haven't, Paolo, please go on."

"I was hoping to share a bite with you. I can see you're a country girl and used to rising early." He saw embarrassment cross her face, as if he'd meant she lacked sophistication. "I envy you, you know. I grew up in a small community and miss the simplicity and clean living of those days."

Carolena was glad he didn't belittle her as a hick-town yokel. "It's I who envy you for your city living. The things you must have seen and done, all the adventures you've had in countries around the world."

"Yes, my life has not been dull." He looked out over the skyline of Charleston. "Count yourself lucky to have grown up as you did. Once gone, those tender days can't be recaptured. I know."

Gwenie had enough of his too personal melancholia. "I'm starving, Paolo. Let's all go into the dining room, shall we?" She put her arm around Carolena's slender waist and directed her toward the enticing smells. "Call me Gwenie. I'll call you Carolena. Let's enjoy a cup of tea while we eat. How's that sound?"

Paolo followed, well aware of what his secretary was trying to do.

In the ensuing days, Carolena and Paolo - and Gwenie - spent hour upon hour discussing and reworking the original designs. Yet, it seemed they could never get them just as Paolo wanted. It seemed, too, he was stalling, deliberately finding fault with the plans, changing his mind, being purposely picky. There were times he'd stand up in the middle of a deliberation concerning the size of a table or the color of a drapery and announce he was in the mood to visit the museum, or the zoo, or a park or that he just couldn't survive another minute unless he had a meal of steak or Spanish mackerel. Whenever that happened, off they'd all go to some fascinating place. Carolena realized this was merely subterfuge, yet it didn't matter. His appearance, his imagination, his creativity, the whole of him, captivated her.

Chapter 14

Time was, Grey never had a spare moment. And he preferred it that way. Alone in Charleston, he found it necessary to fill his hours. He couldn't spend the days with Aunt Coe. He'd be big as a barn from her cooking. He couldn't go to Fries' leather shop. The man had a business to run. The only other possibility, because she was the one other person he knew in town, was Carolena, and she wanted little to do with him.

Grey decided to do what came naturally. He spent many an hour on and about the docks of the city. A sailor could generally spot another of his kind, so he was no real stranger. His amiable ways made for easy acquaintance, and he repeatedly met up with old mates from days past. A party of two never remained such and raucous gaiety grew in direct proportion to the number of seamen present.

The sun spent itself as Hairy Henry Prag, off the *Sacred Sounder,* and Bennie the Whistler, from the *Blue Wench*, met up with shelter, billiards, liquor, and Grey in the colorless confines of the Buried Anchor Bar.

Glad to find men he already knew, Grey soon established he was not at liberty to discuss exactly why he was in town. The boys dropped that subject, but only that subject, respecting Grey's privacy.

They'd completed a few billiard games when Hairy, aptly named, asked, "Hey, Mac? You suicidal or still single?"

A hearty laugh and a, "Still single," was Grey's reply.

"I'm surprised. Ever since we become friends, I seen women hangin' off your heels. Ya know, you're the one and only man I seen who bothers ta make every ugly hag feel like she's the best lookin' thing since Leona Visper, that Songbird of the North. Remember her?" Lost for a short moment in the memory of the enchanting singer he hadn't heard about in years, Hairy composed himself. "What puzzles the piss out of me is why ya do it, man? Why would ya waste time cajoling the ones who'll be of no use to ya when there's plenty enough who'll be happy to cooperate in a little wick-dippin'?"

Grey had never thought about it before. He raised his first finger, and the barkeep poured him another bourbon while the plump waitress who'd brought them boiled eggs, purple cabbage, smoked knuckles, and neck-bones with dill, beat away Hairy's pawing hands. It hadn't occurred to Grey to be civil only to fair maidens. He felt women in general were special and certainly different from men, and not just in appearance. They were creatures of delicacy, and needed, no, deserved a degree of respect and reverence. Without them enduring the pain of creation, where would men be? Admittedly, more than a few females had made him madder than 400 hells. That was all part of the difference, Grey guessed.

"What chu sssay, Mac?" wondered Bennie, his ill-fitting false teeth making a high pitched squeak with every pronunciation of a word spelled with the letter S. He gave his own answer. His front gold teeth caught the light of the gas lamp on the wall. His round black glasses with their thick lenses accentuated his odd appearance. "Women's only good for keepin' varm when they's pruned-up vit age." As the homely man laughed, his lips pulled back exposing pink gums. "I know deese. Mama kick me out ta bed last time I make move in her direction."

Trying not to picture the advances of Benny toward his wife, Grey said, "Well, I'm not about to blow a chance with 'the right one' because I cut to the chase with the first sentence out of my mouth," answered Grey.

"Hell," spoke Hairy, astounded at his friend's attitude. "You're talking like ya plan on getting hitched-up. Sounds like maybe ya got a bead on just who it'll be, too. Ya know damn good and well sailors can never be true, and nobody can expect a wife ta go without for months neither, sometimes maybe years at a time. You're kiddin' yourself if'n ya do. It just don't work."

"I don't plan to marry. What man does? But they do say the best sex is with a good woman."

"Yaw," added Benny, "but ettssss only de married men dat ssssays eet! Like me!"

The hilarity was full-bodied. Unfortunately, all discussions were forced to end because the clock struck four. The lads had to return to their watches. No one knew when or where they'd again meet. Still, all understood the next time would be like this, spontaneous and full of fun.

As Harry exited the bar, he heard him tell Benny, "The first chance I get, I'm polishin' my binnacle." The engineer chuckled and dug in his pocket to pay the tab for the boys.

Grey felt a nudge and was ready to warn Benny or Hairy, that desertion was a serious activity. He knew first hand.

"What the devil are you doing here, boy?"

Grey recognized the gruff voice. "Michael," he said surprised. "So, I assume you haven't heard?"

"Heard what?"

"I left my post," the handsome engineer said simply, taking in Michael's somewhat unkempt appearance.

Michael Dunnigan raised a bushy eyebrow, but found it difficult to question this man he'd become close to over the years. Besides, what room did he have to talk?

"Hey, Samson," Michael called to the bartender. "A stout for me and another of whatever this man is drinking."

Grey placed his hand over the rim of his glass. "No time now, Michael. I have to pick up Carolena. She's expecting me."

"She's doing okay? I miss that girl of mine something fierce."

"She's fine, sir.

"Don't tell her you've seen me here."

Grey figured Michael felt uncomfortable in the Dresher household because of his lack of finances.

"No, sir, I won't. See you around."

As he watched the broad shoulders exit the saloon, Michael was aware he'd never received an answer to just why Grey was in Charleston and not on the *Coral Crown*. He really wished he knew.

***

The day had been especially busy for everyone. Anxious to do whatever it took to finish the plans for the yacht and amputate the girl from Paolo's side, Gwenie offered, "I'm willing to stay longer."

"No, Gwenie. Can't you see how weary Carolena is? She needs to get off her feet. We can work some in the morning, before tomorrow night's festivities."

"What festivities, Paolo? Tell me, tell me!"

He held out his hand to her, indicating she should be patient. "Gwenie, if you do anything else tonight, do a final check on all the arrangements. I certainly don't want an unexpected hitch coming up at the last moment."

"Have I ever let you down?"

Paolo shook his head and smiled.

"What about you, Carolena? May I see you home in my cab?" Gwenie asked.

"Thank you, no. Mr. McKenna will be along shortly," she answered, graciously and gladly refusing.

The mature woman was aware she was getting the bum's rush, but there was little she could do short of staging a hissy fit there in the apartment. Dawdling, she finally left the maiden and mister alone.

Half-pleading, half-demanding Carolena said, "Now please, Paolo, before Grey comes, tell me about tomorrow night!"

Paolo was pleased she had a brain and was so dedicated to her endeavors. He was also pleased this girl was alive with enthusiasm. Her excitement inspired his. Her proximity resulted in a near-delirium of yearning in his mind and body. His need to possess Carolena was controlling his motivation for living. It all had happened more rapidly than ever before.

"Very well, little one. Tomorrow after my final performance, I'm hosting a ball at the Fleur de la Grace."

Carolena had heard of this place. From what she'd read, it was a lavish complex comprised of many chambers, some smaller, some massive, for galas of all types. She'd give anything to be included. "That sounds just wonderful."

He said nothing, watching as she picked up the trash and notes strewn about. Rolling the blueprints to store them in their sturdy paper tubes, her eyes remained downcast. When she looked up, he was gone. Entering the room that was once hers, she took her cape from where it lay on the bed.

"Carolena, would you please come out here?"

"Yes? I was just getting my things to go." She gazed up to see him holding the most magnificent pale blue skirt and bodice imaginable. It looked to be off the shoulder with small cap sleeves dripping pearls. Lace appliqué bordered the V-shaped neck. Iridescent sequins, tiny strings of pearls, and white ribbon rose buds patterned the pointed bodice. The back seemed to sweep low, almost to the waist! The skirt was layers and layers of airy tulle, appearing as if even a whisper might lift it in a dance of gossamer.

"Do you like it?" he asked walking to her and placing the dress in her arms.

"It's the loveliest thing I've ever seen!" She only wondered who would wear it. She felt sad it would not be her.

"Why the long face, Carolena? Don't you want to go my gala? I have to see you in this gown. I have to."

Tears of joy filled her eyes. When he saw them, he felt the heel for keeping the surprise so long. "You must be on my arm, Carolena Dunnigan. I need to show you off. You shall be my hostess."

"Your hostess? Your hostess," she repeated to let the meaning sink in. "I--I'm so flattered, Paolo." So flattered, she was almost giddy at the idea. "You dear, sweet man. How I would love to be your hostess. I can get away with attending the theater and daytime outings here and there in my drab clothes. That's one thing. To wear this gown, though, let alone attend a ball and host it for everyone to see me there while I'm in half mourning, I just couldn't."

He had to play his best card. "It's for a good cause, Carolena. It's for the orphanage. You can't let them down. You don't have it in your heart to begrudge the children. I know you don't. Besides, your name is on the invitation."

"On the invitation?"

"Yes, ma'am." Paolo took the dress and held it to her body, the bodice at her shoulder, the skirt at her waist. She felt it would fit her to perfection. All at once, he dropped the dress onto the floor as he took her in his arms.

"The gown! The gown! Paolo, it's getting all wrinkled!"

He swept it up, to toss it behind him. "Who cares!" he laughed. "That's how Edward earns his keep, remember? Just leave it tonight, and tomorrow after we're through with our work on the yacht, we'll leave directly from here. Come on, let's go out for dinner."

"But I can't go out with you. Grey will arrive momentarily. He'll be furious if I tell him to run along, that his trip to pick me up has been wasted."

Paolo had forgotten she answered to another man, worried about upsetting another man. "Why such concern for him? Is there something between you?" As he asked, he sat on the settee and pulled her down toward him.

She lost her balance, resulting in her upper torso landing heavily against his powerful chest. It stunned her, and her heart quivered.

He took hold of the nape of her neck. He'd waited long enough and, he hoped, so had she. Their lips locked into a kiss that left her panting. Carolena found her hands. She could push herself away. He would let her. She could object if she wanted. Instead, she slid her long fingers up the black silk of his shirt to feel the curve of his collar.

Paolo thrilled that she shared his kiss freely, willingly. He enfolded her in his embrace and twisted her so she was beside him, nearly beneath him.

Her arms found his neck and her fingers his hair. She pulled his handsome head toward her, indicating that she desired his kiss become deeper. Readily obliging, his tongue found hers and with it, he demonstrated what he hungered to do with her, upon her, and to her.

This was so much more than Carolena had experienced with the other men in her life. Paolo was commanding, driving her to places that frightened and yet intrigued her. "Men will be men. Men will be men." Grey! Carolena heard his voice inside her head. She squeezed her eyes tightly. Grey! God, he'll be here anytime. He's probably on his way up in the elevator, she realized. She wiggled beneath Paolo, to free herself.

Paolo took her movements to mean desire and covered her right breast with his large left hand.

Although she didn't want to, she had to speak. She had to back away, to tell him now was not the time. "Paolo," she breathed heavily. "Paolo."

"Yes, darling. Yes, it's so right. It was to be, make no mistake of it. It was to be."

"Paolo." She pulled away in an attempt to focus his attention on her words. "Please, not here. Please."

He heard her alarm and loosened his grip on her. "Am I crushing you, Carolena? You're right. Let me take you to my — "

She took advantage of the moment and managed to extricate herself and stand over him. Paolo got to his feet, embracing her yet again. She turned her head from side to side so he was unable to land his kisses on her lips. "Paolo, listen!"

The knock at the door was unwelcome by both of them. It was certain to be Grey, and he needed answering or he would seek and find his own answers.

"I must get it, Paolo," she whispered. "Mr. McKenna hasn't much patience these days."

"Send him away. I will see you to your aunt's."

"I don't think that will be an easy task."

This time the pounding on the door rattled the pictures on the walls and the vases on the long entry table.

"It's better I leave now."

"Before passion fulfills its quest?" he teased.

She hushed him with her lips on his. She'd meant the gesture to be sweet, with the intention of dousing his smoldering fire. But she let it become more tantalizing. Instead of an innocent peck, her silky tongue followed the width of his mouth.

He reached for her again, and she jumped clear, laughing wickedly.

"This is only the beginning, Carolena. Only the beginning. I'm in no mood to see this McKenna. I may do or say something you might not appreciate. Until tomorrow, and the splendor of it all. It will be a night you'll remember forever."

He left the parlor, heading toward his office. Apparently, she was going to host a spectacular ball, whether she wanted to or not. And she desperately wanted to.

Hurling open the door, she stood with hands on hips. "I wish you'd develop a splash of patience!"

Ignoring her, Grey brushed past, instantly recognizing he'd interrupted something. His confirmation was her ruddy face and puffy lips. It was a blessed good thing he'd come along when he had. "Patience! I've been freezing my ass off outside, waiting for your highness like some lap dog. When you say five o'clock, I damn well expect you to be downstairs waiting for me at five o'clock. I sure don't have to ask what you've been up to. And where is this man who tempts you so much, you're willing to debase yourself at his mere beckoning?"

Carolena looked to the spot where the velvet pillows now lay crushed on the floor. Wadded in the corner was the blue dress. There was little sense denying it. Then again, who was he to tell her what was proper? He'd bedded hundreds of women, she was sure, so he had no room to talk.

Remaining calm, lest her feeling of guilt show, she told him, "Signor Alontti is attending to business. He sends his regards."

"Yeah? I'll just bet he does. Come on. Let's get the hell out of this lair before I find your lover and lay him out!"

Chapter 15

Carolena was reading Peeper's latest letter to Aunt Coe aloud. "Some sailor friend a Waite's give Halley a hen, and she took ta calling it Pretty. That fool chicken follows the child around, even inta the house. Noreen ain't much on animals, ya might recall, and says it's too much trouble. So one day, we cain't find the thing. Guess what we have fer supper? Yup, a whole cluck! That night, Halley comes a-runnin' in with two bits. She found the money in her slipper. Was Noreen's way a makin' it a fair trade, I reckon. Ya know, Halley's still a-lookin' fer that bird."

Everyone chuckled except the usually good-humored Grey. Standing by the fireplace, he watched feather-light ashes disappear up into the chimney. Carolena had informed him of the following evening's dance, and her excitement was apparent. Shrugging his shoulders, he stifled a yawn.

"Sorry if news from home bores you, Mr. McKenna, but we all find it interesting. Must be because you're not family," she said, displaying a deliberately bratty tone.

"Carolena Dunnigan!" Shocked at the ill-mannered remark, Aunt Coe tried to smooth things over with the offer of a gingersnap. "Another cookie, Grey?"

"Just one more, ma'am. Please excuse my sleepiness. I guess it's all that good food you served for supper. And, too, I met up with a couple of old friends. They wore me out with their stories."

"You mean the brown bottle flu wore you out!" the blonde sniped.

In retort, Grey commented casually, "Be sure and send Peeper my best when you write back, Carolena. Now how soon will that be? Let's see, maybe tomorrow morning? No, you still have to do more work on the yacht. Just can't seem to ever get it quite right, can you? How about the afternoon? No, that, too, would be tied up with the same *business*." He spat the last noun in disgust. "Then tomorrow evening? No, you'll be attending that ball thing with Signor Alontti," he revealed, as he peered knives in Carolena's direction. "Or did you forget to inform your aunt and uncle of that fact?"

Rats! Grey had gotten her back for mentioning his drinking. Carolena had planned on disclosing the gala plans at the last possible moment and then immediately excuse herself to retire. She hoped Aunt Coe and Uncle Fries, especially Uncle Fries, would be too exhausted to object. But it was only 7:45. They were wide-awake and more than able to disapprove. "Oh, that's right. Thank you for reminding me, Grey." Her insincerity was obvious, and he returned her nod with an equally artificial smirk.

"Tomorrow night Signor Alontti is giving a ball to raise funds for The Elevation of Euphonious Edification for the Deficiently Parented."

"For what?" asked Fries, confused by the ridiculous name of the event.

Carolena gave a sugary laugh. "Yes, Uncle, it certainly is a cumbersome title, but the cause is quite good, I assure you. The signor holds this same type of party in different cities to raise money to teach orphans about music. Isn't that a generous cause?"

It seemed to Fries the conductor's generosity might be better spent providing nourishing food or sturdy shoes for poor children. Then again, he supposed any aid was good.

"I have read something in the newspaper about it, I believe," said his wife. "It was in the society notices you always skip over, Fries."

"And he's asked me to be his hostess!" Carolena reported proudly.

Grey, who'd taken the gold and white stripped Queen Anne wing chair, raised his eyes from the magazine he'd picked up and stared at her.

Temporarily pinned to her seat by his scrutiny, Carolena pursed her lips and stood to take Grey's place at the hearth.

"Well," her uncle said thinking hard, "I guess it would be all right. It is for charity and, so far, this Signor Alontti has been a gentleman." Suddenly, "He has, hasn't he, Carolena?"

His question demanded an honest answer. To her mind, Carolena's next statement was the truth. Nothing had passed between them thus far that she considered inappropriate. "I've not objected in the least to his behavior, Uncle."

She grinned at Grey, and he wanted to swat her shapely behind. He worried she was caught well over her head in an undertow of Alontti's celebrity and was carelessly ruining any chance she had of delivering herself to salvation.

"What will you wear to the ball?" Aunt Coe queried. "There's no time to have anything made. We'll have to purchase a store-bought gown," as if such a thing were less than seemly.

"I'll bet that's not necessary, is it Carolena?" Grey inserted. "I'm guessing your musician friend surprised you with some fancy frock. Am I right?"

How she wished she were alone so she could clobber Grey yet again with any of the many deadly objects in the room. Her eyes wide in faux astonishment, "You sure are a good guesser."

Unable to let the subject of accepting personal gifts from a man pass, "Honestly, dear," Aunt Coe chided, "I don't understand why you allowed that chap to have a dress made for you."

"Naturally, I thought of refusing such an offering, but it was a kind surprise. It would be mean to say no. Don't you agree?" Carolena's words of defense poured forth. "I hope Grammy is looking down from heaven and understanding this is all for a good cause, that she's not offended at my cutting short mourning for her. I mean no disrespect. Grammy was forever telling me I should attend social gatherings to meet the right man.

It would follow she would want me to be dressed properly. And you remember how much charity work she did for the church, donating her braided rugs to raise money is just one example. Oh, and the gown will be paid for from the yacht profits.

"And to answer your original question, Aunt Coe, I just can't let you and Uncle Fries spend any more money on me than you already have. I mean you're feeding me and letting me stay with you until my business is completed in Charleston. There's no telling how many days or even weeks it might take. Rest assured, I'll settle up."

"You're our niece for land-sakes," said Uncle Fries. "We'll have no more talk of settling up." He dipped his chin and looked at her over the top of his reading glasses. "By the way, where did that music fella get the measurements for your new dress?" Her uncle had asked the unspoken question on everyone's mind.

"Why from the pattern his seamstress traced from my old dress. With that pattern, she was able to make and fit this dress to me. She did the same for my ball gown."

"Doesn't sound like there will be much of anything left you can call profits once you're done paying off all your clothing," Grey said, just in case Coe and Fries hadn't already thought of it.

Trying to take the focus from herself, "I'm so embarrassed," Carolena explained. "I haven't invited you to the party. I realize I've been thoughtless and caught up in my own excitement, but Aunt Coe, Uncle Fries, Grey, I would love to have you all attend tomorrow night's event as my guests."

"Don't you have to ask Alontti's permission?" Grey picked, trying to demonstrate to one and all how she was under the thumb of this musician.

Insulted, she responded involuntarily. "Certainly not! I can guarantee Mr. Alontti would grant me any wish I might have."

Carolena's words confirmed the intimate nature of their relationship.

"Although we'd like to be your chaperons," Aunt Coe looked to her husband, who nodded, "we must decline. We don't go out much at night anymore. It would be inappropriate for me to leave the house, let alone attend a party while I'm in full mourning for my mother. Then, too, when it comes to dancing, your uncle is unable."

"Not too good at it these days, what with this gout in my big toe."

"I'm sorry you can't come. Don't worry though. I'll be just fine."

"Yes, you will because Grey will go in our stead. You know, to keep an eye out for you," Uncle Fries added as easily as if he were ordering a piece of pie.

Aunt Coe's glance toward Grey begged his compliance. "You're sure to have a fine time, son."

Grey hated to refuse such a kind woman, yet refuse he would. The very last thing he wanted was to stand around in some stiff shirt and watch this Alontti guy hovering over Carolena. "I'm sorry ma'am, sir, but I've other plans for the evening." It was a lie, yes. Still, he would damn sure find something better to do than this.

Carolena was thrilled Grey wouldn't be there to spy on her. She'd done the proper thing by inviting all three of them and with their refusal, she was free to do as she pleased.

The meaning of her victorious expression was clear to Fries. This entire matter was distasteful, and he felt he should insert some wisdom here, yet his aches were getting the better of him. Despite the still early hour, it was time to escape to his bedroom. He'd leave this for his wife to handle. Lord knew Carolena was as stubborn as her aunt. With Eckert and Dunnigan blood in her veins, hell, he hadn't a prayer. He knew first hand from living decades with one of them, namely his wife. Besides, Carolena was a grown-up, even though she played cat and rat like a child with poor Grey. She'd do whatever she liked in the end.

After a discussion about how a young woman was to behave at a ball, especially without a chaperon, Aunt Coe said, "There's no need for debate. The good Lord has given you brains and common sense, Carolena. It's up to you to use them both."

"Yes, ma'am. I will."

"Good." With that said, Aunt Coe kissed her niece on the cheek and patted Grey's arm when he stood up at her exiting. "Good night you two. Don't stay up talking too long."

"Don't worry, we won't." Trying to smooth the waters, Carolena said to Grey. "Would you like one more piece of German Crumb Cake? The sugar will keep you warm on your way back to your hotel."

Almost touched at her kindness, Grey replied, "No thanks."

Carolena shrugged. "Suit yourself. I'm getting more cake." She walked toward the kitchen, hoping he'd go away and leave her be. He is so disagreeable anymore, she thought.

***

Carolena washed her plate and fork and put them back in the tall cupboard. She headed toward the guest room. Several candles and holders waited on the square table beside the banister leading from the front hall to the second floor. Taking one, she touched its wick to the gas jet on the wall before lowering the hissing fire on the jet. "I hope Grey has left by now," she whispered to herself. Lifting her skirts, she ascended the steps, careful not to trip in the dim light.

Grey suspected Carolena would avoid him once her aunt and uncle retired. He watched her as she'd casually but purposefully gone from kitchen to dining room to parlor, peeking around corners, as if looking for something--or someone. He expected she was looking for him. Now, here she was, skulking off to the sanctuary of her own quarters.

As she placed her foot on the seventh carpeted step, she heard, "Ready for bed, are you? Or did you have a *nap* earlier in the day?"

He'd scared the dickens out of her! This surprise attack of his could have stopped her heart once and for all! That heart was pounding so hard, she was surprised it wasn't painful. "What is the matter with you?" As she advanced on him, "Why would you deliberately lie in wait for me like this?" Then it dawned on her. "What are you still doing here? I thought you'd gone to your hotel. Oh, let me by!" she commanded.

"I decided to sleep on the sofa, in case you had plans to sneak off in the night."

She let his remark pass because the idea had crossed her mind.

He saw her tight lips and said, "I'll be glad to allow your passage, but first you'll hear me out."

"Again? I know what you're going to say, and I don't care to listen. Oh no!" She panicked. "You haven't changed your mind and are going to the dance, are you?"

"Relax. I'm not interested. Hey, wait a minute. On second thought, from the look on your face, maybe I should go to your gala. Afraid I'll spoil your good time? You just might see me there after all."

"I only invited you in front of Aunt Coe and Uncle Fries so they wouldn't get on to me. You know I wasn't sincere, so don't expect an invitation from me." Her chin high in triumph, she added, "They won't let anyone in without showing one."

"Do you think a piece of printed paper would bar me from doing whatever the hell I wanted?"

He was but a step higher than she. Looking up at him, she clutched the banister to keep from falling backwards. She gave no answer.

"Do you?"

He was right. Grey always did whatever he chose. Discouraged, she blasted, "Good night!"

"Hold on. You will listen, like it or not."

Carolena attempted to shove past him. He stunned her by slipping his hand around her back, pulling her close, and lifting her into the cradle of his arms. As he carried her down the staircase, he pledged, "Raise your voice and wake your Uncle Fries," he warned, "and he'll hear my version of the passionate scene I interrupted this afternoon. I'd bet my rendering will sound quite shocking because I'm certain it was."

She kicked her legs and beat at his back with her right fist. The candle in her holder tipped and was teetering. Some of its melted wax spilled onto her sleeve. She tried to balance it and pummel simultaneously, wanting to blow the thing out so it didn't burn her. Yet, she dreaded being alone with Grey in complete darkness. "Are you threatening me?"

"You're damn right I am," he answered in a hot whisper against her hair.

She was certain if she looked at him, he'd be wearing an idiotic grin, and that infuriated her all the more. "This is stupid. Set me down!"

"If you were a rational woman, we could sit here in this parlor and hold a civil conversation. I have a strong feeling, however, you're not feeling so civil right now."

She stiffened her body momentarily to lie flat across his arms like a piece of lumber. "Ohhhh!" Frustrated to near tears, "If I tell Paolo of this, he'll—"

He suddenly deposited her on her feet in the dining room in order to pull the pocket doors closed. His face was stripped of its usual jovial expression as he eyed the girl across the embroidered table scarf from him. "Do tell, Carolena. What do you envision this man will do to me?"

She never remembered a time when Grey seemed so large, where she felt so small. He appeared invincible. She was certain he felt he was. Paolo was older than Grey, but also a strong man. She'd seen him take charge, give commands. But she would never deliberately pit him against Grey. Paolo was too complicated. He was so unlike this beast she was with now. Her musician was genteel and gentle. Why, one break of a finger and his lifelong career was ruined. To protect Paolo, she had to take back her threat. "Calm down, Grey."

"Me?"

She wanted to run away. Anywhere she might go, he was sure to find her.

"You mean I don't sound calm to you? I thought I was doing rather well considering how irritating you are."

"Me? Irritating?" She giggled.

Grey showed his anger. "Is this all the more serious you take me?" His eyes narrowed. "If it is, you're making a mistake."

Those menacing words sobered Carolena at once. Keeping to whispering, "Listen to me. Please, Grey." She set the still burning candle on the sideboard. Placing one hand on her hip and gesturing pictorially with the other, she tilted her chin coyly. In this dull light, his eyes looked black, as if they'd lost their color. "You're making too, too much of things. Yes, Paolo and I kissed. What on earth could you possibly find the matter with that? Frankly," she hesitated only a moment, thinking of marriage, "I'm hoping it will lead to other things."

He was upon her in three long strides and had her face in his hands. "You can stand there and blatantly tell me you want this man to have you? You will make it so easy for him that all he has to do is name the place and time, and you'll be there? What manner of tramp are you?"

His words were harsh, and Carolena couldn't understand why anyone would say such appalling things to her, let alone fun-loving Grey. "Why are you speaking to me like this? Why? Why?"

She demanded an answer. He sure as hell would give her one. "I address you as the loose woman I'm afraid you'll become if you haven't already."

She didn't care if he were a man, a mountain, or the great Almighty. She wouldn't stand for any more of his vile language. It took all her endurance not to peel Aunt Coe's china from the plate rail and heave one dish after another at him. She had to do something. The only other exit was into the kitchen since he was between her and the pocket doors. She didn't know how, but by the time she'd reached the kitchen, he was there, blocking her way. "Let me pass! You can't hold me prisoner!" With each breath, her voice elevated.

Hell's half acre, Grey thought. This has gotten all out of hand. A simple sincere warning has changed into an ugly scene of--of what? What was it about her that turned a man's usual easy nature to near madness? "Do you want them to hear you upstairs? You're not going anywhere until we settle this!"

"What's to settle? You've done everything except offer a few coins to bed me or is that next?" Her question shocked her while it sickened him.

Throwing his right arm around her shoulders, he covered her mouth with his left hand. He felt her bite and jerked away his throbbing palm. He should have expected it. Dismissing the pain, he held tight, securing her to him.

"Why look so surprised at what I've said, Grey? You've been around, or are you the kind of man who brags he's never paid for a woman? I'll wager that's just your style."

He was determined to silence her. He feared if her ugly talk continued, he might slap her. He didn't want to lose his temper to that degree, not with her, nor any woman. It was not his way.

It was then he saw the whole of Carolena Dunnigan as his gaze magnified, and she, alone, filled his vision. He realized they'd been together this way and that, here and there for years, yet never so close or in these circumstances. He blocked out the sound of her defensive squealing, ignored her struggling in his arms, and saw only a beautiful woman. He had lingered over her face so many times when she was involved in everyday tasks, taking her comeliness for granted. Until this very moment, he'd never truly, *never truly* seen her. Yet even her fury in the dim candlelight couldn't mask the sparkle discharging from her every pore. Her eyes blazed molten malachite while one hand tangled in the hair coming free from her slackened combs.

The seconds ticked by as Carolena realized Grey had tightened his embrace. Somewhere deep inside, she was the tiniest bit sorry he'd forced her to bite his hand. Then again, he had no business suffocating her words like that. She was trying to spit out the reasons he'd been so wrong to accuse her of - she couldn't quite remember what it was he'd said, so she told him, "Just because you're much bigger than I am and can pin me down ..." He was holding the back of her head, and she couldn't break his grasp. "Don't think, I'll ever forgive you." His eyes focused on her parted lips, and she remembered he'd said she'd a lovely mouth. "Forgive you for …"

He was close. So close. And as always, he did not react to her. She'd just have to show him what she wanted. Right here and right now. If he gave no response, she would have her truth. She had to find out if he felt more for her than brotherly concern.

Carolena kissed his smooth cheek, lingering a moment. There. It was done.

The satin of her lips branded Grey's skin. His flesh burned with desire, his mind with surprise. He pulled away to be sure it was indeed Carolena in his arms. His mouth toward hers, he closed the scant inches between them until he was kissing her fully.

She tried to speak and could not as he took her lips for his own. She relaxed into his hard height, letting him support her.

The only barrier between them was clothing. He felt her breasts crush against him, and the thought of her naked body sent ripples of pure delight throughout his own. His kisses were not tender. She returned wild passion, impacted with inexperience and uncertainty.

Gaining confidence as she bathed in the bubbling pleasure of it all, Carolena became aggressive. His scent, his energy, his vitality enthralled her. Maybe it was the taste of him.

In an effort to regain some trace of control, Grey grew gentle. She spun in his loosened embrace to press her back and lower hips into his chest and groin.

Grey's head fell over her right shoulder. His lips danced the distance of her neck, taking time to nuzzle her ear and breathe her name, delivering hot chills that reverberated throughout her body until he felt her tremble. She threw her head back against his chest and his fingers went to her bodice, pulling it open. Carolena grasped his calloused palm and to his delighted amazement, placed it square on her breast.

"Let's get out of here," he rasped.

Let's get out of here. She'd heard him say a similar phrase earlier in Paolo's apartment. Paolo! Paolo! Maybe Grey was right. Maybe she was acting the tramp! Two different men in a day's time had touched her this intimately. And to her shame, she'd welcomed and encouraged them both! At least Paolo didn't always argue with her. Whatever she wanted, he gave her. He did everything he could think of to make her time with him pleasant. Grey was abusive, crude, and disrespectful toward her. He probably figured if Paolo were making love to her, then why shouldn't he? After all, she wasn't married to anyone, so was still fair game. The long tailed rat was using her to satisfy himself and as she'd predicted, he wasn't paying for it. To be sure, she didn't want his money. No, she wanted payment through commitment.

Yet Paolo hadn't proposed either. Why did the maestro seem so much more sincere? The upcoming dance would tell her what she needed to know. He would reveal himself and his regard for her there.

"Grey. Stop it!"

He pulled back, rigid, as if held at knifepoint. Her instantly cold demeanor destroyed his ardor. Her face was stern. Incredibly, she looked mad again!

"What are you doing to me?" she asked, indignant.

He was stunned at her sudden turnabout. When he released her, she stepped away from him to button her blouse over her untied chemise.

The only sound between them was the torturously slow ticking of Aunt Coe's mantle clock in the parlor. Carolena had to speak. "I must think of Paolo."

Had she said she hated Grey's touch on her skin, she couldn't have spoken more hurtful words. He walked to the double doors, slid them open, took his coat from the hall tree, and left the Dresher house.

Carolena was alone in the shadows of the single candle's light. Why hadn't Grey pitched a fit when she stopped his advances? Not even one word. She concluded he was only seeing how far he could get with her, or he'd have been furious she stopped him at the height of his passion. Never mind all that, she thought. Tomorrow he'll be back to the grousing character he'd become of late. I just hope he doesn't make a scene to embarrass me in front of Auntie and Uncle. Worse yet, if he ever meets Paolo, Lord Almighty! Grey is just the kind of man who would deliberately humiliate me in public by speaking of this night.

Exhausted, Carolena ascended the stairs to her room. As she crawled into bed, she prayed, "Give my sick heart enough strength and time so I may know real love in my short life."

Chapter 16

Next morning, Uncle Fries was already downstairs when Aunt Coe heard a commotion and scurried to the top of the stairs to see what was up. Carolena heard, too, and was several feet behind her. They recognized a voice Carolena didn't want to acknowledge.

"Oh, Coe! It's been so long. So long!" The mistress of the house grinned wide and headed down to greet her sister, Ella, in the front hall. "Careful. Don't trip."

Coe laughed, "We always have looked out for each other, haven't we, sis?"

The women hugged as Miss Ella wiped away her happy tears with one of the blue woolen gloves she'd borrowed from Noreen. "You didn't tell her I was coming, did you?" whispered Miss Ella. "I want to surprise her."

"Certainly not, El," Coe whispered back, "but I don't know how much time you'll have together because the girl keeps so busy. In fact, tonight …"

Carolena descended the steps with deliberate pace and hard features. "Didn't anyone ever tell you it's rude to whisper? What are you doing here? Why have you come?"

Her arms outstretched, "Oh, Car--Carolena!" Her mother had almost called her the unthinkable nickname.

Standing three steps from the landing, just out of reach, Carolena spoke. Ice laced her words. "I asked you why you've come. Not enough—" she searched for a word that wouldn't divulge her mother's indiscretion, "stimulation at home for you?"

"Carolena. Please. Let's discuss this. Will you excuse us, Coe? My daughter and I need a moment."

Grey entered the parlor and along with Coe and Fries immediately noticed the uncharacteristic discord between mother and child.

"Do you think a moment's discussion will make a difference? I want nothing more to do with you. I thought I made that completely clear back home," said an angry Carolena, straining with wrath derived from her position of moral superiority.

Grey could tolerate Carolena's rudeness to himself, but not to Miss Ella, the woman who included him in every family gathering the Dunnigans had since he'd met them. "Carolena! You apologize to your mother. I don't care why you think you have reason to judge her so harshly, but no child ever has that right."

"It's none of your business, Grey McKenna. Either you take me to Paolo's this minute, or I'll drop Uncle Fries at work and drive there myself. I want to be away from you as well as her!" Leaving them all in stunned silence, Carolena raced back up the stairs to retrieve her satchel. She came back down and grabbed her cape from the hall tree, nearly toppling it off balance. "And I won't be back until I hear you've left this house!" With that, she walked outside, allowing frosty wind to enter.

Grey shook his head, kissed Miss Ella on her salty cheek, and followed the most hateful and cruel woman he'd ever known out the door.

***

Little work was accomplished in the hours leading up to the ball. Paolo was gone much of the time and Gwenie with him. Edward was a wreck, worrying if the crease in his master's evening trousers was sharp enough and the ruffles on the shirt starched full, yet still soft to the touch.

Visions of high society and glamour replaced Carolena's thoughts of the yacht as she busied herself in preparations. Her hair needed tying to set the curls, her nails buffed, and her body bathed and perfumed. To her dismay, she discovered she'd left her nail file at Aunt Coe's.

She went to the vanity in hopes of finding a spare. There she discovered delicate linen and silk unmentionables. Jealousy took over until she saw they were new. She decided to wear them since hers were plain cotton, not worthy of her gown. She scandalously hoped Paolo chose them and not Gwenie.

Finding no file, she nibbled on the jagged tip of her nail where it had broken and thought of the night ahead. She wasn't sure what to expect. She was familiar with the social graces; she was raised on them. Still, she didn't want to say or do the wrong thing. She anticipated elegance because tonight's affair was under the auspices of Signor Paolo Alontti. She planned to conduct herself with the same degree of sophistication as Paolo by following his lead. He was an expert.

After a leisurely soak in the tub of her private marbled lavatory, Carolena dried herself and stood naked before the mirror while she worked on her hair. That done, she snatched up the sample perfume, Blossoming Ardor, she'd received from the emporium near Aunt Coe's and saved for a special occasion. Ignoring the rule to use a light hand with scents, she dabbed it behind her knees, in the crooks of her elbows, behind her ears, and at the nape of her neck. She saw there was but one drop left. She placed the last of it in the cleavage between her breasts, smiling at the thought of a lover inhaling its floral fragrance there.

Her eyelashes needed curling. Carolena threw on her dingy dark dress and summoned Edward to bring a teaspoon. When he had done so, Carolena stripped off the mourning gown and brazenly naked once again, crimped her lashes over the bowl of the spoon with her finger, just enough to lend a gentle uplift.

Next, she rolled white silk stockings and languidly inserted her pointed toes, pulling the weave smooth to her thighs, and securing each just above the knee. Her garters matched a low-necked chemise with white lace trim and narrow straps.

Putting on her full cut drawers, she tied them at the waist. Carolena checked to make certain the partially opened crotch seam had enough fullness to allow it to overlap for both modesty and comfort's sake. A boned corset followed. Wishing Peeper was with her to help, she turned her back to the mirror and, over her shoulder, watched her hands tighten and finally tie the thing. After two airy silk petticoats, Carolena inspected the buttons and hooks, which would support the train of the satin brocade overskirt, turning it into a bustle for dancing. The lower half of her gown on and adjusted, she centered the embroidered chiffon front panel. The few steps to the bed to pick up the blue bodice in matching brocade were enough to feel the lightweight of the train against the front of her legs. Drawing the blouse up her arms, she worked the concealed side closure, and she was dressed.

The Grecian curls draping over her left shoulder tickled and she smoothed them around her finger. Paolo had suggested Mr. Ramon, coiffeur to Charleston society, come to the apartment to dress Carolena's hair. She'd dismissed the idea, fearing what Grey had said about using all the profit to pay her debts to Paolo might be true. She'd managed an elegant look with a touch of daisies and fern secured on the left. These came from the flower arrangement in her room. With a shy dip of her chin, she blushed at their opposing meanings of purity and allure. "I'll bet Paolo chooses the flowers for each day's fresh bouquet," she told herself. "He's so romantic." She made a sour face. "Grey would never think to do anything like that."

At 8 p.m., Paolo returned. He knocked on Carolena's door to tell her he'd be ready to leave at 8:30. Everything was set, so all they had to do was drive a few blocks to Fleur de la Grace and be there in time to greet the guests. "Do you need my help with anything?" he teased.

Not offended by his question, she said, "No thank you, Paolo." She giggled as she stepped into white slippers and finished with long white gloves. "I'll be with you shortly."

He slid an ivory envelope under her door saying she might like to view the official document required for entrance into the ball. Carolena snatched it up and removed the enclosure carefully. It read:

WORLD RENOWNED
MAESTRO PAOLO ALONTTI
and
Miss Carolena Dunnigan,
Chief Designer, Aqua Verde Passenger Line
Fernandina, Florida
request the honor of your presence at
THE ELEVATION OF EUPHONIOUS EDIFICATION FOR
THE DEFICIENTLY PARENTED
Fleur de la Grace
April 2, 1889
nine o'clock
DANCING / MIDNIGHT SUPPER

She was dumbstruck! She assumed she would stand beside Paolo as he greeted his guests. That was all. This embossed card was her introduction to Charleston's cultured society. She had a skilled occupation, and now everyone at the ball would meet her. Maybe some would inquire about her designs, as had Paolo. And they, too, might want her to build them a yacht or plan a house. Why with enough customers, her financial burdens could be lifted! She sat down on the bed then threw herself back, kicking her feet wildly as she squealed in delight.

The invitation still in hand, she looked upon it once more. Maestro Paolo, Designer Carolena. A strange combination. No, not at all, she thought. Both are creative careers. Both require imagination. Carolena would be lying to herself if that were all they had in common. There was a physical attraction, captivating and powerful. Since Paolo's kiss and her tempting, teasing response, she'd found it difficult to be away from him and impossible to cast him from her thoughts. An increasingly familiar tingle left her skin chilled, and she hugged herself, pretending Paolo's arms were enfolding her.

Realizing she could be mussing her dress or hair, Carolena stood and reached for the hand-mirror she'd deposited earlier on the nightstand. The reflecting surface was small, only large enough to show her face. She looked at herself, checking her skin for unsightly blemishes. Periodically, one would show itself, and her experience told her it was usually on important occasions. Peeper always doctored her with a plaster of white pine rosin and mutton suet, but Peeper was not here.

With a mighty sigh of relief, she found her skin clear. Would she forever be plagued with this problem, she wondered? She let out a small laugh. What was she thinking? Such a malady was so slight in comparison with the deadly serious matter of her heart. She needed to think about little, pleasant things.

Carolena looked still harder at her face, hoping the distraction might help gentle the butterflies flitting about in her stomach. Her lashes were long and full, and she credited their abundance to another of Peeper's concoctions. Every night, she and Breelan would diligently apply a special lotion to their *cheek feathers*, as Marie called them when she was tiny. Peeper had explained how this particular cream was comprised of milk of sulfur, glycerin, and a little rose water. Peeper was the chemist's best customer. Aunt Noreen often scoffed at all the potions, but long ago, Nora informed Breelan and Carolena she sometimes spied her mother sampling Peeper's creams when she thought her daughter was elsewhere.

Carolena placed her hands on her waist, feeling confident in the shape of her figure. With one more splash of rice powder to her nose and shoulders, she stepped before the full-length mirror framed with hand-painted jonquils.

Staring transfixed at her reflection, Carolena forgot to breathe as she saw a princess-pale, stunning woman. She thought of her fine clothes growing up. Her father had seen his children lacked nothing. Some girls bragged they wore gowns from Paris. Carolena judged them inferior to anything made by Grammy and, yes, Miss Ella. Exchanging clothes with Breelan was always fun and doubled their wardrobes. They were the best-dressed young ladies in town. Maybe Carolena was prejudiced. Maybe the love in every stitch and seam added beauty to each garment. Love. Her mother's love. She forced herself to remain hard. She shook her head to clear the tender memories creeping up on her. Carolena refused to think about them, not this day anyway.

Before she forgot, she bit her lips so her mouth was sufficiently red and ready for kissing. Turning the glass knob, she opened the door to see the most handsome of men. His eyes drew hers, and she had no strength to break his gaze. After a long moment, Paolo handed Carolena a tiny bouquet of white rosebuds. She inhaled their fragrance and as she did, Paolo surveyed the tender creature who welcomed him. Sensations churned in him he had not experienced for many years. He was young again.

In silence, he studied her as she did him. His rich hair was freshly trimmed. Not so short as to look scalped, it still had a wild way to it. His black evening dress, with its single-breasted velvet shawl collar frock coat, needed no extra padding. His shoulders filled it well. She imagined the two tails of the jacket would dance when he did, offering a pleasing rear view to curious women. She felt she should blush at her wicked thought, until she decided it was unsophisticated. The fitted trousers hugged his legs down to his empire black pumps. Edward had done a fine job on the shirtfront. The stiffened ruffles didn't look effeminate. They only added to his appeal.

Paolo fetched his grenadier top hat while Carolena returned to the bedroom for Nora's cape. She draped it about her bare shoulders, feeling the itch of the wool and knowing the simple, unadorned garment gave her an odd appearance.

Paolo looked almost shocked when he saw her. "Carolena!"

In his grasp, she spied a glistening cape of blue velvet trimmed around the neck, down the front, and along the bottom in matching ostrich feathers. Iridescent sequins peppered the feathers and she chuckled at the idea of a skinny-legged bird wearing such a fancy covering. Her smile froze in place at the cost of the satin-lined cape. In one smooth sweep, he removed her wool and laid the cool fabric against her skin. The cool of it caused a titillating shiver.

"I'm proud of your costume and prouder still of you. You were willing to wear your wool and not say a word. Though it is a sturdy wrap, did you think I'd let my hostess travel in public in her street cape? I think this will be more appropriate."

"Paolo, dear Paolo."

"Dear Carolena. This gown and cape are my gifts to you. Before you protest, would you accept them if I told you they are an orchestra expense? After all, they really are. I needed a hostess as part of my charity work, and you needed a dress."

"I can't let you do it. What would people say?"

"Be honest. Do you really care what people say?"

She paused to weigh her feelings. "I have to say that, generally, I do. I mean, it's so much easier if you go along with the general rules of society, isn't it? Lately though, I've noticed certain restrictions are downright tedious."

"That's my girl. Shall we go now?"

"Yes, let's do. But Paolo, you do recognize you have a criminal disregard for money, don't you?"

He laughed. "We'll discuss my shortcomings later. Now, we must get along. We don't want to be late to our own party."

His arm around her shoulders, he walked her to the door, ushering her into the elevator. They dropped non-stop to the ground floor.

Cab and driver whisked them to the entrance of Fleur de la Grace. A footman wearing a black uniform with a gold stripe down his pant leg opened the cab door. Paolo was there in an instant and grasped Carolena at the waist, placing her gently onto a flagstone floor under an elaborate portico. A doorman threw open the massive carved door for them.

Handing their wraps to a waiting attendant, Paolo asked, "And the coat-check tickets?"

"Yes, sir. I have yours right here. All the nametags of the guests are ready and await pinning to their owners' cloaks. There will be no mix-ups tonight, I can assure you."

"Excellent."

The first thing Carolena noticed was the scent of flowers. They were everywhere and so varied, she knew but a few. They had to have cost a fortune and been grown in a greenhouse.

Except for servants, she and Paolo seemed to be the only two guests at the ball. She wished it could stay this way, the two of them alone with the glamour, the music, and the romance.

Clutching Paolo's arm, Carolena looked about her. The doorway was framed in greenery dotted with purple and white orchids. They walked down a hallway lined with palms so tall they formed an arch high above, meeting midpoint at the ceiling.

After passing several doors, Paolo explained, "That's the smoking room. Later, I'll find it necessary to leave your side for a short while to visit the gentlemen with deep pockets in there. Let me assure you, I will only be sipping effervescent water. I need my wits this evening, so no brandy for me. I don't want to forget a moment of our magic together. I'll be back before you have time to miss me. Don't worry."

"Do whatever you need to, Paolo. Tonight, I haven't a concern in the world."

He liked her this way, so at ease. It was encouraging.

The staircase was bedecked with fragrant lavender clusters dripping beauty. Climbing the gold-carpeted steps, Carolena's train trailed behind her and she was queen of this palace, at least for a few hours. At the pinnacle of their ascent was the entrance to the ballroom accented with white and gold lilies following the top arch of carved mahogany double doors.

As the musicians began tuning their instruments, Paolo steered Carolena on a slow stroll around the perimeter of the huge room. She spotted Gwenie scurrying about, but Carolena was too excited to pay her any mind.

Fireplaces glowed on each of three rose-flocked papered walls. Their mantles were hung with dogwood-pink satin overflowing with ferns and more wild orchids in a multitude of colors. A half dozen chandeliers, miniature versions of the massive central fixture of the room, were draped with ivy and studded with what looked to be ruby hollyhocks. Ivy garland swirled its way down the Corinthian columns with an occasional china star peeking from behind the waxy leaves. In no particular arrangement, sprays of yellow roses and some odd tiny purple flower hung high from white and yellow dotted ribbons, giving a true feeling of nature indoors. At the far right were round tables with settings for eight persons. In the middle of each was a silver epergne with four fluted vases awaiting the nosegays of the ladies who would need their hands free to dine, talk, and dance. The combination of bouquets would give each table its own personalized centerpiece. Empty food stations hugged the walls, and Carolena anticipated a feast.

A servant in short black jacket and pinstriped pants cleared his throat.

Paolo nodded. "It's time, Carolena."

Unexpectedly apprehensive, "I don't know if I'm ready to meet South Carolina society, Paolo." She found herself griping his arm with all her might.

He placed his gloved hand over hers. "Trust me, angel. Society will fall short of your expectations. You are the queen here."

Before she had time to respond, she was introduced to fine-looking folks, turned-out in all their best. The women were polite, but Carolena could feel the insincerity. Some men dared to leer. Most seemed genuinely pleased to meet her. She did her best, offering her hand, nodding, listening, and smiling until her cheeks ached. She soon realized it was unnecessary to make well thought out comments to people who chose to hear little of what she said and didn't care about her anyway. The guests were here to see and be seen with Paolo Alontti.

Carolena guessed Paolo had been right when he'd told her these people were the same as she and only thought themselves better because of their wealth and probably their lineage. By God, she would never bow before a few overweight biddies. She didn't need anyone but Paolo. Paolo was her shelter in this new and challenging world of the upper crust. She'd only known small-town warmth, and this uneven reception showed her how much she preferred her little Fernandina.

After nearly three-quarters of an hour of endless greetings, Paolo was asked to lead the quadrille. After that, there was a polka and then a waltz, played beautifully by Paolo's musicians. Many men, young and old, tapped Paolo on the shoulder, hoping to dance with the beauty he'd brought. Hesitantly yet politely, he released Carolena from his embrace.

She was thankful for all the years of etiquette piled upon her at home. It would be rude to accept one and refuse another. Grammy's instruction came to her. *A man should never hold a woman's hand at his hip while dancing with her nor high in the sky, flailing it about like a pump handle.*

With all her attention on each partner for the sake of her toes, Carolena was unaware of Paolo's steady eye on her, even though he himself was dancing with others. Finally, he could see she was weary, so to her delight he broke in, taking her from the clutches of a blue-nosed liquor-belly. They went directly to their table, and she was seated for the first time.

"Was it as unpleasant as it looked, having to dance with so many admirers?"

His concern touched her. "No," she laughed. "Not really. The good news is I have two gentlemen, a Mr. Liner and a Mr. Lewis, who are interested in hearing details of my work! Isn't that wonderful?"

"Of course it is." Being familiar with the controlling wives of each man, Paolo wondered if they weren't just toying with Carolena. Still standing, he bent at the waist to speak closely. "That's grand," adding, "You did tell them you're tied up working with me for now, didn't you?"

"Don't look so concerned," she replied. "I won't neglect you." She flashed her eyes and ran a gloved finger along his jaw line.

He looked at his pocket watch. "To my regret, sweet lady, my duty as sponsor calls."

"I'll be fine. I miss you already."

On her own, Carolena watched the others sitting at the table and was surprised to see Gwenie, dressed in a green and black taffeta plaid, join her group. Her escort was an older gentleman from the percussion section of the orchestra. Gwenie's smile was wide, yet her eyes were bored. Another couple was there though their names escaped Carolena. Two cushioned chairs remained empty with place cards for unknown guests.

Sipping the recently poured champagne in front of her, Carolena began, "Gwenie ..."

Before Carolena had a chance to discuss the weather, or anything else, she heard, "Miss Dunnigan?"

She turned to see a tall man with blonde curls and brown eyes addressing her from behind.

"I'm alone and would gladly volunteer to entertain and dance with any unescorted ladies if you will only be so kind as to present them to me." His approach was sweet, his voice soft.

"I'm sorry. I've met so many tonight, I don't recall your name."

"Of course you don't. May I?" he asked, pulling out the empty chair beside her.

She nodded her approval.

"You can't be expected to remember my name though I hope you haven't forgotten my face."

His flirtatious grin and anxious demeanor made Carolena giggle. This pleasant young man rattled on and soon Carolena relaxed, enjoying his witty remarks and sympathetic comments on the crème de la crème of this group of Paolo Alontti fans.

Returning to overhear the banter, Paolo stepped in. "Hey there, Wiley. Are you trying to play fast and loose with my hostess?" His expression clouded.

Carolena was surprised at the anger in his eyes, a look she'd come to recognize whenever Grey's name came up. "Paolo, please help me—"

He misunderstood her words to mean she felt threatened. Rage seared through his body, and everyone at the table noticed.

"—with his name, Paolo. Help me with his name. Tell me once again."

Still wary, Paolo supplied the information. "This is Mr. Wiley Jason, who has yet to answer my question."

She pictured a duel from one of her favorite books and almost laughed aloud that she could be the cause. She was flattered.

"I've no disagreeable designs on Miss Dunnigan, Signor. I was only trying to be sociable and asked her to point out any unescorted ladies I might partner."

Realizing he'd jumped to an incorrect conclusion, Paolo's glowering countenance disappeared. "Sure you were, Wiley. Let me be the one to make the introductions. I'll show you and your good looks off to Miss Peachie Pence over there. You see her, don't you? The lovely in the pink dress with the red flowers bunched at the hips. She's not talking to anyone at the moment. I'm certain she'd enjoy your company and your name on her dance card a time or two. If you'll excuse me once again, Carolena, I'll be back in a moment." He touched her bare shoulder declaring to any on-lookers she belonged to him and was off-limits.

With the shock at seeing Peachie again, Carolena missed the horrified expression on the face of poor Wiley at the prospect of dancing with such a strange woman. And had Wiley not been clamped by Paolo's arm, he would have had to fight Carolena for a safe haven behind the potted palm along the wall where each wanted to dash. Unfortunately, they were out in the open.

The egocentric sprong-head spied her former cabin mate and made a dash across the dance floor, a thing an unescorted woman should never do. Although it would be forward to ask, Carolena wondered what man, if any, Peachie had found to accompany her to this event.

"Why Carolena, dear. My lands! I'm so surprised, and pleased, and everything, to see you."

"Likewise," she lied, repulsed at Peachie's sour smell. Carolena concentrated on Peachie's hairstyle. This time the wiry wisps were pulled forward into a chignon of sorts that sat just above her widow's peak. Hundreds of curling coils protruded in all directions from her skull.

Looking down the bridge of her pointed nose, Peachie quizzed, "How did you come to be at this society function, Cary?"

Back at the table with Wiley, Paolo intervened, "Do you not understand that Miss Dunnigan is my hostess, Miss Pence? It was printed on your invitation."

"Paolo, darling!"

Her words were possessive as she thrust her face forward, intending to bestow a kiss on his lips. Quick to turn his head away, Paolo was thankful her pucker landed on his cheek instead.

Peachie continued, "Once I read your name, I dismissed the rest, and everything. After all, you're the reason I came here tonight, Paolo. To see you, of course, and to show-off my latest conquest. I think this fellow is the one, Paolo. I'm sorry for you, and everything, but he's stolen my heart." When the only comment was the upward roll of eyes by everyone within earshot, Peachie proceeded with her inane chatter. "Cary, you certainly do get around."

"Would you care to define your words more clearly, Madam?" Paolo challenged.

"Only that I first met her aboard the *Coral Crown*. Oh, she had little time for me. She was otherwise occupied, and everything. No dillydallying for her, be it business or pleasure."

Carolena should have been offended. Instead, "Please, Mr. Jason, would you accompany Miss Pence to the dance floor? According to my program, I believe the next number will be a polka."

Wiley held out his hand.

"Thank you, dearie." Peachie tossed a nearly imperceptible nod his way, her tone superior.

"My escort is about. He's only now stepped away for a smoke. Well all right, Mr. Jason. Just so you won't be disappointed and pout, I'll dance with you. Once my beau returns, remember, I'm his."

"Yes, ma'am."

"We'll see you around a little later, and everything, Paolo."

Carolena's sympathy went out to Wiley as Peachie pulled him into the prancing crowd already dancing. Paolo turned to her, and she calculated he was about to apologize for his guest. Carolena placed one gloved finger against his lips, and he understood it was unnecessary.

A sip or two more of champagne, and Carolena was refreshed, thrilled her heart was holding strong tonight. When Paolo took her hand, she stood and followed him. He wove a path through the dancers to the grand piano. They arrived as the final bars of the polka were played. The polite applause for the concluding song grew to a thunderous ovation, as celebrants realized they were in for a treat. The great maestro himself was going to perform. He directed Carolena to stand in the concave curve of the piano's frame where he might see her. The people stilled themselves as he took the bench.

With no fanfare, he spoke, "I call this *Carolena's Imaginings*."

Chapter 17

She heard the first three cords and recognized them as the rich, haunting melody he was playing that afternoon she'd met him in the theatre. It was as if he knew they were destined to meet and had composed this song in advance. It was more stirring than she'd remembered. She realized she was crying when tears dampened the silken skin of her chest. She was unaware of anyone in the room but Paolo. As the music climaxed, it reverberated through her body, and Paolo saw her trembling.

He publicly, yet privately, pantomimed the act of love to this woman before the eyes and ears of the guests. Women flushed and men were anxious to return home, or wherever their ardor took them, in hopes of quenching the carnal thirst raised in them, as well.

The final note lingered in the hushed room. For a time, no one moved. Then Paolo stood. He walked to Carolena and bowed over the hand she extended toward him. Her curtsy in response, her acceptance of his advance, shattered the quiet. The room broke into a mostly male tumult of approval and envy. The noise seemed unending until the first of twelve reverberating strikes to a gong was heard proclaiming the hour of midnight.

The lone drummer played a roll. Doors on either side of the main fireplace opened. Uniformed men in white aprons and tall bakers' hats marched forward, led by the chef in his black and white checkered trousers, white coat with the knotted buttons, and saucy red kerchief around his neck. The formal meal was delivered with the precision of a military drill to stations about the perimeter of the hall. Once it was laid out, the guests scurried like ants.

Carolena sank into her chair. Her personal wonder of this night would probably not end until dawn and, being realistic, she needed to limit the strain on her heart.

Two servers placed china plates piled high with delights in front of Carolena and Paolo. "It all looks so delicious. Is this chicken or lobster or crab salad?"

"Probably all three. I do know the one with the green flecks is chicken tarragon. It's my favorite."

She tasted. "Mmm. This one is lobster." Carolena was reminded of her mother's delight at cooking. It came to her how much Miss Ella, more than anyone, would appreciate the skill with which all this was prepared. Ha, Carolena thought. She doesn't deserve to be here!

While they supped, Paolo explained the intricacies of the German dance program. Carolena had heard of it and even seen it performed, yet had never been a participant. She felt a bit intimidated. "The German is always the last elaborate group of dances to end the ball. You and I will lead the group beginning with a waltz. Then, we'll split as you choose two gentlemen and I select two ladies. We newly paired couples will dance a *tour de valse*. By this time, many couples will be dancing this pattern. We'll do *la corde*, where a rope is stretched across the floor. The gentlemen must jump across it to reach their partners, trying not to trip as it's raised. Another dance will be *les masques*. The men wear masks of some grotesque beast or other. That way, each lady isn't sure who her partner is." He leaned in to her, "I'm hopeful some things are instinctual between certain persons." Grinning, he said, "The final dance will be the *Sir Roger de Coverley*." Paolo caught her scowl. "Take that worried look off your face, darling. It's nothing more than the *Virginia Reel!*"

Her laugh was spontaneous, and he was desperately anxious to kiss her enticing mouth. "The best part will be that in three of the dances we do, favors will be offered. They may be tiny bouquets, boutonnieres, and miniature flags or maybe bonbons, scarves, hat pins, fans, or tiny vials of perfume." He unexpectedly sounded cross. "I hope I haven't given too much away. I wanted you to be surprised."

"Oh no, Paolo," she soothed. "Your telling me about it all just makes it more exciting. The anticipation is wonderful."

"Alright then. After every few rounds of dancing, these gifts are to be presented to new partners, the idea being to eventually interchange all dancers and trinkets throughout the room. No one leaves empty-handed."

"It sounds enchanting. I hope I can keep up."

"Don't fret, my beauty. Just look around and do what everyone else is doing."

"One thing is for sure. This whole affair is a milestone in my social life. Up to this point, I've never cared for frivolous things like receptions and balls. You've changed everything. I will tell anyone within earshot of the glory of it all. I can promise you that."

"Carolena. Oh, Carolena." The more times Peachie spoke her name, the shriller her voice became. Paolo was unsuccessfully trying not to cringe, and Carolena had to smile at his suffering.

"I've finally located my escort! I should have known. That man is simply too attractive for his my own good, and everything. He can't get a moment's peace. Why the way women fawn over him, it would be like me visiting a prison. The men would be drooling so, I'd have to wear waders! Come alone, Cary. You must see my companion."

Paolo was about to tell Peachie to be patient and wait until they had finished eating.

Sensing this, Peachie pleaded. "Oh, Paolo. It'll just take a moment or so. Next to you, this man is the best catch here."

Peachie's aroma remained, driving away the appetite of all those within smelling range. Carolena would be doing everyone a favor if she obliged. Besides, if Carolena knew one thing, it was that Peachie was determined.

"Very well, Peachie. I'll just be a short while, Paolo."

Accepting her decision grudgingly, he said, "Don't be long. We've plenty of dancing to do before the German."

Peachie grasped Carolena's arm in hers and yanked her forward. Trying to keep up in a ball gown was somewhat of a trial. "Peachie. Do slow down. I fear I'll trip on my skirts."

"Just lift them higher, Cary, like I do. I'm anxious for you to meet him."

Down the steps and into the front foyer they scrambled. "Wait here while I have a servant fetch him."

Left alone, Carolena was somewhat uncomfortable. She returned a smile to querying gazes, feigning composure that wasn't there. Shifting her weight from left to right, her mind wandered. She was surprised how perfectly fitted her new shoes were to her feet. The lobster salad was so good, she wanted more. After too many minutes had passed, Carolena made the decision to return to Paolo. Obviously, some complication had arisen with Peachie's presentation of her escort. Climbing the stairs back to the ballroom, Carolena smelled that unappealing aroma.

"You there," was shouted in her ear. "I've found him."

Thinking it rude to be addressed as "you," Carolena considered the source and pursed her lips. Spinning on the carpeted step, she heard the tear of fabric as the hem of her dress gave way to the ungainly gunboats standing on her train!

"Oh dear." Peachie was smiling cruelly. "Have I torn your gown?"

Carolena looked back over her shoulder at the brocade fabric beneath Peachie's shoes. She twisted to see the rear of her skirt. Her petticoat was showing! A gaping chunk, some two feet in diameter, had been ripped off the border!

"Peachie! How could you be so careless?"

"Why, Cary," she innocently said, still wearing a wide lopsided grin. "You act like I did it on purpose. You should apologize to me."

"What? Me apologize for you ripping my gown? It's only because I don't want to embarrass Paolo that I don't push you down the stairs and right out the door!"

A crowd was gathering.

"You are the most vile creature I have yet to meet. You and your *and everything.*"

Carolena wasn't surprised when Peachie turned-tail and left. Actually, she was glad because her own words were fast becoming out of control. She looked about and found herself the center of attention. Doing the only thing she could, she scooped the torn fabric, thinking to head in the direction of the nearest powder room. The attendant on duty would have a needle and thread. Her expression was as pleasant as she could muster since her spirit was so furious. Again, she heard that loathsome voice.

"Here he is!"

Carolena whirled around. She couldn't speak as she gazed in stunned disbelief.

"Well, what do you think of my catch, dear Cary? Why do you look surprised? I told you he was a good-looking thing. What's the matter with you? Don't you recognize your own father?"

The shock of the situation compressed the image of Miss Ella with Uncle Clabe into a tiny ball of nothing. This couldn't be! Never in time could this person replace her mother. There had to be some other explanation. Pray God, there had to be.

Carolena forgot where she was. The orchestra played on. She didn't hear them. The staircase grew crowded with more spectators. She didn't see them. Her focus was Michael Dunnigan and Peachie Pence. They looked like a tableau of a gentleman with his pet scarecrow.

"Father." Carolena spoke slowly. Why had she addressed him so? She always called him *Daddy*.

Michael, dressed formally and wearing a full beard, was weaving on his feet, unsuccessfully trying to free his arm from the clawing fingers of the woman beside him. "Daughter." When he spoke, his voice was strained, his words slightly slurred. He nodded in Carolena's direction.

Peachie just watched and enjoyed. She was caught up in the ecstasy of victory. Since meeting Miss High and Mighty Dunnigan on the *Coral Crown*, Peachie decided Carolena, like the rest of her family, she was sure, was conceited and haughty and self-important. So what, Peachie thought, if that girl's father owns the ship. So what, if she holds a powerful position in his firm. So what, if she designed ship's interiors. So what, if she were pretty. So what! So what! So what, and everything! Carolena has no business, no business ever, patronizing me. I may not have had the advantages the Dunnigans have, but I'm about to have all of Michael.

Carolena saw her father drain the glass in his hand and motion for another. She waited for him to say more. His face had reddened. Could it be from anger? What, in God's name, could he, of all people, be angry about? Containing her growing dread, "Father, I didn't know you were in Charleston. Are you traveling further up the coast?"

"If you must know, Carolena, Michael and I are on our way to New York." Peachie's words hurtled forth, leaving him no time to insert denial. "Yes. He loves to treat me and treat me often."

Carolena felt her stomach's contents lurch upwards, seeking escape. She swallowed back the bile with a painful gulp.

"We enjoy going to the theatre. Although the symphony is all right here, and everything, Paolo just doesn't compare to the talent up north. In fact, that's where I met your father. Didn't you realize he had such a love of music, and everything? Tsk, tsk. You really should have spent more time getting to know him instead of always having your head stuck in some stupid project. Yes, he's told me you're the bookworm in the family, and everything."

Michael tried to interrupt, but to no avail. Peachie would not be silenced.

"Too late for you. He's mine now, aren't you Mike."

Tears were flooding Carolena's eyes. Her heart hammered. She ignored it. Why was her father letting this woman say such things? Carolena had always believed she knew him well, almost as well as his wife did. She'd lived with the man for twenty-eight years, hadn't she?

"Are you going to stand silent?" Looking into Michael's bloodshot eyes, Carolena demanded an answer. "Defend yourself!"

"How can I," he whispered, his head hanging, "when she speaks the truth?"

Shocked to her innermost being, Carolena screamed at him. "You mean to tell me you've deserted your family? For this? Have you lost your senses?"

Carolena didn't notice the hush in the foyer. It meandered up the stairs and into the ballroom like a slithering serpent. The musicians had stilled mid-piece when Paolo and most of the patrons left the hall.

Paolo headed where the gathering was the thickest, parting the inquisitive with the authority of his demeanor. The stairway was filled with folk, yet he easily descended as the spectators plastered themselves against the wall, letting him pass.

"Allow me to answer for you, Mike, shall I?" Peachie beamed. "Your dear daddy told me how his wife neglected him. How she thinks herself capable of butting into his business, the business he began. Where she should be tending his children like I would, and everything, she fancies herself a partner in his firm. She's so caught up in the glory of power, why her poor neglected son has run off. And the rest of Mike's children," she peered at Carolena with eyes lancing accusation, "are trying to push him out of his firm, too. Breelan never consults him about promotion and you, Miss Carolena, have the audacity to produce blueprints of your own. Now, I ask you," Peachie shouted to the crowd, "after all he's done for his family, is it really a surprise a man of the physical magnificence and mental magnitude of Michael Dunnigan here, would seek comfort elsewhere, and everything?"

Carolena's words were low. "And just what do you expect to gain from all of this, Miss Pence? My mother will never divorce him."

"Maybe not." Peachie had thought of that. Did Carolena think her stupid? "He can disown his children, and kick them, and his wife, out of the business. Then together, he and I will manage the profits from the Dunnigan passenger line! You see, I make him happy."

Carolena watched her father stand silent as if a spectator at his own funeral. "Sir," she said to the man who cuddled her when she skinned her elbows, who let her eat the yoke from his fried eggs, leaving him only the slimy remains of the white, who always brought her a tiny surprise when she was sick, the man she had admired for her entire existence. "Do you let this woman speak for you?"

His only reply was a paling of his ruddy cheeks.

"I ask you again, Father. Are her vile words true?"

He said nothing.

Carolena screamed at him. "Answer me, damn you! Answer me!"

His response was swift this time. Looking directly into the eyes of his golden child, his knees buckled, and he collapsed onto the floor.

"Mike, Mike!" shouted Peachie, her voice panicked.

Paolo wanted to help as Gwenie gave him a scowl signaling he should stay out of it. Disregarding her warning, he shouted for a doctor. Footsteps were heard running. As a physician knelt over the man prostrate on the black and white marble floor, Peachie cried, her shoulders heaving.

"What's the matter with his daughter?" Carolena heard a woman in white whisper. "She should be down there with the poor man. She's as cold as Nellie's titties, that girl is."

"Doctor, Doctor? Please say he'll be alright, and everything." Grabbing hold of the physician's lapels, Peachie screeched, "Tell me he's not dead!"

Prying her off him, "No. He's still alive. We need to get him out of here though. Someone, please. We need help here."

Paolo snapped his fingers in the direction of the staff, and uniformed servants appeared. "Do as the doctor orders."

Peachie was all homely smiles again.

Carolena spoke. "Afraid for a moment you'd lost your meal ticket, Peachie-girl?"

With a humph, Peachie followed the men carrying Michael.

"Oh, Peachie, by-the-by," Carolena raised her voice to be certain she was heard. "Just so you're alert to the facts …"

Peachie couldn't help herself. She stopped dead.

Carolena gave an acidic laugh. "Apparently, my father forgot to inform you during your late-night dalliances that we haven't a cent! That's right. That's what I said. The Dunnigan fortune is gone!"

At the unexpected announcement, Peachie's eyes began to lose their green cast and turn a queer shade of yellow.

It was Carolena's chance now. No one could stop her if they tried. "You've wasted precious gold-digging time on a penniless old man? What? You don't believe me? Check around. I don't think it will take too much effort to confirm that the D in Dunnigan stands for destitute!" Carolena mounted the stairs regally, disregarding her torn skirts and exposed petticoat, her family's poverty, her infirm father, and even Paolo. She had long passed the point where her own words and actions seemed inappropriate and even bizarre.

Peachie screeched, "Liar! You're a liar! Michael wouldn't use me like that, and everything. He loves me! There has to be a fortune! There's got to be!"

The onlookers could only stare at the madness they witnessed.

A feeble smile crossed Carolena's lips as she thought how Peachie's ghastly dress would be destroyed before the next sunrise for, certainly, tonight would be classified as a disappointment to her. After that, Carolena saw no more and heard no more because she wanted no more. No more of Peachie, no more of her father, no more of this glamorous ball, no more.

A woman with nary a face wrinkle and wearing beaded black blocked her path. When she spoke, her complexion looked to be crawling with worms of skin. "I've been given the privilege of informing you our husbands, Mr. Liner and Mr. Lewis, will have no need of your services, boat drawing services, I mean. We wouldn't trust our lives in a vessel of your construction if the caliber of your workmanship is in any way similar to the caliber of your personal life."

Mr. Liner looked embarrassed and shrugged his shoulders at his wife's declaration.

Paolo was beside Carolena in time to hear the last of the nasty words. He stilled the older woman with a glare.

Her heart! Carolena pressed her right hand to her chest in panic. Her heart was pounding with the speed of hummingbird wings, but it *was* pounding. She wondered what trauma would finally take hold of the beating muscle to still it. How much more despair could it tolerate in its weakened condition?

"Carolena?" Paolo asked.

The voice was kind and refreshing, reminding her of the cool of an ice cream on one of those Florida days when it's so hot it almost hurts your lungs to take in the air. She walked briskly as if she had a particular destination. She didn't know where she was going. She passed staring faces and kept walking. Paolo followed two steps behind. She wandered to another hall altogether, reaching an intersection of sorts. The common way to the left seemed deserted. She welcomed the privacy it offered, yet she went the other way, lured by the music. It was unlike Paolo's music. There were only violins playing. A door was half-open. She entered the room aglow with candles. It was a wedding celebration. Oak molding framed walls of silver brocade. The table linens were white and the flowers were shades of pink but she didn't notice any of that now.

No one questioned her when she found an empty chair and seated herself because Paolo was recognized and waved anyone away who might give challenge.

He pulled out a chair beside her. She said nothing. He didn't know if she realized his presence. It didn't matter. He was with her to keep her safe. She'd been through so much. If she'd let him, he would make it all right for her. He wouldn't bear her suffering if it were in his power to help.

She wrapped her arms around herself, rocking back and forth. Her head fell to her chest. She was in shock. Paolo snapped his fingers, whispered to an answering servant and in fast minutes, their wraps were at the ready. She didn't resist when he lifted her arm, gently indicating she should stand. His preference was to carry her. He did not for if he chose the wrong door and encountered another crowd, it would cause more questions, more trouble. He, too, was uncertain where the exit was. He randomly chose and was pleased to discover a back staircase. His arm around her waist to catch her if necessary, they descended. The first door they came to was locked. He tried others until he found one that opened onto the street. He impatiently hailed a cab.

He felt Carolena's shivers and covered her with his frock coat. Inside the semi-warmth of the cab, her head lay against his shoulder. At his apartment building, the doorman knew not to offer any assistance as Paolo carried his burden once again. This time Edward had waited up. Dismissing him gruffly after brief instruction, the conductor found Carolena's room down the dark hallway. He laid her on the bed and covered her with two blankets from the armoire.

Still chilled from the trip home, Paolo went to his dining room and gulped a double shot of Crimson Cordial. He returned to Carolena, closing her door behind him. He poked at the fire he'd ordered Edward to light. Paolo had been hopeful of her return to this room tonight. He only wished circumstances had been happier. She required his care. Again. He never tired of giving her whatever she needed. He lifted the blankets and touched her shoulder. Her satin skin was cool to his warm touch. Rolling her on her side, he loosened the hooks of her bodice and skirt and removed both. Doing the same with her petticoats, stockings and corset, he left her there garbed only in her chemise. Tempting. She was so tempting and so asleep. He managed to maneuver her between the soft sheets and covers without awakening her. One kiss on her cheek, and he took himself out of the room. Any longer and he'd have surely warmed them both from the kindled flame each would stoke in the body of the other.

Chapter 18

A scream! Then another! Paolo shook his head once to get his bearings and flew from his bed. Throwing on his paisley robe, he ran to Carolena's room.

Carolena was standing by the window, her blank eyes staring into the black night. The screaming ceased, replaced by a kind of chatter. "I've waited so long. Why don't you want me? Don't touch her! He's wrong! I am strong! Grammy? Mama? Daddy? Fire! Fire!"

Paolo grasped her shoulders in order to guide her to the bed. His touch set off another kind of panic in her. She flailed her arms, her hands in fists. His left cheekbone caught a blow and then another, until he was able to grab her flying wrists. She struggled against him while he pinned her arms to her sides. He whispered in her ear to calm her. It did no good. Half dragging, half carrying her, they landed on the bed. He didn't know why, but that stopped her struggles.

The moon escaped the clouds, and its light streamed through the wide windows. It bounced from the brass catch on the wardrobe, to the vanity mirror and was thrown across the bed. There in the dark, Carolena seemed spotlighted on center stage. Paolo felt they were in an unfolding drama of turmoil and passion, and he was the director of the play.

"Darling, come awake."

She was lying on her back. The bed felt warm and soft, and there was a comforting voice calling her. She wanted to roll to her side, curl into a ball and sleep. She was so tired. The voice still called. Reluctantly, she did its bidding. Seeing a shape against the window's backdrop of falling snow and twinkling stars, she knew her prayers had been answered. Finally, finally, after so much waiting and wanting, he was here, close to her, stroking her brow, kissing her cheek.

Her smile was brilliant. Nibbling her throat, he gently raked the softness of her earlobe with his teeth. She giggled in response, and he sensed her sudden playful mood.

Her hands captured his strong neck. Then she turned her head, her mouth seeking his. It was a sweet kiss at first. Sweet was not what she wanted. Not now. She wanted a man's deep, lusting assault kind of kiss, and that was just what he was giving. She received it willingly, advancing into the depths of desire.

"Oh, Carolena."

Still enjoying the kiss, she pushed him from her, breaking their bond. In the shadows from the moonlight, she studied the man in her bed. She reached for his face and gently outlined his features with her fingertips. As she touched his left cheek, he flinched involuntarily. His movement was enough to awaken her completely. This was not Grey. This was Paolo! How could she have confused the two? Here was a good and decent man, making love to her and the entire time, she was thinking, no, wishing, it were Grey.

He rolled off her as she pushed at him. Sitting up, she stroked his hair, exposing his handsome face. Ever so delicately, she blew on his bruised cheek and then laid her soft lips to it. He took this to be teasing him and couldn't endure it. He held her jaw and again captured her lips with his. The weight of his body laid her back upon the bed. He was atop her. Sometime, somehow, he had removed his robe, leaving him dressed only in his silk pajama pants.

His body was sleek in the charcoal light. She saw him and was unafraid. This was a fine man, an attractive man, a wealthy man, a gentle man. What more could a woman want?

Her heart screamed another man's name, but her brain suppressed it. She would not, she told herself, she would not be settling for second best with Paolo. If Grey didn't feel the way she wanted him to, she would have to accept that truth. She couldn't afford to wait for him forever because she didn't know how long her forever would last. What an idiot you are, Carolena Dunnigan. If the man you want doesn't appreciate you, he doesn't deserve you. To hell with Grey McKenna!

***

"Grey," Miss Ella whispered as she gently shook the thick shoulder of the sleeping sailor on Coe's sofa. So concerned for Carolena, he'd given up the luxury of a posh hotel a block away.

Due to his military experience, Grey was always quick to awaken. But his dreams were disturbing tonight and left him in a foul mood. He came up swinging!

Miss Ella protected her face with crossed arms. Recognizing whom he'd almost struck, he was on his feet, apologizing.

"Never mind that." Her soft voice did little to hide her grave concern. "I can't let another second pass. We have to get to that ball. If we wait any longer, it may be too late."

"Too late for what, ma'am?"

"Carolena. The way she hates me, the way she said she wouldn't return to this house so long as I'm here." She paused, embarrassed. "I'm afraid she'll give herself to this musician."

Grey's stomach knotted. He'd guessed as much. That was why he'd drugged himself to sleep with Aunt Coe's sherry. He'd warned Carolena to be careful, and she'd laughed in his face. If that was what she wanted, was it his business, really? Now here was her mother asking him to butt in. He couldn't very well refuse Miss Ella.

"Coe told me how Carolena stayed with that man when she was sick. How she talks incessantly of him. We all know what lengths that girl will go to when she's determined to have her way. We have to stop this if we can. Please Grey, help me."

In less than five minutes, they were bundled and harnessing Fries' horse to his buggy. Although the snow no longer flew, a cold wind was coming off the ocean. Grey put his arm around his friend and pulled her close to warm her. She smiled dimly up at him. Nothing more was discussed on their trip to Fleur de la Grace. He would leave it all up to Miss Ella. She would somehow convince her child to come home with them or at least he prayed she would.

At their destination, Grey handed her down as they caught the strains of lively music from inside.

"I hope they let us in, dressed as we are and without invitation."

Grey tossed it off, saying simply, "We'll get in."

The door opened before Grey could reach for the latch. He was greeted by a stern man in uniform.

"May I be of assistance, sir?" He was as tall as Grey and looked down suspiciously on Miss Ella.

"You give one more discourteous glance to this lovely lady, and I'll assist you into the street! Understood?"

Comprehending the sincerity of the threat, the doorman nodded and allowed them entrance.

"Good. Just tell us where Miss Dunnigan is."

Duty was so ingrained in the doorman, he hesitated until his brain sounded a warning. Quickly, he said, "She may have left by now. That is--I don't know where she is. There was a bit of a scene. She fled up the stairs and that's the last any of us has seen of her."

"Did she and Alontti have a fight?" Grey asked, hoping it was so.

"Not that I'm aware of. I only came on shift thirty minutes ago. I've yet to hear the entire story."

Grey took one step closer. The doorman lost all his composure. "Honest, mister. I don't know anymore than that."

"Thanks," and Grey flipped him a silver coin for his trouble.

Together, Miss Ella and Grey scoured the building. A curious few wondered at the oddly dressed couple amongst them while most were past caring. Again and again, they asked the question of guests and staff. Had anyone seen Carolena Dunnigan or Paolo Alontti of late? The answer was the same. Discouraged, they concluded Carolena had gone to Alontti's apartment.

Grey was no stranger in Paolo's apartment building. He nodded greetings to the night watchman who let him inside, glad to see a friendly face at so late an hour. Up, up, the elevator took them and in seconds, they were standing at the front door of Maestro Alontti.

Raising his arm to lift the knocker, he stopped as Miss Ella caught his sleeve. "If we warn them, Grey, and they're doing something they ought not, they'll only deny it. Ugly or not, I want to know the truth."

"As you wish." He guessed the front door might be unlocked in this well secured building. He was correct. The parlor was dark. He knew

Carolena's room was off to the left, so he led the way, only to be interrupted by a sleepy Edward.

"Mr. McKenna, what on earth are you doing here and at so late an hour? I'm ashamed for you to see me in my nightdress!"

Whispering, Grey answered, "Forget it, Eddie. Go to your room and let us be. We've got some investigating to do. If all is in order, we'll cause no disturbance."

"But Mr. McKenna ..."

Grey placed his hand on a bony shoulder. "Go to bed, man. Don't involve yourself. You didn't hear a thing."

Those simple words seemed a sensible enough solution to Edward. He was gone and under his covers posthaste.

Carolena's bedroom door let out a tiny squeak as Grey slowly exerted pressure against it.

The man within spoke caressing words. "Carolena. Carolena. I'm happy again."

As the door's opening widened, so did the squeal of its hinges. Paolo heard and sprang up, rolling from Carolena. "Who is that? Who's there?" he shouted. "Edward, consider yourself unemployed! How dare you enter a bedroom without knocking?" The half-naked man found his dressing gown and began pulling it on in time to witness not one, but two people enter the room.

Grey and Miss Ella were too late. It was still dark, but with the assistance of the moonlight, they could see across the room to the woman each cherished in their own way. Finding Carolena compromised, what could they do? Drag her out by her hair?

Grey clenched his teeth. His fisted hands wanted to beat something, no, someone.

Miss Ella grabbed his arm for support.

Carolena screamed as she pulled the covers to her chin.

Miss Ella rushed to the bed. "Darling, it's your mother and Grey. Shhh, sweetsie. No need for talk. It'll be fine. We'll—"

Carolena felt like a rat caught in a trap! "No need for talk? What are you two doing in Paolo's apartment?"

Her pompous indignation tipped the scales. Grey blind-sided Paolo with a right cross and knocked him to the floor.

"Are you crazy?" Carolena yowled as she scrambled from the bed, wrapping herself in the rumpled yellow comforter.

Under other circumstances, Grey would have turned his eyes from her near nakedness. She was his friend. God no, she was more than that. Those innocent days were past. Unpleasant as this situation was, the thought of her wound only in a blanket, titillated him much more than he wanted to admit.

Kneeling, she lifted Paolo's head and rested it on her lap. "Look what you've done, you lumbering idiot! Do you wonder at my behavior with this man? Well, don't. I can assure you, I come by it quite naturally. It's in my blood." She glared at her mother. "Don't stand there!" she ordered Grey. "Light the lamp on the vanity so I can see what damage you've done to his beautiful face."

As the light flooded the room, so did the screams of Miss Ella. Her legs wouldn't hold her weight, and she fell to the floor.

Grey rushed to her. "How hard this has to be for you, to see your daughter sell her soul to the likes of this piano playing swine, Miss Ella. I'm so sorry."

Carolena had no sympathy. "Who do you think you're fooling with this faint of heart act, Mother? Besides Grey, I mean." Still rocking Paolo and stroking his forehead, "Hey Grey," Carolena mocked, "Did my dear mother ever enlighten you to the fact that she and my old Uncle Clabe have been--at it?"

His eyes still on Miss Ella, his back to Carolena, he snarled in disgust. "You'll regret the day you told such lies about this good woman, little girl."

"Lies? Not this time. Go on. Tell him, Mother. How Father had been neglecting you. Oh, and by the way, Mother, you may be justified after all. You'll never guess who Michael Dunnigan, your supposed beloved husband, brought to the ball tonight." She crooked her neck, looking around Grey to see her mother's pale face scowl. "Aha. That's right. Tonight, he was all turned out for Charleston society in the very evening clothes he's always grousing about wearing with you. He was with a Miss Peachie Pence. Frankly, I find her completely repulsive, but then I'm not Father. She must possess some hidden charm because he allowed her to hang all over him."

"How could you tell your mother such a thing? She never needed to know that."

"You don't sound surprised about my father, Grey. Could it be you've known all along? Was Father on the same trip to Charleston I was? Was he drunk and disorderly? Is that the unpleasant business you had to take care of when you abandoned me on deck that night?"

"I didn't know the awful part about him seeing Peachie. What good does it do anyone knowing, Carolena?"

"You lied to me all this time!"

"If I didn't tell you about your father's antics, it was to spare you. Nothing more. But you sure as bloody hell give a man good reason to keep things to himself. You can't control your mouth. You wield the truth like some deadly weapon. Do you feel better having tormented your poor mother with that story?"

"She deserves to suffer for her betrayal. My father and mother both need to pay for what they've done! They're bad people!"

Grey advanced on her and raised his hand.

"No, Grey! Don't hurt my girl," bawled Miss Ella.

Not the defiant look on Carolena's upturned face nor the wail from her mother would deter him. Nothing would stop him from striking her.

Grey's eyes snapped a glance at the man in her arms. This was the first time he'd seen Paolo Alontti. He stared hard at the face with the bruised cheek as his open palm fell slowly to his side. Did he know this man? No. It was not possible. It had been years, so many years.

Miss Ella watched Grey's hand and along with it, her head and body dropped down in relief.

Paolo stirred. Opening his eyes, he found Carolena's smile. He reached to touch her lips and caught the sight of a tall figure towering over them, his face in the shadows. He remembered coming to her room and that was all. Here he was prostrate on her bedroom floor. He attempted to ask what had happened when he felt the ache in his head. Had he been struck?

Raising himself, Paolo stood with Carolena at his elbow. He surveyed the rest of the room to ascertain how much of a struggle there'd been. It was then he saw a small woman, limp on the floor. His thoughts fuzzy, he said, "Carolena, what goes on here? Who are these people? What in God's name happened?"

"Let me enlighten you, Paolo. This is your home after all. May I present Grey McKenna, the man who accosted you."

Paolo stiffened … then laughed softly. "Always good for a sucker punch, weren't you, Grey?"

Flabbergasted, Carolena spoke. "You two know each other?"

Paolo's mood reversed itself completely. "Yes, we do, sweet thing." With a strange calmness to his voice, he said, "You see, Grey is my brother."

Chapter 19

Carolena couldn't believe it. "Your brother? Grey, you lied to me. Again!" she accused. "You told me all your family was dead!"

The truth was obvious from his astounded expression. "I thought they were, Cary. I honestly thought they were."

"Well then, this is a miracle! Shouldn't you two hug or something?"

"You're still such a child, my pet."

She didn't appreciate Paolo's talking down to her. He embarrassed her. He placed his hand on her bare shoulder and for the first time, his touch made her uncomfortable.

Although absurd at this point, he put on his robe for decency's sake. "Don't you know the last thing Grey wants to do is hug me, even if I am his long-lost brother? Why would he ever want to embrace the man who sleeps with the woman he loves?"

Carolena's head snapped from Paolo to Grey. Grey replied with a grizzly glare. Sadly for her, Paolo was wrong. Grey didn't love her. Still, she realized he hadn't denied it, at least, not yet.

Cold and aware of her meager covering, Carolena hauled the blanket higher, concealing her exposed shoulders and at the same time, purposely knocking off Paolo's hand.

A soft sob came from the woman still on the floor. Grey rushed to her, again. "I'm sorry, Miss Ella. Here, let me take you to your sister's. We'll all talk later."

"Ella? Ella?" Paolo said. "Ella, it's me. It's Grant!"

Supporting herself on stiffened arms, Miss Ella remained on the floor. Raising only her eyes, she looked at the man who was Grant. From her position and twisted face, she presented the picture of a wild animal. Carolena had never seen her mother, or anyone for that matter, look so savage. Her heart raced, but she didn't notice because she was desperately afraid of what was coming.

"So Grey is your brother after all. I suspected as much when I heard the name and he told me he was from Johnstown. I only hoped his supposed dead brother wasn't you. Grey is kind, not cruel."

"Don't say that, Ella. I'm not cruel. I've wanted to go to you again and again over the years." Paolo sounded like a small boy pleading for forgiveness. "You'll never realize how often your image has crossed my mind. I've followed your life closely, El. Close enough to know you married another and had a family. I was miserable that you loved Michael more than me, but I consoled myself that you were happy. I adored you too much to come between you and your husband. I am aware, too, of the troubles you've recently endured. Let me help you. I'm well fixed. After all this time, maybe there's hope left for us."

Ella cut his words off with a hiss. Lifting her head, she spoke slowly, her register low. "You abandoned me, Grant. When I needed you more than I've needed anyone in my life, you were gone. And my circumstances caused me to--abandon my child." Sobs resonated from the deep well of her soul.

Paolo covered his face with his hands and his answer, although muffled, was still audible. "I understand that now, Ella. But before God, I didn't know then we had a baby. I didn't find out until the last few years."

"You let me think you were dead. Why did you do that? Fortunately, I found a kind man who would marry a woman with a child, his only condition being I would not call that child his. I needed him to support her because when I told my father and mother of my situation, they couldn't forgive my low morals. I went to New York to live with Coe until the baby was born. I lied to my parents, telling them the child had died at birth. They agreed it was God's punishment on me. We never spoke another word about it."

"Mama, what are you saying? Are you telling me I've an older sister somewhere?"

"Yes, Carolena. That's exactly what I'm saying."

"Who raised her? Where does she live? Tell me, Mama! Please, tell me. There's a photograph of a little girl on Aunt Coe's mantle. It looks like me, but the girl in the picture has darker hair, and I don't remember that picture being made."

"Yes, I have that very one or did have until the fire. Most everyone does think it's you, Carolena. Jack Patrick, Breelan, and--Ellissa took after me and have darker hair. You and Marie are like your father and turned out fair."

"Is that her name? Ellissa?"

"Yes." Miss Ella changed her position. She sat on the floor and leaned on her left hand, waving off Grey who wanted to help her up. Her words were coherent but rambling, as if she were telling a bedtime story, which she was, to her second-born child. "You see, your Aunt Coe and I are very close. In fact, she's the one who named the girl after me. She'd already married Fries by the time I was expecting the baby. She was told she could have no children. When she volunteered to adopt and raise Ellissa as her own, I knew the good Lord heard my prayers. At least, I could keep in touch with my little one and even see her occasionally when I visited Coe. Michael has never objected to any of that. Ellissa knows me only as a distant relative. We feared it all would unravel, so we were very careful. When you went to New York with your father that time you were a teenager, Coe arranged for Ellissa to be out of town, so you'd never find out. If ever any of our family visited Coe, Ellissa would go on a happy holiday of some sort. She never suspected a thing and neither did anyone else.

"After your grandfather, Pap, died, Coe and I toyed with the idea of telling Grammy of our deception. We thought the discovery of another granddaughter would cheer her spirits. We didn't do it though. If Ellissa learned the truth, she might think she was unwanted or unloved, that I had been ashamed of her when all along it was the society we live in that caused my parents to force me to give her away. My undisciplined act of loving resulted in years of secrets and lies. I tell you, I'd lie all over again to spare my child."

Miss Ella had more to tell, "Grammy may have suspected, but kept her own council. She never set foot outside Pennsylvania until she moved to Florida to be with us. Since Coe did all the traveling to see Mother, Ellissa was left to believe her grandparents were dead. When she was older and insistent upon seeing where Coe was raised, it was well after Gram was in Florida. While in Johnstown, Ellissa met and married a coal miner."

Grey wondered if she'd been so kind to him because she'd known his brother. No, of course not. She'd have been kind despite his brother. Grey's attention returned to Paolo, whose hangdog look should have withered his heart. It did not.

"That's where we met, Ella and I," muttered Paolo.

Miss Ella ignored him. "When Grammy's house came up for sale, Ellissa and Burt managed to buy it. She wanted to raise her child where her mother had grown up." Her speech held strong though tears saturated Miss Ella's bodice. "I regret Ellissa never knew she belonged to such a large family. So you see, it's all been our secret, Coe, Fries, your father's and mine. Until now."

"So that's what you meant when you forgave Grammy on her deathbed?" Carolena asked. "You forgave her for separating you from your baby."

"Yes, dear. She sincerely believed I had committed an unspeakable act by becoming pregnant without benefit of marriage." She paused. "If I've learned anything, I've learned that nothing my children could ever do to me or anyone, would drive me to forsake a one of them. Again."

A soft groan emanated from Paolo's lips. All eyes finally found his face, which seemed to have aged 20 years.

"If you can forgive your mother, Ella, then why not me?" he pleaded.

"Because if you loved me, you would have come for me in those early days. You would have let me know you were alive. If it had been before I married Michael, maybe we could have had that life we planned when we lay in each other's arms."

Carolena's heart sickened at the image.

"And if your abandonment wasn't enough, you had to take my Carolena from me. You filthy bastard!" Miss Ella lunged at him, and Grey caught her round the middle, holding her back. He, too, wanted to kill this familiar stranger.

But it was Carolena who flew at Paolo instead, slapping him once. A single falling tear was his only response. She slapped him again, harder. He offered no reaction as his hands remained at his sides. "You took advantage of my mother, the same as you have me, you useless loathsome blackguard!

164

How could you let me believe you loved me? How could you?" No one tried to stop her pummeling of him. When her energy was spent, she collapsed on the floor beside the bed.

"I did adore you. I still do. I'm just selfish."

"Just selfish? Is that all you call it?" quizzed an amazed Carolena.

"Back then, when I was seventeen and Ella was sixteen, I was so mixed up. I was miserable in that big house. My parents were dead. My little brother argued with me at every turn. He hated anything cultural I loved. I didn't know you were expecting a baby, Ella, so when war broke out, I did my duty and joined up without ever telling you. I was despondent away from you and took for granted you felt the same and would wait for me. I wrote you letters. Sad to say, by the time the mail reached you, if it ever did, you'd married Michael. After all the fighting and death I saw, the idea of my return to a home without you left me uncomforted.

"I decided to go to Europe to forget. I changed my name to Paolo Alontti because it had a more worldly flavor. I worked as a pianist and gradually gained recognition. As my fame grew, so did my longing for you, Ella. It was impossible to put you from my thoughts. How could I? I loved you, and it has remained so even to this moment."

Carolena was crying hard. There were so many reasons to cry.

"After some two decades, I returned to Johnstown. I had my secretary, Gwenie, arrange it when Uncle Jax was visiting his brother. My plan worked perfectly. If my living there didn't pan out, I saw no need to upset him with my presence. I introduced myself to the town as Maestro Alontti to keep my past hidden, and said I was interested in buying McKenna Hall. With my well-known professional name, it wasn't hard to gain access to the house even though it wasn't for sale. I stayed in a hotel and tried to get to know the people of the town. Memories flooded back. It was too much for me until I saw a girl at a community dance. She looked so much like you, Ella. Her hair was dark like yours; her eyes were bright as I remembered yours were. I made a point of asking and discovered her name was Ellissa. I told Gwenie to have her investigated. She determined Ellissa's mother was your married sister, Coe. Money will invade any privacy and so my detectives discovered Coe was baron. I drew the only conclusion I could. With a name like Ellissa, she was your child, Ella. And mine.

"Once that all sank in, I wanted to claim her until I realized it would upset the life you'd arranged for her. So, I left Johnstown again, afraid if I stayed, I'd weaken and divulge your secret."

Turning to his most recent conquest, Paolo spoke. "Yes, Carolena, you're right. I am a loathsome blackguard, but not in all things. For thirty years, I've wanted your mother, yet I didn't do anything to come between her and her husband. I understood her well enough to be certain she would remain loyal to Michael for a lifetime."

Carolena sneered softly, "Ha!"

"If I were ever to feel joy again," Paolo offered, "it would have to be at the expense of another. So be it. I decided to steal my pleasure, and the cost be damned. You see, the doctor told me I've little time left. It's no excuse, but my heart is no longer strong."

Carolena broke in, "Did the doctor tell you that on the night I collapsed in your dressing room? Tell me, Paolo. Tell me!"

He thought for a time. "Yes, I think we spoke of it on that occasion."

Carolena sprang from the floor, spinning round and round in delight like a mad woman.

"Cary," Grey yelled. "Cary, stop it!"

She realized how bizarre her behavior appeared and ceased, yet her elation had no bounds. She was going to live! She'd misunderstood. The doctor's diagnosis was meant for Paolo, not her!

"Go on, brother dear. Finish your wretched story."

Paolo continued, "If I couldn't have you in my life, Ella, I might have your daughter. I hoped she carried some of your personal traits. From the first, she was like you with your determination, your intensity, your seriousness, your passion. To my satisfaction." He smiled, "The resemblance was remarkable." His face sobered. "I'm a selfish bastard who tried to recapture his lost youth."

Deep in his throat, Grey gave a menacing growl, staring his brother down. "You sorry sonofabitch!" Grey was advancing, one slow step after another until he had Paolo by the lapels of his silken bathrobe, bunching, ripping them.

Paolo lost all appearance of power. The authority he naturally displayed abandoned him. Instead of defending or at least protecting himself from the blows his brother would throw, Paolo clutched at his chest. The pinch of his face told of the depth of agony he was feeling. Grey released him, and Paolo reached for the bedpost, just managing to collapse across the mattress.

Gasping for breath, he implored, "Help me! Ella? Carolena? Grey? Someone?"

Three pairs of eyes watched him struggle. No one did a thing to ease his suffering. The man before them, once loved, was scorned.

Weighing her surroundings, Carolena came to a cold, hard conclusion. To hell with the lot of them! As Paolo offered one great wheeze, his last, she was reminded of her own father who'd collapsed earlier in the foyer of Fleur de la Grace. "Oh, Mother." Her manner was again glacial. "You might be interested to learn your husband's whereabouts. Last I saw him, he was being carried out of the ball on a stretcher. I don't know any details."

"Oh my God!" Miss Ella's fear for Michael's health instantly cleared her clouded brainwaves. "I must get to the hospital. That has to be where he's been taken."

"Let me drive you."

"But your brother, Grey. He's …"

"He's dead. Let him rot for all I care. Come on!"

"Carolena, come with us. Hurry and dress, dear."

"I'm not going with you. Oh, and Grey, be sure and give Peachie a special hug for me if you see her by my father's bedside. Odds are you won't, now she knows he's broke."

Carolena smiled at their offended glances as they rushed past. Despite finding it necessary to pull a stocking from beneath the corpse on the bed, her bizarrely happy expression held strong. She put on her torn gown and the cape. She would go to Aunt Coe's house while her aunt and uncle were still asleep, pack her things, and get to the train station. After bartering her beautiful wrap for a ticket, she'd be off to Pennsylvania before anyone could stop her! She was on a quest to find her new sister!

***

The next morning Edward discovered his master's body. *Cause of death: Infirm heart* is what the doctor would later write on the official certificate. The butler wondered unashamedly if Maestro Alontti had died in the saddle of love, so to speak. He also wondered if he was left anything in the will.

Chapter 20

The journey was slow, or at least it seemed so to Carolena as the train carried her north. She wished she were the only passenger. The others were an annoyance.

Her mind was swamped by all the deceptions, all the sin. How had her life come to this? More particularly, why? Why had God let it? He'd given her a second chance with good health, yet what had she to live for? A man she adored had used her. Her own mother had built a lifetime on lies. Now her father, who had taught the importance of family, was a fraud and as selfish as the woman he'd married! I have no one, Carolena thought, no one to stand by me.

The faces of her brother and sisters materialized inside her imagination. They were the innocents. Each one of them. By all that's holy, they would remain so if she had her way.

"Good day, miss." She gave no answer, so her new seatmate continued. "Where ya headed?" Still not answering, she stared blindly out the window unaware of the passing fields. "If I'm bothering—"

"Bothering me? Yes, I would have to say that is exactly what you're doing." She was rude, and she didn't care. What right had he to accost her like this? She'd call the porter if he didn't return to his own seat.

"Good to hear you've got a voice." He felt compelled to add, "Even if it is a bit on the harsh side."

That caused Carolena to suck in her breath and choke on her own saliva, hacking and barking. People left their seats in an attempt to offer assistance.

"Give her a spoonful of sugar. That'll help," called a gentle lady with chubby rosy cheeks.

"That's for hiccups, Gran," explained her teenage companion with the same cheeks.

"Oops," chuckled the grandmother. "I do get confused now and again, don't I?" She patted the skirts of her younger relative, forgetting about the stranger still choking.

The porter scurried forward with a cup of water, while the man who had seated himself beside Carolena clapped her on the back. Wiping the perspiration from her upper lip with a handkerchief retrieved from inside her cuff, she looked up to see concerned eyes. Her first reaction was anger! How dare they make a spectacle of her? "If you each pay a penny, I'll do my utmost to reenact my near-fatal performance!"

Her acidic words dismayed the kind hearted. They returned to their seats.

"What an awful creature that woman is!"

"We were only trying to help her."

"Now Henrietta, why do you suppose a pretty lady like that is so bitter and mad at the world?"

Astonished, Carolena didn't realize she was speaking. "They act like I insulted them! They were the ones prying!"

Her seatmate had heard some sad tales. But he would be hard pressed to accept any excuse for her behavior. "How old are you?" he asked.

"I beg your pardon? No gentleman asks the age of a lady. You have no manners, you nasty piece of trash!" Without hesitation, she hollered, "Porter! Porter!"

A different porter appeared this time. A heavy-set black man wearing a white jacket labored over to her as quickly as his stiff knees allowed. "Yes, 'um?"

"See that this man is moved somewhere else. And at once!"

"But—"

"Must everything be an argument? Do it now!"

The man in black rose. "It's alright, Johnny." He touched the stooped shoulder of the old fellow. "I'm doing little good here. Maybe later, huh?"

The porter smiled and nodded in agreement.

"What? There had better not be a later where you're concerned, mister!"

His response was a tip of his hat in her direction.

The other passengers listened. They couldn't help themselves since Carolena had raised her voice. Returning her stare to the darkening landscape, she didn't notice their shaking heads and clicking tongues. She just wanted to get to Johnstown.

***

Through restless dozing, Carolena remembered hearing they were in Philadelphia, then Reading, then Harrisburg. She knew Harrisburg meant they were getting close to the middle of Pennsylvania, so she paid attention as each new destination was reached. Altoona, Cresson, Lilly, South Fork, Mineral Point, East Conemaugh, Wood Vale, Johnstown. Johnstown, Pennsylvania. For a split second, anxiety overtook her, and she contemplated staying on the train until she remembered the stop on her ticket was here. She hadn't the money to travel further.

Trying to bolster her courage, she asked herself, what there was to be fearful of. It's a small town. All I have to do is find someone who looks like my mother and introduce myself as her sister. The rest will be easy. She'll take me in as a long-lost relation, and all will be well.

That decided, Carolena picked up the bag containing her few clothes and many blueprints. She didn't want anything more from them, those awful people she'd left in Charleston. She'd make her way alone.

As she alighted the coach and entered the night, she noticed three other people also got off. They vanished, all having a stride of definite destination about them. Dismayed, she wished she had been a bit chattier on board. She might have been steered to a restaurant or room. "Well, just never mind," she said to herself. "It's too late to grouse about it now."

The two story brick Baltimore and Ohio Railroad station was much larger than she'd expected. It was nearly double the size of the tiny depot in Fernandina. Its door creaked eerily as Carolena closed it behind her. There was a ten-foot counter paralleling the right wall, behind which a fat man snored merrily. A gray sweater with a large snag in the upper right arm covered his limp-collared gray shirt.

She tiptoed past the only other people in the terminal, a young man and woman cuddled in the corner, holding hands, and cooing. In the center of the room was a low to the ground depot stove wearing a freshly applied coat of stove black. The fire inside reflected a welcoming amber on the pressed tin ceiling. Carolena stepped toward it to warm herself. She counted eight pine benches and five pine ladder-back chairs with shadings of red paint left on their well-worn seats and rungs. In the muted light cast from oil lamps, she could see this was a clean place. It felt safe. She hoped the whole town was the same.

As the train pulled out of the station, its whistle made her jump. Her last chance to leave was gone. With a strong sigh, Carolena excited the depot.

Her eyes adjusted quickly to the darkness. She was a little girl lost, so she concentrated on her knowledge of Johnstown. But what she'd heard had mostly been stories from Grammy, personal tales with little information about the place itself. Come to think of it, she had no idea of the name of the street on which her grandmother had lived. She had hoped to feel somewhat at home. She didn't. And it seemed there was no moon, or at least the clouds hid it. Then she remembered how the grade of her journey had increased once the tracks pivoted west at Philadelphia. She'd heard someone speak of the Allegheny Mountains. Maybe they were blocking out the moonlight. Maybe Johnstown lay in a sort of depression, surrounded by mountains!

Carolena could hear faint piano music and walked in its direction. The road was gooey with thick mud. Light from a few buildings showed scattered boards on which to step. Only a handful of people were out at this late hour. All ignored her, though a riderless horse escaping a black alley almost ran her down. Finding her breath, she passed Cally's Cookery to see the recently placed closed sign still swinging slightly from its hook. If only she hadn't dallied in the depot, she might have had a good meal. The last places open that would serve food were the taverns, and the Black Diamond Saloon lay dead ahead. When she pulled open one heavy wooden door, the music blasted her ears. The half dozen or so patrons in the bar were all men, except for one scrawny woman whose toothy smile reminded her of Mrs. Ickles back home. Right about now, Carolena would have gladly sat and listened to some hateful gossip because she was one good cook. The woman advancing on the newcomer was wearing a low-cut, tight-fitting bay leaf colored dress with a matching bow across her behind.

"Good evenin', majesty. Kinda late fer a lass like you ta be out."

"Yes, ma'am, it is. I've just arrived on the train, and I'm hungry. Starved, in fact. I hope you folks have something hot."

"Do I hear a Southern accent, miss?"

Carolena was not aware she carried any inflection in her speech. There was no sense denying it. "Yes, ma'am. I'm from Florida." She readied herself for some Yankee insult.

"How are ya? My name is Jamie Matters and I never afore met a person from clear down there. Is it true it never gits cold nor snows? And that the trees and the grass is green all year round? And that ya can grow oranges and grapefruits in your own front yard?"

Carolena smiled at all the questions, much relieved. "I'll tell you what, Miss Jamie Matters. If you'll kindly gather me some food, I'd be pleased to have you join me while I eat. I'll give you all the details about where I'm from."

"It's a deal, Miss?"

"Car —" She thought for a quick second and the result was, "Dunne. Cary Dunne." Why had she lied about her identity? And to use the name Cary, of all names. Instinct told her the meeting with her new sister might not go as smoothly as she been dreaming it would. Caution would be wise at this point. Ellissa could make a connection between her mother's relative, Ella Dunnigan, and Carolena Dunnigan. What if she began asking questions? When the truth was told, Carolena hoped to put the disturbing story in the most gentle of terms possible.

Jamie shouted to someone on the other side of the swinging kitchen door to hurry up with some beef and noodles. The new acquaintances each had a mission: to pick the brain of the other.

After cleaning her plate, Carolena dabbed the corners of her mouth with a rough napkin. Feeling much better, she wanted to question Jamie about Ellissa, yet it was late, and she was very tired.

"Whenever you're ready, Miss Cary, I'll tell ya how ta get ta Mrs. Learner's place. She'll be hateful for waking her up, but don't let her scare ya none. She does have her good moments. Besides, she needs her empty beds filled to keep food on the table fer that boy a hers that was all messed up in the mine explosion."

Jamie had explained how Carolena could work at the New North Needlework's uniform factory in exchange for a room at the factory's boarding house. It almost sounded like slave labor! Her daddy had never held slaves. Clover, back home, was a black man, yes. He was also a dear friend and had always gotten a salary until her family's recent financial embarrassment.

"Don't look so concerned. You'll get a fair day's wage for a fair day's work with a penny or two to spare. Lots of single women and widows work at the uniform shop," Jamie went on. "With all the coal mines in this part of the state, shirts, trousers, hats, aprons, gloves, and coveralls are always in demand. So, if ya want a job, here's one all laid out for ya. You need look no further."

Carolena asked, "If it's such a gainful situation, why don't you work there yourself?"

Jamie laughed. "I tried it once, but was offered this better proposition. My travelin' man from Pittsburgh, about seventy miles west a here, prefers me in colorful gowns instead of denim aprons, and willin', if you get my meanin', whenever he comes ta town." With a wink, she proudly added, "Daytime, nighttime and anywheres in between."

Not wanting to hear any more, Carolena thanked Jamie and left the saloon to follow the directions to Mrs. Learner's "Lean-to," as the girls who lived there called it.

It took only five minutes to find the place. Carolena's soft knocking produced no answer. Forming a fist, she pounded. This time she heard a woman's cursing coming from inside.

A large female, dressed in a heavy white nightgown pulled her shawl tightly around her, binding her wide shoulders. "Well, what is it? Come on. What do you want at this time of night?"

"Mrs. Learner?"

The woman grunted, "Happy Learner, to be exact."

The depth of the distinctive voice as well as the completely unexpected given name surprised Carolena. All she could think to say at first was, "Unusual."

"Are you saying I'm unusual?"

Rapidly composing herself, "Oh, no, ma'am. Not you. Your name."

"I have a funny name, do I?"

"No, ma'am." This was becoming silly. "No. You have an unusually lovely name. Are you called after someone in particular?"

"It's too cold to stand out here and tell you my life story, girl. Now, what do you want?"

"Yes, you're right, of course. I'm so sorry to disturb you. My name is Cary Dunne. I've just arrived in town, and Jamie Matters from the Black Diamond told me you might have a room to rent."

"Do you frequent saloons often?"

"No, ma'am." Carolena was offended, yet for once, smart enough to keep her reaction to herself. "Of course not. That was the only place I could eat at this hour."

"Hmmm. And did Miss Matters explain how you get the money to pay the rent?"

"Yes, ma'am, she did."

"Very well. Come inside. You're letting one hell of a draft into my house."

Carolena was about to close the door behind her when the wind caught it, causing it to slam.

"If you're gonna be so thoughtless as to go crashing about when others are trying to sleep then I'm afraid I don't need any of your kind."

"Forgive my clumsiness, ma'am. I'm awfully tired."

"One more chance is all I'll give ya. Follow me."

They climbed the stairs and walked to the end of the hallway. Before opening the door, Mrs. Learner whispered hoarsely. "Take the third bed on the wall under the windows. The water-closet will be the narrow door in the corner inside on the left." Catching Carolena's look of surprise, "Yes, we have a water closet. Johnstown may be isolated in the mountains, but we keep up with what's modern. I mean to tell you that just last January we put in a telephone exchange. It's a little pricey, so most of us use the telegraph. Still, we got a system all the same."

Carolena felt as if she should respond and said, "Good for you," hoping that it didn't sound condescending.

"The other girls will wake you up in the morning, and you best be quick about getting down for victuals if you want to get some. You'll have a long day ahead of you." Taking Carolena's empty hand, she raised it up close to the gas light that *sssssed* just above them. Inspecting the palm for calluses and finding none, Mrs. Learner shook her dustcap-covered head. "After I check on my boy, I'm going to try and go back to sleep myself. Good night to ya." She walked down the hall to the last door on the right and entered.

As Carolena and Mrs. Learner made their way to their respective beds, they both wondered the same thing: How long would the new girl last?

Chapter 21

An awful clanging invaded Carolena's dreams. She rolled to her other side, trying to relieve the ache in her back caused by the sagging mattress. Besides better bedding, she needed more sleep. The nasty bell stopped ringing when she began to hear in her dreams her father's funny wake-up song. It had been a daily ritual for his children. "Good morning. Good morning. Good goody-good, good morning. Good goody-good, good goody-good, good good, good goody-good ..."

A woman's lyrical voice seemed to join in at the precise moment needed to complete the piece. "Good morning."

Carolena heard the snap of window shades being rolled up. Someone was shaking her shoulder.

"You'd best get up and around. You won't get any breakfast nor catch the wagon to the mill unless you hurry. Come on, miss."

Carolena looked into the sweet face of a girl only a bit older than her sister, Marie. She smiled her thanks and watched the girl dash over to stand in line at the door of the water closet. The half-dozen women there stared at her, the stranger. They were probably talking about her as well, Carolena reckoned.

She noticed the now empty beds were made up tight, so she made hers as well. She always had a time getting all the wrinkles out of the sheets and blankets down home. With extra effort, she made sure there wasn't a one. She changed into the black dress she'd worn on the train, not knowing yet what kind of work she'd be doing or how dirty she'd get.

Finally, there was only one person waiting for the necessary. Grabbing the towel draped on her iron footboard, she hurried over to stand behind a tall woman with beautiful turquoise eyes who was studying her.

"How do you do? My name is Mildred Frame."

Taking the offered hand, Carolena introduced herself.

"I haven't seen you around town before. Did you just arrive?"

The only way to find Ellissa was to ask questions, and no one would freely give answers unless she was pleasant to them. This woman seemed harmless enough. "Yes, I did."

"Where have you come from?"

"Charleston."

"What brought you here? Looking for a husband, are you?"

Carolena must have appeared stunned by the odd question.

"Don't be embarrassed, Miss Dunne."

"Cary, please."

"That's what most of us are here for, Cary. There're so many fellas working the coal mines and the iron works in town, chances are even the homeliest of girls is likely to find a man. Of course, none of the men is too wealthy, but a poor man warmin' a bed is almost as good as a rich one.

Almost."

Mildred chuckled, and Carolena wondered why the women of Johnstown were so preoccupied with men. She'd had enough of the opposite sex for a good while. Grey came to mind. Grey was as bad as the rest.

"You're a quiet one, aren't you? Don't fret, Cary. The girls here are great. Most all are as friendly as you could want."

The water closet door opened and out stepped a black-haired women with mocha eyes and big hips. "Sorry I took so long this morning, Mildred. I've commenced my monthlies."

"I understand. Would you save me some biscuits and gravy though? Oh, and some for Cary Dunne, here. She's the new girl.'

"Sure enough. See you downstairs."

Talking through the door from inside the powder room, Mildred called, "That was Suzanne Wagner. Her husband was killed in the same blast that crippled Mrs. Learner's boy."

"Is that right?" Carolena listened to the chatter, glad that Johnstown was so amiable. Her Grammy would be proud of the place.

While Carolena snatched a few fast gulps of coffee in the dining hall, she looked at the tables and empty benches guessing they would accommodate three dozen or so.

"Come on, Cary," called Mildred. "The wagons are pullin' out!"

"Coming," she answered, grabbing a biscuit for later and donning Nora's cape. She was surprised at the size of the three buckboards, each pulled by six huge mules. They were full to the brim with the ladies she'd seen at breakfast who gabbed and laughed and offered her a hand aboard.

"Squeeze here between us and share my parasol, miss," someone offered.

Carolena did just that, thinking it can't be hard labor I'm going to because these women seem so carefree. I may have struck pay dirt to find room and board and a job so quickly. Since everyone seems nice, maybe they'll tell me where Ellissa is.

"What a glorious April day," said the girl with dark hair and dingy teeth. It's so balmy, I'm going to have to unbutton my coat."

"Johnstown sure is booming," said Mildred.

Carolena joined in. "From all the folks dashing about, I have to agree."

"You talk fancy, Cary. Have you had lots of schooling?" Mildred asked and several of the girls looked interested.

Carolena made light of the compliment. "I don't know about talking fancy. I did have some very strict teachers growing up."

Mildred explained the topography of the area. "Johnstown lies in a gorge amongst the Allegheny Mountains and is surrounded by pine and fir trees. It's grown up where the Stony Creek and Little Conemaugh Rivers meet," Mildred went on because Carolena seemed so interested. "The river water is always high every spring from the thawing snow melt draining down into town and sometimes flooding us. That's why our streets are so muddy." She pointed toward the fields in the distance. "If you take the time to look, you'll see rubied snap-dragons, purple violets, and ivory and sun-pink azalea buds."

"Don't forget the maple and oak trees," added a brunette with a birthmark on her chin in the shape of a bird. "They're producing fresh waxy leaves already."

"It's all so pretty," remarked Carolena. "The few clouds floating seem to be put there only as contrast to the spectacular cobalt sky."

They drove down Maple Street. Carolena took a good look, noting the close-together white framed houses. Each appeared to wear a recent coating of paint and was so well maintained; she thought she could see the wet brush strokes on the clapboards. "My goodness. The lawns are all clipped and neat. Is that woman over yonder actually sweeping her grass?"

"Appears so," giggled Mildred.

"What is covering everybody's drive?" wondered Carolena.

"You mean that rough black gravel?"

Carolena nodded.

"Those are cinders. They're the trash part of coal that won't burn or something like that."

Cinders? Cinders. It came to Carolena how her mother and Aunt Coe, each, carried a tiny souvenir cinder on her knee, just under the skin, from childhood tumbles.

"So you've never been here before, Cary?" asked the older, large bosomed blonde.

"No, ma'am."

That began a tidal wave of information from nearly everyone in the wagon.

"Some 30,000 people live here and in the nearby valley boroughs."

"We have two opera houses, a new hospital ..."

"A night school, lectures at the library, Saturday night band concerts in the park with the fountain."

"I know about the police force," said the woman wearing brown braids twirled into a bun. "My fiancé is one of nine policemen."

"I go roller skating almost every Saturday night," offered the lady with the under bite.

"And the Hulbert House, a hotel on Clinton Street, actually has an elevator and steam heat!" exclaimed the freckled girl.

Mildred explained, as would a professor addressing a student, "Mostly though, Johnstown is a steel and mining community of German and Welsh inhabitants. Six thousand men work for the Cambria Iron Company, which also owns coal mines, trains and track, a company store, seven-hundred houses, I hear, the brick works, and a woolen mill. Cambria Iron makes steel rails, and it's tied into Gautier Works somehow. They make barbed wire. Naturally, with all the factories and mines, came the saloons, all 123 of them!"

"My gosh!" Carolena was shocked. "Why so many?"

"The men say they need whiskey to wash down the coal dust in their throats. I think men just like to drink. No wonder it's called the *devil's brew* if allowed to get out of control."

Carolena thought of her father and ground her teeth with disgust. "I met Jamie from the Black Diamond last night. She's the one who steered me to Mrs. Learner's place."

Everyone mumbled in agreement saying Black Diamond Jamie was a good old gal.

"Then there's California Tom's. Those two taverns are the most popular, I hear," said the short thin girl in the corner of the wagon. "Of course, this is only hearsay since I personally have never set foot in any of those vile places."

"I was in the Black Diamond because it was the only spot serving food so late last night."

"Oh I'm not judging you, Cary. You did what you had to do. If you hadn't, we might not have met you. No. I was just going to tell you my fiancé has cautioned me to ease up on the boys who drink there, including him. He tells me how the coal dust and dry heat from the furnaces leave a mighty thirst in a man. I told him I will try and keep my disgust to myself only so long as my future husband's identity isn't listed in the newspaper among those who've been caught performing in frontier fashion."

"Seems fair," agreed the girls.

"Men can be so coarse at times," Carolena pointed out.

"Lookie there," another said with disgust. "Those nasty shacks on the banks of both rivers are where some of the more unseemly men live. It's probably 'cause it's not far from Lizzie Thompson's, home of the soiled doves."

Carolena wrinkled her brow in bewilderment. "Soiled doves?"

Mildred leaned over and whispered their occupation. The eyes of the Floridian widened with understanding.

Mildred said, "The real talk of the town is always the South Fork Fishing and Hunting Club of Pittsburg. None of us has ever been inside. All we hear is it's some kind of private summer resort for wealthy steel men from that city. Their compound is to the east, about fourteen miles up-river above the South Fork Dam."

"Really," replied a fascinated Carolena.

"They had the old dam repaired and then built their clubhouse and cottages along the reservoir they called Lake Conemaugh. Lessen you're a servant or caretaker, odds are you'll never get inside."

Carolena took this as a personal challenge, especially because a lake meant boats. She made the instant decision to ingratiate herself with the members of that club for the sole purpose of showing her designs to those who could afford to have them built. Lord knew she'd had no luck with Paolo. Now things were falling into place.

The Needleworks' building was noisy and relatively clean. Something tickled her leg! Fearing a mouse, she jerked her knee to find it was only cotton lint. The circulating air from the opened windows sent weightless bluish lint balls tumbling. It reminded her of the dust bunnies she'd swept from under Jack Patrick's bed when he hadn't done his chores. A parade of people with rakes and brooms were chasing and pushing the fluff into piles. It seemed a hopeless struggle to keep ahead of the stuff.

Having no idea what to expect, Carolena waited in line as Mildred instructed. Then she donned the apron issued her and was told to stand by the window until the supervisor was ready for her. In his forties, he looked like an overweight freshly hatched chicken, his yellow hair sprouting sparsely from his round head. Taking stock, Carolena saw that in this section of the huge plant, they were cutting shirt templates. Forgetting her order to stay put, she wandered the factory. She watched while one woman trimmed several layers of cloth into what Carolena guessed would be sleeves. Another cut collars, and others, the shirtfronts, backs, and cuffs. The pieces of blue cotton work shirts were counted, stacked, and placed on a pulley-cart, finally disappearing into another part of the factory.

"Cary Dunne?" questioned the large man.

"Sir?"

"I don't think it's too smart disobeying a direct order the first day on the job, do you?"

She was sorely tempted to tell him she obeyed orders from few people. She didn't. It was likely he was a former soldier, and this was his way. Proud of herself for her control, she said, "If you mean why have I roamed around the mill, I did it because I can see how very busy you are, and I thought I might familiarize myself with things in order to expedite my training." She forced herself to look sweetly upon his spidery-veined cheeks, her eyes submissive and fluttering, seeking his approval.

Flattered that a girl as lovely as this might find him appealing, the supervisor located his voice after a dry swallow. "The name's Evans," he said pleasantly. "You'd best be tying up all that yellow hair of yours sos it don't get caught in no machinery. Here," he said handing her several wire hairpins retrieved from his pants pocket. "Always carry a few spares. I'm surprised none of the other gals told you about this."

"Actually, sir," she said through tight lips that held the pins while she coiled her locks into a bun, "they were singing the praises of Johnstown to me, and I guess we ran out of time for the particulars about work. This is my first trip here."

"First trip? Sounds to me like you don't intend to make this your home. I supposed you've come lookin' for a man, same as the rest of the gals here."

Unlike those other pitiful women, Carolena was proud she needed no man.

Her hair in place, "My goodness." Almost nauseated by her sugary performance, she remembered her mission and kept on. "Are you hinting something, Mr. Evans?"

He actually flushed!

She tried to get back to business, before she retched right there on the man's dusty shoes, by saying. "Let me assure you, you can count on me. I'm a good worker."

Obviously relieved, he pondered, "Dunne? Dunne? Can't say as I know anyone by that particular name."

"Maybe it's not so common in these parts. Do your people live in town?"

Remembering his position of authority, he growled, "Get over to the packing room, all the way down the length of this building. Take a right and then go until you can't go no further. They'll tell you what to do in there."

"Thank you, sir. Oh, excuse me, but what about the mid-day meal?"

"You'll hear a whistle, and someone will tell you where the lunch room is. You're from Mrs. Learner's, ain't ya?"

She nodded.

"Don't worry none. You'll get fed. Get going! You're on company time, dolly!"

Carolena was glad to be leaving the surly man. She couldn't understand why his attitude had turned so sour. She'd thought she'd been careful to watch her words. She sighed at his moodiness and headed out to find her appointed destination.

The foreman running the packing and shipping department seemed nice enough. Despite his kind attitude, Carolena was cautious and spoke only when addressed. He was patient with his instructions. "Fold each garment exactly the same, stacking three, then putting them in the already formed boxes right there." This didn't sound so difficult to her.

The minutes passed while the hours dragged though the women around her were pleasant enough. By the time the whistle sounded at noon, Carolena was exhausted. 7 a.m. to 12 was long enough to go without rest or even a drink. Her fingertips had the beginnings of blisters on them from buttoning shirts.

Following the others to the dining area, she saw Mildred. "I saved this seat for you, Cary. I imagine you're pretty tuckered. You'll get used to it. Really you will."

"I hope so. My fingers are beginning to burn like fire."

"When we get home, I've got some salve you can use. Eat hearty."

As she devoured the vegetable stew, Carolena thought how pitiful it was a sweet woman such as Mildred referred to Learner's Lean-to as *home.*

By the time they returned to the boarding house, it was well past dark. Carolena chewed her dinner, not tasting. Excusing herself, she went on up to bed. It was all she could do to change into her nightdress. Done in, she forgot her tender fingers and fell into a deep sleep. No prayers would cross her lips this night.

***

Days slipped away as most of Carolena's waking hours were spent working. It seemed she'd been permanently assigned to the packing department. It wasn't that the labor was physically demanding or the workday excessively long because she was used to spending endless hours on her drawings. But no imagination was involved with what she did. The only variation was the type of garment she handled. Fold, stack, pack. Fold, stack, pack. Over and over. Her brain numbed in self-preservation.

She talked with co-workers in her section, getting to know them. Their conversations covered diverse subjects such as last Sunday's public embarrassment when the visiting Lutheran preacher left his podium to ask Mrs. Grubb to take her screaming child to the cry room. Then there was Miss Lula's partial hair loss after using the new purple shampoo purchased from the good-looking traveling salesman. In polite passing, the women asked of Carolena's family. She led them to believe she had none.

When opportunities arose to investigate Ellissa's whereabouts, Carolena posed leading questions, but what she really wanted to do was ask plain out, "Do any of you know a woman who looks like me with dark hair named Ellissa?" She did not.

It would have been much easier to be direct. So very much easier. But Carolena didn't want to interrupt her sister's life if it was a happy and prosperous one. How would Ellissa react after some thirty years of living without the knowledge she had another whole family? What about her birth parents not being the man and woman who raised her? How different would her existence have been if she'd known the truth? Her true lineage was a dirty secret. Ellissa would probably hate them all, Carolena decided. Too, there was a strong possibility she'd hate Carolena for disclosing everything. It struck her that her motivation was selfish. In searching for Ellissa, she was looking for a replacement to fill the void left by the betrayals of her mother, father, and lover. She became convinced she must take it slowly. Exposing her identity to others made for complications, including hurtful gossip. No. If she were to find Ellissa, it would have to be with a little help from fate. Then she could decide whether to reveal herself to the woman she already considered a sister.

Chapter 22

Although she was Catholic, Carolena excused herself from mass her first Sunday morning in Johnstown and made the bold decision to attend services at Bought by Blood Lutheran Church with Mildred, whom she now called Millie, Mrs. Learner, and several of the girls from the boarding house. Lutherans of German descent were plentiful here. Carolena reasoned she was half German herself and it was her mother's faith, or used to be before she became so wicked, and Grammy's faith, too. Her guilt overridden, Carolena entered the church vestibule. With an attitude of pleasant anticipation as the organist pumped out *All Glory, Laud and Honor*, the elders greeted her warmly.

The church bell struck and on the tenth chime, a male voice sounded from the back, "Please rise, and turn to page one hundred twelve in your hymnals. Our opening hymn will be *Safely through Another Week*."

Carolena turned to see who'd spoken. Since they were seated third row from the front and most the pews were filled, she was unable to get a glimpse.

"It's a glorious day," he continued behind her. "Listen to the birds sing to the heavens. If they can serve the Lord so humbly with their sweet song, let us do the same. And I don't want to hear any of you say you're tone deaf. The Almighty gave you a voice. You just give it right back to him!"

The congregation laughed. The first chord was struck and the melodic praise rumbled the windows. Carolena was unfamiliar with the tune and lyrics of this particular song. Encouraged by the pastor's words, she followed along, hoping she wasn't too far off pitch. When she saw the speaker, her mouth dropped open. It was the man from the train to whom she'd been so rude! She was mortified. She wanted to disappear under the pew.

Standing in front to the altar, the minister introduced himself as Pastor Scott Obermyer. As the service progressed, Carolena forgot her troubles. The sermon entitled, *Charity is More than the Tinkle of Coin*, with personal stories and some humor, kept everyone's attention. After an hour, the pastor concluded with a blessing, followed by the slow sounding of melodic chimes. The ushers controlled the filing out of the congregation, front row first, working backwards to the last. This arrangement gave everyone a brief time to address their neighbors as well as a personal moment with the pastor. While she waited her turn to be *shaken out* as her father called it, Carolena analyzed the minister. Reversing her original evaluation, she determined him to be a sincere huggy-bear of a man. She prayed she was right.

"Pastor Scott," Millie said. "May I introduce Miss Cary Dunne? She's new to our town."

He took Carolena's hand. When their eyes met, he was silent for a quick second, as if attempting to remember where he'd seen her. When it came to him, his smile was wide. "Miss Dunne, is it? Welcome to Johnstown and our church. I hope you enjoyed your time spent with us."

This was her chance to apologize. She breathed deeply. "Yes, sir. I honestly did. And may I apologize—"

He interrupted her words. "Apologize for not singing joyously enough? I'm certain you'll do better next time. Often, new folks are surprised at how exuberant we can sometimes be. I hope we'll see you again next week." He released her hand and grasped that of the person behind her, Mrs. Learner.

Millie took Carolena's arm and led her out into the sunshine. The visitor was more than relieved. Pastor Scott had spared her any humiliation. He was a godly man indeed.

***

By the time they returned to the Lean-to, it was nearly noon. After a filling meal of chicken soup and fresh bread, Carolena disappeared. Millie found her upstairs in their dormitory. "What are these, Cary?" she asked with one of several cardboard tubes in her hand. "May I take a look? I've seen you up late at night when the moonlight comes in the window. I've been beside myself wondering what all this concerns," she confessed, nodding toward the papers Carolena was extracting from the cylinders in her satchel.

"Of course you can, Millie. It's no secret. You're just the only one who's been interested enough to ask, is all. Most of the other girls are always busy socializing."

"Guess you and I aren't particularly that way."

"Not so much these days," Carolena admitted. Grudgingly recalling her gay times with Grey and Paolo, "I did have a taste for it a while back."

"It would be prying to ask you for details, Cary. Just realize I'm your friend and if you want to talk, to say what you're thinking aloud, I'll listen. I promise, I won't tell anyone. I'm not like that."

"Thank you, Millie." Despite the sincere sounding offer, Carolena couldn't let her guard down. She didn't like the feeling of vulnerability a loose tongue produced. "Let me show you my sketches."

Together they began unrolling a few of the dozens of designs on the quilted spreads of both their beds. Not having sufficient room, they took the liberty of using a few other cots.

"Cary! These boats are wonderful! Look at this big one. This looks like it could hold hundreds of people!"

Smiling proudly, Carolena replied, "It could and it does! She's called the *Coral Crown!*" Realizing she'd given out information, which could link her to her past, she quickly pointed to another drawing in hopes of deflecting any questions that might arise. "How do you feel about the interior of this stateroom? I'm torn between covering the walls with ebony satin or maybe a rich cherry wood. I want it dramatic."

"Me? How do I feel?"

Carolena nodded, "Yes, you."

Honored to be asked, Millie gave her unschooled opinions. This was exactly what Carolena wanted because the entire picture presented had to appeal to the sophisticated as well as the average person. Her sister, Breelan, had once written a promotion, "A Sale of a Sail." The company tried to do just that, offer the best at relatively reasonable prices, the idea being that every person who wanted could ride the waves in style. They understood their profit margin would be less than other passenger lines. Their hope was to make up the difference by, more often than not, selling the ships out. Hanging above her father's desk had been the Aqua Verde Passenger Line motto her mother long ago cross-stitched, "Luxury, Service, and Comfort for All." That framed sentiment was gone, burned to ashes in the horrible fire. Not forgotten, the credo remained on the brass plaque each ship bore high on the hull.

The afternoon progressed, and the girls talked on. It suddenly stuck Carolena she would eventually have to give her true credentials if she ever wanted a serious nibble for her services. She would have to tell of her professional and technical connections to Dunnigan Shipwrights and the Aqua Verde Passenger Line. Her mind scrambled. I could say I keep my original identity a secret because I want my efforts to stand on their own merit. Who could fault her for that?

Worry would overtake her if she let it. Instead, she concentrated on her favorite subject, her work. "Tell me Millie, if you were having a yacht custom designed, would you rather it had a library or a solarium. Which would it be, hum? No, no, no!" Carolena broke in on her own questioning. Her mind was awash with space and shape and color and texture. "Don't answer that! No reason for you to do without. I could quite easily combine the two so you could have both. How about a hexagonal skylight?"

"What is all this?"

The husky voice surprised them both. It was Mrs. Learner.

"I asked you ladies something, and I expect a swift answer."

"Did you have to sneak up on us like that?" asked Millie, her hand fashioning soothing circles over her pounding heart.

"This is my house, isn't it? I guess I can sneak up on anyone I like."

"Yes, ma'am," answered Carolena quickly. She didn't need a fight, not now. She scurried about, picking up the oversized papers to hurriedly roll them back up.

"Be careful, Cary. You're wrinkling all your beautiful work," said Millie, rerolling the crooked ones.

"It's alright. I can always draw more."

"What? Is Mr. Evans not working his people hard enough? Apparently not, if you have time to attend to illustrations."

Carolena was getting irritated. "Let me assure you, Mrs. Learner, these endeavors before you in no way interfere with my duties at the Needleworks. I do this on my own time. I've worked well and hard all week, and this is my day off. I'm sorry I spread my papers on cots not my own. I didn't think any of the other residents here would mind."

"Well," said the middle-aged mistress of the place looking down at the young women sitting on Carolena's bed, "I don't think any of them would mind either. May I have a look, Cary?"

Taken aback by the interest, Carolena froze. Millie poked her in her ribs, and she presented her work, some of which dated back several years. After examination and general questioning, Mrs. Learner inquired the same thing Millie had been about to ask, when interrupted. "So, are these plans of yours for sale?"

"Yes, ma'am." No sense saying they weren't. Carolena still had her brother and younger sisters to help. "Yes, they are, and I know a shipwright who will build them." Feigning ignorance, "However, I've no idea where or to whom to sell them. After all, we're here in a valley between mountains with only a small river running through town. Who would want to invest money in a yacht with nowhere to sail it?"

Millie and Mrs. Learner looked at one another and laughed.

Embarrassed, Carolena said, "I can plainly see from your reaction, I'm wasting my time staying in these parts. Maybe I should move on." A bit sorry she pretended she didn't know about the big lake upstream, she guessed their ridicule was God's way of getting even with her for her fib. They weren't going to help her. She said honestly, "I'm just grateful I've a job at the mill, good food to eat, and a bed on which to sleep until I do leave."

"Leaving is the last thing we want you to do, Cary. You've got more than a job and bed," Mrs. Learner said patting Carolena's shoulder. "You've got friends and a great, glorious talent! I don't intend to let it go to waste. I know men with money! Remember, I'm in good with the owners of the Needleworks," she paused, "who know the owners of the ironworks, who know the owners of the steel mills, and they know the owners of the railroads."

Dare she hope? Carolena fished more deeply. "That's lovely, ma'am, but what need would they have of my services with no water about?"

"Ah, that's what you don't know, my dear. They all belong to the South Fork Fishing and Hunting Club just east of here, and that club is located on huge Lake Conemaugh!"

Carolena let her mouth fall open and her eyes grow wide. "I remember now. When I first arrived, one of the girls told me there was a lake up there. I thought it was tiny."

"We'll just have to see your designs make it into the hands of men who have more money than they know what to do with! Why, they're all always looking for something to spend it on! Oh, and call me Happy, would you?

My friends always do."

Amazed and pleased at Mrs. Learner's unexpected and generous attitude, Carolena wanted to scream a loud *hurrah*. This could be her first-class ticket to success!

***

"All you have to do is show up at my annual Spring Fling, Cary, look pretty and weave your work into conversations with the men who will come in hopes of a flirtation, permanent or otherwise," Happy said coyly, adding a wink. "I'll point out the fellows with money."

"You've been so wonderful," answered Carolena. "Please, what can I do to help with the party?"

"Not a thing. Really. Committees were set up long ago for the decorations. The food and clean up, as always, will be handled by Mr. and Mrs. Bauer. And I'll be bringing my Tipsy Pudding. It's a tradition.

"Sounds intriguing."

"You'll love it. I'm not bragging, but everybody does," Happy told her.

"I've always heard that if it's true, it isn't bragging."

"That's what I've heard, too. Well, my dance may not be as plush an affair as up at the hunting club, but it's enticing enough that a few single club members and some married couples always attend as a sort of precursor to their own official opening, the day after Decoration Day."

Several boarders and Toby Learner, his wheelchair rolled up to the table, were polishing off the last of the hot gingerbread from his mother's oven. By now, everyone knew of Carolena's work and was hopeful she'd succeed.

"I dare say Cary's dance card will be full as soon as she walks in the door, even before she gets her coat off!" complimented Suzanne, the girl who had awakened her that first morning. "What do you plan on wearing? I haven't seen you in anything except your dark dresses."

Carolena looked down. "Well, I've got one that's a little nicer than the one I'm wearing. It will have to do."

Happy's commanding voice took charge. "I've got some beautiful trimmings. Let's go to my room."

She settled her Toby in the shady front yard with a wool plaid blanket covering his lap. Keeping an eye on him from her bedroom window, Happy asked, "Have you seen the carvings my boy does? Though he won't talk anymore, he surely can handle a knife. I'm so proud of him. That's how I got to meet Mr. Ashton from the railroad. He heard of my boy's skill and asked him to do a whittling portrait of his daughter, Juniata. The likeness was so remarkable that now Toby can't keep up with the demand. He even makes cameo sized brooches and necklaces." She crossed over to her washstand and retrieved a rectangular box from the second drawer on the left. "If you can keep a secret, here is one that he just finished doing for Burt Bauer, the man I was telling you about who helps with my Spring Fling. It's of his wife. He wants to present it to his daughter for her next birthday. I'm to give it to him when the missus isn't around. Such a sweet gesture, don't you think?"

Millie took the oval carving, studying it, wishing she had someone who loved her enough to commission such a gift. "How can Burt work in the mines, Happy, and still have time and energy left for doing work like your party?"

"Oh, he hasn't been in a mine for sometime now. He used to be a hoisterman there. No more. Got trapped in that cave-in, same as my Toby. The poison fumes burned his lungs, which were already full of silicosis. They call it *black lung* around here, Cary. Men get it from breathing all that coal dust. It's far too prevalent in these Allegheny hills. Anyway, Burt had to quit. He was glad to get any kind of work after that. He has a fine reputation and now has a job at the club. He's in charge of maintenance. The labor isn't nearly as strenuous for him and since his wife cooks periodically up there, they can spend some extra time together."

"They sound like hard-working, devoted people," Carolena commented, taking the cameo from Millie. Happy and Millie were engrossed in rummaging through the pine locker at the foot of the bed. Opening her closed hand cradling the cameo, Carolena looked down to discover it bore the likeness of a woman who was a younger version of her own mother as well as herself. This had to be Ellissa, her sister! Can't people see the resemblance? Why would they? Any connection between Ellissa and Carolena would never enter anyone's mind, she told herself. Carolena stared at it until her eyes burned and she had to blink to moisten them. Desperately trying to keep her voice steady, she asked, "By the way, Happy, what's Mrs. Bauer's first name?"

"Oh, it's unusual, like mine," she smiled at Carolena. "Her name is Ellissa."

The hours would drag until the dance at the Johnstown Community Hall. Tomorrow, sisters would meet.

***

Carolena was overwhelmed. She never anticipated such a positive reception of her work at Happy's dance. She had two seemingly sincere buyers, and she hadn't even made it up to the club nor had to give her real name.

Mr. Wilber Birthney was familiar with the Aqua Verde Line and took little convincing once he'd seen Carolena's sketches. Mr. Flegmon, whose wife squinted suspiciously at Carolena until she herself got caught up in anticipation of their finished yacht, took some convincing. Finally, both parties shook hands in agreement to pay half in advance. Carolena explained a few more meetings would be required to determine personal preference with regard to trimmings, and excitement reigned!

186

This would make it possible for her to quit her job at the Needleworks. Carolena quickly found Happy and told her the news. "I understand when I do leave my job, I won't be able to stay at your boarding house any longer. You've been so kind to me."

Happy's chubby face scrunched to form a contemplative expression. Then, "Burt. Burt! Over here!" The man wearing a white smock, though busy, set down his empty sandwich tray and headed in their direction.

"Where's Ellissa tonight?" she asked. "Has she got you doing the cooking now, too?"

Carolena liked her brother-in-law before he spoke. She'd looked about for her sister earlier and been unable to identify her. Not wanting to answer questions, she stayed silent.

Burt replied with an easy laugh.

"No, ma'am. Nothing to worry about but our little girl, our Mary Coe, caught a case of something or other. She'll be fine. You know my wife. Family first. Since all the food was ready to go for your party, we've been keeping the trays filled with the help of a few of your tenants. Everything look okay to you, Miss Happy?"

"Oh yes. I've never had difficulty with your work. You know that. I only wanted you to meet a new and very talented friend of mine. Miss Cary Dunne."

"Glad to know you, Miss Dunne."

Happy explained Carolena's need for a room, and, to her shock, Burt suggested she move in with his family!

"While I'm up at the club," he explained, "my wife and child are in the house alone. I like to be careful because of nasty jaspers from the mines and factories. We often have young women staying with us. If Miss Happy recommends you, it's good with me. My wife has to agree, too, of course. She has a special sense about people."

Gravely frustrated she'd have to wait to meet Ellissa, Carolena was overjoyed at the idea she just might be staying in her home. Things couldn't have worked out more perfectly. God was listening to her prayers.

Participating in easy conversation with so many, Carolena's deeper thoughts were on the revenue she'd produce for her family. She'd save back only enough to pay Ellissa for room and board. The rest would go to Breelan. Before long, her reputation would grow, and the Dunnigans would be back on top. She could return to Fernandina with her head high. No more pitying stares. The triumph of skill and will were within her grasp.

***

Carolena was nibbling a cookie and stopped mid-chew. She wondered if the laughing voice behind her could belong to Grey. It struck her how very much she missed him, missed the carefree, innocent days they'd shared in Fernandina. Missed working with him, missed his teasing. Missed him something fierce.

"If you all will excuse me," she announced. "There's someone I'm most anxious to see. We've a lot to talk about."

Groans of disappointment were heard from the men gathered.

"Lucky dog, that fellow," whispered one portly gentleman.

The closer she drew to the source of the voice, the less right it seemed. It was not Grey. Disappointment swamped her. She drooped her shoulders and expelled a sad sigh.

"If you're not otherwise occupied, miss, would you care to dance with me?"

She lifted her chin to look up into the solid brown eyes of a young man possibly five years her junior. No, she'd never laid sight on him before. So what if he were breaking the standard code of behavior by even talking to her when they weren't properly introduced. So what. He sounded like Grey, didn't he? Even if only a little.

"So what." She'd spoken unintentionally.

"Pardon, miss?"

"Oh, why not?" she said and extended her right hand. "I'd love to dance with you."

Pleased she'd accepted so readily, his response was immediate. "I'm called …"

She stopped him with a bare finger to his lips. He experienced a current charge through him at her bold touch. She did not. Her thoughts were with the tempo of the fiddle and piano. The music, the fragrant perfumes of the night, the interested customers, the anticipation of meeting her sister, her healthy heart, these were the important things. She wanted to put away the ugly. Tonight she would celebrate a renewal of life. Grey would have made it complete. Carolena smiled and told the young man, "No names. Tonight, I'm a woman of mystery. Please let me have my way, will you?"

The minutes waltzed, polkaed, jigged, and reeled away. Finally winded, "Thank you, sir," Carolena said formally. "I've enjoyed myself. You've been most kind. Good evening to you." With that, she slipped outside into the darkness, forgetting her cape. For a brief second, she imagined she was down home and expected the air to be humid. Instead, it was cool and refreshing against the mild perspiration she'd developed from all the exercise. Soon she would chill, so doing the sensible thing, she was about to turn to retrieve her wrap when from behind, something was draped across her shoulders. She spun to find the young gentleman who'd been her partner. He said nothing.

Carolena spoke pleasantly. "Thank you. I think I'll return to my friends. The breeze is picking up." She stepped toward the light spilling through Burt's crystal-clean windows as the air's current carried her words away.

With minimal strides, he was beside her then in front of her. "No need to hurry back, miss. It's really not so cold out here. There's an unoccupied house nearby where we could build a fire and be alone."

Another pesky man! Her response was brusque. "I prefer to gather my warmth from the hearth inside Happy's hall. If you'll excuse me?"

The man would not be dismissed so readily. This woman had teased him. The game she played was silly, childish, and boring. He hadn't the patience or the desire to beg for pleasures. "Let me show you. You'll change your mind soon enough once we're together." His fingers cupping her elbow moved higher and were pressing into her upper arm. "You won't be sorry."

She wanted to cry for help, but she couldn't risk any unprofessional scandal before her new clients. His arm was around her waist, and he was half-dragging, half-carrying her deeper into the dark.

"She might not be sorry, boy. You sure as hell will."

Carolena ceased her tussling and was paralyzed by the voice. This time she knew for certain it was Grey. He had the struggling man by the nape of the neck.

"Alright! Let me go, damn you! Let me go!"

"Apologize to the lady," Grey ordered, adding, "and mean it."

"If she hadn't ground that firm figure of hers into me, none of this ever would have—"

Grey squeezed his fingers another eighth-of-an-inch deeper into the man's neck.

"Jesus! I'm sorry, okay? I'm sorry!"

Released with a shove, the man staggered, grabbing his neck to massage his bruised muscles.

"Be seeing you, son." While Grey's words were casual, his true intention was understood. If the man had any sense, he would avoid Grey and this woman permanently.

Snarling, the defeated suitor spit out, "The hell you say!" and was off, vanishing into the night in the direction of the saloons.

Carolena was all smiles. She opened her mouth to thank Grey with the plan to bestow upon him the fiercest hug she could muster.

He spoke first. "You know, he was right. I've been watching you. The way you were dancing so close to him, you openly invited his advances. He had every reason to expect something more than the polite offer of your gloved hand to kiss once the music ended."

Carolena was dumbfounded. The words she spoke were sarcastic and fury-filled. "I thought that man had some huge ones, but you have the biggest …"

Her unexpected vulgarity turned his bad temper to chuckles.

"Stop that. I'm dead serious. How dare you accuse me of such disgusting behavior? You know me better than that. I would never tease a man, tempt him so far that he would force himself on me."

His expression was again somber. "You sure as the devil have been doing it to me for quite a spell, and I'm sick to death of pretending to have no interest."

Had she heard him right? "Grey?" she whispered.

"What?" he asked roughly.

"I'm sorry. For everything."

She stepped closer, standing in his shadow under the silver moon. Their eyes met and the beam that passed between them threw invisible sparks. His arms reached out and swept her to him. Her hands came around his back to clutch his jacketed shoulders.

He'd missed this woman. He missed her beauty, her intensity and, yes, even her infuriating maneuvering.

Her mouth waited beneath his. All he had to do was lower his head and rest his lips on hers. And so he did. Carolena was small, and he was cradling her, caressing her neck, her back, his mouth never leaving hers. He felt her clinging to him, which invoked a response of want so powerful, he could wait for her no longer. He prayed she would not refuse him.

Carolena was reeling from ecstasy. This was the one man she wanted, always wanted really, more than any other. She'd given up all hope he would love her. He was here, now, holding her in an embrace so fierce and all encompassing, she would do anything as long as he didn't cease touching her.

"This way," she said, pulling away from him, yet not daring to break all contact. Her slender hand tugged at his calloused fingers, guiding him along.

He followed her. He'd let her lead him wherever she chose.

Carolena didn't know where she was going. The woods seemed the darkest, most secluded place available, and she wove a path amongst the hardwoods. They advanced until the songs of night birds and frogs, the chatter of the crickets, and the passing river overpowered the music from the dance.

She stopped then and turned to him. The newly sprouted tree leaves weren't as dense as they would be in another few weeks, so moonlight showed the soft blur of each other's face. Grey was the first to move, snatching Carolena high into his arms. The surprise stole her breath, but not enough to prevent her from covering his neck with kisses.

He set her down, and the loss of the heat of his touch made her shiver. She watched him remove his leather duster, laying the hide side down on a bed of pine needles. He took her hand and her knees folded, allowing her to rest on the lining.

"Deer have laid here, Cary. Gentle animals, free to experience all the peace, power, and pleasure God gave them. That's how I'm feeling at this moment."

In an instant, he was supporting himself over her. In another, he was atop her. His weight was comforting, consoling, not crushing. They took no time to remove cumbersome clothing. They only unbuttoned, untied, and unbuckled what was necessary and even that brief period of adjustment seemed far too long.

Their first lovemaking was intense and fleeting. Their second slow and tender, leaving a brand of ownership upon them both.

After, they huddled together, kissing and touching again. And again. "How did you find me, Grey?"

"Miss Ella steered me here. She figured you'd go looking for Ellissa."

Despite her contempt for her mother, Carolena was grateful.

"I'd have lost my shirt if someone bet me one day we'd be together like this, Carolena."

"Not me. Although I tried to give up the dream you would ever care for me, in my deepest heart of hearts, I imagined us as one. It's what I've wanted from the first time I met you. I feel so wonderful! If I felt any better, I'd be twins."

He laughed. "I'm a damned fool. I thought you were a beauty, make no mistake. I also was sure I was ..." Grey hesitated, swallowing hard once, "the last man you'd ever be interested in."

She knew what he was thinking. "Grey ..."

"Yes."

"I was never *with* Paolo. Thank the Lord, you and my mother interrupted things."

His squeeze of relief and joy were so great, she gasped at his added pressure. Prying his hands a bit from around her ribs, so she could breathe normally, it was Carolena's turn to laugh with happiness. They stayed that way as silence evolved and they watched the stars play hide and seek with the clouds.

After a time, "We're so different, or so I thought," he said.

"That's what I thought, too. That's why I've tried to change, to become someone who could share your ..." she sought words that would not insult him, "your playfulness or at least not be so offended by it. I hope I've shown you I mean that."

Concerned, "I hope tonight meant more to you than proving some point."

She kissed his throat. "You know it did."

"You, Carolena Dunnigan, are the most feminine female I've ever met."

A greater compliment, she could not conceive.

"You know, I've been thinking on it for sometime now, and I need to change my habits. I must make a stab at curbing my wicked seaman's ways. Comes a time when a man has to start behaving himself. He can't be a mischief-maker forever."

"Wait, that's all part of the reason I admire you. I'm so staid and judgmental and so sanctimonious sometimes. Besides your handsome face and physique, it's your personality that fascinates me. You bring fun and excitement everywhere you go."

"And you bring dignity and grace with you, my darling."

Chapter 23

"Ellissa will love you when she meets you, Cary." Happy's excitement displayed itself in her wildly gesturing hands. "Come tomorrow, she and Burt will take you along when they drive up to the Fishing and Hunting Club! It's quite a drive up there, so you'll stay overnight with them. I've talked to Mr. Evans at the Needleworks, and he's given his permission for you to take a couple of days off." Her face slightly pinked as if she'd used her wiles to gain that special favor. "Don't think a thing about your rent. You can pay me whatever you owe me when you have the funds, dear. Burt and Ellissa plan to be here 'round seven in the morning. Did I even tell you what they do at the club? I can't remember."

"You didn't give me any real details."

"Well, they ready the place for the season's grand opening, which happens next week. That is, Burt does. The club has its own chef. This trip, Ellissa is in charge of feeding her husband's temporary work crew. As a bonus, the Bauers are allowed to attend the dinner dance the first night. Burt told me they sent out invites to over a hundred fancy folks for the sit-down meal, though they're actually only sixty-odd members who've RSVPed and will be attending. Burt said he could wheedle an invitation for you. I'm certain you'll find more clients up there."

"Thank you for all your help, ma'am."

"Why shouldn't I help you, Cary," Happy continued. "Maybe I can take my Toby for a ride in one of your showy vessels up on the lake some day. He'd surely love it. Since the mine accident, he's not been quite right, I mean besides his cripplin'." As the woman thought of her ailing son, a sad smile appeared. Recovering, "Mr. Ashton, the one with the Pennsylvania Railroad I was telling you about? Now, he seemed interested when I explained all about your work. Who knows? You might put Johnstown on the map!"

"Cary, you're so lucky to be going up there." Millie took hold of Carolena's shoulders. "Don't you dare be nervous," she commanded. "You're pretty enough to get the attention of any of those swells and smart enough to hold it, just like at last week's dance."

"Remember, when you get there, ask Burt which of the men is Ashton." As if divulging a secret, the older woman whispered, "Burt knows who's who, and I dare say what each one of them is worth!"

As the kitchen clock struck seven times the following morning, Happy called out, "Right on time! The Bauers are here!"

The springs of an old wagon squeaked its arrival, complete with patched canvas covering protecting its contents. Carolena took little time to notice more as she followed Happy Learner outside into the cool spring air.

"Good morning! A finer day there never was, Burt."

"No, ma'am. That was just what Ellissa was saying a minute ago. Once those swells arrive at the club, they'll be some fine fishing takin' place. There's always extra fish. I'll drop off some trout first chance I get."

"That would be wonderful. Thank you. Toby surely loves his fish."

The face of the woman beside Burt was shadowed by the hand-stitched deep brim on her bonnet, the cotton of it printed with orange peonies on a black background. Then she spoke. "Morning, Happy. I hope those workman are hungry up there."

The sound of the words carried a lilt Carolena recognized instantly. This woman had the voice of their mother! Anxiously, Carolena darted past her landlady to stand near the rump of the mule hitched on the right.

Mrs. Bauer looked at the beautiful stranger and gathered from what she'd heard that this was the young woman with the drawings of ships to sell to the club members. "Might you be Miss Dunne?" Ellissa asked kindly.

Carolena wanted to cry with joy. Yes, yes! I'm your little sister! Call me Carolena. I'm thrilled to meet you. I've come from far away to find you.

Happy wondered where Cary's tongue had gone as she looked upon her wild-eyed younger friend. "Yes," she answered in her stead. "This is Cary Dunne. Tell us, how's your daughter feeling?"

"Oh, much, much better, thanks. It was some kind of stomach ailment. And thank you for understanding about my not working your party, Happy. Burt told me how kind you were. Here." She reached into her wool coat pocket and pulled out dollar bills. "I can't accept payment for work I didn't do."

Not reaching to take the money, Happy answered, "Look on it then as pay for Burt having to stay a little longer to finish up."

"Thank you, ma'am You're very generous. Still, we just can't."

Carolena could see plainly this was a woman of honor and dignity, like ... with great effort, she smothered the image of her mother and substituted another. Ellissa was a woman of honor like Aunt Coe.

Happy buried her hands inside her crossed arms, offering no place for Ellissa to put the money. "I'll make you a deal. Make my girls a cake, and we'll call it even."

Satisfied this wasn't charity, Ellissa said, "Deal."

"My mouth is watering already." Happy was determined to get back to the business at hand. "Wait 'till you see what Cary can do with a pencil."

Carolena realized what a single-minded woman Happy Learner was, and she was glad of it.

"I'm most anxious," Ellissa said sincerely.

"You folks have simply got to use your influence with those rich men up there."

Burt laughed. "Although we don't carry much of that, Miss Happy, we'll do what we can, of course. How does that sound, Miss Dunne?"

Carolena found her tongue. "It sounds fine, Mr. Bauer. Mrs. Bauer."

"We can have none of that. Please, please address me as Ellissa and my husband as Burt. Now, Miss Dunne, if you'll climb on up, we'll be off."

"And you call me Cary. I have a feeling we'll be good friends." At least I hope so, she thought.

"That would be lovely." Ellissa's eyes reinforced her words. "Cary it is. Burt, lend a hand, would you?" He was already on the ground, had stashed her tote in the wagon, and was supporting Carolena's arm as she hiked her skirts and climbed inside.

"Sorry, dear. You'll have to have a seat on that crate."

"That's fine, Ellissa. My goodness," she said settling herself between boxes and baskets covered in varying calico prints. "Whatever is it that smells so delicious?" She cooks like our mother. Damnation, Carolena chided herself. I have to stop making comparisons.

Ellissa turned in her seat to look over her shoulder at Cary. "Just some food for the workers."

"Gotta be going, darling," Burt gently reminded his wife.

Smiling from beneath their bonnets, Carolena and Ellissa waved goodbye as the wagon pulled out.

Her hand high in the air, Happy hollered, "Good luck, Cary. I'll say a little prayer for your success."

***

They took their time climbing east into the Allegheny Mountains. The chatter was easy. They talked about Carolena's moving into the Bauer's spare room as soon as possible. Burt, bragging about his wife's cooking, was excited to have a regular boarder who could enjoy it, too.

It occurred to Carolena that these people were kind and giving. They didn't fret at being less than affluent. They weren't driven by money. They were motivated by pride for a job well done compensated by a deserved wage.

They talked of Ellissa's only child, Mary Coe, a soon to be nine-year-old. The child spent nights with a neighbor while her parents worked. Carolena wondered whom her niece resembled, but kept this and other questions within. She realized it would take time for Ellissa to acclimate herself to having a new sister.

Despite her fascination with Ellissa's gestures, voice, carriage, and everything about her, Carolena noticed the beautiful surroundings as they traveled. In the distance, was a large geometric-looking cloud laid against the green hillside. The closer they drew to it, the clearer it became. Soon she could see its sharp edges were the outline of someone's huge mansion. "My goodness," Carolena called out. "What a monstrosity! It's massive! Who lives there?"

Burt laughed. "Just a couple of staff members with an occasional visit from a man who keeps the accounts, I hear."

It was much more than a house. It was almost palatial. "What about the outside? It's hard to tell from here. Although it is rather rambling and conspicuous in its structure and size, it's architecturally fascinating."

"Actually, it's in fine shape. Every year a crew comes to assure it's in good repair, a lot like what I do up at the club."

Ellissa added, "It has a history behind it, naturally. The man who owned it kept building additions once he remarried. People say he couldn't do enough for his wife. It was his way of trying to show her how much he loved her. Every year for their anniversary, he'd build another room or make some significant improvement to the property."

Burt coughed hard twice. Clearing his throat, he spat into the tall spring wildflowers they passed. "Excuse me ladies."

This was the first sign Carolena saw that Burt wasn't one hundred percent healthy.

"Seems to me," he continued, ignoring his voice that now was coarse, "With all that building going on, the constant hammering would drive a family batty."

Ellissa put her hand on her husband's arm, "Mrs. Dreggers, she's the town librarian, Cary, told me the family used to travel for six-weeks each year. That way they missed the mess and came home to a surprise. It's amazing how differently folks show their love for one another, isn't it?"

"Yes," answered Burt. He looked down at his wife's hand on his jacket and covered it with his own.

Witnessing this gesture, Carolena was reminded of her parents and of their lost love.

Ellissa saw her face drop and became concerned. "Cary, what's the matter? Are you getting an upset? This is an awfully bumpy ride."

Recovering, at least on the outside, she flashed her brilliant smile. Ellissa mustn't learn of their mother's foibles. "Just some dust in my eye." She blinked rapidly several times. "There. I think it's all gone now."

The road followed the curves of the Little Conemaugh River. In the daylight, Carolena saw the tiny towns she'd heard the porter announce on the train. Although they each had different names, they seemed linked because all sat on the river that sliced through them.

"If you're hungry, Cary, feel free to nibble anything in the square wooden crate right behind you. I always make extra for the trip."

"Thank you. I'm not so much hungry as I am tempted. Would either of you like something?"

"I'm fine for now. Ellissa fed me full just before we left."

"Nothing for me either. I have to watch what I eat if I want my Burt to continue watching me." She glanced at her husband, and he threw a wink right back.

Carolena untied the string holding the lid secure atop the crate. A package wrapped in two blue and white striped tea towels was the first she saw on top of the others, so she took it out and set it on her lap. It was pound cake. Salivating, she wanted to take a bite immediately. As if reading her mind, Ellissa said, "Oh, there's a sharp knife, handle up, in the corner of the crate if you need it."

"Thank you. I do." With that, Carolena cut the heel off the cake and took a lady-like nibble. A soft "Mmm," was the result.

"I hate to say I told you so, but didn't I tell you my Lissa is the best cook around?"

"Mmm," Carolena repeated.

Ellissa looked over her shoulder and smiled when she saw Carolena slice off a second helping.

"You caught me," the blonde admitted, a little embarrassed.

"I'm glad you like it."

"I think it's the best pound cake I've ever had."

"It may be the cream that makes the difference. It's called Heavy Whipping Cream Pound Cake."

"If this cake is a sample of your culinary capabilities, I can't wait to try something else."

After noon, and while sampling an oatmeal raisin cookie, Carolena heard the sound of rushing water. Dead ahead was a wall of huge boulders covered with wild grass, flowers, and saplings. It seemed solid except for the wide sheet of water pouring through a hole in the far left side of it. "What on earth is that thing?"

"That *thing* is the South Fork Dam. It holds the reservoir the rich folks named Lake Conemaugh," Burt told her. "The dam is 72 feet high and 930 feet long."

"I hate to ask," queried the girl from Florida, "but is the dam strong enough to hold an entire lake?"

"Sure it's strong," he answered. "At least we all hope so."

A look passed between the Bauers. "Lake Conemaugh is about three miles long and a mile wide, and the dam is supposed to be the biggest earthen dam in the country. It's owned by the members of the club. You may have heard of some of them. Mellon, Laughlin, McClintock, Carnegie, Phipps, Frick? The group formed in '79 after Benjamin Ruff bought the property from Congressman John Reilly who'd bought it from the Pennsylvania Railroad in '75. The dam was originally built in the latter part of the 1840s so there'd be water for the canal and railroad system connecting Philadelphia and Pittsburgh. A few years later, the waterways were converted to steam railroad. Then in 1857, the Pennsylvania Railroad purchased the whole thing, including the crumbling dam and its lake. It wasn't needed anymore and was left to continue to deteriorate. It broke once, but since the water loss was slight, little damage was done to anything. Another seventeen years passed until the men from the club bought it. The leaks were plugged, and the break was filled in by dumping layers and layers of dirt, tree stumps and logs, gravel, brush, and whatever else was around. They topped it off with a layer of boulders."

Burt heard the concern in Carolena's voice. "That seems a little haphazard."

"A rubble dam is strong so long as water doesn't wash over it. Of course, you can't tell 'cause it's covered with lake water, Cary, but I'm told the wall is around 270 feet thick at its base. Look there." Burt pointed toward the top of the dam. "See that wagon up yonder? Probably workers. There's a two lane road atop it."

Just then, they heard the unmistakable sound of a rifle being cocked. A man in a black coat and hat was pointing a shotgun at them. "Who goes there?" he demanded.

"It's me, mister, Burt Bauer. Me and my wife here work part time for the club." Burt turned to his companions to whisper, "This must be a new guard." Digging into his hip pocket, he produced a wrinkled card. Still speaking in hushed tones, "I usually know the men who patrol the perimeter. They don't like trespassers or poachers. The general public is allowed only as far as the small waterfall at the foot of the dam. Ellissa and I had a picnic or two there ourselves before we began working here."

They were now even with the guard. Burt halted the wagon, showing his pass to the man. After reading it carefully, the watchman handed it back, waving the Bauer wagon to proceed.

Carolena had never seen anything like this. These people were either very snooty or had great and vast possessions to protect. She hoped they were so stinking rich they would drop their funds in her lap without a second thought.

Burt clucked his tongue. "Get to goin', mules."

They responded quickly to make the last of the trek up the hill to the crest. There, Carolena saw Lake Conemaugh. Burt was right. It was huge, and she observed its surface lay only five or six feet below the top of the dam itself.

"When the season is in full swing," he informed her, "you'll see all manner of craft on the water. Everything from rowboats, canoes, and sailboats to a miniature-sized steamboat and even an electric catamaran!"

All that maritime activity is nothing compared to what my talents will bring them, Carolena wanted to say. She kept her thoughts to herself, thinking how conceited she would sound.

Unexpectedly, Burt handed the reins to Ellissa, and he coughed hard. With one hand, Ellissa pulled the wagon to a halt while she rubbed his back with the other.

"Pardon," he said apologizing.

Carolena noticed the bright stain of red on Burt's white handkerchief. Following Ellissa's lead, she filed her concern for later.

Regaining his breath, Burt continued as if nothing were ailing him. "The lake is stocked with black bass, so the fishing's always good. You see, Cary, these industrialists escape from Pittsburgh, and the very air and water they themselves pollute, to come up here to enjoy their profits."

Carolena noted his bitterness.

Burt cleared his throat twice, reconsidering. "I shouldn't feel resentful because they provide work for so many families below."

Forcing her eyes from the body of water that would bring her good fortune, Carolena saw the South Fork Fishing and Hunting Club complex off to the right. From a distance, it looked like doll houses. She counted five cottages connected by boardwalks, then a huge building she assumed to be the main clubhouse, then another eleven cottages. Some of the so-called cottages were two-storied with long windows, full and steeply gabled roofs, and deep porches which would soon, she imagined, service cigar-smoking tycoons in dark suits and round derbies. Discussions of finance or whatever subjects men of power deem interesting would ensue on those porches.

"The club house has forty-seven rooms." It was Ellissa's turn. "The dining room seats 150 people, and there's always plenty of banjo music. Or at least that was popular last summer. Oh, there's a huge patch of wild strawberries over there. I pick them and make jam."

Jack Patrick entered Carolena's mind. How many times back home had the whole family gone berry picking and returned with him all sticky, his face striped in red strawberry juice, his version of Indian war paint.

"The ladies mostly wear white and stroll the grounds carrying their parasols or wearing their picture hats. From a distance, they look like drifting fluffs of cotton or burst dandelion pods, depending upon your mood." They all chuckled. "Hammocks are hung between the massive trees, and servants in uniform offer refreshment."

"I could get used to that kind of treatment real quick," offered Burt without hesitation. "Maybe someday you'll have the chance to be pampered, Lissa, the way you deserve."

Carolena wanted them to have a taste of luxury aboard an Aqua Verde ship, a luxury she had taken for granted too many times. For all her intelligence, this was the first moment Carolena understood the true meaning behind the company's motto. Her family wanted to provide relaxation and coddling for the common man. Not that Ellissa and Burt were common. Lord no! She just wanted to do something for them, to treat them, but that was impossible right now. "You both work very hard. Too hard."

"Oh, we're not complaining, Cary. We have a good life."

Ellissa spoke the truth. If the Bauers never discovered the pleasures of a holiday aboard a luxury liner, they would still have rich lives because love cushioned all burdens.

Carolena was unwavering in her desire for them. Some day, if it were within her power to give, Ellissa and Burt and Mary Coe Bauer would enjoy the high life.

Chapter 24

Cary Dunne was the talk of Johnstown. Another yacht had been ordered, this time by Mr. Ashton himself! Ellissa realized Cary was hard-pressed to keep up with her new workload. Yet, it was that demand for her work that was all consuming. Almost.

When the subject of Cary's love life surfaced, she tried to explain away her relationship with Grey as casual. From the dreamy expression in her eyes, it was apparent things went much deeper.

When Carolena came downstairs the first evening of her stay at Ellissa's, she asked, "May I help with dinner?"

"If you'd fill the water glasses, please."

"Of course. I have to tell you, I love your home. Despite its good size, it's cozy and welcoming."

"That's what I want. I'm glad you feel it, too."

The kitchen was enormous, and the table round. Carolena imagined Grandpa Pap sitting there, tapping the saltshaker with his index finger as she'd been told he did, seasoning his fried eggs. The spiral newel post in the front hall was the same dark walnut Grammy had spoken of, polished to gleaming from the fannies of her girls who had ridden its length. There was a chicken coop out back. Carolena recalled her mother's childhood fear of chickens had come from peckings received while gathering eggs. To this day, it was a chore Miss Ella eagerly gave to others. Miss Ella, Miss Ella. Her mother was always creeping into her thoughts!

The front door slammed, knocking all bygone days from Carolena's mind.

"Cary, may I present my daughter?" Ellissa said, putting her arms around the shoulders of a youngster carrying a small box decorated with lace, buttons, and ribbon.

Carolena was taken aback. Standing there was a child who could have been herself almost twenty years ago! The girl had blonde hair and large green eyes. When she smiled, that grin was Carolena's own! Surely, Ellissa had to see this resemblance, didn't she?

"Miss Cary Dunne," Ellissa cooed with pride, "I'd like you to meet the light of my life, my little angel, Mary Coe."

"Hello, Mary Coe."

The child in the blue-dotted dress and grimy apron from playing, curtsied. "Hello, Miss Dunne. You're very pretty, almost as pretty as my mama."

This brought a tear to both women. As Carolena held out her hand, her face showed a newly found serenity, a look Ellissa hadn't seen before.

"Why are you two crying?" asked Burt when he entered though the back door. "Is everything alright?"

"Oh!" exclaimed Ellissa. "Yes, everything's fine, honey. Just women being women," and she kissed her husband's stubbled cheek.

"Is that all? Ellissa is so sentimental, she cries at the drop of a hat. Looks like you do, too, Cary."

Carolena smiled and nodded.

"I'd best be getting cleaned up, Lissa. I know how you like a man with a smooth face." He winked at Carolena, then kissed his wife's check with a loud smack and chucked his daughter under the chin.

Mary Coe reached into the pocket of her formerly crisp white pinafore and pulled something out.

"What cha got there, girlie girl?" her papa asked.

"It's a secret." It was clear she wanted to share that secret and was only hesitating because she didn't know Carolena.

"I think I'll fetch a handkerchief from my room if you all will excuse me," said Carolena.

"Don't be long, dear," Ellissa called after her.

"No. Just long enough," Carolena replied knowingly and disappeared upstairs.

"I'm glad she's gone. I didn't want her to hear."

"Hear what?" Burt asked his child.

"Well, Sadie, you know her. She lives across the street from the bandstand. She's my best friend this week. Me and she was—"

"She and I were," corrected her mother.

"Right. She and I were playing a fast game of Kick the Can along with Rudy, Andy, Bobby, Betsy, and Rose. My team won. Anyhow, when I went to put on my sweater to come home, I found a surprise under it. It's the prettiest thing I've ever seen. There's a note with it that says it's called a Secret Pebble. Sadie gave it to me so I can remember the fun times we have together. Like when old lady Shunk sits on her window balcony in the shadows so we don't see her till we cut across her yard, and she hollers, 'You awful children. Don't make me have to come down there and chase you with a stick.' Then her dog, Punky, begins barking and she starts throwing potato peelings at us over the rail. We can't just let her get away with that, can we?" Allowing no moment for reply, Mary Coe added, "So we put a frog in her milk box or something." She stopped suddenly, not wanting to reveal too much, or her mother would call her a dickens and tell her how that wasn't what young ladies should be doing.

Mary Coe went on, "Every time I look at my Secret Pebble, it'll remind me how lucky I am to have Sadie as a friend. She said I could keep it or give it to someone else I've shared a memory with or have a secret with or somebody I love. All I know is, it made me feel special, and I like feeling special. I might never give it away."

"And you are special, darling." Ellissa bent over and took her little girl in her arms.

"Wanta see it, Daddy?"

"Sure," Burt told her.

Mary Coe opened her hand flat. Lying across her dirty palm was a small, round, glass stone with a hand painted yellow flower on it.

"You're right, child," Burt said. "That is pretty. Though not quite as pretty as you are."

"Oh Daddy, you're always saying things like that." She carefully placed the pebble in the center of her mother's hand.

Ellissa held it to the light. "It almost looks like it's lit from within. You're so right. It is a special treasure. What a lovely thing it is."

Mary Coe took the pebble and slipped it back into her pocket. "I'll never lose it!"

As children often do, she changed the subject. "Daddy, I don't understand two of the arithmetic problems in my homework today. Would you help me with 'em after supper?"

"Sure thing." His mouth curled into a smile as he passed Carolena on her way down the stairs. "Just want to remind you," he told his wife, "how both my girls are answered prayers from God."

The scene made Carolena think of Grey. He probably would never say such touching sentiments. They'd embarrass him. It was fine. He had other ways of expression. Carolena blushed, and Ellissa saw.

"Cary, would you mind taking the cake out of the oven. I can smell that it's done."

"My mother says that same thing," Carolena said in passing and gritted her teeth when, again, her mother emerged. Wait- their mother. She grabbed the woven potholders from the hook near the stove and removed the white cake, spotting the bowl of chocolate nut frosting on the drain board.

"Funny. My mother says it, too. I guess practiced bakers use common expressions."

Carolena quickly replied, "I guess," and changed the subject. "I'm sorry. Here I am daydreaming, and there you are slaving away."

"I'm hardly slaving. I set the table earlier, and I'm just stirring the soup. It's ready to go. We usually eat here in the kitchen. Tonight, though, we'll sup in the dining room."

"I appreciate it, Ellissa. Don't think you have to go to any extra effort for me."

"I love to cook, so anything I do is never trouble. Did I mention we're having company?"

***

Carolena wondered who would be drinking from the fifth water glass she'd filled. She wished Grey were the company coming. Since her landlords had yet to make his acquaintance, it would be one of their friends. Friend. Grey was so much more than a friend to her. He was a lover. She tightened her lips so as not to smile at the very idea. Straight-laced Carolena Dunnigan had taken a lover! Aw, but he was the man she adored. How she longed to be with him, and he felt the same.

The only time since Happy's party that Carolena and Grey had been alone together had been when he escorted her to the library or the emporium after work. "We must talk," he'd said. She'd agreed. Instead, they'd filled those too few seconds locked in an embrace. "We have to be alone. Not touching you, not laying my hands against your satin skin is … is making me crazy. You're all I think about."

"We just don't have the opportunity since I'm on a deadline with my work, Grey. You know how important my success is for my brother and sisters."

He'd replied with a resentful and honest grunt as he nuzzled her neck.

"I can't think when you do that. You know I can't. Besides, we don't have a site to go to."

"Quit sounding like an architect, would you? If you weren't the woman you are, I'd find a *site*, as you call it, fast enough. That's not what I want for Carolena Dunnigan. A bed of pine straw was fine for our first time. It fit the wild feelings we shared. I want more now. I want to take my time to show you my heart." She had been startled and pleased he was able to speak such delicate words of love and wanted …

"Look who I found wandering about town," announced Burt as he ushered Grey into the parlor. "We got to chatting about this and that and discovered we had a mutual friend in Cary, the girl who draws pictures of boats. And well, here he is."

Carolena was shocked and extremely pleased. Approaching him in greeting, she retrieved her handkerchief from her sleeve and dabbed at the raindrops on his face. She halted, catching her breath, realizing she was performing a personal act, a thing one would never do in a platonic relationship with a male.

"Good evening, Miss Carolena."

She smiled in polite response, "Mr. Grey."

"May I present my wife, Ellissa, and daughter, Mary Coe?"

It came to Carolena she had never told Grey of her plans with Ellissa, nor had she inquired about her family or her father's condition or even what Grey was doing with himself while she worked. What if he inadvertently blurted out something she wasn't ready to reveal? Dear God! Too many secrets.

While Grey recognized the family resemblance, his face wore only the pleasant mask of a new acquaintance. "It's an honor, ma'am," he replied in truth, bowing over her extended hand.

"My goodness," the big sister remarked at his gallantry.

Grey turned to Mary Coe. "Hello, Princess. It's good to meet you. Your father brags about you."

"He's nice, Mama. No one has ever called me a princess before."

"It's high time we did, darling Princess." All eyes twinkled, especially

Carolena's and Grey's.

Ellissa and Burt could see right through Carolena's pretense of innocent friendship with this man. And as dinner progressed, Burt asked in a teasing, formal fashion, "Why are you so jittery, Miss Dunne?"

Grey heard the strange name and his gaze traveled up from his meal to look upon a fidgeting Carolena. Concentrating on her eyes, he attempted to read her mind because, clearly, she was sending him some sort of message.

Those green eyes begged him caution as to how much he revealed about her.

"Could it be that our dinner guest makes you nervous?"

Mary Coe giggled.

Ellissa stepped in. "Burt Bauer, don't be mocking Cary. She's worn out from all the effort she's been putting in on her drawings."

"Sorry, Cary," he said easily. "Mr. McKenna, have you seen her work? It's a marvel what that girl can produce on paper."

"Call me Grey, folks. Please. Yes, I've seen her work first hand."

Carolena was shaking now. She sat on her left hand to keep it from tapping the silverware while her right mercifully was occupied with twirling the dinner fork. Unable to swallow food, she set down the fork and grabbed at her dress, balling its skirt into a wrinkled lump. She rose from the table, heading toward the kitchen. "Anyone need more coffee? No? Well, I could use another cup. If you'll excuse me."

"Where do you work, Mr. Grey?" Mary Coe asked.

Seeing no need to complicate matters by telling of his unexpected leave of absence from Aqua Verde, he answered, "I'm on a sort of holiday right now, Princess. I've been making sure things are in order at my house."

"Here in town?" Ellissa asked. "You have a home here?"

"Do you know that big old house up yonder?"

"You mean McKenna Hall?" Burt asked.

"Yes, sir."

McKenna Hall? Was Carolena over-hearing correctly? That was Grey's house? In the excitement of being with her sister that first trip to the club, the name of the owner of the property had never come up. She imagined a life with Grey in his ancestral home, with Ellissa and her family below in the valley. She'd miss Fernandina mightily, of course, but she'd have her new family here in Johnstown, and Jack Patrick and Bree and Marie could visit. It would be a happily ever after ending for everyone!

Burt was talking. "I figured you might be related to the family."

"I used to live there as a child. Haven't been back since I was in my teens. No one lives there but the housekeeper, groundskeeper, and my uncle on and off. I'll have to oversee the overall upkeep now my brother, Grant, has passed away."

Grey displayed no remorse in his voice, sounding strangely indifferent to Ellissa and Burt.

"I'm sorry to hear that," Burt told him. "We heard some fancy musician owned it."

Grey answered simply, "It's still in my family."

"Does that mean you're planning on moving in permanently up there?"

The stress of mention of his brother plus hoping she would hear him answer yes to Burt's question became too much for Carolena. Her quaking hand lost its strength, making the blue spatter-ware pot of hot coffee feel like a twenty-pound iron. Her grasp on the woven potholder covering the handle loosened, and the thing crashed onto the stove and bounced once as it hit the wooden floor. The din was quickly followed by a tiny scream as hot coffee landed on Carolena's skirt.

Grey was the first to respond. He found Carolena on her knees, dishrag in hand, mopping up the mess, and sobbing. Relieved, he took hold of her arms and helped her up. "Hey now. What's this all about? I'm sure Miss Ellissa won't throw you out into the street just because you spilled a little coffee."

"Oh, my dear," her sister rushed in. "Please, don't cry. I'll clean it up. It's nothing. Why you should see the messes I make. Burt, remember the time I dropped the crock of honey, and it smashed right here on this very floor? Then that dog we had ran through and tracked it clear up the stairs before I could catch him. Took me two days to get up all the sticky."

Carolena was still crying.

Burt held a chair, and Grey led her to it.

"Maybe," said Mary Coe with concern, "maybe Miss Cary got burned."

The adults all looked at one another. "Cary, is that it? Were you scalded?" Grey took hold of her tear-streaked face.

She had to think, to make her mind feel her body. Her emotions were such a wreck, she'd been unaware of much else. Suddenly, she realized her leg felt like fire. "Yes, yes! It's my right leg!"

Although, he'd seen her leg in the moonlit darkness, Grey knew she'd protest in front of the others. He ignored her modesty and snatched up her skirt and slips. Her stocking was wet. Pulling it down, he exposed her ivory skin, red and blistering. "Ellissa, quick! Get me the biggest butcher knife you've got."

Dear God, what's Grey going to do to me? "Grey, don't cut me?" she panicked. "It's just a little burn!"

Ellissa handed him the gleaming blade she'd pulled from the drawer.

"Are you all crazy? No, no! Don't," she screamed, and Burt came around the back of the chair and grasped her shoulders.

Grey looked at her as if she'd lost her mind. He proceeded to place the three-inch blade flat against her scorched skin.

She stopped struggling when she felt the steel's icy coolness begin to absorb the heat of her burn. Feeling utterly foolish, she tried to apologize to them all.

"No need, Cary. You just didn't know what we were going to do. The key to forgiveness is understanding," said Ellissa, wringing cold water out of a clean cotton dishcloth and laying it over the wound.

It sounded as if her mother had just spoken. Same voice, same wise words. But this wasn't her mother. Ellissa was a better woman than her mother was. She would never do anything despicable.

Propping Carolena's leg on another chair, Ellissa poured more cold water over the cloth without removing it. She let the excess drip into a large pan below. Burt fetched his shaving mug for his wife and she spread foamy lather on the burned area. The pain was gone and the doctoring completed with an application of egg white and a bandage.

Grey carried Carolena upstairs to her bed. All followed to tend her. Ellissa supplied a snifter of brandy with a cinnamon stick while Burt stoked the fire.

Mary Coe retrieved the Secret Pebble from her skirt pocket. "Here you go, Miss Cary," said the little girl, presenting the glass stone to Carolena along with a soothing pat to the forearm. "This is my Secret Pebble. You can have it until you're feeling better. Then, I need it back, please."

"It's so pretty, Coey. I'll take proper care of it and give it back to you in the morning, after I've had sweet dreams."

"Coey," the little girl said. "I like that name. Mama, you can call me Princess Coey, if you ever want to."

"I'll be happy to, Your Majesty."

Looking about the room at her smiling family, Carolena's eyes filled with tears again. "You all have been so good to me. I hope I don't cause you too much trouble. Thank you. Every one of you. Thank you."

Ellissa kissed Cary's forehead while Burt gently pinched her toes under the covers.

"Come along, you two." Ellissa directed her husband and child. "You can both help me finish the dishes. Let's let Mr. McKenna be the one to tell Cary a bedtime story." Leaving the door slightly ajar, she led Burt and Mary Coe down the stairs like chicks after a mother hen.

"Grey, Grey." Carolena was in his arms, and he was stroking her long, loose hair. "I've made a mess of everything. They must think me mad, the way I took on so downstairs. And how am I going to explain to Ellissa why I haven't told her we're sisters? You do realize we're sisters, don't you?"

"Yes, honey. I put it all together."

Her chatter continued. "And my dear little niece. She looks just like me, don't you think? And my completed drafts are finally the way the clients want them. At least I hope they are. They have to be because Breelan and the children need the down payments so desperately. Which means, of course, I'll have to bite the bullet and take on the distasteful job of contacting my father. Assuming he's still alive?"

His expression impartial, Grey nodded. "He is."

"Hmm," was her only reply. "I'll tell him I've commissioned yachts for the company to build. And I want to be with you again. To have you hold me and make love to me. Soon, soon."

As she eased into sleep, Grey watched, wanting to make it all right for her in every way, if only he were able. Putting aside unsettling thoughts for the time being, he looked at her face, peaceful in its slumber. His eyes moved down her body and back up. He wanted her. He would never tire of her. He bent, tasting her sleeping cinnamon lips an instant longer than he should have. His mind consumed, he walked to the stairs and down to the front door, exiting without a thought of goodbye or thank you to his hosts.

Watching from the parlor, Burt turned the page of the newspaper he was reading. "That man's got it bad, Lissa."

"There's no mistaking it. You were right to be concerned for Cary. I'm glad we invited Mr. McKenna to supper tonight. That couple is in love. We've got to see to it the two of them get together, legally, I mean, before it's too late - if it isn't already."

Chapter 25

Ellissa witnessed rain often. Too often. Damage from that God-awful flood two years ago was just now abating. Today, Thursday, the thirtieth of May, she counted as the eleventh day of rain this month. Moreover, the previous month, she'd been told the heavens had dropped some 14 inches of snow in the mountains. The rapid thaw ran the rivers deep. Still, the citizens made light of it. Her own husband laughed at the weather, saying it was the price paid for living in so beautiful an area of the country among all the great and thirsty hardwoods.

Cary was expected in a few hours. She and Burt had ridden horses to the club yesterday, so she could check in with Mr. Ashton. That was fine. The part Ellissa didn't care for was Cary returning all that way, alone, with a stop at McKenna Hall to see Grey's home. Ellissa contemplated Cary's definition of *stop*. She thought again of the softly spoken question asked her by the flushed unmarried miss as she put on her coat to leave. "Are your monthlies ever irregular?"

Burt had entered the front hall ready to leave just then, so there was no time for an in depth discussion between the two women. Although Ellissa understood the importance of the question, her simple answer of reassurance soothed Cary's worry for her immediate health. Did she think no further than that, Ellissa pondered? For such an analytically minded person, Cary's naiveté came as a surprise.

"No sense looking for trouble," Ellissa reminded herself out loud. "Cary assured me she'd be back in time for the Decoration Day festivities. I'll just be glad when she's here safe and not in a situation that could put her in harm's way."

Ellissa picked up the photograph of her husband from the parlor table. "My poor Burt," she said. "You've got duty for another forty-eight hours up there. You'll miss the ceremony at the cemetery. I can hear you saying it can't be helped. A responsible man isn't likely to risk his job unless dire circumstances arise." She sighed and looked out the window. The road was slick with mud. Clouds tormented the sunshine. Thunder snapped and dishes rattled in the corner china cabinet. Ellissa hoped the rain would hold off at least long enough to have the parade.

Ellissa called to Mary Coe, home from school for the holiday. "Time for piano practice, Princess Coey."

"Coming, Mama. Then can we play tic-tac-toe?" came the voice from upstairs.

"Yes, ma'am. Sounds like fun." The doting mother picked up her sewing basket from the tri-legged stool beside the old rocking chair and sat down. She straightened out the rolled strips of red, white, and blue fabric and proceeded to weave two patriotic medallions. Each would have a brass button stitched in its center. One would be for Cary to pin to her collar and the other for Grey. As her daughter pounded out her scales, Ellissa forced all worry from her mind, concentrating on her daughter's even rhythm and the fact that, so far in this lesson, she'd only hit three clinkers. Ever hopeful, she imagined young Mary Coe's musical future. Ellissa smiled, unaware her toe was tapping. Her beat was irregular because it wasn't the tune from the piano she accompanied, but the pounding raindrops, dancing on her roof.

***

"Grey! Grey!" Please be home, Carolena thought. Please be home!

The right side of the front double-door opened to reveal the wood paneled welcome hall of the man Carolena loved. There he was. Saying nothing, he ignored her wet cape to pull her into his house and into his arms. Pushing the door closed with a mild slam, he looked into her face and told her, "It's been an eternity since I've kissed you, Carolena Dunnigan."

She breathed him in and held him tight. She couldn't get enough of him. They clawed at each other. Her sopping wrap was getting his shirt front wet. He didn't care or even notice. Neither did she. Suddenly something came to mind, and she stilled.

"What is it, darling?"

"Are we alone? Are there servants about? Workmen? I don't want anyone walking in on us."

He answered her with more kisses. "No, no, my conservative pearl. No one is around. Uncle Jax, my lawyer and dear friend, is up in his room in his favorite chair going over the household finances. He's retired and lives here when he's not traveling. Our Mrs. Grossmyer is in the kitchen."

"Good," she whispered, rubbing the front of his chest through his wet shirt.

Helping her off with her cape, he flung it in the direction of a chair, not noticing it landed on the floor. Grey off-handedly remarked, "You weren't so careful that night in the woods. What makes you shy now?" He was teasing, complimenting her on her wild and pleasure-giving ways.

She colored, and he felt the immediate change between them.

Holding her face, he scoured it with questioning eyes. "What's wrong?"

She couldn't speak.

Smiling, he said," Why are you blushing, Cary? Believe me, I'm sincere."

Pulling from him, "Remember what I told you about calling me Cary? I hate that name! It's okay for Ellissa and her family because they don't know who I am, but not for you. And there I was displaying raw emotion for maybe the first time in my life, and you made me feel like a tramp."

Damn it! He took her to him again. "That's the last thing I'd ever mean. You've misunderstood, Car - Carolena." He gently nibbled on her delicate earlobe.

She wanted to stop him. She could not. What he was doing felt too delightful.

"I'm only happy you're comfortable enough with me to be spontaneous and impulsive. I swear that was all I meant. I don't want to hurt you. Ever. I love you."

It had been a whisper, but it was as if a multitude had spoken his last three words. Although the phrase was simple, the depth of its meaning was a lifetime commitment from him to her.

"Oh, Grey! My darling. I love you, too. I have for so long."

He had been the first to actually say the word *love*. He'd thought it plenty of times. Irrational jealousy surfaced when his mind showed him the vision of her with another, his own brother. The image of the two of them repulsed him. He could mention her past indiscretion to punish her. He did not want any of that.

Before this minute, his all-consuming question was when would they next lie together? He realized he'd been thinking only of the present, the immediate. Not the future. Suddenly, it was he who became pensive. His hold on her loosened.

Unfounded insecurity swallowed Carolena. Had his interest somehow waned? "Grey?" Surely he wasn't tired of her, was he? How could he be? They'd only been together that one tree-sheltered night. Why, only seconds earlier, he'd declared his love for her. She'd simply have to get used to his moods, as he would hers …

She switched topics and began studying her magnificent surroundings. "Come and show me your McKenna Hall, Grey." She was anxious to see the home in which they would share their lives.

He didn't seem himself. He was more sober, though he hadn't had a drop to drink. She led him from room to room asking questions. Obviously, Mrs. Grossmyer loved the house as her own because it was spotless. They made a pass through the dining room and walked into the huge kitchen where Carolena met a large woman wearing a sweet, knowing grin. Her German accent was heavy, so Carolena thought it best to smile her most winning smile and nod in agreement.

They went through the parlor then on to the study. Grey pointed out the library and the music room, where he'd been made to practice. Carolena figured he preferred outdoor activities. While there was nothing wrong with that, she would see these rooms, particularly the library, were put to good use. On up to the bedrooms. "What are the carved notches on the corner molding here in the hall, Grey?"

He smiled. "It's a growth chart. Look, closely and you'll see the faded pencil markings on the wall telling my name and dates as I grew. "

His neglect to mention his brother's ever-increasing height was fine with her. She would have the wall painted over. It would be a shame to loose Grey's history, yet removal of negative reminders was sometimes the better thing to do.

Grey knocked on Uncle Jax's door, and a tall thin man with remarkably black hair for his advanced age answered. "It's grand to meet you, Miss Dunnigan. Grey's a changed man just from the knowing of you. I was planning on coming down and properly welcoming you until I discovered our boy here got his hands on my accounts. I'm having a devil of a time trying to figure out his numbers."

Many men would have been embarrassed by the remark. Not Grey. He understood his limitations and balancing accounts was one thing he never cared about doing.

"I hope you're handy with figures, Miss. Someone needs to be."

Simple exchanges from Mrs. Grossmyer, whatever it was she had said, and now from Uncle Jax, made Carolena feel like part of the McKenna family already. Modest in her response, since mathematics was a thing of sheer enjoyment to her, she said, "I've been known to cipher a column or two. After all, I managed to sum up Grey McKenna, didn't I?"

Uncle Jax roared, "My girl, my girl. You have beauty and brains. Welcome." He leaned down to place a kiss on her temple.

Smiling again, yet still looking somehow vacant in his expression, Grey said, "See you later, Uncle Jax. Don't be too long. I don't want you to over tire yourself."

With a wave of his bony hand, the old gentleman's kind face disappeared behind the six-paneled walnut door.

In the master bedroom, Carolena hurried over to the window to see the view from the second story. It was then she noticed some script etched in the glass on the lower right pane.

The gray light of the cloudy day illuminated the sweeping cursive. "What is this?" she asked, bending to read the signature of Lettie McKenna.

"My mother wrote her name on the glass with the diamond ring my father gave her." He said no more, and Carolena wondered what happened to the ring. She hoped Grey would give it to her so she could carve the name Carolena McKenna there, too.

Finishing the tour, they re-entered the parlor and sat close beside one another on the leather sofa facing the fireplace. The length of their bodies touched. She took his hand and asked, "Who decorated this house? It's a real showplace."

"My mother."

Getting no more information, she ceased further questioning, commenting only on the beauty and good taste of the mansion. Her gaze settled on the picture above the mantle shrouded in a sheet. Springing from her seat, she grabbed the corner of the cloth to peak beneath just as Grey shouted, "No!"

Startled, her hand jerked, and the covering floated down, draping her shoulder and arm. She looked first at him and gasped at his ghostly coloration. Then, she looked up at the oil portrait of a man, a woman and two boys. This was his family.

There were tears in his eyes now and he stood, turning away so she wouldn't see. He left the room and went directly into his father's study. He was pouring some whiskey into a glass when Carolena entered.

"I'm sorry. I didn't mean to upset you." She crossed to him and placed a comforting hand on his arm. "Don't worry, darling. Once we're married and living here, we'll fill this place with life. We'll —"

"We'll do what?" he exploded! "Don't you at least think you ought to wait until you're proposed to before you move into my house?"

What had seemed a natural assumption was now clearly stupid conjecture. She was mortified. She wanted to disappear. How could he say he loved her and treat her so miserably? Fleeing him, his tempers, and his precious McKenna Hall, she exited the front door, the same one he'd welcomed her through only an hour earlier.

Spurring her horse, she heard him screaming after her, "You will never live here! Do you hear? Never!"

Chapter 26

"Wasn't it a wonderful Decoration Day, Cary? Red, white, and blue was everywhere. And so many people. Mama said they came from Somerset and Altoona and New Florence just to hear the speakers and the music." Mary Coe caught the clean stockings Carolena tossed at her. "I hope Mama can't get out all this mud. Those dirty things are the most uncomfortable pair I own. They bunch up in my shoes." Donning a yellow plaid skirt from her armoire, the little girl continued. "I can't understand how you keep yourself so clean. We all walked on the same ground, didn't we? Just look at the hem of my skirt. I'm glad the rain held off until now, aren't you? Mama said if it lets up again, we'll go to the cemetery and pull weeds around the graves. We do that to honor the war dead, Mama said."

Coey continued chattering. She reminded Carolena of Nora. Was Nora still being courted by that volunteer fireman? Carolena thought of her family in Florida. Since the telegraph office was closed because of the holiday, she decided to send a wire the next day saying she'd been successful in her bid to sell her work. This evening, she would take the time to write a long letter home. She missed everyone so much. She worried Marie was still excruciatingly shy and hoped Jack Patrick was helping Bree more than hindering. How were crotchety Peeper and dear Clover? Carolena knew her father was still alive and that was enough information where he was concerned. As she mused, Carolena made up her mind to tell Ellissa everything, and soon. She could not continue to live with her under a false identity.

They were interrupted by Ellissa's knock on Mary Coe's open door. "It's just me, girls. You both dry? Good thing. It's nasty outside, so chilly and damp. Supper will be ready in a few minutes, but I'm afraid we'll have to eat fast. The rain's been coming down hard for a long while, and it's time to start toting some of the lighter things upstairs. We'll find a neighbor man to help with the heavier pieces. I'm afraid the rising water will be inside the house before we know it. It's already half-way up the first step of the porch."

This amazed Carolena and excited her, too. She had heard stories of such things, never thinking she would be involved in a flood! Besides, it took her mind off that horrible Grey. When she'd arrived back at Ellissa's before the ceremony, her sister had only asked how her business had gone. Ellissa appeared sincerely pleased at Cary's potential success, yet was preoccupied herself. It seemed best for both not to speak of their worries.

Once the dinner dishes were dried, the women struggled with the dining table, moving it into the kitchen in order to roll up the rug beneath. Mary Coe began to gather the irreplaceable glass, porcelain and other delicate sit-abouts without having to be told. The photographs, the green and white plate commemorating the end of the war, the golden quartz rock whose facets made it look like a toad, the family Bible. All the treasures went into a wicker basket until it was full. Mary Coe set it down in search of another container.

There was a knock on the front door and Mary Coe ran to answer it. "Cary, it's for you."

Carolena and Ellissa were on their knees still rolling the parlor carpet, wondering who would come out in this weather. Just as she recognized the large figure in black rain-gear, lightening cracked, accompanied by a clap of thunder sounding so loud, it jarred the chimneys of the oil lamps. Carolena jumped. It was as if the heavens were announcing the arrival of some kind of god, she thought, as she took in the hard, still appealing face of Grey. He was no god to her, she countered silently, and her crooked smile was cold.

Rushing past Carolena, Ellissa reached for his wet sleeve, inviting him in as she pushed the door shut against the wet wind. "My soul! I can't believe you'd brave this storm!" She looked to Cary then back to Grey. "Well, maybe I can." It was obvious from Cary's unenthusiastic welcome they'd had some sort of row.

"It's the devil's own night out there." Grey spoke as if nothing had happened.

"Please the Lord, it'll soon stop, Grey."

"Amen to that. I put my horse in your stall, if that's all right. I fed him before we left so he's good with the fresh water I gave him."

"Certainly. There's feed if you need it, just in case."

"Thank you, ma'am." As innocent acting as Jack Patrick speaking to a nun at school after he'd put tacks on her seat, Grey said, "When Miss Cary stopped to visit me this morning, she mentioned Burt would be up at the club for a couple of days. I came to check on you ladies and see if there's anything I can do to help."

"You dear man! Come in, come in. Let me have your coat." Ellissa hung it on the newel post and set his gum-rubber boots on a tray in the corner. "Have you had your supper?"

"Yes, ma'am. I stopped at a restaurant on my way here."

"Pshaw! Next time, if you don't come on directly and eat my cooking, you might as well trample my feelings as soon as look at me."

"Wouldn't want to do that. I won't be making the same mistake twice. You can count on it."

He stepped closer to Carolena. She stood her ground, ignoring the heat radiating from his body. Restaurant, huh? It was probably a saloon. He did look a little peaked beneath the surface. Probably hung over, she reckoned. I hope your head pounds so hard and loud, I can play piano to the metronome of its throbbing beat.

"As a matter of fact, I was just going to go 'round to see if I could scout up a neighbor to help us carry the heavy furniture upstairs. Now you're here, Cary and I can get on one end and you on the other. No need to bother anybody else. Their own families need them."

They took the sofa and the rocking chair upstairs and arranged them in the hallway, leaving a clear path. Next they stacked the two other parlor chairs atop the sofa along with the side tables and hall tree. With the aid of a hammer, the dining table collapsed and found its way to the higher floor, followed by its matching cushioned chairs. Then, Ellissa directed Grey to the basement to retrieve some bricks and wood. When he returned, they stacked the bricks four high, added the wooded planks, and set the piano on top.

"Mary Coe? Mind you don't bump into the piano when passing it. It might topple over. It feels pretty stable, but still ..."

"I think it'll be fine, Miss Ellissa," Grey reassured. "Don't worry."

Although she knew she was going overboard, she had Grey remove the pictures from the walls. The water had never come up so high before. Still, Ellissa knew she'd feel better when most of their things were jumbled together upstairs.

"Grey, Burt will be so grateful you've helped us. You will stay the night, won't you? You mustn't try to go back up to McKenna Hall in this weather. Cary can sleep with me, and you can have her bed. Alright, Cary?"

What choice did she have? "Yes. It's late and I'm tired. Do you care if I retire after we tuck in Coey, Ellissa?"

"I don't mind. Then again, I can't speak for everyone."

Not wanting to acknowledge Ellissa's meaning, Carolena called to Mary Coe. "Time for bed, sweetsie," unaware she'd spoken the same endearment toward her niece her own mother so often used. "Are you washed up, yet?"

"How did you know that's what my mama calls me sometimes, Cary?"

Careful to be casual, "Oh, it's a name I heard once. It suits you."

Downstairs, feeling very unwanted and unneeded now the chores were done, Grey thought hard about returning home. He entered the kitchen to say goodbye to Ellissa.

She anticipated his reaction without having to look at him. Stacking the muffin tins, she said, "Don't be disheartened, Grey. This is just the first of a long line of squabbles the two of you will have. It's all part of being in love."

He should be embarrassed by such talk. He wasn't with Ellissa. He already felt she was family because she was kin to Cary. Hopefully, that would one day make her part of his family. "I wonder. I said some pretty ugly things to her."

"You probably thought she deserved them at the time."

"No one deserves to be treated as hatefully as I did her."

"Then apologize."

"She won't talk to me, so I don't think she'll have much patience for my explanation as to why I said what I did."

"As long as you have reasons, though they may not fully justify your behavior. Cary is an intelligent person. Her curiosity will compel her to hear you out. She's a forgiving woman. I'm sure of it."

"I hope you're right, Miss Ellissa." He turned and said, "You'd best get to bed yourself. You'll need your sleep if the water keeps rising and we have a mess to clean up."

"I'll be up shortly. Here is your candle. Oh, towels and wash clothes are in the linen closet to the right of the necessary. Night-night."

"Good night, ma'am."

Pausing at the top of the stairs, Grey couldn't remember which room was which, and he didn't see Cary or Coey around to ask. He slowly turned the knob on the first door to the right. Holding the light high, he surmised it was the master bedroom when he saw the shotgun standing in the corner and the mix of perfume and men's hair tonic bottles on the vanity. This was where Cary would be sleeping tonight. She wasn't yet here. He advanced to the next room and immediately recognized it as hers. This was where he would sleep, that is if he could find sleep at all. He didn't see how it would be possible to drive her from his senses. Sighing, he needed to try. He was tired. He'd had a hellish lot to drink after Carolena left this morning. So much in fact, he was glad he'd thrown most of it up. If not, he'd still be soused. The ride in the rain did nothing to help his head. He figured he deserved all the pain delivered him for what he'd said earlier.

He was clean enough. He'd washed up before he'd come. Removing his shirt and boots, he stoked the fire in the room and then nuzzled under the coverlet. The pillow smelled of her as did the sheets and the blanket. Idiotically, he envied the sheets because they were privileged to have been rubbed and rolled upon by her.

The door was ajar and a tiny creak announced its further opening. Someone was entering on tip-toes, sneaking over to the dresser and retrieving something long and flowing from a drawer. The lighting flashed again as it had all evening, and Carolena jumped. She was still wearing her day dress, but she'd let loose her long hair. It reached just past her waist.

The sight of her made him forget the apology he owed. "Don't you think it's a little dangerous, you slinking in here like this? Did you forget there's someone sleeping in your bed? Or what manner of man he is?"

Whispering, she answered, "I know well what kind of no-account you are!"

He sprang up and was at her in an instant.

She couldn't scream. It would frighten Mary Coe. "Let me go. I can't stand you!"

He found her angry, hoarse whisper fetching. "Is that why you refused to look at me all evening? And here I thought it was because you were afraid you'd attack my body if our eyes locked."

She squealed in disgust.

"Shh. Your sister will come up. Don't force me to tell her all your secrets."

Carolena's intake of breath was so sharp it hurt. He was a user of women, which was obvious by the way he'd led her to believe they had a future once they'd made love. Made love! Her skin iced. Dear God, could she be in a family way? She was late. Could she be expecting a child without benefit of marriage like her mother? Why hadn't she thought of the possible consequence, no probable consequence? Why? Now, the man she would always love, the father of her child, was going to betray her secrets. She never would have imagined him capable.

He'd hated to pretend he'd tell Ellissa the truth. It was the only way he could think of to hush her. Grey wanted to believe Carolena would forgive him. "Now. Just one kiss and I'll let you alone - until the next time."

He was fast in taking what he wanted, giving her no time to reject him. If the truth be told, she disgusted herself as she enjoyed that smothering, marvelous kiss. It was rich and full and pressing, leaving the promise of more of the same and beyond. As quickly as he'd secured his prize, it was over. He pushed her away. "Good night, sweet angel. I shall dream of you and your yellow tresses, and in those dreams, you will come to me. Run along now."

He was dismissing her like some concubine! She left gladly.

When Ellissa joined her sister under the covers, Carolena feigned sleep, listening to the wailing wind and the lashing rain, and thinking about Grey. He was not to be trusted, that was evident. Nevertheless, she was obsessed with him. His last kiss had raised a fever in her. Damn him. She didn't understand the man. He was a hopeless blackguard with a loose tongue who would turn on her. When finally she dropped off to sleep, her sporadic dreaming bounced from Grey's kisses, to a fatherless baby, to her sister learning the truth unexpectedly. Tossing and restlessly awake again, Carolena renewed her vow to tell Ellissa everything first thing in the morning.

Chapter 27

Burt stood under cover of the clubhouse porch, looking at his well-worn pocket watch. Just after seven. He placed it beneath his rubber great coat and stepped back into the blinding downpour. The sun was up or at least he reckoned it was. If he hadn't verified the early hour, he'd have bet it was nigh onto twilight. He hadn't rested any last night. The wind, the rain, and the rising level of the lake wouldn't let him. This was the hardest rain he remembered in all his years of living in the valley. How much longer could he wait before he went to his family?

Tromping through the squishy sod, he glanced back to see his deep boot prints already filling with water. He found it necessary to bow his head into the wind. Gusts always whistled louder and pushed harder once you left Johnstown below. Today it seemed even more so. At the edge of the dam, the rain was heavier. Through squinted eyes, he looked at the level of Lake Conemaugh. Yesterday, the water had been at its usual level, about five feet below the crest of the dam's wall. He made out the rise in the water level at two, maybe three feet. And it didn't help matters the iron fish screens were clogged with broken limbs and other debris. If they were clear, he wasn't certain they could let enough water through to alleviate the pressure from all the rain anyway.

***

Ellissa awoke just after 7:30 a.m. When she'd slept, she'd slept hard, yet she did recall getting up and placing the alarm clock inside the wardrobe under several sweaters, trying to silence its irritating ticking. Maybe her sleep wasn't as sound as she'd thought.

There was no need to push back the curtains to know it was still raining. Dressing quickly, she tucked the covers over Cary's exposed shoulder then checked on her daughter who continued her slumber as well.

Headed downstairs to begin cooking breakfast, Ellissa was forced to stop mid-staircase. The muddy water was inside her house and up to the second step.

Without the usual pleasantries, Grey waded in from the parlor, wearing hip boots. "I'm sorry, ma'am. I hoped it wouldn't get this high. I was going to let you all sleep a little longer. You'll need your strength."

Through the front door pane, she spied water where the street used to be. "Have you been out in it?"

"I got up just before sunrise to survey the area. There's fog in the low lands and heavy mist between bouts of rain. Listen," he said, cocking his ear toward the roof, "I think it's let up for a spell. I sure hope so. It looks like most of your neighbors are up and at it and have been for some time. The lamps are lit in most every house.

"There're some families leaving. I heard folks who're staying hollering out their second floor windows. They were laughing, saying the deserters would never live it down, being so faint of heart and all. Most men have left the mills, I understand, to be with their families." As soon as he'd said it, he wanted to take back the thoughtless words. All he could do was apologizing and go on. "I'm sorry, ma'am." When she lifted the corners of her mouth only slightly, he continued, randomly telling her the little he'd found out. "Some storekeepers have opened their shops real early to sell whatever they can to help and/or make one last nickel, I suspect. They'll be out of business for a day or two with all the mess. Men are hauling their teams and whatever livestock they can handle up into the hills. I imagine they'll be some critters wandering the mountainsides until this is all over. I tied Cary's horse and mine to your front post for easy access. They're wearing no saddles though. I'm thinking they don't need the extra weight of a wet saddle.

"Folks will have to abandon their wagons soon. A horse will have all he can do to carry a rider, let alone pull an overloaded cart. They won't be able to keep their footing. Some people are walking, carrying their bundles on their heads and shoulders in efforts to keep their possessions out of the knee-deep water. There are even some make-shift rafts." Saying more to himself, "It's the damnedest thing to see a row boat paddle down the center of the street." He removed the smirk from his lips wanting Ellissa to know he realized the severity of the situation. "Some seem to be rowing around as if on a Sunday afternoon on the lake, just out for the air. I saw a lone man with a dog and three cats in his canoe. He was being a Good Samaritan is all. He told me he was taking the animals back to a hayloft he was filling with strays. Said once the water recedes, he'll let worried folks know their pets are safe and cared for. Oh, I also heard all the schools will be closed today, and of course, no milk deliveries or mail."

"Tell me honestly, Grey, what about the rivers?"

He kept his voice steady. "It's been raining on and off, mostly on, since last night. They say the river is rising at better than a foot an hour. There's a powerful current coming down from the mountains, and it's carrying logs and brush and dirt right along with it. By noon, they expect Johnstown to be covered in water anywhere from two to ten feet deep."

Finally, dull fright won out and a grave look overtook her. "Grey, I want you to do something for me."

"Yes, ma'am?"

"As soon as I've fed you all, I want you to take Mary Coe and Cary to higher ground. Take them up to your house. Just in case."

He didn't argue. He only hoped Ellissa would go, too.

Once everyone was up and dressed, Ellissa insisted her daughter and Cary stay upstairs. There was no reason for them to get wet before it was necessary. Grey carried up a tray of bread and jam and some sliced apples and raw carrots for everyone. All found a seat on Ellissa's bed. No one was eating much, and the talk was minimal.

When Mary Coe spoke, she avoided mention of the rainfall as did the adults. Seeing and smelling the filthy water inside the house, Carolena felt foolish she'd thought a flood would be exciting. Even her small niece recognized the seriousness of it. They watched as Grey stoked the fire and was very glad he was nearby.

It was his turn to look at her. Wearing Ellissa's black wool sweater, Carolena folded her arms. "I thought it was supposed to warm up some by the end of May," she said through chattering teeth.

"Alright, little one. Time to go on an adventure with Mr. McKenna and Cary," said Ellissa with a command in her voice her daughter recognized as meaning no arguing allowed. "Be sure and take your memory box."

Carolena watched Mary Coe retrieve a small box covered with colorful ribbons and lace from atop her mother's dresser. It clearly contained tiny treasures that reminded her niece of fun, family, and love.

"Got it. I won't lose it, Mama. Where are we going?"

Carolena wondered the same thing.

"Mr. Grey will take you to his big home high up on the hill. You know the one."

"That'll be grand! I've never been in such a fine place as that, I don't think."

"You deserve everything fine, sweetsie. I want only what's best for you." Ellissa went to the child, falling to her knees. Hugging her closely, fighting tears, she said, "If you remember nothing I've taught you, sweetsie, remember to keep up your schooling so you'll be able to take care of yourself and your children. You never know what the future holds. We've been blessed with your father, but I'm too dependent upon him, angel girl. Not all men are as fine as he is. Even if they are, there's no telling when the good Lord will take them from us. Always use your intellect and be strong. Don't ever be ashamed of being independent and self-reliant and smart. Ever!"

Mary Coe didn't understand why her mother was telling her this. It seemed important so she replied, "I promise to remember, Mama."

Watching this exchange of mother-daughter devotion, Carolena became more worried about the weather. No, not worried. She was scared. She wished her own mother were here to hold her. Why? Why? Because it was the truth. She'd always felt so secure in her mother's arms. The short school piece she'd written about Miss Ella when she was near to Coey's age crept inside her head. It had somehow been published in the Fernandina newspaper. Until the fire, her mother kept the clipping tucked inside the frame of her vanity mirror, so she could read it every morning because it had meant so much to her, she'd said. Carolena remembered the simple words. With them returned the tender feelings that inspired her to write it.

My mother is wonderful because she can do almost anything. She can cook the greatest food and sing the prettiest songs. She helps me with things I'm

having trouble with. My mother is the greatest person and always will be the greatest. Forever!
        Carolena Dunnigan

Carolena started recalling bits and pieces of lectures her mother had given her over the years. At the time, she'd found most of them boring and only listened because Peeper threatened to tan her hide if she showed any disrespect. She now realized all those endless instructions had formed her into the person she was today. She was smart and independent. She could care for herself. She was a woman of honor or, at least, that's how her mother had meant her to be, just the way Ellissa wanted Mary Coe to be. From Grammy to Ella and Coe, from Ella and Coe to Carolena and Ellissa, and now from Ellissa to Mary Coe. Different approaches, yet always the same meaning.

God, why had she been so judgmental toward her mother, so deliberately brutal in her words and actions toward the woman who'd loved and served her family her entire life? Carolena admitted she'd made many foolish mistakes and here she was condemning her mother without giving her the chance she begged for to explain why she'd let Uncle Clabe kiss her. Except for that one ugly moment, Carolena couldn't think of another single time her mother had ever disappointed her.

So many other mothers were fat and frumpy. Hers was still slender and beautiful. She'd successfully run a household with a husband, four children, two grandmothers, dogs, cats, birds, chickens and goats. She gardened, cooked, sewed, nursed, repaired, and maintained, taught religion, did charity work, socialized and now she was almost single-handedly managing a huge business that employed hundreds, and had, as Grey informed her, the compassion to care for a sick, unfaithful husband. Ella Dunnigan was a marvel! She was also an interesting, complicated woman.

Recognizing her mother's depth of character was a release for Carolena. Hatred's hold lifted because of the scene she'd just witnessed between Miss Ella's daughter, Ellissa, and her grandchild. Carolena wanted to tell Ellissa everything. And she wanted to go to her dear mother and ask to be forgiven because she, herself, had forgiven.

"Cary, please come on. Grey's waiting."

Carolena was lying across her sister's bed. She didn't know just how much time had passed, yet in that time, her thoughts had changed her life. She wanted one thing at this moment, to get home and take Ellissa and Coey and Burt and yes, Grey, with her.

"All right. I'll just bundle up." She hurried to her room, found her warmest things, her umbrella, and boots and met the others in the upstairs hall.

Grey and Mary Coe were ready. Ellissa wasn't yet wearing her coat and galoshes. Answering Carolena's puzzled look, Ellissa said, "I'm not going, Cary. Someone needs to stay behind with the house. There are always looters at times like these, not to mention crazy drunks prowling about, just waiting to raid unoccupied homes. Don't fret," she pointed toward her room. "I've got Burt's shotgun and plenty of loads. He always says there's no sound like the cocking of a shotgun. That alone is enough to scare away most anyone. I'll be fine."

Carolena opened her mouth to speak. Before she could emit a sound, her sister stopped her. "I need you to care for my daughter, Cary. Please. Do it for me," Ellissa leaned close and whispered in her ear, "and for our mother."

Astonished to her core, Carolena could only whisper back, "How did you …"

"Years ago, I overheard my parents speak of details they wanted to remain private. I decided if it was the Lord's will that I meet my sisters and brother," she paused, "and mother, I would be patient and let Him lead me."

Grey guessed the essence of the exchange when he saw Carolena's eyes grow wide and fill with tears. The two women pulled back and for a long moment looked hard, each on the other. Then they embraced with the full power of family found, family acknowledged.

The water was a third of the way up the four-paneled front door. It would be difficult to open. Grey unlocked the brass catch on the front window, lifted the sash, and climbed out. Extending his hand to Mary Coe, he said softly, "Ladies, time's a-wastin'."

Mary Coe returned to her mother for one more kiss. Now ready to go, the little girl stepped into the water covering the polished pine floor. "If the water weren't so cold, I'd go barefoot, Mama. My boots are already filled up. This is fun! Who would have thought I'd be allowed to go swimming in my own parlor!" She waded to the windowsill. Standing in the fast flowing water on the front porch, Grey helped her through the window. Not letting her hand go until he was sure she was secure, he said, "Hold on to the front rail there, Coey, while I help Miss Cary."

"Got it, Mr. Grey." The water was up just past her knees.

"Good girl. Come on, Cary. You're next."

Concentrating on the unceasing rain on the porch roof, Carolena let it obliterate her desire to turn around and look at Ellissa. She accepted Grey's assistance. Once through the window, she took hold of her niece's gloved hand. Her own skirts sucked up the cold water and in a few moments, her bodice would be saturated. They were all certain to catch pneumonia, but she did her best because the same was happening to little Coey, who, though silent, was still smiling. Carolena had to be as brave as the child. And she prayed she'd have courage beyond that.

Ellissa handed Grey Mary Coe's memory box and the family treasure basket now inside a knotted pillowcase. "I'll wave to you from my bedroom window! Remember, Princess Coey, you'll always be our precious angel.

Blessings on you all!" Racing upstairs, she threw back the curtains and looked down. Ellissa focused on her daughter wrapped in Grey's capable arms as they shared a horse. Cary was beside them on her own mount. They all waved and were off, their animals visibly stressed by their lethargic pace in the deep, cold flowing water. When they were gone from view, Ellissa glanced at the bedside clock. It was nearly 9 a.m.

Returning her gaze to the window, she watched many of her friends fleeing. A family on foot struggled through the street, trying to keep a child upright as well as a good grip on a wooden vegetable crate with a chicken inside.

Ellissa's mind wandered to the shopkeepers. She guessed they had long since closed their doors. It was too late for anyone to buy supplies. If you didn't have it by now, you'd have to make do. Everyone understood this. Lord knew they all had enough experience over the years.

The rattling of what sounded like the parlor window broke into her thoughts. She was surprised to see almost an hour had passed since she'd said goodbye to her little girl and sister. Ellissa couldn't imagine who would be knocking. The water inside was up to the fifth step, so she stood on the sixth and bent down to see who had come calling. There, with paddle in hand, was her neighbor, Snavely Tanks. Apparently, he had rowed his way over to check on her.

He'd pried up the window a bit from the outside and turning his face to the side, he yelled through the two-inch crack. "Morning, Miss Ellissa. I saw from my house you'd sent the child off. Heard the mister is up at the lake. Filomena sent me to see if you'd like to come over to our place. We're brewing tea in the upstairs bedroom, and we've got a cloth on the floor, like a picnic. The children are having a good time, even if their mama is getting a little tense."

Touched by his concern, "Thank you most kindly, Mr. Tanks. I think I'll stay here in case Burt comes home early. I don't want him to worry about us."

As his small canoe bobbed from the wake of a passing team of mules, the neighbor's tone changed. Almost pleading, "Please, ma'am. My wife needs help. She's getting' real concerned, and I'm afraid she'll scare the little ones. Another female with a calm way will aid matters mightily. You can leave a note high-up somewheres for Burt. Besides, he probably wouldn't want you to be alone anyhow." Using the last of his persuasive arguments, he said, "From across the street, you can keep one eye out for him and the other on your house. Our bedroom window looks right down on your own front door."

Not wanting to leave her secure surroundings and her property, Ellissa felt the pressure of friendship take hold. "Yes. You're right. I'll be glad to do whatever I can to help. Just let me get my wrap and boots."

"Hey, I've got a great idea," he said excitedly, but she didn't hear.

When Ellissa had returned with her gear, she was amazed to see Mr.

Tanks in his boat, in her house! Wearing a big grin, he offered his hand. Ellissa held tight and stepped from staircase to boat.

"There," he said proudly, "and you didn't even get the hem of your skirt wet!"

Exiting through the wide open window, Ellissa smiled tightly while a voice inside her head repeated, this is just another adventure. Remember, another adventure.

Chapter 28

By ten o'clock, Burt, a few worried local residents from down below, a group of men building a club drainage system, and Colonel Elias J. Unger, the manager and only club member present, were swinging pick axes to the point of exhaustion, in an attempt to loose the iron fish grates in the dam. Leaks were beginning to appear in its face. Everyone knew the rising lake would be level with the crest soon.

After a while, one plump fellow, looked to the dripping cloud covered heavens and guessing the hour, "To hell with this. It's dinner time boys." His crew took his lead and dropped their tools, preferring to wrap their blistered fingers around a hunk of crusty bread to that of a wooden handled pick.

Watching them walk toward the shelter of the horse barn, Colonel Unger shouted to those remaining, "This is no use, men. We've one last hope. Let's try and make a second spillway."

"Are you crazy?" screamed Burt. "If you can't pry away an iron screen, do you really think you can cut a hole through solid rock?" Then he coughed and spit up the corruption he'd dislodged in his lungs from his exertion. He didn't care if he lost his job. He spoke his mind. Through gritted teeth, he shouted over the roar of the downpour. "You goddamned millionaires! You took off three feet of dam at the top to make it wider so your fancy carriages could drive on two lanes up to your private resort! All that did was let the rising lake reach the crest faster. If that wasn't enough, we peasants suspected the dribbling dam was declared unsafe. And that just before your club opened, you allowed them to dump trash, trash," he bellowed, "in the center of the thing. I saw the straw and manure, the brush, the stumps, whatever they cleared. That's what they used to pack the holes. A temporary fix at best. Then you blocked the spillways with iron grates to make certain your precious fish couldn't escape from your lake. Now, no one may escape! We all trusted you. And I'm the worst because having seen it, I still trusted you!"

Burt threw his ax with all the fury in him. It lodged in the earthen wall. As he ran for his stabled horse, some followed. He didn't see the ashen faces or the frightened eyes of those who watched him go. They knew he'd spoken the truth. They all knew.

***

Around noon, Frank Deckert, freight agent, and George Myers, ticket clerk of the Johnstown depot, were jawing about the condition of things.

"Trouble's comin', I'm thinkin'," said Mr. Deckert. "What with the 8:10 Day Express from Pittsburgh not arriving until 10:15 and how it was ordered to run east to East Conemaugh on the west-bound track on account of the east-bound rails bein' washed out … Then there's that log jam from the boom that busted up river. It's become wedged against and between the Stony Bridge just below town."

"If I didn't think it was serious before, I do now," concurred Mr. Myers.

The door flew open and a sodden boy of sixteen waded into the station, proudly extracting a dry envelope from beneath his slicker. "A wire for you, Mr. Deckert!"

Deckert opened the letter and felt those present had a right to hear it. "It's a warning, come by way of the Pennsylvania Railroad telegraph system. Says that the South Fork dam might give way."

A woman screamed and fell faint against her hapless husband who nervously patted her limp hand.

Two regulars in the station began to laugh. They'd heard the warnings so many times before.

"Hell," said one man, "Folks say if it ever does let go, they guess it'll raise the rivers about two feet is all."

***

"I can't stay another minute, Grey. I have to go to Ellissa." Carolena was in tears as she pleaded with him. "Coey will be fine here with your Uncle Jax. Although he says I shouldn't go, he told me the other town folks sheltering here will help him look after my niece. Some of her friends are already here for her to play with."

Grey understood her wanting to go, but he would not be moved. "Ellissa knows the danger, Carolena. If I were her husband, I'd have hog-tied her to get her out of there, but I don't have Burt's permission to force her. One thing's sure. I will not allow you to put your life in danger."

"What life do I have without my family? Never mind that I didn't know her until a few weeks ago. Never mind it was only just today we acknowledged the truth of our relationship. She's part of me, the same as Breelan and Marie and my mother. I won't desert her. I can't." Carolena was resolute. Her niece was safe. She'd fulfilled her promise. All her attention was on Ellissa. If Burt were unable to get to her, by God, Carolena would. She would not allow Ellissa to suffer this hardship alone. Eyeing a gun in a holster hanging on a wall hook, Carolena crossed toward it.

Grey's eyes followed her. He expected her next move because he knew her so well.

As her hand wrapped around the barrel of his gun, he said softly, "No need, Cary. I'll let you go."

Ashamed, she released the weapon without ever having lifted it. She turned to him and threw herself into his arms. "I'm frightened, Grey. I've never been so frightened. What if that dam won't hold? What if I can't get to Ellissa in time?" She trembled. He squeezed her more tightly, trying to still her shudders. Neither had any idea of what to expect.

Looking up into his face, she blinked away her tears. He studied her moss green eyes.

"Kiss me, Grey. Kiss me hard."

To her it was a kiss goodbye. She might never again see this man she loved. They had shared so much in the years they'd known one another. Arguments and misunderstandings aside, none of it mattered because standing like this, she was content.

Grey tasted the kiss and read her meaning. He heard laughter from the kitchen and was pleased his uncle had the good sense to give them privacy. On his way here, he'd expected Carolena would insist upon returning to Johnstown. The kiss he returned to her was not of goodbye, but of courage and support.

She broke away from him. He did not try to hold her. She gathered her wet cape and scarf, sat down on the chair in the foyer and began to pull on her boots, boots which were saturated inside.

"Just a minute, Cary. Uncle Jax assembled some dry things for us. They may be a little big for you, but at least they're somewhat waterproof."

Had she heard him correctly? "Oh no, Grey. You're not going. I won't let you. I won't let you put yourself in danger for me. I love you too much."

His smile was wide, "And I adore you, Cary. You can't expect me to stay all dry and cozy in this big house while you're out there facing," he paused, "God only knows what. I don't want to live unless we're together."

She opened her mouth to speak.

He silenced her words with another deep, lingering kiss. He forced himself to stop. "To be continued. We'd better dress and go. We'll ride down as far as we can and then get a boat from someone. Boats are a hot commodity right now, but, as always," he patted his breast pocket, "money talks. Uncle Jax will keep everyone entertained with his sculptures of vegetable animals. If we say goodbye to Coey, I'm afraid she'll start to cry, and you don't need that. He'll tell her we've gone after her mother once we've left."

Carolena Dunnigan and Grey McKenna went to the barn to get fresh horses. She and her man were off on a dangerous mission to rescue a member of her family. No, Carolena thought, a member of our family.

***

The little girl laughed at the silly grown-ups. They thought they'd fooled her, but Princess Coey was too smart for them. Securing the bottom clasp on her coat, she went out the side door to follow Cary and Mr. Grey back down the big hill to her mama.

Chapter 29

The delivery boy entered the Johnstown train station a second time. Ignoring Mr. Deckert's hello, "Mrs. Ogle and her—" He saw the questioning faces of the stranded travelers and explained, "She's the mistress of Johnstown's telegraph office. Anyway, her and her crew was working out of the second floor. Said the water's so high in some parts, she don't know how much longer it would be before the telegraph wires was grounded out."

Looking at the large round clock on the wall, Agent Deckert took the wire from the boy. It was just before one p.m. He read:

WESTERN UNION   31 May 1889
    TO: Agent Deckert
Johnstown Penna Depot

    FROM: C. P. Dougherty
Penna RR Ticket Agent
South Fork Penna

WATER RUNNING OVER LAKE DAM IN CENTER AND WEST SIDE STOP BECOMING DANGEROUS STOP

At one o'clock, another warning came:

WESTERN UNION   31 May 1889
    TO: Agent Deckert
Johnstown Penna Depot

    FROM: J.P. Wilson
Superintendent Argyle Coal Co
South Fork Penna

DAM MAY BREAK STOP

***

After reassuring the neighbor lady as much as possible, Ellissa was back in her own home. Worry had exhausted her, so she lay down to rest her eyes. In scant minutes, she was asleep and dreaming there was a woman calling her name. The voice kept on calling. Ellissa smiled as she thought how strange it is that dreams can seem so real. The voice wouldn't hush and oddly, it sounded like Cary. Cary. Ellissa's eyes flew open.

"God, no. Please don't let her have come back for me."

When she heard Grey, too, she scrambled from beneath the blankets, rushed to the window, and opened it.

"Can you come out and play, Miss Ellissa? Lovely day for a row boat ride, don't you think?" Grey continued, his hands cupped at his mouth. "Found this ship stuck in the mud. It mightn't be up to the standards of the Aqua Verde Line, but with the right crew, she's passable."

"Coey is fine," Carolena shouted up through the rain. "She's at McKenna Hall with lots of folks. That's where we're headed. You can bail the rainwater, sis," Carolena addressed her as casually as if she'd said it a million times before. "My arms are tired."

The sight of the two drenched angels in slickers caused Ellissa's throat to constrict with a gratitude so overwhelming, she bit her lip to stem her thankful tears. Then reality struck her the same instant more thunder clapped. "No, Cary, no! You must go back. Both of you!"

Carolena's answer was simple. "Not without you. If you stay, we all stay."

Ellissa knew she meant it. She recognized the determination in her sister's eyes because she'd seen it in herself, her own child, and her adopted mother, Coe. She might foolishly risk her life for the sake of what little property she and Burt possessed. She would not risk the life of her family and friend. Of course, her Burt would expect her to use her head and go on without him. Ellissa smiled, giving in.

There was no time to spare now. Grey had one mission: To get these women to safety before it was too late.

***

Burt urged his horse through the deep mud and random pools of water paralleling the river on the way to Johnstown. The only saving grace was it was downhill. Yet as the time dragged on, it felt as if they were making little progress. Near exhaustion, the animal chose to ignore the repeated sting of his master's hand on his backside. Burt was praying the horse wouldn't collapse under him as they slid and then somersaulted down the incline with Burt's foot caught in the stirrup. Deep inside his head, he heard the sharp crack of his spinal column. Pinned beneath his dead animal, Ellissa's husband felt no pain. Unable to move from the neck down, he wondered what was causing the quagmire beneath him to vibrate so. With the last swallow of air leaking from his lungs, he sent up one final plea for his wife and child.

The smashed face on the watch in his pocket read 3:08. Burt did not witness the emptying of the dam in less than ten minutes, nor would he see or hear the forty-foot wall of water drive down the South Fork Creek to its mouth two miles away. The fury would hit the north bank of the Little Conemaugh, sweep away the town of South Fork as swiftly as a broom does a dust bunny and make its way fourteen miles through the valley to Mineral Point, East Conemaugh, Woodvale, and on to a waiting, but ever-hopeful, ever-prayerful Johnstown.

***

Tying sheets together and securing them to the bedstead, Ellissa climbed down from the second floor of her house to Grey's waiting arms as he balanced in the boat some ten feet below. Then Carolena, Ellissa, and Grey paddled their way through the cross streets, trying to reach high ground. They saw people hanging out attic windows calling for help while many more waited on their rooftops. To prevent anyone from slipping off, whole families were joined together with ropes lashed to chimneys. Gunshots sounded as men and boys picked off the rats who'd surfaced in the light of this miserable day. Carolena tried to ignore the drowned chickens, cows, cats, dogs, sheep, mules, and horses that streamed by. She was doing a fair job until she saw a woman's body. All in the boat watched as the corpse bounced off each obstacle in its way. Until the water receded, there was little anyone could do to put the dead to rest.

Carolena's spirits sank. Looking to her sister, she masked her despair. She didn't want to give the impression that any daughter of Ella Dunnigan was a coward. Instead, Carolena nodded at the sight of a man and woman sailing past on what appeared to be the ornately carved front panel of an upright piano.

"Grey." She jerked her chin toward the heavens. "The sky seems a little lighter. Maybe the worst of it's over with."

He welcomed the clearing skies and replied with a doubtful empty grin as a railroad whistle sounded. It wasn't the usual short blast that announced the arrival or departure of the train. It was a continuous, piercing, irritating noise. "Never heard anything like that before," said Ellissa wondering. Her common sense told her it was a warning.

All curiosity was interrupted by an explosion so powerful the oarlocks buzzed from the vibration of it. Within five seconds, the water churned as the three held fast to their small boat, fearing it would capsize.

Grey shouted over the screams and panic surrounding them, "The cold water must have hit the boilers at the iron works. If that's what happened, barbed wire will be everywhere! Watch out for it!"

Carolena felt a violent rumbling in her chest. An earth-shaking roar in the distance grew louder. And louder still. The only other sound every man, woman and child in the town could hear was his or her own heart. Instinctively, each knew the time of their passing had come.

A living, seething, tumbling mountain of debris headed for them. It toppled trees, houses, and buildings like so many dominoes. Friends, animals, the spring-sprouted blades of grass, all life itself, disappeared into the churn. Nothing was spared.

Grey stopped rowing. Ellissa laid her head in her lap and wailed silently. Carolena crossed herself then threw her body over the hunched shoulders of her sister and prayed for them all. With the speed of a winged cannonball, the towering tons of rubble and water lifted them in the air, high above the rooftops. For a single infinitesimal moment, the boat sat on the crest of the wave. The view was bizarre. To the east lay black jagged ocean, to the west below, a city doomed to be shredded by a whirlpool of death. The moment ended. They sailed through the air and landed in a suffocating gruel of icy water laced with anything and everything that makes up a town.

Carolena and Ellissa held hands but were torn apart as a great surge of foul liquid pulled Ellissa under and away. Carolena, who'd always loved the sea, loved to swim in it, loved to wonder at its corralled power, was defenseless. This was more than water. This was annihilation. Like a bobbing cork, she tried keeping her head above water. Her hair was loosed and the strands were twisting around her neck, strangling her. Half-treading, half-hand-paddling, she managed to dislodge herself from the worst of the tangle while just out of her reach, she watched a child go down for the last time.

Grabbed and pulled down, Carolena gulped the filthy water, having no moment to snatch a breath. She spun underwater and punched someone in the stomach who was using her as a stepstool. Freed from her frantic attacker, she surfaced to be forced below again by a wild current. Fighting the undertow, she clawed her way up to feel the cold air buff her face while she tried to take hold of the flailing arms of the female who'd pushed her down. Dear God! It was Ellissa!

Carolena used all the strength left in her to holler, "Lissa! Lissa!" Slapping the girl's face as hard as she could, "Lissa! I'll help you, but don't climb on me. You'll drown us both!"

Overjoyed to see Cary, Ellissa defied the overwhelming awfulness to read her little sister's lips as much as listen.

Holding Ellissa's collar, Carolena ordered, "Roll over on your back and kick your feet! You've got to work with me!"

They floated together as Ellissa struggled to overcome her panic. Although they went under again and again, they somehow managed to keep their arms linked as they floated fast and chaotically, covering what seemed like miles. They saw others go by, mostly dead, but there was no time for pity.

"When that table leaf is within reach, grab it, Lissa! Grab it! Don't worry about me. I'll latch onto something else. Now! Grab it now!"

Reluctantly, Ellissa let go of Carolena and ignored the pain when the smooth plank hit her shoulder. She threw herself on top. It rolled over with her still hanging on. Struggling savagely, she managed to emerge on top of the wood. Ellissa inched her way up the board as another wave struck. When she surfaced again, Carolena heard a long, pitiful wail, "Burt ..."

"God keep you, Ellissa." Carolena was caught. A cutting, slicing web of barbed wire assailed her from behind! The more she struggled to free herself, the more it pierced her flesh. Her golden ropes of hair wound around the spiked iron threads. And in turn, the coiling cables captured scraps of floating projectiles, filling the web to capacity. Its weight increased until it hung from her like an anchor, her hair the chain. Her screams mingled with hundreds of others. When the current threw her forward and jerked her under, she let the tainted water have her. The knifing pain she felt in her lower abdomen went unnoticed because her last thought was of Grey.

Chapter 30

Saturday night, late, Breelan Dunnigan Taylor rode unaccompanied to the Fernandina newspaper office to deliver her advertisement for the ship line. Her husband didn't approve of her riding alone after dark, but she thought she'd be back before he had a chance to miss her. Her ad needed to be on Mr. Whitney's desk first thing Monday morning. Business was steady. Her father had mentioned much was due to her contribution. Breelan smiled. Michael Dunnigan almost seemed his old self now he was recovered from his collapse. They'd roughed in the beginnings of a new Dunnigan Manor. While her mother and father weren't happy like they used to be, Bree had seen her father give a playful wink to his wife and witnessed Miss Ella's surprise. Breelan had no idea of the cause of the disharmony, but she hoped his efforts would lead to a complete reconciliation between them.

She thought of her wonderful Waite and how he'd exhausted himself getting the walls up for their new house. With the help of Jack Patrick, Mickey, Warren, and even dignified Uncle Clabe, he'd managed to make the place livable. It would be a while until the final touches were completed. That was of minor concern to the boys who were sleeping at the Taylors' home these days. This took much of the pressure off Aunt Noreen, though it did little to reduce auntie's irritable ways.

"Oh, never mind her," Breelan told Noir as he trotted west. He had become used to his mistress's conversations over the years. "Aunt Noreen's the one to be pitied. It seems the older she gets, the more she focuses on her own suffering and martyrdom. She thinks life is incomplete unless there's something to complain about. Ain't never gonna change, boy," and Breelan fingered the mane of her favorite animal friend.

"I wonder what Carolena is doing right now? I miss my big sister."

So often, as children and on into young adulthood, they'd fussed and feuded. Those times were long past. Breelan wanted Carolena to come home. Her mother's eyes saddened whenever Carolena's name came up. All Miss Ella would tell everyone was Carolena had a difficult romance and was in Pennsylvania to see where Grammy had lived. It was so beautiful she'd decided to stay, getting a job in a shirt factory.

Dismounting and tying her horse to the hitching rail in front of the newspaper office, Breelan entered, still mumbling. "Well, when I have the time and the extra money, I'll go to this Johnstown and bring her home. Yes. For the sake of family unity, that's exactly what I'll do!"

"What's that you say, Miss Breelan?" asked the copy clerk.

"On nothing, Sam. Just talking to myself. Wanted to drop this off for Mr. Whitney." She handed him her paperwork. "Would you please put it on his desk?"

"Sure thing."

"See you on Monday. Oh, and would you tell him I'll be in at 9 a.m. sharp? That should give him a good two hours to have gone over my ad. We'll finalize it then."

"Yes, ma'am. Have a good evening. "

"Sam! Sam!" Henry Rogers ran in from the telegraph room. "Sam! Miss Bree! News just coming in there's been some horrible disaster up north. Some place called Johnstown has been wiped off the face of the earth by a flood from a busted dam in the Pennsylvania mountains!"

***

Waite was about to leave for the newspaper office in search of his wife when he heard the pounding hoof beats of a horse galloping in his direction. He saw Breelan, skirts and hair flying out behind her.

Pulling Noir's reins in sharply, she leaped from his saddle and ran to her husband, breathless. "Waite! Oh Waite!"

He heard the despair in her greeting and took hold of her shoulders. "Breathe, sugar, breathe. Calm down and tell me what it is. Are you hurt?"

"No, no. It's not me. It's Cary! She may be gone forever! Look at all these reports I got at the Mirror. From New York and Pittsburgh, from Philadelphia. It's all the same. It's the worst disaster in the world. So many lost. So many."

"Come away from here. We don't want to worry anyone until we have to."

"Waite! Breelan! Tell me," commanded Michael Dunnigan, who rose from the rocking chair he occupied on the spot that would eventually become Dunnigan Manor's front porch. "What more can God do to us, to me? My home is gone, my business is struggling, my wife is estranged, and my oldest daughter is disillusioned over me. What else is left?"

It was folly to try to hide the news. Michael was sure to find out. Like flood waters, news spreads fast and recklessly.

Breelan handed her father the clippings. Scribbled across the top of each: "FOR IMMEDIATE RELEASE." Michael read aloud:

PENNSYLVANIA TOWN WIPED OUT BY FLOOD

PITTSBURG, PA - Reports coming out of the valley community of south-central Johnstown, Pennsylvania, are still scarce. Survivors say on May 31, 1889, sometime between 3:00 and 4:00 p.m., more than 2000 people lost their lives in a sudden and massive flood when the Lake Conemaugh Dam, fourteen miles east above the town, burst and emptied in minutes. Record-breaking rainfall in the Allegheny Mountains where the earthen works were located is said to have contributed to its weakening.

BURST DAM DESTROYS JOHNSTOWN

HARRISBURG, PA - The dam is estimated to have cleaved at 3:15 p.m., releasing its raging waters to go on to destroy most or all of the smaller communities of South Fork, Mineral Point, East Conemaugh, Clover, Woodvale, Conemaugh Boro and then on to Johnstown itself.

Located at the fork of the Stony Creek and Little Conemaugh Rivers, Johnstown's population of 30,000 supplied much of the tri-state area's coal and steel. The 40 to 60 foot wave of debris, oil, wire and mud, obliterated the town except for the four-story Alma Hall, the Presbyterian Church, the Methodist Church, the B&O Railroad station and one brick building belonging to Cambria Iron Works. Wreckage is piled up to 30 feet high. The air is permeated with an overwhelming stench of death.

ENTIRE PENNSYLVANIA COMMUNITY RAZED

PHILADELPHIA, PA - Human and animal corpses could be seen floating or half-buried in the mud. As night fell on the last day of May, a fire erupted in the debris that jammed the arches of the Stony Bridge. Survivors who sought refuge were trapped and cremated before the eyes of their families and friends. Some 80 people are thought to have died there.

Emergency morgues and hospitals have been established. As word of this disaster spreads, an abundance of medical supplies, blankets, food, and clothing is expected to be sent from all across the United States.

Handing the papers back to his daughter, Michael went in search of his wife.

***

Miss Ella was inconsolable. No one but Michael understood the depth of his wife's torment. She would not eat, nor could she sleep. She refused Peeper's soothing dandelion tea with honey and Doctor Tackett's tranquilizing pills. She wanted to be left alone to suffer as her daughters who were dead had suffered. Thoughts of her first child and how she had let society cause her to give the girl away pounded inside Ella's head. Coe had done a fine job raising Ellissa. Still Coe was not Ella. She pondered how different Ellissa's life would have been if her birth mother had been able to nurture her. Michael would not let her keep the baby. She hated him for it. No, despite everything, she loved her husband. She loved her husband more than her own flesh and blood. She had turned her back on her first-born so Michael would marry her. She realized she didn't hate Michael; she hated herself!

Ellissa's face merged into Carolena's before Ella's eyes as she stared at the ugly image of herself in Noreen's vanity mirror. Her beautiful, smart, independent Carolena. Gone. Gone. Pictures of her dead children, broken and bleeding, filled her mind. Tears were no release, though she shed them. Screams brought no peace, though she emitted them with regularity. They only added to the misery in her ears. Mary Coe and Ellissa and Carolena and Grey and Burt, all gone.

"I deserve this woe," she told Michael. "If I'd never given Ellissa away, I would have moved from Johnstown to prevent gossip. I could have gone anywhere, pretended to be a widow, and saved the life of that dear child." She cocked her head in confusion. "Then again, I probably would have never met you or had Carolena."

Her howling was heard throughout the Duffy house, and no one could calm her. Upon the suggestion of Clabe, Michael removed anything sharp from the bedroom. In Ella's state of torment, she had abandoned her faith, and they feared she might take her life.

Michael tried and tried to help his wife. Miss Ella turned from him, leaving him to think she blamed him for everything. "I've earned all her hatred, Blackie," he told the dog as he sat on a stump behind the cowshed, mindlessly stroking the animal. "If it weren't for the rest of my children and grandchildren, I think I would succumb to the suffocating loss of Carolena, just like Miss Ella. Pray God, I can keep myself together for them. I've been so weak before in so many ways."

To the shock of everyone, Aunt Noreen pitched in, doing as much of the uncomplicated portion of office work for the ship line as she was able. Peeper and Nora and the rest of the adults used all their courage and strength to show a brave front.

When Halley asked in front of the others, "Mama, what is the matter with Gramma Ella? Why does she cry all the time? Will she ever not be sad because Aunt Carolena and Mr. Grey died? I'm sad too."

"Yes, darling," Breelan told her child. "Gramma Ella is ill with a thing we call grief. It's a very strong, strong sadness."

"Is her sad stronger than my sad because she's older than I am?"

Her mother tried to smile. "Yes. That's exactly it. She's lived longer and can remember things about Carolena you never knew, so her loss is greater. Eventually, though, she'll come out of it. I'm sure she will."

Chapter 31

When something grabbed her left arm, wrenching it from the socket, Carolena screamed until the filthy water filled her mouth and cascaded down her throat and into her windpipe. She kicked and popped to the surface to catch a breath of the mud-misted air. There was a painful pulling, a kind of sawing around her head. She couldn't escape the constant tugging and twisting of her hair, clear to the roots. The chemicals in the water seared the raw crimson spots on her scalp. Her neck muscles were cramped from struggling against the attack of whatever it was. Or did the frigid water cause the pain? She was so cold her teeth vibrated like singing saws, making her vision unclear. It was almost as if her eyes had come loose and were bobbing about in her head.

Someone had her around the waist. She tried to pry the arm off away, but her left arm and shoulder would not move, could not cooperate. Her right hand was weak and of little use. Her strength had left her.

"Cary! It's Grey! I've got you! Grab on!"

Grey, her Grey, was with her. She wasn't alone. "I can't move my arm."

"I said do it!" he raged, knowing it would cost her life if she did not obey.

Trying to steady a crude raft, which may have been a window shutter once upon a time, he managed to hike one of her legs over so she was straddling it. "Hang on. For God's sake, hang on!"

Drawing her knees toward her chest in an attempt to squelch the needles in her belly, she looked to him for courage. Despite the blood gushing from his face, he smiled at her. Together they rode the wild wood wherever it would take them.

After an eternity of lost grips, regained holds, and piercing splinters, they headed toward a huge brick building, one of the few still holding against the powerful currents. Dazed, Carolena wondered if what she was seeing was really a blanket thrown out the window in their direction. Whatever it was, Grey snatched hold of it, just as they were about to pass on by. Carolena watched his teeth grit. He refused to release his grasp.

When a strange man from inside clutched her bare knee and pulled her in, she felt nothing but gratitude. There were hands all over her and Grey, both.

"Lay them out over here," called a voice.

"We need some dry blankets," called another.

"We got nothin' dry," was the reply. "Nor do we got medicine, food, fresh water, not even whiskey ta drink. And for mercy's sake, nobody strike a match if'n ya got a dry one in a case somewheres. Odds are there's a natural gas leak in the basement, and we'll all get blowed ski high!"

"It'll be dark soon, and we'll have no light. All we'll hear is screams!

We're in hell!" shrieked a woman at her wit's end.

Carolena was unaware of most of the frantic chatter going on behind her. Although she was on a hard still surface, she felt as if she were still bobbing up and down and her legs were moving.

"You can quit treading water now, girl," an older woman told her. "You're on dry land. Try and take a deep breath."

"Go ahead, Cary. Breathe for me. Breathe!" Grey took her in his arms and laid her across his knees right there on the floor for all to see. Neither of them considered the proprieties at this moment. No one else did either.

She looked up to see him holding a tattered cloth to his right eye. When the pain grabbed her again, her lids closed and she gave into it and screamed.

A man in wet black clothes, who had been consoling a woman cradling a lifeless older man, came to kneel beside Carolena and Grey.

"I'm Pastor Obermyer," he told Grey. "I know this woman."

In stark contrast to the icy cold shreds of cloth she wore, Carolena felt a gush of liquid run warm between her legs. She shrieked again and yet again.

Grey saw the blood spill from his beloved and instinctively understood their mutual loss. More frightened than he'd ever been his entire adult existence, Grey pleaded, "Please, you've got to marry us right now. That was the passing of our child you just heard in her scream." Tearing his panicked stare from the minister, Grey looked down at the woman he supported. "Cary. Cary!" Grey was slapping her face. "Don't leave me. Don't ever leave me." Nearly hysterical, he got hold of himself. "Look, angel. A minister is here, and he'll marry us. I want that more than anything. Cary? Cary?"

Grey was calling her nickname. In the flickering light of the fire from the massive pile of burning debris and bodies caught against the arches of the Stony Bridge, she slowly opened her eyes. Her smile was weak, but visible. She nodded.

The pastor began quickly, "Dearly beloved, as we gather here under difficult circumstances, we beseech thee to bind Cary and ..."

"Grey," she supplied in a whisper.

"And Grey in holy matrimony. They come before you seeking your grace to be life partners. As proof of your tender mercy, they have survived this horror. Wherefore they have consented to become husband and wife, may thou grant them affirmation of the same. Grey, forsaking all others, will you love, honor and keep Cary all the rest of your days?"

"I will." With this, Grey's lips kissed her third finger where the wedding band would have rested.

"Cary, forsaking all others, will you love, honor and keep Grey all the rest of your days?"

Grey leaned down to hear and felt her breath on his cheek.

"I will."

"By the power invested in me by the God of our fathers and the laws of the Commonwealth of Pennsylvania, I pronounce you husband and wife." After a moment's pause, "You may kiss your bride."

Their lips touched in a swift yet enduring promise of forever more.

Pain took over. Neither bride nor groom heard the soft applause sent their way by the other survivors on the third story of Alma Hall.

***

He heard agonized moans and opened his eyes. Or tried to. Something bound about his head wouldn't let him. He raised his right hand and touched a rag. Pushing it up onto his forehead, he felt it pull at his right eye and pain him like the devil, as if it were stuck to a wound. "Jesus!" Grey cursed. "What the hell's the matter with me?"

A soft hand clasped his and pushed it down to his side. The voice of an older woman spoke. "There now. No need to be playing with my dressings. My name is Clara Barton. I'm with the American Red Cross. We've come to Johnstown to lend a hand. Our people have been caring for you since you were brought to us."

He knew he should thank the kind woman, yet the throbbing in his head wouldn't let him. What had happened? Obviously, he was in a hospital. He recognized the sounds and smells from the war. Still, if this wasn't the hardest damn mattress he'd ever ridden.

"You're in a church, lying on a wooden pew, a makeshift bed of sorts. I'm sad to say there's been many a casualty from the flood. Caught everyone unawares."

"Flood?" Memories assaulted Grey as he struggled to sit up. The woman pushed him back with little difficulty. His strength had left him. "Cary? Carolena Dunnigan? Do you know where she is?"

"I'm sorry, I don't."

Overhearing, a coarse female voice broke in. "I know a name that's close."

Grey interrupted, "What is it? Tell me."

The woman wiped her freshly washed hands on her apron. "Cary Dunne."

"Yes! Yes, that's her!" Grey defied his weakness and threw his body into a sitting position.

"Mr. McKenna, is that you? It's Mrs. Learner. Cary's old landlady. Remember me?"

"Yes ma'am." Grey couldn't take the time to ask after her own condition. He had to know about Carolena. "Please, is she alive?"

"She's alive, son. That much is for certain. I'm told her sister identified both her and you at Alma Hall. She's over at the Methodist church."

"Thank God," he exhaled. "Thank you, God."

"Yes, indeed," Mrs. Learner agreed as she looked about at the survivors.

She tried to close her thoughts to the tormenting images of her dead son washed up in the mud, his chair still upright, the wheels stuck in the mire. And Millie was gone and so many of her other girls.

"Get a move on everybody," shouted Mr. Evans from the shirt factory. "Get the last of those patients fed breakfast or it'll be dang-near time for lunch!"

Happy Learner tried to focus on helping the living. "If you'll excuse me, I've got to feed my charges. Feel better soon, Mr. McKenna." Rapid footfalls carried her away before he could thank her.

"I've got to go to Cary," Grey pleaded. "I've got to see for myself she's alive and do what I can to help her."

"In good time, in good time," responded Miss Barton firmly. "Right now, you need to mend yourself."

"Mrs. Learner said we were at Alma Hall together. I don't remember exactly." Grey's uncertainty left him angry and frustrated.

"Well, I'm told you're quite a hero. It was you who helped a blonde woman tangled in a knot of barbed wire. You nearly scalped her to do it, but free her you did. You saved her life. Given a little time, her hair will grow back and her cuts and scratches will heal. She's mighty lucky you were there. Could that be your Cary?" asked the woman kindly.

Nodding, he began to weep with happiness. Salt from his tears scalded his facial wounds, and he grimaced. Refusing to give in to the misery, he gasped between stabs of shooting pain, "What's the matter with me?"

"I'm sorry, Mr. McKenna. As you were freeing Cary, the wire attacked you. You've bruised your left eye and lost your right."

***

Despite the sling on one arm and the bulbous bandage on her left thumb, Ellissa managed to spoon oatmeal into Carolena's smiling mouth.

"Don't we make a pair, Sis? Me with my left arm all trussed-up and you with your right. I guess together, we'll just have to manage. Together. I like the sound of that." As soon as the words were out of her mouth, Carolena watched Ellissa's face drop. How thoughtless she'd been to say such a thing. Her dear sister's husband was dead and her child missing. The word together would never, could never, feel the same to Ellissa again.

Shaking her head as if refusing to let grief overtake her, Ellissa spoke. "It's alright, Cary. I will have to learn to go on living. I have no choice." Feigning brightness, "You and I are alive. And Grey. And some of my friends. With so many gone, God chose to save us. We're meant to be a family." Giving Carolena no time to respond because she knew tears would come to them both, Ellissa wiped a drop from her sister's chin, "I'm through here, so I'll go over to Grey and then report to you. After that, I'll see if the telegraph is back up and running. I've got to get word to the family about what's happened. They must be sick with worry. Rest now so you and Grey can be together soon." She kissed Carolena's forehead.

"Anything you want me to tell him?"

"Tell him," she paused, closing her eyes, lifting the words from deep inside her heart, "I love him."

"I will. And Cary,"

"Yes?"

"Tell him every chance you can. Do it for me."

"I will. Oh, I promise I will."

After Ellissa left, Carolena adjusted her sling, sliding the knot from behind her neck to a more comfortable position. The ongoing clattering of washbasins and chamber pots could not distract her from counting her blessings. The general commotion was a reminder of the massive suffering.

Ellissa had told her she couldn't remember any of her own ordeal, only that she was found tossed high on a hillside three miles down river.

Carolena was not so lucky. Her dreams, over which she held no power, would be nightmares of death and devastation, probably for the rest of her life. She could see the battle to push them from her waking thoughts would be constant. If she let the horrors have control, she might easily loose her mind to them.

Gently touching the gauze cap she wore, she made certain it was secured over her stitched skull because she wanted her wounds to heal quickly and her hair to grow back as full as possible. Between the wire ripping away patches of the golden fleece, Grey's hacking off huge clumps with his pocket knife, and the doctor shaving away most all of the rest, what remained was a scant curl at the nape of her neck some three inches long. But she didn't care what she looked like. She was alive and going to live out her days with Grey.

With this last thought, Carolena rolled to her side in hope of finding rest. Something small and hard was under her right hip. Reaching into the pocket of a kind stranger's dress, she pulled out the Secret Pebble that had been Coey's! Surprise lit her eyes as Carolena tried to think how it got there.

A woman beside her saw the wondering furrow between Carolena's eyes and explained, "You weren't wearing much other than a ragged coat when they brought you in. They found that pretty stone in the pocket."

Carolena realized Coey must have slipped it in at McKenna Hall. It had remained with her despite everything.

Those passing by noticed the sweet smile on the sleeping face of Cary McKenna.

Chapter 32

WESTERN UNION   3 June 1889
  TO: Michael Dunnigan
  Fernandina, Florida

  FROM: Fries Dresher
  Charleston, South Carolina

WORD FROM JOHNSTOWN STOP BURT DEAD STOP MARY COE MISSING STOP CARY ELLISSA GREY ALIVE STOP WILL REQUIRE RECOVERY TIME STOP TO ARRIVE CHARLESTON THEN FERNANDINA LATER STOP GOD IS GOOD STOP

Nigh onto a month passed. In that time, letters were written and received, injuries discussed, assurances given, and comfort, great and small, was the result.

The people of the world, including many from Fernandina, sent crates of supplies to Johnstown addressed in care of the newly established McKenna Haven, an orphanage opened for homeless children. With the help of Carolena, Ellissa, Uncle Jax, Mrs. Grossmyer, a recently arrived and dedicated Gwenie, and Paolo's fortune left to Grey, the huge mansion was transformed from idle to cheery and useful. More than fifty orphans, infants to teens, were and would be cared for there.

"Sit down for a while, Cary, would you? You'll have a relapse if you don't take care of yourself." She flitted past, and he caught her wrist on the cuff of the too short brown gown she wore. Looking down on her, "Please?"

"I admit I'm a little tired. One of the babies fussed all night. We couldn't get her to quiet down before she woke up half of the rest of the infants." She put her finger to his lips. "And before you apologize for not getting up yourself and helping, don't bother. There is no need for excuses. You've been working so hard getting these rooms turned into dorms for the children, it's small wonder you're not nodding off right now."

"Don't give me too much credit. We've all done what's been needed."

"Boys!" hollered Gwenie from down the hall. "If I have to speak to you one more time about hiding the girls' shoes, I'll sic Uncle Jax on you!"

At that, the boys laughed. "Ooh," a wise guy replied. "That's a good one. Who do you think suggested the game in the first place?"

"Now you've done it!" whined Uncle Jax. "That part was a secret,

Georgie."

"Oops. Sorry."

"There's too much racket in here, Cary. Come on outside with me for a bit, would you?" Grey asked. "I want to talk to you."

"Not unless you kiss me first, Mr. McKenna."

"If I must, Mrs. McKenna."

The kiss was not passionate. After only a few rapid heartbeats, their lips parted, anxious to reunite at a more appropriate place and time. Hand in hand, they walked out into a beautiful summer morning where Grey led his wife to the iron bench under cover of the old apple tree.

"Sit down, honey. I need to apologize to you."

"Apologize for what?"

"I've had something weighing on me for a while now. I need to explain why I was so hateful to you the first time you came to McKenna Hall and talked about us living here after we were married."

Carolena colored. "You owe me no explanation, Grey. I overstepped my bounds. I don't know what possessed me to assume you'd marry me and we'd live here."

He took her shoulders and turned her to face him. "You had every right to assume such a thing because you felt my love for you. That's exactly how it should have been."

She sighed with relief. "I'm glad you brought it up. It was one of those subjects I wasn't about to mention unless you did. I've been terribly embarrassed by it."

"No, darling. What's unforgivable was my over reaction. I have a reason if you want to hear it. It's the best excuse I can figure out."

Carolena could tell her husband needed to bare his soul. "Whatever it is, Grey, tell me. It's okay."

"When we were up in the master bedroom, I told you my mother had etched her name with her diamond ring. I would have loved you to wear her ring, but it was not mine to give. What I didn't tell you was she was murdered on a trip with my father to Pittsburgh."

"Oh Grey. No."

"What I also didn't tell you was the thief who killed her severed her finger to get that ring."

Carolena watched the blood drain from Grey's features. She was sure she was as ashen as he. All she could do was take his head in her hands and bring it to rest on her bosom. "Shhh," she whispered and rubbed his broad back.

He dried his tears with his sleeve, lifting the black patch that covered his sightless socket. "I can't have the children see me crying. They've had enough awful to last a lifetime. Anyway, I guess the remembrance of my mother's suffering made me momentarily crazy. I've faced it now. My sadness is slowly dissolving with the certain assurance my parents would have approved of our efforts to help the homeless children of

Johnstown."

"It's true, Grey. Add to that the fact Gwenie was once your brother's tutor. Since she never had children, it makes perfect sense for her to be here and part of it all because she possessed a maternal love for him. She told me she wants to live out her days working in his memory." Carolena smiled. "She also said, like most mothers, she felt no girl he'd known had ever been the right girl for him, including me. I have to give her credit for recognizing what I couldn't. Paolo and I were never meant to be together." Carolena took Grey's hand. "Ellissa told me once that with understanding, we can find forgiveness." She added, "... or at least peace."

***

It was a confusion of emotions for everyone. So much lost, yet so much for which to be grateful. Keeping busy was the tonic that seemed to best bury grief.

Carolena stirred one of three big pots of stew Ellissa had prepared for all the children. "Since your house was taken in the flood and the South Fork Fishing and Hunting Club disbanded, it worked out perfectly, especially for the little ones here, that you should head up the orphanage. Lord knows you're desperately needed."

"Yes," Ellissa replied somberly. "It's almost as if it were meant to be."

Trying a different angle, Carolena said, "I know the kids will miss you something fierce, Ellissa, but now that we've set up the basics, Gwenie, Uncle Jax, and the staff can run things until you get back from Fernandina. You've got some anxious family to meet. Are you almost packed?" Carolena bit her lip. "I'm sorry. I wonder if I'll ever remember to think before I speak."

"It's alright, honey. Yes. What little I have, that too big dark blue hand-me-down dress, a hairbrush, and a coat are up in my room, ready to go."

"I have about the same. We can put all our things in one bag. At least Grey will appreciate the fact he won't have to tote three trunks of stuff just for me."

"Sounds like you're trying to find the silver lining in everything," Ellissa noted. "Good for you. I need to focus on that myself."

"You don't need to change a thing," Carolena told her sister as she put an arm around her shoulders and gave a squeeze. "You're perfect the way you are."

The next morning, the McKennas and Mrs. Ellissa Bauer were on their way to Philadelphia by buggy, arriving in time to meet the *Miss Breelan* at the dock. The only words Ellissa could find to say were, "I never imagined I would enjoy such luxury," and "This is more than I deserve."

Carolena hoped the voyage might take Ellissa's mind off her loss. It did not. She spent a great deal of time staring out over the water, her look vacant, her face wet with tears.

As Carolena and Grey lay in bed that night, each tried to touch as much flesh of the other as was possible. "Surely, Grey, time with Aunt Coe and Uncle Fries, the only parents Ellissa's ever known, will be a comfort to her," Carolena confided.

"It can only help. And maybe a new dress, too?"

She sat up suddenly, the covers falling away to expose her upper torso. "I've been so wrapped up worrying about her, I forget about how we must look."

He pulled her back down to him and bent over her. "You look gorgeous in rags, or finery, or my favorite ... nothing at all."

"You're supposed to say that. You're my husband," she giggled. As he capped her shoulder with his warm palm, she tried to keep her mind on the subject at hand. "I can't wait until morning! What time does the Demure Damsel Shoppe open on the promenade deck? Do you know?"

"I'm sure the literature in the desk over there says, but I'm guessing 9 a.m."

"Great. Wait! What am I thinking? We can't get pretty colorful gowns. We're in mourning. Thank goodness I remembered before I rushed in, grabbed Ellissa's hand, and dragged her out to buy a party dress! I don't know where my head is these days."

"Whatever colors your dresses, they'll be new and fresh, and will make you both feel a bit better."

"You're right. We can have an early breakfast and be there when the clerk unlocks. Do you think it would be alright to charge two dresses to my family's account?"

"I guarantee it'll be alright to charge some clothes. However," he replied, good-naturedly stern, "it won't be on any Dunnigan account. It'll be on mine. Remember who you are, Mrs. McKenna. While you're at it, you and Ellissa should get several gowns each. You need them desperately anyhow."

Carolena buried her face in his neck. "I keep forgetting I'm married to my very own pirate with an eye patch."

"Let me help you remember." And he pressed himself upon her with a welcome weight, hungering to possess his wife.

***

Coe and Fries Dresher were waiting at Charleston's dock. As Ellissa ran into the arms of her parents, they saw where her tears had dripped on her black bodice. The white collar she wore represented the loss of her innocent child.

Pulling Ellissa's wrap closed, subconsciously protecting her from the chilly air as mothers do, Coe wept, "Oh my baby, my baby. We have so much to talk about."

"Yes, Mama, we have."

After a week in the South Carolina city discussing the distant and not so distant past and a future for Ellissa without her husband and child, Grey and Carolena were on the sofa in the Dresher parlor. Aunt Coe and Uncle Fries sat in individual rocking chairs across from them, and Ellissa was pouring coffee and serving brandy.

Fries sighed, "Thank God we have no more secrets. Thank God it's over."

Ellissa bent her head to hide her weeping eyes. When a teardrop plopped into her coffee cup, the sound was audible to all. They looked into each other's eyes and then began laughing. The release was cathartic, and the healing began.

"I think it's time to continue our journey to Fernandina," Ellissa said and saw her mother's face drop. As Coe dabbed her napkin to her eyes, Ellissa comforted, "Mama. You will always be my mother in my heart. Don't ever doubt that. I need to see Miss Ella. It will take me full circle and give me more knowledge of what makes me tick. I expect I'll find a kind, smart, loving, pretty woman, just like you."

Chapter 33

Waiting for the *Coral Crown* to pull into Fernandina, Ellissa drummed her black gloved fingers on the teak rail of the main deck.

"It will be fine," Carolena assured her. "We're almost there. Ellissa?"

"Yes, Cary," she replied. When Carolena didn't answer back immediately, Ellissa turned and looked at her. "Did you want to tell me something?"

Carolena shook her head. "No," she said. "I want to show you something." She opened the drawstrings of the reticule bag hanging from her wrist and retrieved a small object. "Give me your hand."

Wondering, Ellissa did as asked. Carolena placed something onto her sister's cloth covered palm. It was the Secret Pebble Mary Coe had given her. Ellissa stared with wide eyes. Forming a fist around the precious gem, she put that fist to her mouth as tears spilled from her eyes.

"But how?"

"Mary Coe must have slipped it in my pocket before the flood. It survived, the same as she survives in our hearts."

"Thank you, Cary. Thank you," Ellissa whispered, throwing her arms around her sister.

Grey saw their private moment and didn't want to interrupt. After a bit, he walked over to join them as they studied the folks on the overcrowded pier.

"Listen!" called Carolena. "That's our own Fernandina Concert Band. I think they're playing *For He's a Jolly Good Fellow*."

Grey cocked his head to get a better earful. "Yup. That's what it's supposed to be. I have to hand it to those men. They must have practiced for your arrival," Grey laughed, realizing how much effort it took on the part of the band members to keep the beat, let alone play the right notes more often than not.

"Can you read some of the signs, Ellissa?"

"You read them for me."

"*Welcome Ellissa! Love, Marie!*, *We've Missed Carolena and Grey*. Oh, and there's one that says *Bless You All from Dotterer's Grocery, 2 for 1 Soap Powder Sale*."

Grey grinned. "Leave it to them not to miss a plug for their store."

"Look there, Lissa. Right in front. That's our niece, Halley, on the shoulders of our brother Jack Patrick! Remember, he likes to be called *Pat*."

"Like you like to be called *Cary*?" Grey winked at her.

"I was such an idiot before," Carolena admitted. "I don't care what you call me, just as long as you always do." He kissed her and a cheer went up in congratulations to the newlyweds.

"Looky here, Aunt Carolena," Halley hollered as loudly as a child can.

Proudly displaying her little thumbs, "I don't chew my nails any more!"

Carolena threw her niece a kiss then waved a thumb's up sign in return.

Still wearing a stained apron from his job at the Watermelon Gardens, Jack Patrick was unsmiling. Carolena saw his quivering chin and realized her brother was fighting for control. When their eyes locked, she mouthed the words, "I'm fine. I'm fine." Comprehending, Jack Patrick lowered his head. When he raised it, there was his usual grin, but somehow changed. Pat Dunnigan had grown into a man while she'd been gone.

"And there are the Taylors," Carolena pointed out. "The dark haired beauty is our sister, Breelan, and beside her is her husband, Captain Waite Taylor. And the redhead is Nora, our cousin, Aunt Noreen's girl. She's lived beside us and been our close friend ever since I can remember. You can tell Nora anything."

"I'll remember that," Ellissa replied.

"The fat lady beside her is Aunt Noreen. We all pretend she's as trim as a ballerina. No sense getting her riled." Carolena saw Uncle Clabe and concentrated on not picturing him kissing her mother. Still, she shuddered once.

"You chilly, darlin'?" asked Grey, ever attentive.

"No, just excited and so glad to be home."

"That fella with Nora is her volunteer fireman, Austin. According to Nora's letter, he's a pig farmer by trade. Aunt Noreen isn't crazy about his occupation, but Nora doesn't give a hoot. She sure looks like she's in love. Again." Carolena explained. "We tease Nora and tell her she needs to start an organization called *Nora's Beau of the Month Club.* Pretty soon, there won't be a hall in town big enough to hold them all."

"I'll bet she's just looking for the perfect man ..."

Carolena saw the sadness in Ellissa's eyes and hoped to distract by saying, "Hey, where are Peeper and Clover?"

Grey craned his neck, looked about, and pointed. There in the shade of the depot overhang was the grand lady herself, sitting in a wheelchair with Blackie-White-Spots sleeping on the stoop beside her. Clover was resting his weary self against the nearby railing and holding Halley's big white stuffed Martha Bear.

Carolena waved and waved until Peeper and Clover both waved back. "Peep is the most wonderful woman, Ellissa. You'll love her. Her feet must be swole up like poison pups for her to be in a wheel chair. Poor thing. It won't slow her down much. It never does. As for Clover, he can repair anything and is so good to the animals. You can see by the bear he's taking care of for Halley that the children just love him."

Carolena's eyes filled with wonder and tears. "I never expected anyone to meet us but the family. It seems the entire town is here!" Yet, there were two people missing. Where were her mother and father? She looked to Ellissa, who was so anxious to see her real mother, she could hardly contain her excitement.

"Glad you're back among us, Grey!" shouted a man from the pack on shore.

Mickey and Warren Lowell broke ranks and were first to dash up the newly laid gangplank. Stopped midway up the ramp by a burly seaman, Warren Lowell seemingly stumbled, acting as if he were about to fall into the drink. The sailor's attention fell on the boy headed toward the water, and Mickey dashed past and on up to the rail to plant a fast kiss on his Aunt Carolena's cheek!

The crowd howled with laughter, understanding the boys were up to their usual antics. The recipient of the unexpected pucker darted a quick glance at Aunt Noreen, expecting a sour look. Instead, Noreen was laughing along with all the rest!

Grey was the first of the clan to disembark. Ellissa followed. Though a stranger to the townsfolk, she carried a family resemblance to Carolena and was thought to be kin of some kind to the Dunnigans. The lively response of the Fernandina residents was welcoming and warm, and greatly appreciated by the newcomer.

Just before Carolena reached the dock, she adjusted her bonnet, only slightly self-conscious of the short hair beneath and the healing cuts on her face. When the hot Florida sun illuminated her features, she heard a man shout, "You look beautiful as ever, Carolena Dunnigan!" It was Charlie Beason, a former classmate. She waved at him and to all her friends.

Grey heard the remark and was in full agreement. However, he found it necessary to correct a misconception. With a proud smile, he added, "That's Carolena McKenna, if you please, sir!"

Applause and whistles mingled with the cheering. Charlie smiled back and doffed his hat to Grey.

Looking to her husband through salty tears, she watched him shake hands with Captain Rockwell. "Captain," said Grey respectfully.

"Mr. McKenna. Welcome home," he replied sincerely and clapped his officer on the back.

With relief, Carolena knew Grey's job was secure. Slipping her hand into her husband's, Carolena decided Grey was more handsome than ever. Quickly she whispered in his ear, "That black eye patch lends you an even greater sensuality, if that's possible. Just so you know, I'll fight to the death any woman who tries to take you from me."

Her unexpected words shocked and pleased him. Had it been possible, he would have taken her back to their stateroom, or any room for that matter, and made wild love to his wife. There was no chance of that because the family swarmed them like an army of ants.

"I have so much to tell you about Austin, Carolena," Nora bubbled. "We've been talking marriage! I'm thrilled to meet you Ellissa. You're one of us now!" Nora sobered, "God bless you."

Overhearing, Aunt Noreen refrained from her usual negativity. "God bless all of us. We can't ever have too many blessings, mind you."

Torn between the loss of her family and the discovery of new kin, Ellissa replied, "You're right, ma'am."

Michael was waiting beside the carriage, his head low, his cheeks wet. "Daddy, oh Daddy. Don't cry." Carolena put her arms around her father's stooped shoulders. "It will be fine. Everything will be fine."

He hid his face against his oldest girl's shoulder and let forth great, heaving sobs of release.

"Shh. Shh," Carolena consoled.

The crowds had scattered, recognizing a private time. Carolena gave her father the handkerchief stashed inside her cuff. "Dry your eyes now. I've got someone for you to meet."

"Ellissa." Michael's delivery of her name was raspy as he searched for his voice. "I'm so ashamed."

With kind eyes, she said, "We'll all move forward from this point. That will be best for everyone. Don't you think?"

Michael could only nod in appreciation of her tolerance.

"Ride with Ellissa and your father, Cary," said Grey. "I'll follow with Clover, Peeper, Marie, and Halley. The boys will ride their horses."

Before getting into her carriage, Carolena looked up at Clover holding the reins as he waited for his buggy to fill. Martha Bear was still in his arms. Carolena stretched to pat his calloused hand, the back of it wet where he'd wiped away his own tears. "It's okay, Clove. Really it is."

Waite drove first rig with Breelan beside him. In the back seat, Michael was happily sandwiched between Carolena and Ellissa. He closed his eyes briefly and was finally able to speak. "With all my sweet Carolena's efforts to bring in money and those efforts nearly killing her, her reward wasn't financial. It was emotional. She has her Grey and found a new member of the family for us all to love."

He cleared his throat twice and went on, "I will now talk of things usually left unspoken."

Postures stiffened, wondering what was to come.

"I am blessed to say your mother, my Miss Ella, has forgiven the unforgivable. She is once again mine."

Breelan and Carolena let forth soft sighs of joy. Prior to her arrival in Fernandina, Ellissa was told some of the recent ugliness. As the newest member of the tribe, she was pleased to hear the good news.

"We're all adults here," Michael told them. "I ask you to listen in silence. Some of this may be new to you. Then again, living in such close quarters as we have in the recent past, I suspect that secrets are few." After a deep intake of air, "So while we needn't go into the inadequacies of Miss Peachy Pence, let's just say I chose her, that most gruesome looking, acting, and smelling woman, as my punishment for having been dishonest about problems with the business. I thought of her as my penance."

Before deep thought could be given his words, Michael went on to say,

"And when Miss Ella told me she kissed Clabe, I wanted to kill him. That's a part of what got me to drinking so much, though I'm not making excuses. Clabe would have made advances to someone sooner or later, since kind words at home were sorely lacking. I hope it's better between Clabe and Noreen these days. It seems it is. I'm focused on making up for my neglect and cruelty to my wife. It was unjustified. Perhaps, in my deepest heart, I hoped Ella would forgive me because she loves me. I counted on her to come through, and she did.

"One thing's for sure. Her heart nearly stopped beating when she heard the news about the flood and family being gone. I honestly didn't know if she'd come out of it. News that you three were alive restored her, but not to her old self. She's changed. She will always be scarred because I kept Ellissa from her and she never got to know Mary Coe, her first grandchild, or her son-in-law, Burt.

"The good Lord made her strong. Miss Ella realizes how much she still has left on this earth and that keeps her going." He looked to Ellissa. "I imagine you're a lot like her, dear."

Ellissa's gaze dropped to her folded hands in unspoken agreement, glad her mother had passed on her inner strength.

"We have our life back. We have our life back. Thank you, God. Thank you." With that, Michael Dunnigan wept again. This time his tears were cleansing tears of deep gratitude. The girls joined him in weeping for their own happiness, their own sadness, and Waite clenched his teeth to keep from doing the same.

Turning south, town-side of Clark Creek, they were soon on Dunn Road. Pulling out his own handkerchief since Carolena's was saturated, Michael wiped his face dry. "We'll be home in a moment, Ellissa. I intend to be the one to deliver my Ella's beloved Ellissa to her as I should have done so many long years ago."

The team of horses halted in front of a large clapboard two-story house. "Except for painting the outside yellow, adding the Charleston dark green shutters, and some old rose curtains to fan the front window sills, the new place seems to be exactly the same as the old!" Carolena marveled. "How did you get it done so quickly? I had no idea it was ready!"

"The whole town came together to help in time for your homecoming," said Waite.

"And all the colorful flowers around the porch and the base of the trees," noted Ellissa. "How perfectly lovely."

"We always help Mama plant fresh petunias and tend the day lilies and roses, but she's gone all out this season. There are more and bigger beds than ever before!" Carolena explained.

"Miss Ella always says the amount of flowers on the outside of a house tells the amount of love inside," Michael told Ellissa.

"I've heard Aunt Coe say that, too," Breelan said.

"Another family tradition."

"It would seem so, Cary."

"Now don't expect the inside to be the same, Carolena," Breelan explained. "The walls need to be finished and the trim and much of the detail work, as well. We have to be patient. Oh, and it'll smell different. Instead of chicken potpie, like Grammy used to make, or coffee roast beef, there will be the scent of fresh sawn lumber. Eventually, we hope to replace the original furniture with similar pieces, depending what our pocketbooks can afford, of course. It's still pretty empty, although it won't seem so when all the family is gathered."

"No matter the walls or the furniture, Bree, it's home," cried Carolena. "We're home!"

After helping Carolena and Ellissa down from the carriage, "Come on," Michael invited. "Your mother is waiting for you." With that, he put his arms around both the girls before ushering them into Dunnigan Manor.

Within moments of all wagons pulling up in front, the entire welcome hall filled. After a quarter hour of kisses and hugs, Carolena's disappointment was apparent.

"Where is Mama?"

Ellissa looked concerned until Michael said, "She's up in our bedroom. Go to her." He kissed Carolena's forehead then Ellissa's, adding an extra-long embrace. He was seeking the reassurance of Ellissa's forgiveness for keeping her from her mother for so long. Taking his face in her hands, Ellissa's lips touched each of his cheeks.

"Thank you, daughter," he said meekly.

Pulling Clabe back into the parlor for privacy, a nasty click of the tongue came from Aunt Noreen. "I simply don't approve of Michael referring to that girl as *daughter*," she whispered into Clabe's ear. "She's not his daughter. She's a stepchild and steps are steps. It only confuses the generations." Despite the unsavory circumstances, Aunt Noreen still managed to smile sweetly up at her husband.

Clabe stepped away from his wife and motioned to Nora and Warren Lowell to join him. Keeping his voice low, "Your mother is sometimes misguided. This idea about steps is totally incorrect, unkind, and uncharitable." His children dismissed her remarks, as was their usual, for they understood her backwards way of thinking. She'd given them plenty of lessons over the years.

Clabe realized, too, that Noreen's overly gushing adoration of him, of late, was not genuine. He was surprised by and appreciated her efforts at being an attentive wife since she'd heard about his indiscretion. Family, friend, or foe, she ran hot and cold. That was her way. He expected many an in depth replay of his sins and their torturous effects on her in the near and distant future, but that was a punishment he deserved.

Quiet wafted through the welcome hall and beyond as all eyes watched Carolena and Ellissa ascend the staircase, side-by-side. In the brief moments it took them to climb to the second floor, Carolena's thoughts highlighted how, since leaving Fernandina, she had suffered, struggled, and survived. The others had suffered, too, and much more so. It had taken tragedy for her to realize she, herself, had erred and undoubtedly would again despite her best intentions to always do the better thing. She'd received forgiveness. Offering the same, her burdens had lifted. She'd learned and would never, ever forget that no matter their deeds or misdeeds, family was the center of life.

Ellissa took Carolena's hand and, between palms, they held the Secret Pebble. Looking at each other and with mutual nods, they agreed Miss Ella should be the next recipient of the treasure.

Mary Coe's words sang through her mother's mind. "I won't ever lose it." No little girl, Ellissa thought. We won't ever lose it. Your pebble is safe now and will shortly be in the care of your grandmother.

The sisters turned the corner and were out of the line of sight of the family. A gentle knocking was heard, then a soft, "Come in ..."

Chapter 34

It was still two hours until sunrise. Neither Carolena nor Grey had slept well. But his frustration wasn't due to her tossing every night. He was certain nightmares followed her as she unconsciously tried to out-run the torrents of deadly water.

In her waking, although she was able to speak about the gruesome flood if the subject arose, he'd noted one peculiarity. She managed to avoid the sight of water. Aboard ship on their way back to Fernandina, Carolena stayed in their stateroom, the dining hall, the library, or any part of the ship that kept her eyes from the sea. He'd watched her as they'd docked in town. Normally, she'd have looked over the rail, trying to spot dolphins or sea turtles just below the surface. Instead, her eyes drew a bead on the folks on shore, welcoming them, but not on the Amelia River. Since they'd been back - and it was going on eight weeks now - she declined going to Amelia Beach with family or friends. That first fortnight before Ellissa returned to Pennsylvania, the family had frequently taken her for picnics on the Atlantic shore. Conveniently, Carolena had an upset stomach every time. She even allowed Peeper to pour some bitter-tasting potion in her mouth to be convincing. When Carolena couldn't resist the intense pressure to go along, Grey realized she kept her back to the sea, refusing to even look at the ocean. Her rosy cheeks and bright smile prior to the mention of a picnic left her husband certain her torment was fear of water and that torment was all-consuming.

Shaking her gently so as not to startle her, he whispered, "Carolena. Cary. Come awake. Let me take you away from your troubles."

She was too tired to argue and allowed him to help her into britches and a loose shirt. He lifted her into his arms and carried her down the freshly sanded boards of the Dunnigan staircase. The last of the moonlight illuminated Pat, Warren, and Mickey who'd made their pallets, Blackie-White-Spots and Monstie included, among the last of the stacks of lumber and brick in what was beginning to resemble the parlor. Grey chuckled at the uncomfortable-looking positions in which they lay, but he could guarantee they loved every stiff joint and sleep-interrupting sawdust sneeze they experienced.

Having already brought out Breelan's Noir, Grey hoisted Cary up onto the horse's bare back. With graceful agility, he swung up behind her, causing the animal to snort at the unaccustomed extra weight. Grey enfolded his wife with his body and tugged gently on the tangle-free mane of the animal, directing him out into the moonlight. When Carolena asked where they were going, Grey turned her chin to the right and kissed her to silence.

As they traveled the sandy shell-covered road east, they passed the Amelia Light, its beacon standing sentry over the marshes before it. The smell of the salty ocean invaded their nostrils, the even rhythm of the waves their ears. In the past, this had been pleasant. For Carolena, it was no longer so, and she began to tremble.

Murmuring endearments against her neck, he felt the silk of her short hair tickle his cheek. Her lacerations and bruises had mostly disappeared. Only the blackened abrasions on her mind's memory were left. As long as she knew the water only as an all-consuming beast, she had no hope of leaving her terrors behind if they continued to live on an island in Florida with the family business dependent upon the ocean. Her entire life would be hopelessly burdened should he be unable to convince her the sea could be as appealing as the flood had been terrible.

The sound of the water was almost deafening to her. She wept, understanding he would not let her escape without facing her demons. When he halted Noir on the shore and pulled Carolena down, her knees buckled. He held her against him.

"Cary. Cary."

Grey half carried, half dragged his wife to the water's edge. She clung to the security of his arms and voice. She tried to center all her energy on his soothing tone. It was no use. Fear obliterated reassurance.

She felt hands tugging at the buttons on her blouse. Grey was with her. The man she'd loved for so long was with her. He could be her strength if she'd allow it.

When her trousers dropped to the sand, Carolena made a weak cry. Grey tossed her into the air, and she landed against his naked chest. Then, Grey was running with her, splashing through shallows. The moonlight waltzed on the frolicking waves and the ruffled water sparkled like a floating field of stars. It was beautiful.

He slowed, turned, and carried her deeper into the breakers.

"No! No, Grey! Don't make me! I'm afraid!" She let out a scream of dread so ugly, he revisited the grotesque faces and floating death of the flood himself.

"Cary. Trust me. Trust me!"

Hearing no reply, he put her down to stand. The water was just past her knees, but her legs wouldn't hold her. Pulling his arm around her waist, she sobbed against him. He shook her hard.

"Do you trust me?"

He could just make out her closed eyes. He read the yes on her parted lips then felt her weeping convulsions.

Carolena had a death-grip on his neck as he slowly bobbed them deeper and deeper into the ocean. "Don't think about the cold, Cary, or the bad. Think only of me... and my touch. Think only of us, here, alone together. Let me make love to you."

The idea shocked her. Ugly visions were replaced by those of lovers lusting one after the other. But within seconds, her ghouls returned, and Grey felt her tremors renew themselves. It would be the power of his love versus her haunts.

With the water to his chest, he wrapped her legs around his hips. Smothering her sufferings with his mouth, Grey lingered on her lips until either exhaustion or pleasure quieted her. He hoped it was the latter. Randomly, he kissed her neck, her ears, her shoulders. When he pushed her from him, she whimpered. Pulling her back, he covered her cries with his own groans. Again and again, he forced her from his sheltering caress. And each time, her tears returned until she again felt the security of his embrace. Closing his eyes, he prayed his proven devotion would relieve her. His eyes opened as he felt her teasing touch beneath the waves. With delight, he caught the sparkle of her growing smile in the last rays of moonlight.

She saw herself in the mirror of her lover's eyes and, in that reflection, she confronted the undertows that had delivered her here - the undertow of unholy romance, the undertow of hatred for her own flesh and blood, the undertow of the extinction of life.

With an over-due delirium of pleasure, she and Grey welcomed a velvet undertow of revisited passion. The passing birds, the creatures beneath the swirling seas, and the sunrise were solemn witness to their unspoken vow to savor each passing second of the precious days reserved them.

At last, at long, long last, all was as it should be.

POSTSCRIPT

Authorities list the lives lost in Johnstown, Pennsylvania on May 31, 1889, at 2209. At least 900 people have never been accounted for. Over 700 bodies were never identified. Those innocent souls found their final resting place in a plot marked "Unknown" in Grandview Cemetery.

It took mere minutes for the city of Johnstown to wash away and five years before Johnstown returned to its former stature, proving the courage and tenacity of its residents.

Although lawsuits were filed against the South Fork Fishing and Hunting Club of Pittsburgh, none were successful. The official cause of the flood? An act of God.

***

"Nature never deceives us; it is always we who deceive ourselves."
Jean-Jacques Rousseau, French philosopher (1712 – 1778)

SECRETS OF THE COVER ART OF
Amelia Island's VELVET UNDERTOW

After I drafted four books in THE GOODBYE LIE Series, I thought about what the book covers should look like. I wanted them to be similar to tie the series together, but since each story stands alone, the covers had to be distinct.

The background element of my Amelia Island's VELVET UNDERTOW cover photo is actual sand from Fernandina Beach on Amelia Island, the first barrier island in north Florida, and home of the fictional Dunnigan family and my family as well.

A sheet of antique music, entitled Mosquito Waltz, lies upon the sand. I found it in the antique organ book I keep on my patented February 24, 1897, Ontario, Canada, working Guelph (brand) pump organ. This song, mentioned in the first book in the series, THE GOODBYE LIE, will remind the reader of the notorious insects of Florida. More importantly, the sheet music represents Paolo Alontti, the world famous conductor, whose life is a tangle in VELVET UNDERTOW.

The antique wood and brass 24-inch folding ruler inspired me to give Carolena Dunnigan the occupation of interior designer. This ruler belonged to Ed Harkins of Erie, Pennsylvania. Uncle Ed was a master carpenter and brick layer from the 1930s until the 1980s. He built our family home in 1950 for his mother, my grandmother, Jane Dunne Harkins, after whom I am named. When she passed away in 1951, my father, Leo, and mother, Marie, purchased the house. In the mid-1960s, Uncle Ed helped our father with an addition. I remember seeing Uncle Ed use this ruler though I don't know exactly how I came to have it. The ruler measures on both sides and folds into four parts with brass hinges, brass ends and sides. It reads: Stanley No 62, Stanley Rule and Level Co., New Britain, Conn., Boxwood, Warranted.

From my courtyard garden on the island, I gathered orange hibiscus flowers to represent the tropics. The pansies remind me how my mother and I annually planted them on either side of our front door steps, just as Miss Ella, the Dunnigan matriarch, plants her flowers with her children.

The red ribbon represents the storyline meandering throughout each novel.

Especially dear to me is the rhinestone jewelry that belonged to my mother. Its glitter represents the world of high society in which Carolena becomes involved. The key-shaped brooch specifically represents the moral of VELVET UNDERTOW, which is: The key to forgiveness is understanding.

For recipes, crafts, jewelry, and more fun and interesting articles about Amelia Island's VELVET UNDERTOW and THE GOODBYE LIE Series, please visit GraciousJaneMarie.com, and Jane Marie, Jane Marie Malcolm and GOODBYE LIE at Facebook and Twitter. See you there!

- Jane Marie

Watch for other titles available or coming soon by Jane Marie Malcolm

Amelia Island's

THE GOODBYE LIE

Series

"where Little House on the Prairie meets Gone With The Wind"

"A rollercoaster of emotions ... [which] include ... loving the characters. ... The unexpected ending makes a jaw dropping jolt to the senses."
                                    - ReaderViews.com

"A well thought out and designed mystery. The ending was most definitely a surprise."
                                    - HistoricalHearts.com

***

THE GOODBYE LIE
Breelan Dunnigan's foolish vault into folly may destroy her once upon a time carefree existence. Strong family bonds are pitted against lurking treachery, jealousy, and much, much worse in this 1882 twisting escapade.

***

Amelia Island's VELVET UNDETOW
Carolena Dunnigan's life turns to ash and she is lured to Charleston, South Carolina. Decades old lies are uncovered, taking Carolena to Pennsylvania and into the deadly Johnstown Flood of 1889. Who will survive this tangled undertow of mystery, family clashes, and love?

***

Amelia Island's MARK OF A MAN
Pat Dunnigan faces the Spanish American War and Mother Nature in this wild 1898 tale, laden with jarring conflict. Will all this drive away the woman who loves him? Some call her unsuitable.

***

Amelia Island's SAND AND SIN
A letter written, a letter found, bring the Dunnigan family full circle in the sultry tropics set in modern times.

ABOUT THE AUTHOR

JANE MARIE MALCOLM

Known to her fans as *Gracious Jane Marie*, Jane Marie Harkins Malcolm, originally of Erie, Pennsylvania, celebrates heart and home every day with roses, recipes, and romance at GraciousJaneMarie.com. Her complimentary and always tasteful on-site newsletter includes Martha Bear® short stories for MarthaBear.com. She is the creator of Secret Pebbles™, hand painted glass treasures, featured in her *GOODBYE LIE* Series. A mother, grandmother, and former first lady of Fernandina Beach, Florida, Jane Marie makes her home there with her charming husband, Bruce, and several enchanting cats. She is an avid handbell ringer and artisan, as well as a member of the American Legion Auxiliary, the Amelia Island Museum of History, and the General Duncan Lamont Clinch Historical Society of Amelia Island. Jane Marie is a practicing rosarian and quilter, and has fashioned family christening gowns by way of French heirloom hand sewing techniques. She dabbles in playing the musical saw and has mastered the harmonica to the best of her ability.

Jane Marie invites you to enter her world of lace and laughter at GraciousJaneMarie.com. Discover the fascinating Dunnigan family recorded in the historic *GOODBYE LIE* Series set on Amelia Island, Florida. Let her imagination embroider your realm with mysterious wanderings and delightful rainbows because Jane Marie Malcolm believes in happy endings.

LaVergne, TN USA
20 August 2010
193961LV00005B/2/P